Until Death

Holly Copella

In Loving Memory of
Michael Wetzel

"Goodbyes hurt the most, when the story
was not finished..."

Michael & Lynne
Forever

ACKNOWLEDGMENTS

Copella Books: First Paperback Edition 2018
Cover Artist: Daniela Owergoor
Dani-owergoor.deviantart.com
Model by MJ Ranum
Printed by KDP, an Amazon.com Company

PUBLISHER'S NOTE

Chapter 1

Homecoming

A new, black sports car drove the long, winding back road that seemed to extend forever before turning onto the private lane. Just ahead was a well-maintained, stone bridge over a gently babbling brook. The car crossed the bridge then drove through the imposing, wrought-iron gates onto the enormous country estate nestled in the middle of nowhere. It drove up the long driveway, which extended a quarter of a mile. The private lane was lined with towering, weeping willow trees, which created more of a tunnel than a driveway. It was early evening, so the private lane was already dark beneath the trees.

The car appeared in the clearing before the elegant, two-story mansion, drove along the circular driveway around the large fountain, and parked not far from the set of stone steps leading up to the home. The mansion was more than one hundred years old and appeared almost medieval. The beveled glass windows on both levels were arched with a church-like beauty. An attractive young woman, who barely made the legal drinking age, got out of the sports car and walked along the stone terrace before the steps.

Raina Steele wore her long, dark hair in a messy ponytail. Despite her expensive car, she dressed casually in worn jeans and a black blazer overtop her white tank top. Her 'not your ordinary rich girl' outfit was completed with calf-high black boots that looked like a feminine version of military boots. She crossed the patio and attempted to open the main door, but it didn't open. Raina was a bit surprised since the door was rarely ever locked, and she hadn't brought her house keys home from college. Rather than go around back to the kitchen entrance, she admitted defeat and rang the bell.

On the other side of the door, a young, proper looking butler stood in the foyer before the double doors and kept a close eye on his watch. The thirty-one-year-old butler, Dane Kingston, was devilishly handsome with dark brown hair and a clean-shaven face despite the evening hour. His butler's uniform was an expensive, three-piece suit without a crease or wrinkle. His wardrobe was as impeccable as his hygiene. When the second hand on his expensive watch hit twelve, a devious smile crossed his face.

"Dane, who's at the door?" a woman called from the front sitting room.

Dane unlocked the door while straightening proudly. His devious smile turned proper as he opened the door to reveal Raina. She glared at his pleasant smile and became further agitated.

"Good evening, Miss Steele," he announced almost charmingly despite that his blue eyes mocked her. "We weren't expecting you until tomorrow."

Raina sneered and pushed past him with annoyance. "Save it for your adoring fans, bellhop," she snarled. "Bags are in the car." She tossed him the car keys, purposely aiming for his face. "Knock yourself out."

Dane shirked back but managed to catch the small key ring, thankfully containing few keys on the off chance he would have missed.

"Is that Raina?" the woman from the front sitting room excitedly called out.

An attractive woman in her early forties appeared from the nearby sitting room, saw Raina, and squealed with excitement. She hurried up the foyer steps and happily hugged Raina. Brenda Steele was a gracefully stylish woman with shoulder-length, raven hair, an alabaster complexion, and large green eyes surrounded by thick lashes. Her regal beauty gave her the appearance of royalty, but her down-to-earth personality was far more humbling.

Brenda pulled away and looked over her stepdaughter. "We weren't expecting you until tomorrow," she announced gleefully. "What a pleasant surprise!"

When Brenda magically appeared in Raina's life more than ten years ago, Raina wasn't receptive to the idea of a stepmother. By her own admission, Raina treated her poorly in the beginning, but Brenda's charm and persistence eventually won her over. Her thirteen-year-old baggage, the son she'd brought with her, was a train wreck waiting to happen. Raina didn't want a stepmother, and she certainly didn't want a teenage stepbrother. Unfortunately, she'd taken to her new stepbrother and out of respect for their newly found friendship, Raina had little choice but warm up to Brenda. Once she conceded, Brenda easily won her over even if she never once called her 'mom'.

"My final exam was pushed back until next week," Raina announced and smirked almost deviously. "My professor was arrested for indecent exposure."

Brenda gasped dramatically. "Oh, that's terrible!"

"No, that this is the second time is what's terrible," Raina remarked then eyed her stepmother slyly. "This is what happens when you send your children to an Ivy League college, Brenda."

"Don't start that again," Brenda boldly announced and offered a teasing smile. "It's a fine school. Miller graduated from there, and he loved it."

"Of course he did," Raina remarked matter-of-factly. "He was in the wildest frat house on campus." She shook her head. "I still don't know how he managed to graduate."

"Now be nice," Brenda teased, although she didn't seem to mind Raina taking shots at her son. It was all in good fun. Her stepmother beamed. "I have a little surprise for you."

Brenda took Raina's hand and led her into the lounge as Dane entered the foyer with her duffel bag. He dropped it on the foyer floor with a plop and was about to step away.

"That goes upstairs, bellhop," she called out in a gruff tone without even glancing at him.

Dane sneered, snatched the bag, and headed up the massive grand staircase. Brenda practically pulled Raina into the front sitting room where an attractive woman in her early twenties stood alongside a lanky man a few years her senior.

Raina stared at the handsome couple with surprise. "Miller? Alicia? What are you two doing here?"

There was a small, joyful reunion as all three happily hugged. Raina's stepbrother, Miller, was only three years older than she was. He was a handsome man with his light brown hair kept businessman short and his youthful face clean-shaven. He was a fashionably snappy dresser, even more so since he'd been dating the beautiful Alicia, who helped improve his wardrobe. Alicia was as beautiful as she was intelligent. Her long, golden-brown hair was straight and silky. Despite not wearing much makeup, her skin was almost flawless. With her newly acquired tan, she was even more breathtaking.

Raina wasn't expecting to see her stepbrother and his girlfriend this particular weekend. They'd snuck off to the family beach house in Maui and had been gone the better part of the month. Alicia grinned and eagerly extended her left hand to reveal a one-karat diamond solitaire on her finger. Raina saw the sparkling diamond ring and cried out excitedly. She hugged both again with a little more enthusiasm. Alicia squealed with delight then clung to Miller's lean midsection.

"He proposed last weekend in Maui," Alicia announced while bubbling over.

"We wanted to surprise you and Dad tomorrow when he got back from his business trip," Miller informed her. "I didn't expect you tonight."

"I wasn't expecting you either," Raina announced cheerfully. "I thought you were staying in Maui until the end of the month."

"I heard Mom was going to be alone tonight, so we decided to come home early," Miller replied.

Brenda playfully slapped Miller on the arm and pretended to pout. "It's awful that you've been dating this girl almost a year, and I've seen her less than a dozen times."

"Alicia is busy with college," Miller insisted. "We don't get much time away from her studies. Becoming a doctor is a lot of work."

Raina waved off the couple. "Eh, I see enough of her at college."

Alicia playfully smacked Raina on the arm.

"If you prefer," Miller announced. "You can always come out with the guys and me tonight. Nothing too wild, I promise. I'm practically a married man." He laughed. "I love saying that."

Alicia squeezed him affectionately. He leaned down and kissed her warmly.

Raina rolled her eyes and groaned playfully. "Oh, give the happy couple thing a break," she muttered. "It depresses us single girls."

"I offered to fix you up with my friends," Miller announced with little sympathy. "As I remember; you not so politely declined."

"No offense, but your friends are too much like you, and I'd never want to date you," Raina scoffed.

"Good thing too, considering he's your brother," Alicia giggled.

"Stepbrother," Miller reminded her. "Technically, we're not related."

"I keep forgetting that," Alicia remarked then grinned. "I guess that's because you two act too much like brother and sister."

"Yeah, he was a pain in the ass at thirteen, and he's still a pain now at twenty-four."

"Yeah, you're brother and sister all right," Alicia muttered and laughed.

Miller eyed his stepsister. "So did you want to come along tonight?" he asked then grinned. "My friends love tormenting you."

"I drove five hours to get here," Raina informed him. "I don't feel like going out, especially with those perverts you call friends." She hesitated then looked around with bewilderment. "Where did Dad go? I didn't know he was going away on business."

"He had to fly out to the New York office early this morning and straighten something out," Brenda informed her. "I think one of his executives is in some sort of legal trouble, but I don't really get involved in his business. I just know he won't be back until tomorrow afternoon. It'll be us girls tonight."

"That's more my speed for tonight," Raina announced almost happy to have a quiet evening at home. Despite being away at college for long periods of time, she still considered the mansion her only home. "I'm going to go to my room and freshen up, see if Levi baked any of my favorite cookies, and then join you guys."

"See if you can squeeze a few extra cookies out of him for the rest of us," Brenda remarked and made a face. "He's pretty tightfisted with those things. I'm not sure if he's trying to help me maintain my girlish figure or keep his robust one."

Raina laughed. "I'm thinking the latter," she teased at the cook's expense.

Chapter 2

A Dish Best Served Cold

Raina entered the large, bright kitchen from the back stairs. She wasn't certain if any of the staff would be around after seven o'clock in the evening. To her surprise, both the cook and the upstairs maid had gathered in the kitchen. The cook, Levi, was a heavy-set man in his mid-thirties. He'd been working at the mansion for the last fifteen years since he was twenty, which gave Raina many years to adore him. Levi always wore a crisp white, neatly pressed cook's uniform, which almost resembled a Navy uniform with side chest buttons. As his yellow high-top sneakers suggested, he had an abundance of personality and, apart from his cooking, rarely took anything seriously.

Despite being robust, Levi was also tall, which only added to his presence. His dark curly hair just about touched his collar, and his sideburns attempted to form a beard, although his face somehow remained baby smooth. Rumor had it; Levi couldn't grow a beard or mustache, which is why he allowed his sideburns to grow out of control. The upstairs maid, Sloan, was only a few years older than Raina. Sloan was a natural beauty and could pass for the 'girl next door'. She was slightly taller than average at about five-foot-seven and was in excellent physical shape.

Sloan started working at the mansion when she was eighteen and Raina was sixteen, which gave them more than two years to develop an unsanctioned friendship before Raina went off to college. Having Sloan around was almost like having a sister. Raina often wondered if Miller would have made a play for Sloan had he not been off at college already when she started working for their father. Sloan was dressed for a night out. By the flattering, form-fitting dress she wore, Raina guessed she was heading out to some posh nightclub in the city. Sloan was careful only to wear flat shoes, so she wouldn't scare away potential suitors by appearing taller than them.

Levi leaned over the counter and flipped through a cookbook while Sloan stood at the end of the counter and sipped on a bottle of sparkling water. If they had been having a discussion, they had already wrapped it up. Raina approached the island counter catching their attention. Raina was always quiet on the back stairs, which would often startle the staff while gossiping. Most times, they would hear someone entering the kitchen and pretend to be busy. Levi straightened when he saw her then grinned and met her at the end of the counter. He gave her one of his famous bear hugs, practically smothering her and pulling her off her feet. She was like a rag doll in his arms.

"You're home early," he cried out with enthusiasm. "It's good to see you, squirt."

When he released her, she just about lost her balance then laughed. "I was just home last month."

Sloan gave Raina a sly once-over and smirked. "If you think I'm hugging you, you're out of your mind," she scoffed teasingly.

Raina raised a cocky brow and eyed her. "Good," she announced. "I don't want to reek of ode de' toilet the rest of the night."

"In that case," Sloan announced then laughed and hugged her. She purposely rubbed her wrists on Raina's blazer before pulling away.

Both women laughed like old friends. Levi grinned and extended a container of cookies to Raina. She grinned and accepted one of the large, chocolate chip cookies. Sloan leaned on the counter and smiled at Raina.

"So," Sloan announced. "Tell me about the rich boys at that Ivy League college of yours."

Raina groaned and waved her off. "Stuffy and pompous," she muttered with little interest. "What more do you need to know?"

"Better than community college," Sloan insisted with a dreary sigh and made a face. "Immature and supporting two or more kids."

"Why are you even looking?" Raina asked. "I thought you were dating the new, insanely cute chauffeur. What's his name? Titan."

"Titus?" she questioned then rolled her eyes. "We dated a few months until he dumped me for a slightly younger, perkier version of myself."

"How's that?" Raina asked seeming uncertain what she'd missed.

"Callie."

"Callie?" Raina squawked. "I thought she was dating Hanson, the gardener."

"She was until she discovered I was dating Titus," Sloan remarked. "I swear she didn't have any interest in him until she found out I was dating him." She shifted and placed her chin in her hand while leaning over the counter. "They're going out tonight with her sister, little Miss Hitler."

The back kitchen door opened and a handsome, neatly dressed man in his mid-to-late twenties entered. Sloan caught a glimpse of the chauffeur, Titus, and straightened while frowning her distaste. As Sloan turned away, she discreetly unbuttoned the top button of her dress to reveal additional cleavage. Raina saw the action and knew she did it to flaunt what he gave up. Raina felt bad for Sloan. The maid was head-over-heels for the chauffeur, and just like that, he was dating her co-worker. It had to be hard on her.

Titus was a ruggedly handsome man. The term 'tall and strapping' came to mind. He was moderately muscular, and his impressive build could be seen beyond his neatly pressed suit. His fashionable evening attire wasn't much different from his chauffeur attire. There was no denying the dark-haired, bronze-skinned, suave man was handsome. He'd only been working for them the last year or so after Raina was already away at college, so she didn't know him all that well. Seeing the handsome man, particularly with another woman, had to make Sloan insane. Raina could just about see the rage in the young maid's eyes, although she seemed to hold it together fairly well. As expected, Titus didn't acknowledge Sloan to avoid a confrontation. He must have realized it was best to play it cool with her, particularly since Dane would not tolerate fighting among the staff.

"Miss Steele," Titus announced cheerfully when he saw her at the counter. "I wasn't aware you were coming home this weekend. Your father will be disappointed he wasn't here for your arrival."

"I'm staying a few days," she informed him. "Just long enough to annoy the staff."

Sloan chuckled at the comment. The staff wing door opened and a young woman no older than Sloan entered the kitchen. Callie Burton was a stunning woman with long, blonde hair, which never seemed to be out of place. She was fashion magazine beautiful with the body straight from the pages of a girly magazine. She was dressed to kill in a form-fitting dress popular at most city nightclubs. Callie started working at the mansion a little less than four years ago, a few months after Dane had started. She came highly recommended from the Nixon's; their distant neighbor.

Callie was high maintenance from her makeup and hair to her professionally manicured nails. How she could afford to look as good as she did was almost puzzling. Although the chauffeur was paid handsomely, Titus wasn't a wealthy man by any means. It was obvious he wasn't paying her high maintenance price tag. He smiled when he saw Callie. She purposely posed seductively for him almost as if attempting to get a rise out of Sloan.

"How do I look?" Callie cooed.

"Stunning," Titus announced then fidgeted slightly while glancing at Sloan's profile. He seemed uncomfortable around his ex-girlfriend. "We should probably get going if we're going to pick up your sister and her boyfriend."

Callie noticed Raina and immediately smiled. "Oh, Miss Steele," she announced with some surprise. "I didn't know you were coming home this weekend."

"That seems to be the theme," Raina teased.

Callie offered a tiny grimace. "You know your father had to go away on business," the young maid offered. She then turned enthusiastic. "You could come out to the club with us tonight. It'll be fun."

Titus tensed but didn't comment. Raina found the invitation a little forward considering she didn't know Callie or Titus very well. She'd known Sloan for several years growing up, but Titus had only been working for them a little over a year. Despite that Callie had worked for her father for the last four years, Raina's interaction with the downstairs maid was minimal.

"I appreciate the offer," Raina announced while attempting a smile, "but it was a long drive, and I'm exhausted. I plan on going to bed early."

"Yes, you must be exhausted," Callie announced then smiled and clung to Titus' strong arm.

He seemed uncomfortable with her public displays of affection, although it was uncertain if it had more to do with the boss's daughter being in the room or his ex-girlfriend. Maybe it was both.

"If you need anything tomorrow," Callie announced cheerfully, "just let me know."

"That's my job," Sloan huffed with irritation and raised an arrogant brow. "I'm the upstairs maid, in case you've forgotten."

Callie glared at Sloan and released Titus' arm. "No, I didn't forget," she snarled in response while placing her hands on her dainty hips. "I can't forget, because you keep reminding me."

Sloan turned to face Callie and appeared annoyed. "I keep reminding you because you're constantly weaseling your way upstairs into my domain."

"Oh, get a life," Callie snapped back then sneered at her. "Oh, that's right. You don't have one." She linked onto Titus' arm and nuzzled it.

Titus became uncomfortable and attempted to stop a fight before it started. "Okay, that's enough," he announced and attempted to pull Callie away from the island counter.

Sloan glared at Titus with hostility. "I certainly hope you weren't talking to me," she launched. "Because you forfeited the right to tell me what to do when you started dating that little skank."

"Who are you calling a skank?" Callie suddenly cried out while attempting to break free from the chauffeur's firm hold on her.

"Whoa, whoa," Levi cried out in a whisper and hurried between the two women. "Let's not raise our voices. There's no need to bring the wrath of Dane upon us."

Despite the looks the women gave each other, Titus managed to scoot Callie out the back door. He obviously wanted nothing to do with Dane's vindictive side. Once they were gone, Sloan finally exhaled then held her head with a trembling hand. She looked at Raina and frowned.

"I'm sorry about that," Sloan announced timidly. "I shouldn't have exploded like that in front of you. It's just that, well, she loves to flaunt her relationship with Titus, and it burns me."

"It's okay," Raina assured her. "I understand. Guys can be jerks, but women can be vindictive bitches."

"I appreciate that." Sloan managed a smile despite her depressed state. "I'd love to stay and gossip, but I have a class tonight. After that, it's out with the girls for a wild night of wishing the cute guys were single. If you're bored, you know where to find us later."

Raina chuckled with amusement. "Thanks for the offer," she announced. "But I'd rather get my jollies reading a good thriller or horror book tonight."

Sloan shook her head while laughing, obviously understanding the comment all too well. She then left through the back door.

Levi didn't comment after the maid's departure. He finally smiled at Raina. "Is there anything you and the other ladies need before I turn in for the evening?"

"I'd heard a request for some cookies," Raina informed him.

He groaned teasingly and shook his head. "Oh, I suppose," he announced then grinned while laughing. "I made four batches when I heard you were coming."

"You're the best, Levi," she replied then appeared bewildered and eyed him. "I can't believe you go to bed so early."

"I'm up at the crack of dawn. Breakfast doesn't make itself," he replied. "Besides, I have to be up before Commandant Dane. You don't want to talk to him before he's had his morning coffee."

Dane entered the kitchen then hesitated while casting a look at Raina and Levi. Levi fidgeted despite that he was off the clock. He placed several cookies on a plate for the ladies then replaced the container to the counter. Dane ignored them and proceeded for the teapot.

"I'll be serving tea in the lounge in ten minutes," Dane informed Raina.

"Well, it's off to bed with me," Levi announced while seeming tense around Dane. He smiled politely at Raina. "I have a grisly horror movie coming on in ten minutes, and I'd like to be asleep before the second body falls. See you in the morning. Goodnight."

Raina laughed as Levi left the kitchen through the staff wing doorway. Once he was gone, Raina's mood immediately dropped as she looked at Dane. He leaned his back against the counter behind him and glared at her.

"The good ship lollipop has sailed," Dane scoffed. "Kindly vacate my kitchen."

She shook her head with irritation. "I'm amazed at how quickly you go from a proper butler to a surly prick," Raina snapped. "It's got to be a world's record."

"What can I say? You motivate me," he growled then glared at her and straightened. "Now be a good, little girl and leave me alone."

"You're so charming," she snapped back while sneering at him. "I wish my father could hear the way that you talk to me."

"You've been trying to get me fired for four years now," Dane scoffed. "He's not going to believe anything you say about me."

She rolled her eyes but withheld her disgust despite her rising blood pressure.   "Always a pleasure talking to you, Dane."

Raina headed across the kitchen and stormed out the hallway door.

Chapter *3*

Gossip Hour

The three women talked and laughed cheerfully together in the front sitting room while drinking tea and nibbling on cookies. The room was decorated with antique furniture and had an Old Victorian feel to it. There were two sofas placed facing the center of the room with a large coffee table in the middle. A wing-backed chair was off to the side allowing a view of the massive, stone fireplace. There were several larger sitting chairs toward the corners of the room with small end tables and antique lamps to provide additional light. Several expensive paintings hung on the walls, completing the elegance of the room. Large floor to ceiling windows surrounded the room, although the gaudy tapestry curtains were currently closed. Dane entered the lounge and paused within the doorway. Raina rolled her eyes when she saw him and silently fumed.

"If you won't be needing anything else, Mrs. Steele, I'll be turning in now," Dane announced.

"We're fine," Brenda replied cheerfully revealing her fondness for the surly butler. "Goodnight, Dane."

Dane politely nodded to Brenda, cast a dirty look at Raina, and then left the room. Raina sneered her distaste. Brenda caught the look from her stepdaughter. She shook her head and held back her laugh.

"What is it with you two?" Brenda asked while smiling doubtfully. "I swear the two of you hate each other."

"You're just realizing that now?" Raina teased while attempting to hide her sneer. "Where have you been the last four years?"

"I guess it's your similar personalities clashing," Brenda remarked.

Raina glared at her stepmother and nearly gasped. "I'm nothing like him."

"So what is it?" Brenda demanded. "What started this feud between you two?"

"He's had an attitude ever since he started here," Raina remarked. "I was seventeen or eighteen when Dad hired him. He'd only been here a couple of weeks."

§

Four years earlier. Eighteen-year-old Raina lay on the game room sofa with a tall, lanky boy from her school. Her boyfriend, Jeffers, had sandy brown hair and a baby face, which was why most of the girls at her school were attracted to him. Raina couldn't believe that he'd asked her out, considering he could have any other girl at school. The couple kissed passionately while Jeffers firmly caressed her body as he partially lay on top of her. Raina was slightly uncomfortable and stopped his traveling hands several times, although he didn't allow her protests to distract him.

Jeffers broke off the kiss, pulled back to meet her gaze, and grinned. "It's quiet around here," he announced. "Where is everyone?"

"It's Sunday. The staff has the day off," Raina informed him. "They went to that picnic in town."

"What about your father and stepmother?" the teenage boy asked.

Raina grinned slyly and caressed his broad shoulders. "They're visiting Miller at that overpriced college of his."

His eyes seemed to sparkle at the response. "So we have the place to ourselves all afternoon?"

"All afternoon," she replied and kissed him affectionately.

Jeffers returned the kiss with increased passion and aggression. His hands firmly caressed her body then attempted to unbutton her pants. Raina broke off the kiss and stopped his hand.

He appeared disappointed while staring at her. "What's wrong?"

She shifted uncomfortably beneath him. "I don't know if I'm ready for that."

"You're going to graduate soon," he announced while grinning. "I want us to be exclusive."

She stared at him with some surprise then smiled in response. "Me too."

"You don't want to be a virgin when you go away to college, do you?" he asked.

Raina tensed slightly while staring into his eyes. What was he saying? He responded as if reading her mind.

"Being at two different colleges is going to be difficult. You're going to be five hours away," he insisted then grinned. "If we're sleeping together, we'll be exclusive, and it'll make it easier."

Jeffers kissed her neck and continued running his hands along her body.

She considered the comment and was puzzled by it. "That doesn't make any sense," Raina informed him.

Jeffers pulled back to meet her gaze and groaned with some irritation. "There's going to be a lot of temptation for both of us," he insisted. "If we're exclusive, there won't be any temptation, but we can only be exclusive if we're sleeping together."

He kissed her passionately and aggressively on the mouth. Despite that his explanation troubled her, Raina reluctantly gave in and returned the kiss. He again attempted to unbutton her pants. She again stopped him. She was still troubled by his reasoning of why they couldn't be exclusive unless they slept together.

Jeffers groaned with annoyance and glared at her. "What's your problem?"

Raina felt her frustration rising to match his. She was feeling pressured, and his hostility regarding her feelings wasn't helping any.

"I think it's you," a gruff male voice responded. "Time to go home, Romeo."

Jeffers jumped off Raina and sat up on the sofa with surprise as he looked across the room. Dane casually stood in the doorway conveying little emotion, although he didn't appear pleased. Raina saw Dane then sat up while groaning and rolling her eyes.

"Who the hell is that?" Jeffers demanded, indicating the man in his late twenties dressed neatly in a suit.

"No one," she scoffed while avoiding looking at Dane. "Just the butler."

Jeffers snorted a laugh and smirked. "Get lost, butler," he launched.

Jeffers moved against Raina and attempted to lower her back to the sofa despite that she no longer seemed interested. She gave him a slight shove to show her disapproval. She certainly had no intentions of making out in front of the newly hired butler. Raina was irritated that her boyfriend somehow thought she'd be okay with it. Jeffers was suddenly pulled off her. She cried out with surprise as her boyfriend let out a sharp scream. Dane twisted Jeffers arm behind his back and forced him across the game room and into the hallway. Dane escorted Jeffers along the hallway keeping his arm pinned while Raina ran after them.

"Damn it, Dane. Let go of him," she cried out. "Stop this!"

Dane forced Jeffers up the foyer steps and carelessly tossed him out the front door. He slammed the door behind him then turned to face the irate teenager standing behind him.

"What the hell is wrong with you?" she cried out with surprise and anger.

He stared into her eyes without flinching. "Your father expressly forbids bumping and grinding under his roof. You have a reputation," Dane scoffed while remaining unusually calm. "One of us has to protect that."

"You bastard!"

§

The following evening. Eighteen-year-old Raina followed a distinguished looking man in his early forties along the hallway. Her father, Otto Steele, was a handsome man with a little gray peppered into his short brown hair. Her father was a tall, sturdily built man, who sometimes looked more like an Army sergeant than a businessman. At times, he acted it too. Raina couldn't control her anger any longer.

"I can't believe you're siding with the butler, Dad," Raina launched while her father practically ignored her emotional outburst. "He roughed up my boyfriend. Jeffers was so upset over how he was treated that he dumped me!"

"I'm not taking sides, Raina," her father insisted while refusing to face her. "I commend Dane for looking after you while I'm away."

"Yeah, for protecting me from my own boyfriend," she snapped. "Real classy."

Otto turned to face her and stared into her eyes with little sympathy. "I'm sorry you feel you're being disrespected, but I'd have done the same thing if I'd been here," he announced then held his breath a moment. "I know Dane may seem a little rough around the edges, but I trust his judgment." He placed his hand on her shoulder and stared into her eyes. "If the world ever falls apart, stand behind Dane."

"So that's it?" she squawked. "He's allowed to treat me however he wants."

"No, but I trust his judgment," her father again announced. "I'm sorry, Raina."

§

Later that evening. Raina sat at the kitchen island counter with a cup of tea before her and watched Levi mixing a batch of cookies. As he added some chocolate chips, Raina watched him closely. Her eyes narrowed. He caught her stare.

She raised her brows with disapproval. Levi laughed and dumped the remainder of the bag into the mixture. They exchanged humored looks and laughed. She swore he tormented her on purpose, but she adored him. Dane entered the kitchen from the hallway entrance.

Levi caught a glimpse of Dane and muttered to Raina, "Virgin alert."

She sneered at the cook. "That's not funny."

Despite her venomous look, Levi chuckled. Dane cast a glance at Raina and continued with his work. She was still mad at him, and the tension between them was enough to make Levi uneasy.

Callie entered the kitchen from the back stairs, which struck Raina as odd since Sloan was the upstairs maid. The new downstairs maid wasn't good with boundaries and seemed to step on Sloan's toes every chance she had. Dane's attention briefly shifted to the attractive, twenty-year-old maid. Raina noted his gaze and watched the exchange while keeping a low profile at the island counter with Levi. Callie walked behind the island counter and talked with Dane. Raina continued to watch their interaction closely. It was more than obvious that Dane was falling all over himself in her presence.

"I'll be sure to take care of that first thing in the morning, Callie," Dane announced while smiling almost boyishly.

"Thanks, Dane," Callie practically cooed and returned the smile. "I appreciate that. I'm clocking out."

Dane nodded in response. Callie headed for the servant's quarters entrance on the other side of the kitchen not far from the counter. Dane hesitated then hurried after her. He stopped her short of the door and appeared tense while fidgeting.

"Callie," he announced timidly, "I was just wondering if you'd like to--"

Although neither seemed to notice her, Raina now stood alongside the island counter not far from them with a piece of paper in her hand.

"Excuse me, Dane," Raina announced in all seriousness. "You had a phone call earlier."

He gave her a bewildered look and appeared almost unable to comment. Her interruption was throwing off his already awkward attempt to ask out Callie. Raina looked at the paper and read the message aloud.

"He said his name is Bud and that you'd met Tuesday night at that bar downtown," Raina announced while keeping a straight face. "He wanted to thank you for a wild evening and hoped you could get together real soon." She waved the paper while grinning. "He left his number." She stuffed the paper in his hand.

Dane glared at her with a hostility she hadn't seen before. Raina didn't let that interfere with her revenge scheme. She flashed a smile and lustfully raised her brows.

"Sounds like you made a new, special friend," Raina announced and drove her revenge home.

Dane crumbled the note while maintaining his glare. Levi watched the exchange with shock or possible horror. Raina grinned, spun on her heels, and headed for the back stairs. A hasty retreat seemed to be in her best interest.

§

Present day. Brenda and Alicia remained sitting silently on the antique sofa and stared at Raina with shared looks of surprise at the story they'd been told.

"You didn't--" Brenda finally gasped and shook her head with disbelief.

"Hey, he started it," Raina insisted without remorse as she nonchalantly leaned back on the second sofa across from them. "I was handling Jeffers just fine. He ruined my chances with the only guy I really cared about. I was just repaying the favor."

"That's awful, Raina," Brenda announced while maintaining her stunned look.

"It wasn't that big of a deal," Raina remarked. "He ended up dating Callie anyway." She rolled her eyes and shook her head. "Although, I can't imagine what she saw in him. Talk about a mismatch. I'm not surprised she dumped him after only a few weeks."

"He's not that bad," Brenda insisted and appeared disappointed. "You two just got off on a bad note."

"Which he started."

"I remember a time when you thought I was your evil stepmother," Brenda reminded her. "You didn't like me much either."

"That was different. I was ten, and I thought you were replacing my mother," Raina remarked. "I was wrong about you. Dane's a prick."

"Raina!" Brenda chided despite attempting to hide her smirk. Perhaps she knew the statement was partially true.

"He's had it out for me from the moment we'd met," Raina insisted. "I can't stand being in the same room with him."

"You've never given him a chance," Brenda criticized then sipped her tea.

"Because he hates me," Raina protested. "Why should I tolerate him when he doesn't make any effort?"

"He doesn't hate you," Brenda huffed and shook her head. "If you tried being nice to him, you'd see that."

"Perhaps when hell freezes over," Raina scoffed and avoided looking at her stepmother.

"Maybe we should change the subject," Alicia remarked as she shifted uncomfortably from the exchange.

Chapter 4

All is Fair

As the grandfather clock on the staircase landing struck midnight, Raina appeared on the steps wearing a pair of shorts and an old, worn tank top she used as her sleep attire. She headed down the many steps in her bare feet, rounded the banister into the grand hallway, and approached the library. Raina entered the library and nearly collided with Dane. She jumped with surprise, sneered at him, and then walked past him. She shouldn't have been surprised to find him in the library. From her experience, he'd spent a lot of his free time there. Dane replaced the book he had recently finished without comment and searched several titles on the shelf near the door, better known as the stuffy section. At least that's what Raina liked to call it. To her knowledge, Dane's taste in books seemed limited to deceased authors. The silence between them was unsettling as both searched for a book and pretended the other didn't exist.

The library was practically medieval in appearance and considered a work of art to those who were serious about their books. The room had a high, vaulted ceiling with chandeliers throughout. Sculpted wooden bookcases took up nearly every available wall with shelves high enough that a rolling ladder was required to reach some.   A large window contained beveled glass and a deep, padded window seat allowing a breathtaking view of the mansion fountain and the weeping willow trees covering the driveway.   There were assorted antique sofas positioned strategically around the room on many throw rugs over top the marble floor.   The room offered one desk for anyone interested in research, although it was rarely used.   The library had always been Raina's favorite room in the mansion, and she'd spent hours on the window seat reading books since she was a child.   When she was little, her grandfather, DawDaw, would sit with her on the window seat and read to her.   Those were her fondest memories.

Raina removed a book from her personal section of the library consisting of little-known authors.   She flipped through the book, uncertain if she'd read that one before or not.   When she lived at home, she had a system.   Books she'd read were on the bottom two shelves while those she hadn't read were on the two higher shelves.   Once she went away to college, someone took it upon himself to arrange the books in alphabetical order.   Raina was certain Dane did it on purpose to piss her off.   She hesitated then apprehensively cast a glance at Dane across the library.   There were times she'd take in a sweeping eyeful of the man and admire his striking features.   There was no denying he was a handsome man.

The first time she'd laid her eyes upon him, his mesmerizing blue eyes captivated her.   He also had a charming smile.   He had smiled at her many times, although usually with a grin meant to mock her.   Despite the devilish look behind that smile and sinister eyes, he was still a handsome man.   Although athletically built, he had a hint of body mass beneath his meticulously pressed uniform suggesting he had at one time worked out.   She looked back at the open book in her hand and frowned.   There were moments when they were alone together, silently loathing each other, that she admired his handsome features.   She hated those fleeting moments of attraction toward the insufferable man.   Raina counted the seconds until he'd inevitably do or say something to put an end to those feelings.   Her thoughts strayed to Brenda's words earlier that night.   Maybe she didn't give Dane enough credit.   Maybe she should give him a chance.

"I, uh, didn't think anyone else was up," she said aloud before she could stop herself. The moment the words left her mouth, she cursed herself for not coming out with some scathing insult instead.

"I wouldn't be either if Levi wasn't snoring louder than the volume on his television," Dane casually remarked and avoided looking at her.

She was almost stunned that he responded with something polite rather than his usual insults. Raina raised a brow and smiled more naturally. The prospect of having an actual adult conversation with Dane was almost exhilarating.

"Is his snoring really that bad?"

"The walls vibrate," Dane muttered with little interest in their conversation while keeping his nose in his book.

She turned with surprise while lowering her book and looked at him. "Really?"

Dane shut the book he held and turned toward her with a look of impatience and involuntarily tensed. "Why are you talking to me?"

Raina was slightly surprised by the hostility directed at her. He was in rare form tonight. "I'm trying to be nice," she launched back.

"I sincerely doubt that, Miss Steele," he sharply responded and took a quick step toward her, startling her. "Any time you've smiled at me, some sinister plot to get me fired usually followed." His brows rose while making his point. "Any pleasantries were always followed by some degrading insult usually at the expense of my manhood." Dane cocked his head while glaring at her through narrow eyes. "So you'll forgive me if I'd rather not talk to you." He then shot a glare at the tank top she wore as if pointing it out with his eyes. "And consider covering up, for God's sake. This isn't 'girls gone wild' on spring break."

The remark nearly floored her. She glanced at the worn, white tank top she wore and realized it was practically see-through in the library lighting. Despite wanting to hold the book over her chest to hide her body from him, she refused to comply with his request. She sneered at him despite the color rising to her cheeks and chose to keep her perky breasts visible just to spite him.

"You really are a repulsive prick," she scoffed while staring into his blue eyes. "And if you find my ta-tas so offensive, maybe you should stop staring at them."

Although she knew he wasn't staring at her chest, she was certain it would embarrass him. He fidgeted despite being offended by the insinuation but refused to back down or look away. They stared into each other's eyes for an awkward moment. It was obvious he was searching for a quick comeback but was rendered speechless by the insult. Raina knew she had the upper hand and couldn't relinquish her power by looking away first. She wasn't sure if it was the sudden rush of adrenaline or her dominant upper hand, but as she stared at him, she felt an uncontrolled desire to kiss him. She allowed the thought to invade her mind only a moment before thinking better of it. Raina turned and stormed from the library. The moment Dane was out of her view, she insecurely held her book across her chest with embarrassment.

Chapter 5

Love and War

Raina stormed into her bedroom, shut the door behind her, and tossed her book with disgust onto the tall, frilly looking bed. On the nightstand next to the picture of her mother and father was a large vase filled with fresh yellow roses. Even the beautiful flowers couldn't soothe her hostile mood. She paced the length of the large bedroom like a caged animal, alternating running her fingers through her hair and insecurely rubbing her shoulders.

"I should have hit him," she muttered while pacing. "I should have slapped him across the face." Her brows rose as everything she should have done now surfaced with her rising frustration. "I should have called him a pervert. That would have pissed him off."

She continued to pace then paused before the free-standing, full-length mirror and looked at her reflection. She eyed the partially see-through tank top revealing her perky nipples that were practically poking through the thin material. There wasn't much left to the imagination. She rolled her eyes, embarrassed that Dane had more or less seen her breasts. She groaned with disgust.

"I'm never going to live this one down," she muttered while again running her fingers through her hair.

Raina frowned with disgust at herself and entered the bathroom. The massive bathroom was mostly marble and wood, giving it an elegant appeal. There was a large garden tub, a clear glass standing shower, and a double marble sink. She approached the garden tub and turned on the water. She needed a long, hot bath to settle her frayed nerves. She needed to get Dane from her mind. Despite the running water, she heard a faint thump. Raina looked around the bathroom then shut off the water to listen for the sound. She didn't hear anything.

She was about to turn on the water again when she heard another thump coming from the room next to hers, which belonged to her father and stepmother. Raina appeared bewildered, decided to investigate the sound, and hurried from the bathroom. As Raina entered her bedroom, a man wearing a mask grabbed her from behind. She only caught a glimpse of the intruder before he tossed her onto the bed, momentarily disorienting her. She barely managed a scream as the man leaped on top of her. Despite taking self-defense classes in college, she found herself unable to think straight until she saw the hunting knife in his gloved hand.

A rush of adrenaline coursed through her and her reflexes took over. Raina struck him in the nose with her palm in what had to be a precision shot. He cried out in surprise and pain as he fell off her while clutching his bleeding nose. She sprang to her feet and ran for the door. Before she reached the door, the intruder again grabbed her from behind and stopped her from escaping. She kicked behind her, ramming her heel into his shin, and then jabbed him twice in the ribs with her elbow. Raina clutched his arm and tossed him over her hip. He struck the floor with force and a loud thump. Raina saw the discarded knife on the floor and lunged for it. The intruder swept her legs out from under her. She crashed to the floor and attempted to brace her fall with her arms.

§

Alicia ran into the hallway from her bedroom while tightening the sash on her robe, having heard the loud thump from one of the nearby rooms. She heard a crash from the master bedroom next to Raina's room and ran to check on Brenda. Alicia darted into the dimly lit bedroom and turned on the light by the wall switch. Brenda half-lay on the bed with blood soaking the sheets and dripping down her arm as it hung over the bed. Alicia suddenly cried out, but her scream was cut short as a man dressed entirely in black and wearing a mask grabbed her by the throat. He slammed her into the nearby wall, which temporarily dazed her.

The masked intruder raised the large, bloodied hunting knife, prepared to strike. Alicia screeched with horror as her knee instinctively connected with his groin. He cried out and released her while clutching himself. As she attempted to bolt for the door, he recovered enough to slash at her from his doubled over position and sliced her thigh. She screamed and struck the wall. The intruder straightened, bolted for the door, and slammed it shut. Alicia darted away from the door while clutching her bleeding thigh and faced her attacker.

"Raina!" she screamed, hoping to alert her friend in the room next door.

§

Raina was on her bedroom floor beneath the first intruder, who now straddled her waist and held her down with his gloved hand on her throat. He raised the knife and was about to plunge it into her. She struggled to hold back the hand with the knife as well as the hand on her throat. As she heard Alicia scream her name from the nearby room, Raina's look of horror turned to anger. She released her attacker's hand gripping her throat and grabbed his crotch with a vice-like grip He cried out as she violently twisted until she felt as if her wrist would snap. While he was crippled in agony, she bit his wrist near her face. He screamed in pain between her teeth on his skin and her grip on his crotch. She released his crotch and punched him in the mouth, knocking him off her and to the floor. Raina scrambled to her feet and kicked him in the groin before running from the room, leaving the intruder writhing in agony.

Raina skidded across the hardwood floor in the hallway in her bare feet and ran for the master bedroom next door, which is where she heard Alicia's cry for help. She attempted to open the door, but it didn't budge. Without hesitation, she stepped back and gave her best karate kick to the door. It flew open with a thunderous crack. Raina blindly bolted into the partially lit bedroom and suddenly stopped when she saw Brenda sprawled out in a bloody mass on the bed. She then saw the second intruder only a few feet to her right with his hand on Alicia's throat. He tossed Alicia across the room, forcing her to stumble and fall, before leaping for Raina with his bloodied knife. Raina saw Alicia on her knees but kept her focus on the man with the knife.

"Raina, run." Alicia screamed loud and shrill while she remained on her knees near the dresser.

Despite hearing her scream, Raina didn't bolt and kept her eyes locked on the man in black. The killer lunged at her with the hunting knife raised above his head. She dived to the floor for him and tackled his legs, knocking them out from under him. The killer flew over her and roughly struck the floor. Raina sprang to her feet as her attacker moved to his hands and knees. She kicked him in the abdomen and sent him rolling across the floor. He again moved to his knees while still clutching the knife.

Raina screamed with anger as she kicked him in the face just narrowly missing his nose. The masked intruder was thrown to the floor, writhed in agony, and finally dropped the knife. Raina grabbed the discarded knife and ran to Alicia's side. Alicia clung to Raina while sinking in her arms. It was then that Raina saw the blood covering her friend's hands. Her eyes immediately strayed to the young woman's nightgown now saturated with blood over her abdomen. There was so much blood! She met Alicia's gaze with her own horrified one.

A relieved smile crossed Alicia's face. "I knew you'd save me," she gasped while offering a soft laugh before falling limp in Raina's arms.

Raina stared at her friend with horror. "Alicia?" she gasped. "No, Alicia. You can't die!"

Tears streaked Raina's face as reality swept over her. Alicia was dead! The killer groaned and attempted to stand, alerting Raina to the danger still present. Raina gently lowered Alicia to the floor and moved to her feet with the knife in her hand. She sneered at the writhing man while clutching the knife.

"You fucked with the wrong woman!"

Raina took two quick steps toward the man now on his knees and raised the knife in both hands above her head. He looked up with surprise as she was about to plunge the knife into his throat. Raina felt a painful surge to the back of her head. The room spun as she caught a close-up look of the floor not even realizing she had fallen. The intruder from her bedroom stood over her as she attempted to pull herself up with little success. She could do little more than scratch and claw at the floor. Raina attempted to look at the man who'd hit her, but she couldn't focus. He turned his attention to his partner, who was still on his knees not far from Raina, and appeared angry with the injured man.

"Get up, you idiot!"

The killer slowly moved to his feet and stared at Raina, who lay on the floor attempting to remain conscious. The little voice inside of her was screaming for her to get up, but she couldn't seem to move. The killer held his bleeding mouth and eyed his partner with anger.

"I thought there was only one woman in the house," he launched. "What the hell? We're not being paid enough for this shit!"

"Don't worry, we're going to take the rest out of her ass," the first intruder announced gruffly. "Help me get her to her room, and then I want you to make sure the butler is out of the way."

§

The two intruders each took an arm and easily dragged Raina down the hallway toward her bedroom as her heels dragged along the hardwood floor. Her vision was blurry, her head seemed fuzzy, and her ears were ringing loudly. For a moment, she had forgotten what had happened. She had possibly blacked out a minute. When her heels hit carpeting, she realized the intruders were taking her to her bedroom. She struggled with consciousness as they tossed her onto her bed. The moment her back hit the bed, her head seemed to clear, and the ringing in her ears subsided. The first intruder unbuckled his belt. After her assault on his crotch, she knew he had to be hurting.

As he reached for her sleep shorts, Raina felt her adrenaline return. She flew upward into a sitting position and rammed her palm into his nose. He cried out while clutching his bleeding nose and stumbled backward. The second intruder leaped on top of her, but she managed to wedge her knee between them. He caught her wrists and attempted to pin her to the bed while she concentrated on getting leverage with her leg.

"Hold the bitch still," the man with the bleeding nose cried out and grabbed her ankle in an attempt to pull her knee out from his partner's midsection.

"What's going on here?" Dane's familiar voice boldly demanded.

Both men looked behind them and saw Dane standing in the doorway with his hands behind his back and a bewildered look on his face. Raina just about had her foot into the man's abdomen while he was distracted but became distracted herself. She looked at the doorway as well and stared at the clueless look on Dane's face.

"I'm calling the police," Dane boldly announced, as if that would be enough to stop the two men.

Horror swept over Raina, knowing Dane was going to be torn apart by the two men. "Dane, run!"

With her wedged foot now in her attacker's abdomen, she attempted to push him off her despite her poor leverage, but he refused to release her wrists. Alicia's killer stormed across the room with the knife in his hand and nearly reached Dane in the doorway. Dane revealed a two-shot, double-barrel shotgun carefully hidden behind his leg and barely aimed before pulling the trigger. The sound of the blast filled the bedroom. The killer barely saw the shotgun before taking the full brunt of the buckshot at close range to his chest, throwing him backward and onto the floor. The intruder holding Raina released her and spun to the deafening sound. The sound of the shotgun blast had nearly paralyzed her as well. Raina scrambled on her backside across her bed. Horror filled the man's face as he stared at the shotgun now aimed at him and raised his hands in the air.

"Don't shoot!"

There was no emotion in the butler's eyes as he pulled the trigger. Raina gasped and curled into a ball on the bed to avoid the shot that would be too close for comfort. The intruder immediately cringed and shut his eyes. All three were stunned when the shotgun clicked and nothing happened.

"Ah, fuck!" Dane cried out.

The intruder opened his eyes then sneered as he removed his own knife and lunged for Dane. Dane flipped the shotgun in his hand and swung it like a baseball bat. He struck the man on the shoulder, narrowly missing his head, knocking him back several feet and to the floor. Dane bolted for him and swung again. The intruder ducked the swinging shotgun and stabbed Dane in the upper thigh. Dane cried out in agony and dropped the shotgun. Before the intruder could pull the knife out, Dane punched him in the face. Dane stumbled back a step and looked from his injured leg to Raina, who stared with horror at the knife now stuck in the butler's thigh.

"Get out of here," Dane shouted the order.

Raina sprang off the bed but was reluctant to leave him. Instead, she ran for the dresser and grabbed her cell phone. The intruder scrambled to his feet with the shotgun in his hand and swung for Dane's head. Dane blocked the swinging shotgun with his forearm and was nearly driven to his knees from the pain and force. The intruder took advantage of Dane's helpless position and swung the shotgun for his head. Dane caught the shotgun with his left hand and punched him in the face with his right. The intruder dropped the shotgun and attempted to punch Dane in the face.

Dane caught his fist and twisted his arm, driving him to his knees. While he had the man on his knees, he pulled the knife free from his own thigh. Raina stared with horror as Dane's blood flew from the blade. He flipped the knife in his hand and plunged it into the man's throat. The intruder stared at Dane with horror as blood poured from his mouth and down his chin. Dane showed no emotion as he stared into the man's eyes then released him, allowing him to sink to the floor. As Dane stared at the dead man on the floor, Raina hurried to check on the injured butler.

As she reached him, his look softened as he stared into her eyes with concern.

"Are you okay?" Dane asked while panting heavily.

Raina stared at him with shock as her mouth hung open, and she slowly nodded, uncertain how to respond.

Dane straightened without taking his eyes off her. "You should probably call an ambulance," he announced just before he collapsed to the floor.

Chapter *6*

Sitting up with the Dead

Two days later. The viewings for both Alicia and Brenda were held at the Steele mansion within the formal sitting room. Alicia lay within the plush satin liner of her decorative casket surrounded in flowers. She wore a lacy, white wedding dress while holding a bouquet of yellow roses. Even in death, she was beautiful. Miller stared blankly at the love of his life while standing solemnly over her casket. Raina's father stood over the second casket on the opposite side of the room while clinging to his daughter. Brenda, who was dressed in her favorite peach evening dress, lay peacefully within her casket.

A room full of mourners grieved along with Otto, Raina, and Miller while the staff stood lined along the back wall. Each wore the same glossed over expressions on their faces. For some of the older staff, Brenda wasn't the first lady of the house tragically taken from them. Dane stood just inside the double doorway while leaning on a cane to support him after his injury. As Otto's friend and business partner approached, Raina released her father. Nole Oaks was a distinguished gentleman in his early forties, only a few years younger than Raina's father. Most women considered the man to be quite handsome with his ginger hair the perfect length for running fingers through. He had a neatly trimmed, ginger beard that gave him a slightly rugged, lumberjack appeal. His expensive taste in suits and watches only added to his physical appeal.

Unfortunately, he lacked charm and had a way of turning women off the moment he opened his mouth. He often made women uncomfortable with his constant, inappropriate touching. Despite that his touching wasn't necessarily sexual, it had a certain creepiness to it. Nole hugged Otto sympathetically and attempted to console him in the loss of his second wife. Raina slowly approached Miller, who still hadn't moved from Alicia's casket. Raina gently clung to his arm and rested her head on his shoulder. Miller couldn't tear his eyes away from his dead bride-to-be, and his expression never changed.

"Those men," he announced in an almost sedated voice. "They suffered, right?"

Raina patted his arm. "Yes, they suffered," she replied then drew a shaken breath while attempting to keep from reliving the events from two nights ago. "She tried to save Mom, Miller. She was very brave."

Miller seemed to hesitate then looked at his stepsister with surprise. "You called her mom."

She eyed him with bewilderment. "What?"

"You'd never called her mom before," he announced then managed a tiny smile. "She'd be happy that you called her mom."

Raina suddenly lost control of her emotions and started sobbing. "I was so close, Miller," she practically cried out. "A minute sooner. A minute sooner, and I may have been able to stop them. If I'd only been in my room. I should have been in my room." She placed her hand over her mouth to hold back her sobs. "But I had to get into another *pointless* argument with Dane!"

All eyes were suddenly on Raina as her voice rose above the low murmur of the crowd. Dane stared across the front sitting room at Raina. He lowered his head while fighting his tears and limped from the room. Miller pulled Raina against him, burying her face in his chest, and attempted to keep her from causing a scene.

"She thanked me for saving her, but I didn't save her," Raina sobbed then shook her head despite Miller keeping her face buried against him. "She died in my arms!"

Raina managed to pull back and met his tear-filled gaze. Miller was close to losing it himself from her words.

"All I could think was I wished it were me instead," Raina continued to sob. "Because I didn't know how I was going to tell you I couldn't save her!"

Miller clung to Raina to keep her from becoming hysterical while he sobbed uncontrollably onto the top of her head. Otto hurried across the sitting room and helped Miller escort Raina from the crowded room. Once they passed through the doorway, Levi rushed after them.

§

Once the wake was just about over later that evening, four of the six mansion staff gathered around the island counter in the kitchen for their own farewell gathering. Levi, Dane, and the two maids wore somber looks on their faces while empty shot glasses set on the counter before them. Despite their silence, all four were clearly drunk. Raina entered the kitchen from the back stairs. She looked heavily sedated and wore frumpy clothes, no longer dressed for the wake. When they saw her, Levi attempted to hide the nearly empty bottle of scotch. Everyone stared at her except Dane, who kept his eyes on his empty shot glass.

Raina slowly approached the counter while clinging to her arms folded over her chest. She uncrossed her arms and removed the partially hidden bottle from Levi. She filled Sloan's shot glass and drank the contents in one swallow. When she attempted to refill it, Dane took the bottle from her without making eye contact.

"Alcohol and sedatives don't mix," he gently informed her.

"Are they gone?" she practically whispered without looking at those staring at her.

"Mr. Oaks and the Nixon's are with your father in the study," Sloan replied timidly.

"Miller?" Raina asked.

"In the crypt saying goodbye," Levi gently informed her then fidgeted. "Titus and Hanson are keeping an eye on him for you."

Sloan caressed Raina's shoulder while leaning closer. "Can we do anything for you, Raina?"

Raina pushed the shot glass toward the bottle of scotch without response. Sloan frowned and looked at Dane while raising her brows. Dane reluctantly filled the shot glass. Raina drank the contents and nearly collapsed on the vacant stool. She finally looked up and eyed Dane across the island counter. He met her gaze and immediately looked down.

"I should check on Mr. Steele," Dane gently announced then drunkenly limped from the kitchen while leaning heavily on his cane.

A moment or two after he passed through the doorway, Raina leaped up from her chair and hurried from the kitchen after him. She saw Dane several feet down the hall where he had stopped. He leaned his back against the wall and attempted to restrain his emotions. Raina approached him in the hallway. When he saw her, he straightened, avoided eye contact, and turned to leave. Raina touched his arm, causing him to stop and turn to face her. He met her gaze for the first time and appeared to fumble over himself.

"I'm so sorry," he gasped with drunken emotion, his guilt clearly showing. "None of this would have happened if I'd gotten there sooner."

Without commenting, Raina placed her arms around his neck and clung to him while burying her face into his neck. Dane placed his arms around her and held her against him in a tight embrace while holding back his emotions. They held each other a long moment without saying a word. Raina finally pulled back to meet Dane's gaze and gently wiped the tears from his cheek. He smiled timidly and appeared embarrassed that he'd been caught crying. Raina stared into his blue eyes a moment while touching his damp cheek. Between the sedatives and the alcohol, her emotions were running rampant. As they stared into each other's eyes, she couldn't seem to control herself and kissed him quickly but warmly on the lips. Dane tensed slightly, surprised by the kiss, but didn't hold back as he pulled her against him and eagerly returned the kiss with added passion.

In that brief moment, a thousand inappropriate thoughts raced through Raina's mind. Every indecent thought she'd ever had regarding the butler seemed to surface. His kiss was intoxicating, and her inhibitions seemed to be taking a break. She somehow knew what she was doing was wrong, but she had a difficult time telling herself to stop. She wanted to feel something other than anger and sorrow even if it was only temporary. She heard the staff rustling around within the kitchen, jolting her back into reality. Raina hastily broke off the kiss and pulled away from Dane with some embarrassment while wiping her own tears. She managed a tiny laugh and smiled uncomfortably.

"You're right," Raina announced and had to avoid looking at him after the thoughts she had going through her mind. "Sedatives and alcohol are a bad combination."

Dane shifted with embarrassment and shook his head in her defense. "No, that was entirely my fault," he announced a little too quickly. "I wasn't thinking. It's been an emotional couple of days. I should know better--"

Raina gently touched his face, which immediately silenced him, and met his gaze. "Dane, it's okay," she announced almost timidly. "I think we both needed that."

He stared into her eyes with some surprise. "Really?" Dane shifted uncomfortably. "So we're good?"

She managed a warm smile and nodded. "Yeah, for the first time in four years, I think we're finally good."

The way he stared at her, she could tell he was surprised to hear her say that. "You don't know how much that means to me," he responded then smiled. "Thank you."

Chapter 7

The Happy Occasion

Two years later. Raina's black sports car pulled up to the mansion a little before five o'clock that Thursday evening and parked alongside several other, newer and much fancier cars. Raina and Miller got out of the sports car and stared at the mansion with matching frowns. Neither moved from their respective sides of the car. An attractive woman got out of the back seat of the two-door sports car. Raina's friend, Jenna Ford, was around the same age as Raina. She had dark nearly black hair carelessly pulled up into a ponytail and wore faded blue jeans and a black leather jacket. She looked more like the lead drummer in a rock band than someone attending a mansion party.

Jenna shut the passenger side door, straightened her leather jacket, and took a step toward the mansion. She hesitated when she realized Raina and Miller didn't follow. Jenna looked back at the brother and sister duo who hadn't moved from the car and continued to stare at the mansion as if a monster had come to life. She eyed them with a bewildered look and raised her brows in reaction. Neither Raina nor her brother had been back home since the funeral, which seemed like a lifetime ago. Raina could almost feel herself transformed back to two years ago and remembered repressed memories she'd forgotten after the tragedy.

§

Two years earlier. A paramedic, who had placed his jacket over her shoulders, assisted Raina from the mansion. She remembered being cold, which seemed strange considering how warm the night had been. She could still see the fleet of police cars swarming the fountain and their red and blue flashing lights brightening the exterior of the house as she was escorted onto the porch for the awaiting ambulance. She remembered the paramedic clinging to her almost weighing heavily upon her shoulder. She noticed his bloodstained hand clutching hers as tightly as she clutched his back. They paused on the porch a moment for her to stare at the media circus outside the house. She wondered why the paramedic weighed so heavily upon her, but she was almost glad since it comforted her.

As they continued across the porch, she caught the paramedic, who had been guiding her, and kept him from falling. As she again looked at the hand clutching hers, she saw the familiar, expensive watch. Raina hesitated a moment and realized she wasn't wearing a paramedic's jacket but a more familiar black suit jacket. She felt some of the fog within her head clearing and looked at the man she seemed to be assisting across the porch. It hadn't been a paramedic at all but Dane. She'd never seen Dane looking so pale before. He strained while limping alongside her, clinging to her for support.

Raina then saw a familiar car stop behind the fleet of emergency vehicles. She felt herself tremble as she stared at the newly arrived car. Miller got out of the car and stared at the house with a look of indescribable horror on his face. The moment Raina saw him; she screamed and sobbed uncontrollably as her legs gave out beneath her. The paramedic ripped Dane's hand from hers and kept him from falling to the porch with her. He protested as two paramedics forced the belligerent butler onto the waiting stretcher. Raina could only stare at her brother as he weaved through the emergency vehicles to reach her. She continued to sob knowing his world was about to end with what she couldn't bring herself to tell him.

§

Present day. Jenna's voice brought Raina back to reality. Her friend sarcastically pointed and indicated the mansion to her friends.

"Aren't we going inside?" she asked, seemingly snapping Miller out of a similar trance as well.

"Forget it. No way. I changed my mind," Raina blurted out as she came to life and adamantly shook her head. "I can't do it."

Miller eyed his stepsister across the roof of the sports car and reached for the passenger side door. "If you're not going than neither am I," he announced and was about to open the car door.

"Seriously?" Jenna suddenly launched with surprise and mild irritation. "We just drove five hours for you to drag me to your father's wedding. My ass is killing me!" She shook her head with some hostility. "I don't care what you two do, but I'm going inside."

Jenna spun on her booted heels and headed for the house. Raina and Miller exchanged looks overtop the car roof, frowned, and followed Jenna with less conviction. Jenna had been their wild card. Bringing Raina's friend along essentially forced them to go through with the visit. As they crossed the front patio and approached the mansion steps, Raina leaned closer to her brother.

"I can't believe he's marrying *her*," Raina muttered with disgust while shaking her head. "I mean, how can he do this to us?"

Miller folded his arms across his chest in a cross between childlike insecurity and annoyance. "I thought I'd be happy for him when he started dating again, but why her?" he scoffed then shook his head as if in shock while staring almost blankly. "I mean, seriously, why her?"

"Right place at the right time," Raina muttered as they lagged behind Jenna up the steps.

"But *her*?"

Raina and Miller joined Jenna on the stone porch before the double door. When neither stepped forward to get the door, Jenna glared at both, shook her head, and approached the door.

"Big babies," Jenna scoffed and without hesitation rang the bell.

Only a moment passed before the door opened to reveal Dane looking handsome in his expensive butler's uniform. As Raina stared at him, her heart suddenly skipped a beat. She hadn't seen him in two years, but it felt like yesterday. Dane appeared surprised to see them then offered a tiny, almost sympathetic smile.

"I'm a little surprised either of you showed," he announced and stood aside while showing them in with a slight bow. "I guess I'm out twenty bucks."

"I like him," Jenna announced while grinning and entered the house.

Miller looked at Dane with some surprise as he entered with Raina. "You were taking bets on whether or not we'd show?"

"Are you kidding?" Dane remarked as he shut the door behind them. He briefly met Raina's gaze, immediately fidgeted, and then resumed his cheerful demeanor. "Levi has odds on whether or not I'd show." His pleasant smile turned to a sneer. "The happy couple and their guests are celebrating in the game room."

Jenna stood on the elevated foyer and marveled at the nearly medieval appeal of the marble, grand hallway and elegant staircase. She nodded her approval then cast a look at Dane and smirked.

"Is anyone happy about this wedding?" Jenna finally asked. "I know those two weren't the ideal travel companions on our long drive here."

"Well, the bride and the groom seem to be happy about the wedding," Dane announced before considering Jenna's sarcastic question and raised his brows. "The bride's sister would probably be happy for them if she wasn't so busy seething with jealousy." He appeared falsely cheerful while avoiding looking at Raina. "I'll announce your arrival." Dane was quick to head down the foyer steps.

"Wow, that's one unpopular bride," Jenna muttered then eyed her friends. "What's the deal? When you invited me to this wedding, I think you may have neglected to tell me a few details."

Chapter 8
Friends and Foes

A small group of selected guests had gathered in the game room for the intimate pre-wedding celebration. The game room had a large, hand carved, wooden bar with enough seating for twelve guests and plenty of standing room. There was an expensive slate top pool table with thick pedestal legs and clawed feet near the back wall not far from the large, beveled glass window similar to the one in the library. There were two pub tables with tall seats not far from the pool table. A faux antique jukebox contained every imaginable song in digital format, although it had the appearance of a spinning record. There was a large, eight-person, felt-top poker table in the back corner. A set of sofas and a coffee table were strategically placed in the center of the room for entertaining many guests. Naturally, the room wouldn't be complete without the large, stone fireplace.

Several guests sat at the large bar while others played pool. The remaining guests stood around and socialized. Judging by their fancy outfits, Jenna was grossly underdressed in her faded blue jeans and worn leather jacket. All three followed Dane into the game room.

"When you told me your family was rich, I didn't realize you meant filthy rich," Jenna announced to her friends while eyeing the meticulously dressed men and women. She eyed her less than impressive wardrobe choice. "I would have worn my nicer jeans."

"I told you it was a semi-formal party," Raina remarked without sympathy.

"Yeah, semi-formal," Jenna scoffed. "No tee shirts and flip-flops. You should have told me to wear a dress."

"Do you own a dress?" Miller teased.

Jenna glared at him without humor. He grinned and laughed at her expense. Raina looked across the room and immediately tensed while linking insecurely onto Miller's arm. She gripped his arm so tight, he nearly yelped.

"Showtime," Raina muttered through a faux smile and gritted teeth.

Miller scanned the room and saw what his stepsister saw. He groaned with disgust. Callie approached them while decked out in an expensive, slinky dress.

"You made it," she squealed with delight. "We were worried you wouldn't show!"

Callie thrust her left hand out to reveal the large, almost gaudy diamond ring. Raina put on a false smile at the former maid and could barely look at the mutant diamond ring. Obviously, her father hadn't picked it out. His taste ran solitaire simple not crown jewels extravagant. Miller tightened his arm on Raina's hand as he attempted to control his building hostility. Raina slipped her hand out from his arm to avoid the intense pain. Otto crossed the room toward his children while beaming with delight. He gave Miller a manly hug then affectionately hugged Raina.

"I'm so glad you came," her father announced cheerfully. "I'll admit; I had my doubts."

"Of course we'd come to our father's wedding," Miller announced while putting on a false smile. "What sort of children wouldn't attend their father's wedding? That would be rude." He then muttered under his breath. "Or so Raina keeps telling me."

"It's just, well," he fumbled with his words. "Neither of you have been home since--" Otto hesitated and smiled timidly. "Well, since the funeral. Two years is a long time to stay away."

"That had nothing to do with you, Dad," Raina assured him. "You know that."

"I know. It's just when I visit you, I end up spending most of my time at the hotel," Otto remarked then smiled more naturally. "It'll be nice for us all to be under one roof for a change."

"Odd that the two of you share an apartment," Callie announced with a bewildered look. "I would think you could both afford your own places." She then giggled at the comment while eyeing them. "I mean, with the size of your trust funds and all."

"Miller and I like sharing an apartment," Raina remarked with little emotion.

"In all fairness, it's not really an apartment. It's actually a three-bedroom penthouse," Miller informed her through a fake smile. "Neither of us sees the point nor the added expense of having our own places."

Callie eyed them then grinned slyly. "You two aren't secretly *dating*, are you?"

"Callie," Otto practically scolded. "They're brother and sister."

"Not really," Callie reminded him. "Not blood siblings. Only by marriage."

"Close enough," Otto remarked and seemed tense by the entire conversation.

"Yeah, Callie," Raina reconfirmed while hiding her sneer. "Close enough."

Otto was desperate to change the subject and turned his attention to Jenna, who watched the sideshow with great interest.

"You must be Raina's friend, Jenna," Otto announced pleasantly while extending his hand to her.

"After five hours stuck in a car with these two, that might be debatable," Jenna informed him then smiled and politely shook his hand.

"They haven't changed much since they were kids," Otto remarked with a chuckle. "Why don't the three of you get something to drink and relax after your long trip? I'll introduce you to some of the other guests once you've had a chance to unwind."

Otto escorted Callie away from his daughter and stepson so the happy couple could mingle with their other guests and possibly avoid the conflict he was almost certainly expecting. Miller and Raina stared after the couple with matching frowns and hidden hostility.

"They seem *happy*," Miller muttered.

"Yes, they do," Raina replied with little enthusiasm and stared across the room.

There was a moment of awkward silence as both continued to stare at the couple. Jenna eyed both but didn't comment.

"I still hate her," Miller scoffed without emotion, refusing to look at Raina.

"Yep, me too," Raina announced with a sigh then looked around. "I need a drink."

Jenna groaned and shook her head. "Not nearly as bad as I do."

Chapter 9
The Snarling Beast

The intimate gathering of twenty was still going strong a little after eight that evening. Everyone continued to drink and socialize, particularly since they all knew one another. Raina and Miller played a game of pool while Jenna sat at a nearby pub table and watched the game. She occasionally scanned the room as if looking for something or someone. She seemed to zero in on what she'd been seeking.

"Who's the cute, distinguished looking man at the bar with your father?" Jenna finally asked.

Raina glanced across the room, although she already knew who occupied her father's time. "That's Nole, my father's business partner," Raina replied then returned to watch her stepbrother make his shot, sinking the nine ball. "You'll want to avoid him."

Jenna's eyes remained on the handsome, older man. "But he's cute," she insisted.

"He's creepy," Raina corrected with distaste. "He likes to touch when he talks. Trust me, if you as much as smile at him, you'll never get rid of him."

"He doesn't seem creepy, and I don't mind a little harmless flirting from cute guys," Jenna assured her then grinned playfully while giving her a quick once-over. "You should try it some time. You might like it."

Raina didn't seem impressed. "Don't say I didn't warn you," she muttered.

As Jenna stood and was about to approach the bar, Miller straightened after his shot and looked at her while leaning on his pool stick.

"Isn't he a little old for you?" Miller asked.

Jenna flashed a lustful grin. "Not too old for what I want," she announced then headed for the bar.

Miller shook his head and lined up his next shot. "How are you two friends?" he finally asked. "She flirts with every man she meets, and you're practically a nun."

"She doesn't flirt with every man," Raina scoffed then glared at him, offended by the comment, "and I'm most certainly not a nun."

He cast a sharp look at her. "Oh? When's the last time you had a boyfriend?" Miller asked then considered the question. "When's the last time you've even been on a date for that matter?"

"I had a date two weeks ago; I'll have you know," she announced defensively.

Miller straightened and glared at her. "With who?" he demanded then laughed. "The computer repair guy? He fixed your computer, and you offered him coffee. That's not a date."

"College taught me that guys are immature and should be avoided at all costs," she insisted while proudly raising her head. "Too many guys like you."

Miller studied her a moment with a strange look and appeared distant. She caught his stare and became defensive.

"And what's that look about?" she demanded, uncertain if it was actually directed at her.

"It's just, well, I think maybe you should talk to someone," he gently informed her.

Her eyes widened with surprise. "You think I need therapy?" Raina suddenly demanded. "Hey, you don't date, and I don't get on your ass about it."

"Yeah, I don't date. That's my point," he launched back. "That night fucked us both up." He moved closer to her and attempted to keep his voice down. "I don't date, because I lost the woman I loved. You lost all interest in men the same night. I don't understand the correlation, but it's all connected." He then hesitated while staring at her. "You told me everything that happened that night, right?"

She stared at him while feeling her defenses rise. Raina wanted to lash out, but she held back. "Yes, I told you everything," she snapped. "I'm just not ready for intimacy with anyone right now."

"Are you sure that's all?" he asked while eyeing her then shifted uncomfortably. "I know what those men tried to do and something like that can emotionally scar a person. If that's what's bothering you, you need to talk to me or someone about it."

She groaned with annoyance. "We're not having this discussion again," Raina retorted while attempting to keep her voice down. "Those men are dead. I watched them die. That's the best therapy I know." She hesitated and drew a shaken breath. "It's just--I just don't want to care about anyone right now." She met his gaze, revealing her emotions. "It hurts too much when you lose them. One day, those feelings will go away."

Miller frowned at the comment. "I can't argue with that," he muttered with understanding. "You're not wrong." He glanced across the room at Jenna laughing and talking with Nole. He met Raina's gaze. "I'm actually surprised you allowed Jenna in your circle if that's the case."

"Jenna's the exception to the rule," Raina replied and finally smiled. "The more I pushed her away, the harder she pushed back. We were meant to be friends. Besides, when provoked, she's a nasty, snarling beast. Who wouldn't love that quality in a friend?"

"Nasty, snarling beast?" Miller questioned then snorted a laugh. "Seems more like a little tease to me."

Both felt compelled to look across the room at Jenna, who now attempted to put some space between her and Nole. He kept moving closer and touched her arm while they talked. She was obviously regretting the decision to meet Otto's friend.

"So when does she turn all green and snarly?" Miller teased while grinning.

"Give her time."

They watched the scene a moment longer.

Miller then frowned. "Should we rescue her?" he finally asked.

"Nope," Raina replied with little care. "I warned her, but she didn't listen."

Chapter *10*

The Enemy of My Enemy

Raina and Miller had resumed their pool game when Raina's father and Callie approached them at the pool table. They had another couple in tow. They were Callie's sister, Elana Burton, and her boyfriend, Keefe Osborn. Elana was a slender, beautiful woman with distinctively strawberry blonde hair where her younger sister was more blonde. Elana's long hair was neatly styled in an elegant French twist in an attempt to look the part for the semi-formal gathering. Elana wasn't much taller than Raina, although she was about as thin as a woman could be without looking malnourished. As with her younger sister, Elana wore excessive amounts of makeup to give her face that flawless appearance. Elana was bustier than her sister, and it was entirely possible her breasts were fake, although Raina didn't usually see that outside her father's wealthy friends.

Keefe was built moderately muscular much like the chauffeur, Titus. He had perfect, nearly black hair with a classic Italian mobster appeal. The chances of Keefe being anymore handsome was almost physically impossible. His only flaw seemed to be the facial stubble most men seemed to think made them attractive. Raina didn't particularly care for the faux five o'clock shadow that had been trending for decades among handsome men. She was glad her stepbrother shaved daily and didn't go for the 'popular' look since she had to live with him. Miller was a bit of a neat freak when it came to his hygiene and wardrobe.

"Raina, Miller," Otto announced pleasantly. "This is Callie's sister, Elana, and her boyfriend, Keefe." He then eyed the young couple. "This is my daughter, Raina, and my son, Miller."

All four politely shook hands.

"Elana's my maid-of-honor," Callie boasted.

Naturally, her sister would be her maid-of-honor. It would have been odd if she wasn't.

Miller eyed Elana and appeared curious. "You look familiar," he announced while studying her. "Did we go to school together?"

Raina mentally rolled her eyes at the thought. It reminded her that her new, soon-to-be stepmother was only two years older than she was.

"No, we didn't live around here until after I graduated high school," Elana replied while clinging to Keefe's moderately muscular arm.

"You do look familiar," Miller pressed.

Naturally, Raina wondered if Miller had a one-night-stand with the attractive woman and that's why he thought she looked familiar. Miller wasn't a womanizer by any means, but he had gotten around before meeting Alicia.

"You've probably seen her with me," Callie announced while grinning. "She'd drop by and pick me up when we'd go out to nightclubs."

Miller nodded. "Yeah, that must be it."

Otto and Callie excused themselves so they could talk with their other guests leaving Miller and Raina alone with the couple.

"Didn't you work for the Nixon's?" Raina asked the attractive young woman.

"Actually, I still do," Elana replied then grinned deviously and nodded across the room.

Elana indicated a wealthy looking couple in their early forties, Farley and Gilda Nixon. They appeared to be watching

Elana and her boyfriend as well. Their dislike for the couple was evident. Raina had some knowledge of the Nixon's since they were what qualified as neighbors. Neighbors in the sense that they sort of lived next door, except that next door was technically three miles away by car. They'd moved in during Raina's sophomore year in high school, which would have been Miller's first year in college. They'd attended a few of her father's parties, but she didn't know them exceptionally well. Apparently, her father was acquainted with Farley from their trips to the country club.

Farley was a shorter, smaller man with dark hair and just a hint of graying on the sides. He was only an inch or two taller than Raina, making him under five foot eight. With his lean frame, Raina envisioned him making an excellent jockey. He was actually quite attractive, particularly in his expensive suit. Supposedly, Farley was an amazing golf player, although that was according to her father, who couldn't even make par for as often as he played. His reluctance to take lessons indicated he wasn't nearly as serious about his game as he was with socializing at the club with its well-to-do members.

Mrs. Nixon, or Gilda as some were allowed to call her, was the classic rich snob. She was refined and proper, so it was no surprise that she didn't socialize with those she considered beneath her. Raina was almost certain that included her since she refused to act like the daughter of a millionaire business tycoon. Gilda was wealth from her perfectly styled, always meticulously dyed hair, to her expensive shoes that undoubtedly cost more than Raina's entire wardrobe. Gilda wore a layer of carefully applied makeup and still only qualified as somewhat attractive. She was a tall woman, much taller than her husband was. She was a tick under five foot ten and was built more like a farmer's daughter than a fifth-generation heiress.

Little was feminine about Mrs. Nixon's physical appearance, although she attempted to achieve a feminine look with the clothes she wore. She had broad shoulders, and her waist gave way to slender hips, keeping her from being curvaceous. Raina sometimes wondered if it was physical looks that made some women more attractive than others or if it was actually their attitude and personality. Mrs. Nixon was a pretentious snob who thought very little of most women. Raina had even heard rumor Gilda looked down upon Otto as well, which wasn't surprising. Her father wasn't exactly the typical millionaire.

"They're not really comfortable being at the same party where their maid is a guest as well," Elana bubbled over with a giddy laugh, humored at the image. "Can you believe we're actually in adjoining rooms with a shared bathroom? Not sure whose idea that was. It's too funny though. The world suddenly makes no sense to them."

"They're old money," Raina announced and easily dismissed her father's rich friends. "They play by a different set of rules than the rest of us."

"It's nice to hear that," Elana remarked with relief. "Keefe and I were feeling a little out of place, and this is only a small gathering. I feel like everyone is looking down on us because we're commoners."

"I know how you feel," Miller announced with a dreary sigh. "My mother and I lived in a rundown apartment before she met Otto. For a long time, I felt out of place and as if everyone in his world of wealth looked down upon me." He cast a look at Raina and smiled. "Fortunately, I had Raina watching my back. I never wanted a sister, but I consider myself lucky I had no say in the matter."

Raina rolled her eyes at the sideways compliment and gave him a playful shove to shut up.

"That's right," Keefe announced with realization then grinned at Miller. "Otto adopted you after he married your mother."

"What happened to your real father?" Elana prompted then shifted uncomfortably. "If you don't mind my asking."

"I don't really know, and I don't care," Miller scoffed. "He ran out on my mother when he found out she was pregnant. He wanted nothing to do with her or me. Otto is the only father I've known."

"Callie and I never knew our father either," Elana remarked then frowned. "We weren't so lucky. Our mother took up with any creep who'd help pay the rent. As soon as I turned eighteen, I left home and was lucky to land a job with the Nixon's. I convinced them to hire Callie as well. Of course, she was only sixteen at the time, but no one knew that. Our mother certainly didn't care that we were gone, so she wasn't reporting us."

"I was lucky enough to have two wonderful mothers," Raina confessed then sank into her own thoughts along with some depression. "Unfortunately, both were tragically taken from me."

"How old were you when your real mother died?" Elana asked.

"I was six."

"What happened?" Elana pressed.

"Car accident along a dark, back road one rainy night," Raina replied in a timid tone. "It wasn't anyone's fault. She never liked driving stick shift, but it was the chauffeur's day off, so she took my father's Ferrari. It was too much car for her, especially in those conditions."

Miller eyed her with a strange look. "What are you talking about?" he asked with surprise then shook his head. "She wasn't driving."

She glared at him and turned impatient. "Of course she was," Raina snapped. "I think I'd know how my own mother died. How would you know? You weren't even around back then."

"Levi told me she was afraid to drive the Ferrari, so the butler drove," Miller explained.

"What?" she gasped while staring at him. "Levi told you that?"

"Yeah, Dawson died in the crash with her," Miller informed her. "He was driving the car."

"Dawson?" she demanded with confusion. "I don't remember a butler named Dawson."

"He had to be about sixty," Miller remarked. "He took his grandson in after his daughter died. Surely, you'd remember his grandson. Levi said the poor kid only lived here a few months before losing his grandfather. I guess he was pushed off on an uncle."

"I don't remember any of that," Raina insisted. She couldn't believe she was just hearing this now. It was a large home, so it was possible plenty was going on she didn't know about.

"Well, you were only six at the time," Miller reminded her. "I'm just relaying what Levi said. You'll have to ask him for the details."

Keefe managed a tiny laugh then turned apologetic. "Sorry, it just sounds like we're all damaged goods."

"Maybe we're not so different after all," Elana added almost cheerfully.

Miller raised his glass. "To damaged goods!"

All four smiled and laughed while clinking glasses. The mellow music from the vintage jukebox suddenly changed to a hip-hop song. Elana nearly choked on her drink and grabbed Keefe's hand.

"I love this song," Elana cried out and started dancing seductively.

Miller stared at Elana's risqué dance moves and immediately tensed. Elana pulled Keefe across the room so they could dance together. Miller grabbed Raina's arm and pulled her to the opposite side of the pool table out of earshot of the other guests. Raina nearly cried out in pain and pulled her arm free from her stepbrother then glared demandingly at him.

"What's so important that you practically tore my arm off?" Raina launched.

"I just remembered where I'd seen Elana," Miller gasped as his eyes widened.

"Where?"

"That strip club on the edge of town that I used to frequent before I'd met Alicia," he announced in a hushed gasp. "She's a stripper!"

Raina wasn't impressed with the new revelation. She wasn't big on gossip, and Elana's side job was of little relevance. "Everyone needs a hobby, Miller," she remarked with little emotion. "So she's a stripper. You're the pervert who pays to watch women take off their clothes. If you ask me; that makes you the one with the problem." She shrugged without care. "She seems nice enough."

He eyed the woman dancing seductively across the room. "And surprisingly flexible."

She groaned and shook her head. "Callie's sister being a stripper isn't going to stop Dad from marrying her," Raina boldly announced. "He'd probably marry her even if she herself was the stripper. Face it, Miller; nothing's going to stop this wedding."

Miller sulked and took a large swallow of his drink. "I blame Sloan."

"Sloan?" Raina demanded and stared at him with surprise. "What did Sloan ever do?"

"Nothing, that's the point," Miller muttered into his drink. "Why couldn't she have seduced Dad instead? She's twice as attractive, four times as smart, and has a level head."

Raina groaned and shook her head. "Get used to the idea," she announced. "Now let's put on our false smiles and get hammered like good children."

Chapter 11
All Bets Are Off

Ten o'clock that night, Raina and Jenna entered the kitchen and found the entire staff hanging out around the island counter. They appeared unusually quiet when they realized someone had entered.

Jenna felt the tension and eyed the five at the counter. "I'm guessing we interrupted gossip hour," she muttered.

"It's okay," Levi announced while relaxing. "It's just Raina."

Raina and Jenna approached and joined them at the island counter.

Dane eyed them and appeared curious. "Is the party breaking up?" the butler asked.

"No, not for a while," Raina announced and removed the bottle of vodka Levi had been attempting to hide. Raina eyed the bottle and raised her brows. "Hmm, the good stuff." She set the bottle on the counter and looked back at Dane. "Miller took a walk, and Jenna needed to escape Nole."

Sloan held back her gasp and sympathetically eyed Jenna. "Oh, you poor baby," she announced. "Didn't anyone warn you about him?"

Jenna rolled her eyes in response. It had been her own fault since she'd been warned. Levi opened a decorative tin to reveal cookies and placed it on the counter. Raina smiled and helped herself to a cookie. As Raina picked at her cookie, she noticed she and Jenna were receiving odd looks from the entire staff. Something was going on, but she didn't want to ask. Maybe she and Jenna *had* interrupted something.

"So," Titus boldly announced nearly startling them then grinned almost mockingly. "Anyone rip the blushing bride-to-be a new one yet?"

The remaining staff shot looks at him to the comment, although they seemed more irritated then surprised by the remark.

"Titus!" Dane scolded.

"Hey, I'm just curious, that's all," the chauffeur announced then leaned on the counter and grinned at Raina. "Did you crack yet, Raina?"

"I call foul," Levi suddenly proclaimed while pointing at Titus. "That's against the rules!"

Raina and Jenna eyed Levi then the rest of the staff in an attempt to understand what was happening.

"Did I miss something?" Raina asked feeling a little anxious herself.

"We have a small wager placed on who's going to go off on Callie first," Sloan announced then smiled mockingly at Raina. "Big money's on you."

"Okay, the bet's off," Hanson proclaimed with annoyance. "No stacking the deck. I want my money back."

"Hanson put his money on Miller," Sloan muttered while indicating the brawny gardener.

Raina eyed the staff with surprise. "You guys were taking bets on whether Miller or I would flip out on Callie?" she demanded.

"Not me," Levi announced defensively while holding his hands in the air. "I went with the wild card." He then grinned and indicated the butler. "My money's on Dane."

Dane glared at him with disapproval.

"Sorry, dude," Levi announced. "You've had that look of instability for weeks now."

"Well, if the bet's off, I'm going to bed," Titus announced with a defeated groan.

Titus and Hanson bickered between themselves as they left through the outer kitchen door. It wouldn't be the first time they got into a fight over a wager.

"I should probably check on the guests," Dane announced then left through the main kitchen door to the hallway.

Jenna glanced at the remaining staff consisting of Levi and Sloan. "So how unpopular is this bridezilla?" she asked. "It seems like everyone hates her."

"Pretty close," Sloan replied and sighed while frowning. "She used to be one of us. Rumor has it Mrs. Nixon shipped her over here six years ago because she was having an affair with Mr. Nixon." Her brows rose daringly. "After she arrived, she promptly slept her way through the ranks. She cozied up to Dane first, since he's in charge of the staff. After she got what she wanted from him, she tossed him aside for Hanson. Then she tossed him aside and stole Titus from me." Sloan sneered. "When Mr. Steele suddenly became available, she made herself at home in his bed." She shifted uncomfortably then eyed Raina and appeared embarrassed. "Sorry. I shouldn't have said that. That was insensitive."

"It's okay," Raina replied not even slightly bothered by the comment. "My father's only human."

"Sloan, shame on you," Levi scolded and wagged a warning finger at her. "What have I told you about gossiping?"

Sloan rolled her eyes and groaned. "Save some for you," she muttered.

"Exactly," he scoffed then grinned.

"So you're the only one not pissed at her?" Raina asked the cook.

His eyes widened while staring at Raina. "Are you kidding?" Levi balked with astonishment. "While she worked here, she tried several times to get me into trouble for things she would do." He offered a tiny laugh. "I guess she overestimated her grip on Dane because he never even said anything to me."

"Did anyone warn my father about her?" Raina asked with surprise while eyeing the two. "Is he aware she'd slept with the entire male staff?"

"Whoa, wait a minute," Levi suddenly chimed in. "I never slept with her."

"Dane was going to have a talk with him," Sloan replied with a defeated sigh. "No one knows what became of that. He's been unusually tight-lipped about it. We were sort of hoping you and Miller would protest their wedding and maybe cause a big enough rift."

"We agreed we wouldn't interfere," Raina reluctantly informed them.

"Instead, they bitched for five hours straight on the car ride here," Jenna announced.

"Well, on that depressing note, I may as well go to bed too," Sloan announced and groaned. "We have a full house tomorrow night for rehearsal. I'm the last maid standing, and I have a lot of rooms to freshen."

"Dad hasn't replaced Callie yet?" Raina asked with some surprise.

"We think Callie's attempting to get him to hire her sister," Sloan remarked then rolled her eyes. "You can imagine how that would work. I'd have to do twice the work while her sister sits around and chats with the lady of the house."

"My father didn't agree to that, did he?" Raina just about gasped.

"No, not yet," Sloan replied. "That's why the search for a replacement is taking so long. Callie has nixed all the applicants and chased away all the temporary maids in a 'not so silent' protest." She shook her head. "I don't even want to think about it, or I won't sleep."

Sloan headed into the servant's quarters through the connecting door. Once she was gone, Levi leaned on the counter and boldly stared Raina in the eyes.

"Okay, now that it's just us," Levi announced. "What will it take for you to have a psychotic episode and stop this wedding?"

Raina shifted uncomfortably. "I'm sorry, Levi."

"Did you offer her a bribe to stop the wedding?" Dane suddenly proclaimed from across the kitchen.

All three looked at Dane as he approached.

Levi quickly straightened and frowned with noted embarrassment that he'd been caught. "We need to get him a collar with a bell on it," he muttered to Raina then looked at Dane. "It was worth a shot. It's going to be hell taking orders from her. She's been impossible the last few months, and she doesn't even have any official power yet." He adamantly shook his head. "What happens when she starts giving the orders? You know she has it out for you."

"I've been up against others with more influence than Callie," Dane announced boldly as he eyed Raina then raised his brows. "And I haven't been fired yet."

Raina caught his not so subtle dig and hid her embarrassed smile.

Dane looked back at Levi. "We'll get through Callie's reign of terror," he announced. "I have faith that Mr. Steele values our loyalty."

Levi snatched the bottle of vodka from the counter. "You can have faith," he muttered. "I'm going to bed."

Jenna raised a brow and watched the cook leave through the servant's entrance. It was unclear what Jenna thought about the soap opera unfolding before her. Raina almost felt bad for dragging her friend along for the ride. Almost.

"I think I'm ready to turn in myself. It's been a long, weird day," Jenna announced and eyed Raina. "We should probably get our bags from your car."

"Your things are already in your rooms," Dane proudly informed them.

Raina eyed Dane as she tensed. "Oh, we probably should have discussed sleeping arrangements earlier," she informed him while fidgeting then adamantly shook her head. "I don't care what you have to do, Dane, but I'm not sleeping in my old bedroom."

"You don't have to worry about that. Your father considered that two years ago," Dane replied while adding a tiny smile. "The contractors completely gutted the upstairs bedrooms. The three master suites now overlook the garden."

"Really?" she asked with surprise then managed a smile and felt less uncomfortable with the situation. "That makes me feel better."

"I assure you; your father felt the same way about his master bedroom," Dane informed her. "I'll show you and your friend to your rooms."

They followed him to the kitchen stairs. As they walked behind him up the narrow back stairs, Jenna eyed Dane on the steps ahead of them then nudged Raina and indicated his backside. Dane's pants were tailored perfectly and hugged his buttocks in all the right places. Jenna raised her brows seductively in gesture. Raina rolled her eyes at her friend's dirty mind and shook her head despite secretly taking in an eyeful herself.

Chapter 12
A View to Die For

Raina and Jenna followed Dane along the second floor hallway and past several bedrooms. Raina instinctively stopped and looked at what would have been Brenda's bedroom. A strange chill raced down her spine. Dane and Jenna looked back at her, realizing she'd stopped, and noted her slightly pale expression. Echoes of that night haunted her. She could hear Alicia screaming for help. Dane approached and paused alongside her with a sympathetic look.

"I assure you," he announced delicately startling her. "There's nothing left of the old master bedroom. Perhaps you'd like to see for yourself--"

"No, I'm good," Raina replied a little too quickly then met his gaze despite her many attempts to avoid looking into his eyes.

When she looked into his blue eyes, images of Dane in her bedroom doorway with the shotgun flashed through her mind. Horrible images plagued her mind as if she were watching some slasher movie playing on an endless loop.

§

Two years ago. Raina hovered over Dane as he lay unconscious on her bedroom floor. She held pressure to his bleeding leg with one hand, putting the weight of her entire body behind it. She had her cell phone in her free hand and talked with the police.

"Please, hurry," she cried into the phone. "He's bleeding pretty badly."

Raina set the phone down on the floor just short of the swiftly collecting blood from the dead intruder with the knife embedded in his neck. She pressed the button marked 'home' from her contacts list on the blood-covered cell phone. The mansion phone in her bedroom rang in unison with the call she was placing.

"Come on, Levi," she groaned with increasing anxiety. "Pick up."

When the answering machine picked up, she disconnected the call and cursed under her breath. Raina kept pressure on Dane's leg. The blood had soaked through his black pants and oozed between her fingers. She looked around her room for something to stop the blood then stared at the dead intruder only a foot or more away from them. His eyes were open, and he seemed to be staring at her, but she knew he was dead. Raina forced herself to look away and continued to scan the room. She avoided letting her eyes settle on the second dead man and the gruesome shotgun wound that had torn apart his chest. She then looked behind her to the bed.

Raina sprang up from the floor and bolted across the blood-spattered carpet for her bed. She snatched one of the pillows from her bed and tore off the pillowcase. Raina cast the pillow aside and returned to Dane's side. She rolled the linen, wrapped it around his bleeding thigh, and tied it as tight as she could manage. She again hovered over Dane. As she reached out to touch his face, she saw his blood covering her hand. Her hand trembled. She drew a deep breath, wiped his blood on her once white tank top, and gently touched his face.

"Dane," she gasped while attempting to wake him. "Dane, wake up. I'm scared, and I don't know what to do."

Raina held back her sobs and attempted to keep her emotions in check. She had to hold it together, but she felt so alone. She eyed her cell phone and was about to reach for it when Dane slowly woke. He looked at her and appeared puzzled. To her surprise, he sat up, eyed the dead men, and attempted to stand.

"Mrs. Steele," he announced.

She attempted to stop him, but loss of blood stopped him for her. He held his head and swayed slightly. Raina clutched his free hand in both hers.

"You've lost a lot of blood," she informed him. "You need to remain still."

He looked at the pillowcase tied around his leg then looked back at Raina. She stared at him with an indescribable look of horror.

"Are you okay?" he asked and gently touched her face.

She shivered and nodded, although her eyes told a different story. Dane saw the look in her eyes. He slipped out of his jacket and placed it around her shoulders.

"I need you to concentrate on breathing," he announced firmly. "You're going into shock. Just stay with me, okay?"

Raina drew a deep breath while staring into his eyes through the dim lighting and nodded. She slowly slipped into his jacket and bundled it around her from the unexplained cold chill sweeping over her. He continued to stare into her eyes, forcing her to focus on him.

"Did you call the police?"

She nodded.

"That's good," he replied. "I'm going to check on Mrs. Steele and Miss Dunkirk."

Dane attempted to stand. Raina caught his hand and gripped it hard enough to stop him. He looked back at her while remaining on the floor with her.

"They're dead," she whispered then trembled and fought her emotions.

Dane stared at her with a horrified expression then pulled her against him with his left arm and held her head to his chest. She didn't release his hand and held it against her chest for comfort. She resisted the urge to break down. As he held her in silence, she concentrated on listening to the beating of his heart and his hand clinging to hers against her chest.

§

Present day. Raina twitched and realized Dane was still staring into her eyes as if reading her expression. She almost forgot they were still in the second floor corridor outside the old master bedroom. Her eyes subconsciously strayed to his leg. She could almost see the knife embedded in his thigh and the chilling moment when he ripped it from his own flesh. She again witnessed his blood flying from the knife. Surprisingly, she could feel the pain that he hadn't shown. Dane turned to show them to their rooms across the hall and intentionally leaned toward her in a secret motion.

"It's over," he whispered. "Let it go."

Raina snapped out of her trance and exhaled, realizing she'd been holding her breath. Jenna had turned as well and hadn't even noticed the exchange between the two. Dane's motion was seemingly flawless that he was already heading down the hall with Jenna. Raina inhaled deeply and followed. Dane paused before the bedroom door, which would have been Miller's old room on the other side of Brenda's old suite. He opened the door, switched on the light, and indicated the room to Jenna.

"The lavender room will be your room, Miss Ford," Dane announced while offering a pleasant smile. "There's an in-house directory alongside the phone on the nightstand. Dial nine for an outside line."

Jenna hesitantly approached the open door, glanced inside the room decked out in varying shades of purple, and then looked back at Dane. "No one died in there, right?"

"No, not that I'm aware," he replied reassuringly.

Jenna grimaced and looked at Raina. "See you in the morning, I hope." She disappeared into the bedroom and shut the door behind her. They heard it lock.

"You're across the hall," Dane announced and led her across the corridor.

Dane opened the bedroom door and stood aside. Raina uncertainly entered, stood just in the doorway, and looked around the breathtaking bedroom suite. There was a large window with a wide seat built into it that faced the garden, an elegant fireplace, private bathroom, and all new furniture. The room seemed to be filled with fresh flowers. The vase containing yellow roses on the bedside table, in particular, caught her eye. They were her favorite, and her father always seemed to have them by her bedside when she would return home. She was surprised he remembered after two years of absence. Raina approached the window while marveling at it, sat on the padded seat loaded with throw pillows, and looked at the garden, which encompassed the area around the pool. In the distance, she could see the family crypt, which contained her mother, stepmother, and Alicia. She turned on the window seat and eyed Dane.

"I'm surprised my father thought to put in a window seat," she announced with an almost humored look while reflecting back. "He has no idea how many hours I'd spend in the library on that window seat."

"He was made aware of that," he replied while offering a tiny grin.

She stared at him a moment and considered the comment. "Did you suggest it?"

"I may have mentioned it."

Raina hid her smile then stood and approached the large bed. Although she would miss her old bed, she was actually happy to be rid of it. She didn't want to be reminded of the two men struggling with her and what almost happened there. As she stared at the bed a moment longer, something about it seemed almost familiar. She realized it closely resembled the bed from one of her favorite books. She hesitated then glanced around the room and noticed other similarities from that particular book.

It seemed almost impossible that her father would have known any of those things. Although he knew which section of the library contained her books, he certainly wouldn't have known which book was her favorite. She supposed he could have seen her reading it numerous times, but he wasn't much for picking up on subtle details.

Raina approached the nightstand and picked up the old framed photo of her mother and father. She stared at it a moment then set the photo down and eyed the book on the nightstand. She appeared curious and picked it up. It was the same book she'd borrowed from the library the night of the murders. Raina returned the book and looked at Dane, who remained in the doorway. Judging by his expression, he had been closely watching her. She then realized every detail within the room had to have come from him. Between the two of them, they'd spent the most time in the library out of anyone else within the mansion. He had a keen eye for details and would probably be the only person in the house who would have noticed or cared what book she was reading.

"Will there be anything else, Miss Steele?" he politely asked snapping her out of her trance.

For a moment, she couldn't take her eyes off him. She then realized why her stepmother loved him so much. This was the sort of royal treatment he gave Brenda. He needed someone new to make a fuss over. Her nerves were suddenly on fire. Too many emotions were fighting for control of her. Anger over her father's choice of brides, an uneasiness of again being in the house that filled her with nightmares of the brutal slayings, and her renewed lust for the handsome butler. Now that she was no longer feuding with Dane, she had nothing to hold those feelings at bay.

She gently rubbed her chilled shoulders and managed a tiny, nervous laugh. "A strong sedative, if you've got any," Raina teased, although she was actually serious.

Dane approached the small bar and opened the door. There was a wide selection of beverages, alcohol, and mixers. His mocking smile was enough to humor her.

"You really have thought of everything, haven't you?" she remarked with a laugh.

"I try," he replied while grinning then indicated her private bathroom. "Incidentally, the Jacuzzi bathtub wasn't exactly authorized, so that'll be our little secret."

Raina smiled and laughed softly while staring at the handsome man. "I won't tell."

As she stared at him, she remembered their brief but passionate kiss in the grand hallway the evening of the wake.

Her heart skipped a beat while reflecting upon the intense moment. She never told anyone that she'd kissed Dane or that he'd kissed her back. It was one of the many new secrets they now kept between them. She wasn't sure how long they stared at each other, but when Dane tensed, she wondered what had been going through his mind.

"If you need anything, I left my cell phone number next to the phone," Dane informed her. "You'll be able to reach me at any hour."

She stared at him with some surprise. "I thought that number was reserved exclusively for my father?"

"I thought--" He hesitated, reconsidered his words, and smiled timidly. "I just want to make sure you're comfortable and feel *safe*." He offered a warm smile that nearly melted her heart. "Goodnight, Miss Steele." Dane turned to leave then hesitated and glanced back at her. "I'm glad you've come home."

He left the room, shutting the door behind him. Raina stared after him and felt her heart pounding in her chest. Keeping her attraction for the handsome butler at bay was much easier when they were at each other's throats. She looked at the card next to the phone then removed her cell phone and eagerly added the number to her contacts.

Chapter *13*
The Good Old Days

It was a little after six o'clock on Friday morning. Raina wearily entered the kitchen from the back stairs. She hadn't slept well despite the amazingly comfortable mattress in her new bedroom. It was going to be a busy, exhausting day for everyone, so she wasn't surprised to see Dane was already up and working. Dane stood by the main counter preparing the massive coffeemaker for their arriving guests, although the smaller coffeepot typically used for the household was also in use. He glanced back as she approached the island counter and appeared surprised to see her up already.

"Miss Steele," he announced pleasantly. "I didn't expect anyone to be up this early considering how late the party went last night."

Dane prepared a cup of tea as she nearly collapsed at the counter. He placed the mug before her along with the container of sugar substitute. She eyed the cup of tea with some surprise then managed a smile.

"How do you know I prefer tea?"

"I have a very good memory," he replied.

"I don't remember you ever making me tea before," she countered.

He placed his palms on the counter and leaned across it toward her while smirking. "That's because I was being a prick."

Raina glanced at him and the look on his face. He stared back with all seriousness. Was he baiting her or looking for an apology? For a moment, she felt a hint of their old rivalry. She desperately wanted to counter with something insulting to fire him up but decided against it.

She smiled with some embarrassment and took the mature approach. "Sorry about that."

"Don't be," Dane replied almost cheerfully and straightened. "I deserved it. Lord knows I called you a bitch enough times."

She gave him a bewildered stare. "I don't remember you ever calling me a bitch."

"Not to your face."

Raina saw his tiny smirk and hid her smile at his ability to laugh at their past feud. "I have to be honest with you, Dane," she announced. "I prefer being on your good side for a change. It was probably only a matter of time before we killed each other."

He smiled reflectively and sighed. "Ah, the good old days," Dane announced.

Raina looked at his teasing smile and laughed. She wasn't sure if he secretly missed their fierce fights. Although their current relationship was preferable, she did miss their verbal assaults on each other. Call her nostalgic.

She raised her teacup to her lips and scoffed, "Prick." It just slipped out.

"Bitch," he muttered then grinned with satisfaction.

Raina had to keep from laughing. It actually felt good. She sipped her tea and cast a look at him. "So what's on today's itinerary?" she asked as she set her cup down.

"Guests for rehearsal will arrive this afternoon. Rehearsal starts at four with dinner at seven," he announced as if reading from some invisible itinerary. "The caterers show up tomorrow morning promptly at nine, at which time the staff has been given the rest of the day off to either attend the wedding or skip town."

"Oh?" she replied with some surprise. "That's nice of the happy couple to invite the staff to join in their day."

"Just the wedding," Dane corrected and raised his brows. "Not the reception."

"Their generosity only goes so far, huh?"

"I assure you, I'm not complaining," Dane announced and withheld his grin. "In three days, your father and his bride leave for their month-long honeymoon. The entire staff has off with pay. Our only responsibility during that time is that one of us remains on the premises for security reasons."

"Now that's generous," she announced with some surprise although she shouldn't have been. Her father always treated the staff as equals. He knew the house would fall apart without them to hold it together.

"I suspect Sloan will use that additional time off to find a new employer," Dane announced and returned to his work at the main counter.

"Really?" Raina announced while feeling her heart sink. She adored Sloan and couldn't imagine ever coming home and not seeing her.

"Her position as upstairs maid puts her in close proximity to Callie and her reign of terror," Dane offered while looking over his shoulder at her. "She'll suffer more than the rest of us. She'll never be able to take orders from that one."

Raina looked at her tea and frowned. "I like Sloan," she pouted.

"Yes, me too," Dane replied. "I never had to lurk over her shoulder to make sure she did her work." He shrugged and turned to face Raina, leaning his back against the main counter. "She'll be graduating from community college with her registered nursing degree in another year. It's only a matter of time before she'll be finding work at some hospital anyway."

Titus entered through the outer kitchen door and cast a glance at Raina on his way to the smaller coffeepot. "For someone with nowhere to be, you're certainly up early," the chauffeur scoffed hoping to get a rise out of her.

"My inner demons wouldn't let me sleep," she remarked then eyed the moderately muscular man. "What's your excuse?"

"I'm playing chauffeur today," he announced while grinning playfully. "Wait, I am the chauffeur." He chuckled at his own comment. "I'm picking up our overnight guests to conserve space in the driveway for the big day. I suspect there will be a dozen or more limousines and dozens of cars clogging up the driveway." Titus chuckled more to himself. "Hanson is already wigging out that guests will park on his lawn. He's more of a prima donna over that lawn than Dane is about muddy feet on the kitchen floor."

"This is coming from the guy who pulls out the dust-vac every time there's a speck of dirt inside the limo," Dane remarked.

"Hey, I'm on top of my game," Titus announced and sipped his black coffee. "The rest of you are just anal retentive clean freaks."

"Would you girls like to be alone so you can bitch-slap each other?" Raina announced while casting glares at the two handsome men.

Both shot surprised looks at her.

Chapter *14*

Bridezilla

While both men were taking a break and enjoying their coffee, Raina kept the mood light with her not so charming personality. Callie appeared on the back stairs and hurried to the island counter with her long satin robe flowing behind her. Both men tensed by her presence. Dane easily pretended to be working, but Titus had coffee as his only reason for being in the kitchen. Raina minded her tea and didn't bother acknowledging the woman, who seemed to have a mission in mind.

"Titus, I'm glad I caught you before you left," Callie announced almost dramatically. "Elana needs a ride to the jewelers in the city."

"Mr. Steele has me picking up overnight guests the entire day," Titus informed her. "I don't have two hours to run to the city--"

"Find time," Callie snarled while glaring at him.

Titus and Callie stared at each other in a small battle of wills. Titus shifted uncomfortably, obviously hating having to take orders from his former equal and the woman who'd dumped him

"I'll need to clear it with Mr. Steele," Titus informed her with a hint of annoyance.

"*I've* cleared it with Mr. Steele," Callie practically snarled. "Do what I tell you."

Titus stared at Callie with a cold look, set his coffee cup down with enough force to nearly break his favorite mug, and then left the kitchen without further comment. Dane returned to the main counter and continued with his work. Callie looked at Raina as if finally realizing she was there and smiled sweetly.

"Thank God the wedding planner is arriving this afternoon," she announced and appeared relieved. "I'll tell you, Raina, a wedding planner is the way to go. I thought having the wedding here would simplify things, but it's just one, big headache."

"So I noticed," Raina replied with little interest. "I think I'd prefer a smaller wedding myself."

"Tell that to your father," Callie announced. "Most of the guests are his. Friends, clients, and business associates. I'm afraid the reception may turn into a convention." She sighed and shook her head. "I only invited about fifty people. I don't have any relatives." She considered the comment. "At least none I'd want to invite." She then eyed Dane while he worked. "How about some coffee, Dane?"

"I'm brewing a fresh pot," he announced without looking away from the main counter. "It'll be a few minutes before it's ready, Ms. Burton."

"I can't function without my morning coffee," she pouted in response then groaned while covering her eyes with her hand. "It's going to be a long day."

"Tell me about it," Raina muttered into her tea mug.

Callie spun toward Dane's turned back. "Dane, when the wedding planner arrives, I expect you to give him your full cooperation."

Dane finally turned and placed a plate of scones on the island counter with enough added force to make Raina jump. He met Callie's gaze and attempted to remain polite, although it had to be difficult.

"I've spoken with Mr. Love on the phone," Dane informed her. "Everything is in order for his arrival."

"You'd better give him the respect he's due," Callie practically huffed while pressing the issue as if purposely attempting to get a rise out of the butler. "I don't want you upsetting him with that surly personality of yours."

Dane didn't react, but the irritation showed in his blue eyes. "I've never been rude to a guest since I've worked for Mr. Steele," he informed her.

"Maybe not, but I know two women in this room who you've been a little more than snarly with," Callie boldly announced.

Dane remained rigid while staring at Callie. He appeared ready to explode but somehow seemed to hold it together. Raina watched him closely in silence as she held her tea mug to her lips.

"I will treat Mr. Love with respect," he responded almost through gritted teeth.

Raina knew his politeness at that moment had to be difficult. She wondered if what was playing out before her was what it had been like when she got into it with him.

"His room is ready, I trust," Callie pressed.

"Yes, Ms. Burton."

"The lavender room across from mine," she insisted with little emotion.

"Miss Ford is in the lavender room," Dane replied. "Mr. Love will be in the gold room."

Callie's expression immediately dropped, and she reacted as if it were the end of the world. "That won't do, Dane," she squawked. "I specifically asked that he be put in the lavender room. Purple is his favorite color. Besides, if he's in the gold room, he's sharing a bathroom. It's bad enough my dear friends, Tia and Olivia, are sharing a bathroom."

"Then he can have the silver room, which has a private bath," Dane informed her. "We can move Mr. Oaks to the gold room."

"Mr. Steele wants Nole in a room with a private bath," she interjected.

"We have no other rooms with private baths," Dane reminded her. "Unless, of course, you'd like to put him in the servant's quarters."

Raina's eyes widened with surprise at the remark. Thankfully, she hadn't been sipping her tea at the moment, or she would have spit it out. She secretly commended Dane on his snarky comeback.

"So move Miss Ford to the gold room and put Mr. Love in the lavender room," Callie snarled through gritted teeth and put on a false smile. "As I had requested in the first place." She then turned to Raina and smiled sweetly. "Your friend won't mind, I'm sure."

"No, probably not," Raina replied.

Callie spun back to face Dane and sneered at him. "There. Problem solved."

"But I mind," Raina casually replied.

Callie looked at Raina with surprise as her mouth hung open. "Excuse me?"

"Jenna is already unpacked and comfortable in her room," Raina informed Callie as she leaned back in her chair at the counter. "Moving her would be an inconvenience to her and Sloan, who would be required to change the sheets and scrub down the bathroom, which I'm sure she just did yesterday." Raina straightened proudly in her chair and stared into Callie's eyes without flinching. "Jenna stays in that room." Raina raised her brows and mocked the woman with her look. "I guess your wedding planner will just have to rough it in the gold room."

Callie spun to face Dane, who hadn't moved and seemed a bit surprised by Raina's scathing remarks, although it was possible he was secretly smiling.

"Move Miss Ford," Callie fumed. "Now!"

Dane gave Callie an innocent look. "I don't have the authority to override Miss Steele's orders," he announced without emotion.

"What the hell are you talking about?" Callie bellowed in an explosion of hostility. "You've never done anything she's ever told you to do in your life. You've made it your mission to defy her."

"I'm sure I don't know what you're talking about," Dane remarked with an innocent look. "Our relationship has always been mutually respectful."

Raina couldn't keep from giggling into her teacup. Callie didn't seem to notice her reaction since her wrath was aimed at Dane.

"Don't fucking play games with me, Dane," Callie lashed out while practically jumping in place.

The coffee machine hissed having finished the brewing process.

Dane cocked his head while smiling. "I believe your coffee is ready, madam," he announced politely.

"Don't you fucking 'madam' me, you little prick," Callie cried out while pointing demandingly at him. "I'll have your balls on a platter!"

"Hey!" Raina suddenly shouted in a commanding tone that startled both.

Callie and Dane shot surprised looks at Raina, who appeared ready to jump out of her seat while glaring at her future stepmother.

"You don't talk to the staff that way," Raina lashed out in rage. "If you don't want a fat lip to go with that big mouth, you'd better watch your language and rein in that condescending, bridezilla attitude."

With his arms folded across his chest, Dane shot looks between the two women while holding his fingers to his lips to hide his humored smile. He was enjoying their clash a little too much.

"How dare you speak to me that way?" Callie gasped. "I'm marrying your father tomorrow!"

"Which means precisely jack shit to me," Raina launched back. "Marrying my father doesn't give you any authority over me, Callie." Her eyes immediately narrowed. "I know where you've been and *who* you've been under, so drop the superior attitude."

"I'm talking to your father," Callie cried out. "You won't speak to me this way!"

"Oh, I'm through speaking," Raina boldly remarked. "My next course of action will be a fist to your face."

Callie stared at Raina, unable to respond, and appeared slightly alarmed. She hurried from the kitchen by way of the nearby stairs. Dane stared at Raina, who still sat perched forward in her seat ready to strike. He allowed his arms to fall to his sides.

"If you don't blink or breathe soon, I'm breaking out the sedatives," Dane announced with concern.

Raina slowly sat back and exhaled as her entire body trembled. She stared blankly at the counter.

"Are you okay?" Dane asked while watching her as he took a step closer.

"I--I don't know what came over me," she gasped as she opened her clenched fist and flexed her hand. "I wanted to rip her face off." She met his gaze. "I mean, *literally* rip her face off."

"Yes, I believe you," Dane replied. "She has that effect on people."

Raina relaxed and leaned on the counter while holding her head. "I don't know what's wrong with me," she groaned. "My emotions are all over the place."

He stared at her a moment in silence then appeared curious. "Just recently?" he asked. "Or since *that* night?"

Raina tensed but couldn't bring herself to look up. "Since that night," she replied softly. "Usually I'm fine, but sometimes, for no reason, I'll become extremely paranoid, uncontrollably violent, or a sobbing mess."

"Sounds like PTS. Post Traumatic Syndrome," he informed her. "It's not just for soldiers anymore. You survived a horrific trauma, and I suspect you're repressing your emotions about what happened."

"No kidding. Do you think I want to talk about it?" she snapped while finally glaring at him. "When I talk about it, I get angry. You saw me at the funeral. Nothing's changed." She shook her head and straightened. "Miller wanted to talk about it once, and I ended up smashing the television. I scared him and myself." She studied him a moment while attempting to relax and gave him a curious look. "How are you able to hold it together?"

"We all wrestle with our inner demons in different ways," he informed her.

"So you're saying I'm emotionally weak," she scoffed and added a laugh. "That's perfect."

"I didn't say that, but I do think you hold in your emotions," he replied.

"So I should break a few more televisions?" Raina demanded.

"Perhaps," he replied then appeared curious. "Did you tell the police everything that happened that night?"

"I think so."

"The things you said at the funeral weren't in the police report," he informed her.

"How would you know what was in the report?" she asked with surprise.

"Detective Payne let me read your account of what happened," he informed her. "You didn't mention Alicia speaking to you before she died, just that she died. I think that's been weighing heavily on you."

"I don't want to talk about this, Dane," she announced in a firm, cold tone.

"You're holding back," he insisted and shook his head. "That's not healthy."

She glared at him and sneered with annoyance. "You and I having this conversation isn't healthy."

He studied her and attempted to read her expression. "Did something happen that you're repressing?"

"I'm not repressing anything," she snapped at him. "Nothing happened. This conversation is over."

Raina stood and left the kitchen.

Chapter *15*
The Rehearsal Dinner
AKA
Get with the Program

Later that day, Raina sat on the half wall of the back terrace while staring out at the garden. The garden was filled with a variety of flowers in full bloom, and there wasn't a blade of grass out of place. The meticulous lawn and garden had little to do with the outside wedding. Hanson, the groundskeeper, was a garden Nazi and protected every flower with his life. Despite his somewhat frightening relationship with the estate grounds, Raina had to admire his dedication to his job. Her father walked onto the terrace from the kitchen entrance, approached, and sat alongside her while sighing deeply. He placed his hand on her hand.

"Are you okay?" he gently asked.

"Why?" she immediately demanded and glared at him. "Did Callie tell you I flipped out on her?"

"She mentioned a disagreement," Otto announced then stared at her with some surprise. "This is the first I heard about flipping out." He appeared curious. "Did you flip out on her?"

She frowned and shrugged. "Maybe a little," Raina remarked then looked up and met her father's gaze. "She's being unreasonable, and I don't appreciate you siding with her on this."

Her father stared at her with surprise. "Who said I was siding with her? I'm not siding with her," Otto insisted. "She told me about her request to change your friend's room, and you refused her request."

"Yes, I refused."

"So your friend stays in the lavender room," he replied and shrugged. "No big deal."

"That's not how Callie saw it," Raina informed him while raising a cocky brow.

"My daughter's friend trumps the wedding planner," Otto proudly announced. "For what I'm paying that guy, he can buy his own damned house." He affectionately patted her hand. "I'm happy you and Miller are here. I'm not going to let Callie's pre-wedding jitters chase my daughter and son from my house." He shrugged with little concern. "All brides get a little crazy before their wedding day." He chuckled while fondly reflecting back. "Your poor mother gained a pound and thought it was the end of the world. In the end, the dress still fit." Otto considered something else. "Brenda obsessed over the wrong flowers being sent, but the wrong ones actually looked better in the photos." He sank into thought and sighed. "Callie is obsessing over the wedding planner like he's God himself." Otto laughed and shook his head. "Wait until you meet this guy. He's as flighty as he is flashy. She's afraid he'll throw a tantrum and leave her in total chaos."

"Remind me not to get married--ever," Raina muttered without looking at him.

Otto squeezed her hand. "No, never," he proudly announced as he straightened. "I want to walk my daughter down the aisle."

There was an awkward silence as Raina considered the promise she and Miller made regarding the wedding. Raina tensed and glanced at her father.

"Dad, can I ask you something personal?"

"As my daughter, it's your prerogative," he announced cheerfully.

"Have you ever considered Callie might be after your money?" she asked and attempted to keep from cringing at the question.

Otto tensed then drew a deep breath and sighed. "Raina, I know you and Miller don't approve of Callie," he announced. "You haven't exactly disapproved, but your lack of enthusiasm speaks volumes." He stared into her eyes. "I know she loves me, and there's nothing you can say that'll stop me from marrying her."

"Yeah, I told Miller that," she muttered.

"You didn't let me finish," he announced. "I know there's a very real possibility I may not approve of the young man you bring home either, so that being said, I required Callie to sign a prenuptial agreement the same as I'll require your young man to sign one. I couldn't possibly expect you to do what I wouldn't."

She stared at him with surprise. "And she signed it?" Raina gasped.

"Yes, without protest," he replied. "Does that make you feel better?"

"A little," Raina announced then stared into his eyes. "I want her to love you for you, not your money. You deserve to be happy, Dad."

He hugged her affectionately. "Thank you, Raina." He pulled away and gave her a serious look. "Now can I ask you something personal?"

She tensed at the question then laughed it off. "How can I refuse?"

"You've been in this house over twenty-four hours," he announced. "Why haven't you and Dane clashed yet? There hasn't been a single explosion, one hurled accusation, or even a scathing insult. What gives?"

She hesitated, drew a deep breath, and smiled timidly. "It's hard to fight with the man who saved my life," she replied.

Otto stared at her a moment and nodded. "Yes, I suppose so," he announced then frowned. "I guess I'm out twenty bucks. I should have known Levi was fleecing me."

She stared at him with surprise to the confession involving another wager at her expense then shook her head in disappointment. "I think the people in this house need to find more constructive hobbies."

§

Later in the afternoon, the rehearsal party of seventeen gathered in the garden before the gazebo, which wasn't yet prepared for the lavish wedding the following day. Hanson stood fifty yards away and closely watched where every person stood and stepped on his precious lawn. The minister stood inside the gazebo with Callie and Otto, who faced each other while holding hands. Nole, Miller, and Farley stood alongside the groom, while Elana, and Callie's two friends, Tia and Olivia, stood alongside the bride-to-be. Everyone was dressed formally informal, which in the world of the wealthy had the men wearing casual suits and the women wearing simple yet nice dresses. Even Jenna was wearing a dress for the rehearsal party, despite that she borrowed it from Raina. Her friend wasn't about to be caught wearing her nicer jeans as originally scheduled.

The minister instructed each on their job throughout the ceremony and even had some fun at the expense of the groomsmen regarding their missteps.

"Then we'll exchange the rings, and I'll say those most important words," the minister announced while grinning. "You may kiss your bride."

Otto grinned and, on command, kissed Callie. She returned the kiss as several within the rehearsal party clapped and cheered. Miller frowned and clapped his hands with mild disinterest. Jenna and Raina glared at him from the area on the lawn where the chairs would be set. Miller caught their disapproving stares and sneered back in return.

§

The back terrace was set up for the after rehearsal party with three, large round tables. Each contained six elegant place settings, which included the good china, rarely used silverware, and the crystal champagne glasses. In addition to the wedding party, the seventeen guests included Gilda Nixon, Keefe, and a lanky man sporting a blue rhinestone jacket, Jimmy Love, the wedding planner. Jimmy Love was possibly in his mid-to-late thirties, although it was difficult to tell since it appeared as if he wore makeup or concealer at the very least. Raina couldn't even tell if he was a good-looking man beneath his makeup. His over-the-top personality was as flashy as his jacket and somehow made him that much more appealing to the eye.

Jimmy Love had his head shaved on both sides with a mound of Buddy Holly hair on top. It was difficult to tell what color his hair would have been since it was an array of colors streaked throughout. He wore a large, diamond stud earring in each ear, flashy rings on every finger, and an expensive, glittery watch on his left wrist. His skin was heavily bronzed, but it was impossible to tell if he'd spent too much time in the sun, had a spray on tan, or if it was his natural complexion. Raina's best guess on his ethnicity was that he was from Venus or possibly Saturn.

The guests sat at the three tables and enjoyed their elegant meal, which Dane, Sloan, and Levi busily served. Dane was in charge of champagne and beverages. Levi and Sloan served the meal and cleaned away dirty dishes with their usual efficiency. Raina, Miller, and Jenna occupied a table with Jimmy Love and Callie's two attractive bridesmaids and longtime friends, Tia and Olivia. Tia and Olivia were the same age as Callie since she knew them from high school. Tia was a perky blonde bombshell with her greatest assets being her hair and her large bosom. She fancied her makeup and wore it a little on the heavy side.

Olivia had sandy brown hair almost in the same style as her friend wore. She was just as attractive as her counterpart, except she wore less makeup. Her large brown eyes seemed to make up for her less ample breasts. Both women wore revealing dresses that displayed their cleavage and plenty of leg, which they willingly flaunted while giggling as they listened to Jimmy Love's animated conversation. Miller attempted not to stare at the women's cleavage while Jenna gave him disapproving looks.

"For a guy who's not looking; you're certainly looking a lot," Jenna remarked to Miller regarding his straying eyes. She almost seemed jealous of the fact.

"They're practically spilling out onto their plates," Miller muttered while leaning closer to Jenna. "How am I supposed to *not* look? Besides, who says I can't look while I'm not looking?"

Despite his overwhelming feminine characteristics, Jimmy Love appeared to shamelessly flirt with both of Callie's friends. His enthusiasm was nearly exhausting as the man never stopped to take a breath.

"And I said to her, 'girl, if it works for you, work it'," he cried out in a shrill wail while dramatically snapping his fingers in the air.

Both women giggled and touched his flashy, rhinestone jacket. They loved his unbridled attention.

"I just love good wedding gossip!" Jimmy Love squawked in his voice that turned shrill the more animated he became.

Raina leaned closer to Miller while watching the exchange across the table. "He's gay, right?"

"I don't know," Miller remarked while knitting his brows with confusion. "His outfit screams Elton John raided Liberace's closet, but he's working those girls like Don Juan had overdosed on Viagra."

"A simple yes or no would have worked," Raina muttered in response.

Dane approached their table and refilled Raina's champagne glass once again, barely allowing it to go below half-full. She glanced up at him and offered a humored smile.

"I've had three glasses already," she informed him.

"Me too," Dane responded.

She looked at him and eyed his cheap grin. She hid her smile and had to look away.

"Woohoo, cutie pie," Jimmy Love cried out while pointing to Dane from across the table and dramatically motioned to himself and the ladies. "Bring some of that expensive bubbly this way!"

"Did he just call me cutie pie?" Dane asked under his breath.

Raina smiled and shrugged. "I've heard plenty of men say you have a cute butt," she announced while grinning.

Dane sneered at her then rounded the table and refilled Jimmy Love's glass. The flashy man gave his backside a quick once-over while he poured the champagne.

"Hmm, you are delicious," Jimmy Love declared loud enough for the entire table to hear.

Dane straightened with surprise, eyed him, and backed away, uncertain how to take the strange compliment.

Jimmy Love squealed and laughed. "Oh, I scared another one straight!" He returned his attention to Tia and indicated her cleavage. "Tell me, honey. How do you keep those things from just jumping out?" he asked while waving his hands around. "You have me in a tizzy with anticipation!" He gave her a quick once-over. "You, me, and your little honey there are going to jump, jive, and wail tomorrow night! Oh, baby!"

Miller leaned closer to Jenna without taking his eyes off the flashy, flamboyant man across the table. "Okay, now I'm really confused."

"Not nearly as confused as Jimmy Love," Jenna teased while grinning.

Chapter *16*
Another Party?

Later that evening, the dirty china dishes and crystal glasses had been cleared from the tables allowing the guests to socialize and have drinks from the portable bar set up on the patio. Dane tended bar, although that was usually Levi's job during parties. Levi undeniably had the better personality to play bartender. Jenna spent half the evening attempting to elude Nole, who now had his sights set on her after last night's introduction. Music had been piped onto the terrace through hidden speakers. At the bride's request, the music was more modern club music. Jimmy Love danced spiritedly with the lovely Tia and Olivia on the stone terrace. He had some impressive dance moves, and the women seemed to enjoy his company. They danced seductively around him, which he was giddy to reciprocate.

Elana and Keefe danced slowly despite the fast-paced music. Their dancing, which included a lot of bumping and grinding, was to the point of obscene. Otto attempted to learn some new dance moves with his future bride and the younger crowd. As expected, the Nixon's stood together yet acted as if they didn't know each other. Their marriage had to be a cold one. Raina felt a little sorry for Farley Nixon. He was a docile man who pretty much jumped when his wife said jump. When Raina looked at her friend alongside her, Nole had crept his way back to Jenna and resumed his play to win her attention. Raina almost felt sorry for her friend, but she had warned her about Nole. Although she wouldn't admit it, Raina was a little perturbed that her friend seemed to have gone out of her way to make Miller jealous by approaching Nole in the first place.

Jenna had been pursuing Miller since she first met him; not that Miller had any clue how Raina's friend felt about him. Raina grew bored with the game and desperately wanted to tell her brother about Jenna's feelings for him, but she promised to keep out of it. Jenna didn't want Miller playing ball in her court until he was ready. Raina hated to tell her; that day may never come without the proper prodding. Miller, who had disappeared for a while, made his reappearance and approached Jenna, who was still unable to escape Nole's pesky persistence.

Miller politely extended his hand to her. "May I have this dance?"

Jenna appeared relieved and accepted his hand. "I thought you'd never ask."

Raina was actually surprised her brother stepped up to the plate. Not that he hadn't danced with Jenna at the nightclubs when they'd go out, but the intimate setting dictated he might shy away from dancing with a woman who wasn't Alicia. Raina was interested to see how it played out. Miller led Jenna to what had been designated as the outside dance floor just as the song turned slow. Miller groaned and reluctantly caved to dancing the slow song with Raina's friend. Jenna didn't seem to mind and was grateful to escape Nole.

"That Nole; he's--"

"Creepy?"

She groaned displaying her annoyance. "Oh, I hate when Raina is right all the time," Jenna scoffed. "I can't believe I'm going to spend the entire reception avoiding him and his tentacles."

"Yes, he's pretty persistent with his testicles," Miller remarked.

Jenna glared at him while they danced. "I said tentacles," she insisted.

"I know," he replied then laughed at her expense. "Relax. There'll be plenty of other guests. Over two hundred, I believe. I'm sure he'll latch on to someone else."

"I'm not so sure," she remarked. "He seems pretty persistent."

"Well, there is the extreme option," Miller announced almost teasingly.

She gave him a puzzled look. "What's the extreme option?"

"You could come as my date," Miller stated matter-of-factly. "That'll get rid of him."

"You and me?" Jenna announced then chuckled while studying him with a sly smile. "I thought you had a prudish reputation to defend."

"Hey, I was just trying to be nice," he remarked somewhat defensively. "You don't have to get snarly."

"Yes, I'd like to be your date for the wedding," Jenna quickly responded before he'd change his mind. "You're certainly a step up from my original date."

"Who was that?" he asked with surprise.

"Raina," Jenna replied while grinning. "At least with you, there's the option of a goodnight kiss."

Miller hesitated and stared at her a moment at the last comment. He immediately covered and offered a grin. "Oh, Raina's not your type, huh?"

"Now who's being snarly?"

Raina watched her friend and stepbrother share a slow dance and hid her devious smile. Maybe it would work out between them after all. Finally realizing she was now bored, Raina noticed Farley Nixon had been abandoned by his wife. Raina decided to make a little small talk. The poor guy looked like he needed a little light conversation. Raina approached Farley and attempted her best, approachable smile. She barely knew the man, which would make for awkward conversation, but he looked like he could use the company.

"Hey, Mr. Nixon," she announced in a cheerful tone. "Are you enjoying yourself?"

He smiled when he saw her. "Raina," Farley announced. "It's nice to see you again. You *can* call me Farley."

So he said. She remembered calling Mrs. Nixon by her first name a few years back and was immediately corrected by the insufferable woman.

"Beautiful night, isn't it?" Raina asked while scrounging for something to say to the man who was her neighbor for years yet practically a stranger to her. She mentally rolled her eyes at her own words. She couldn't believe she was actually talking about the weather.

He looked up to the clear sky and the many bright stars then smiled as he looked back at her. "Yes, it's an astronomer's heaven out here," Farley informed her. "I always wanted to study the stars." He grinned. "Or be the captain of my own starship."

Raina laughed at the comment. Her amusement with his conversation allowed him the opportunity to relax, and he spontaneously combusted into a charming man. Farley indicated the nearly full moon with a gentle nod.

"When I studied abroad, I'd spent time in a small village," he informed her. "They believed getting married at midnight under a full moon would bless the couple with a lifetime of happiness."

She found that interesting, although she couldn't imagine it would help her father's marriage to Callie. His marriage was almost certainly doomed before it began. Raina grinned and eyed him.

"Were you able to prove that theory?" she couldn't help but tease.

He considered the comment as Gilda approached. "I can't say for certain," Farley replied then raised his brows. "But being married under no moon spells doom for a marriage."

Raina stared at him a minute with bewilderment as Gilda paused alongside her husband. The look his wife gave him was enough to make Raina understand the significance of the comment. Despite his warm smile, she knew he was secretly crying for help. Gilda seemed to effectively silence her husband with her mere presence then eyed Raina and put on a false smile.

"Raina," she announced with a strange hiss to her voice. "We were surprised you actually showed up. You and Miller haven't been home in years."

"No, we haven't," Raina replied and shifted uncomfortably. "Not since the murders."

"Yes, I'm very sorry about that," Gilda remarked even if her tone didn't convey sorrow. She gave her a strange look while cocking her head to the side. "I heard you and Miller share an apartment together. A bit strange. I mean, strange for brother and sister, but almost unusually strange considering you're technically not blood relatives."

Raina found it odd how so many people wanted to put her and Miller in a relationship just because they were close but not technically related. In her mind, Miller was her brother. On the few occasions she'd caught him walking to the kitchen in nothing but his briefs, she found it mildly creepy and disturbing. Miller was a handsome man, and she loved him to death, but she wasn't the least bit attracted to him. Raina brushed off Gilda's tone and attempted to be polite, despite what her instincts were telling her.

"It's not strange at all," Raina announced proudly. "In our souls; we're brother and sister. The trauma the murders had on us made us that much closer. We share an unbreakable bond."

"It must be awkward for your boyfriend," Gilda remarked while eyeing her.

Raina knew the woman was fishing for information, but she wasn't sure what information and for what purpose. "I don't have a boyfriend."

"Oh, then that probably explains why you looked so cozy talking to my husband," Gilda announced while displaying little to no emotion.

She stared at the woman with shock and surprise, although not nearly as much as poor Farley. He appeared embarrassed and couldn't even look at either of them.

"That's not what was happening," Farley insisted in a timid tone to his wife.

Gilda didn't take her eyes off Raina and smirked almost evilly. "If you're done fawning over my husband, you can go back to your friends now."

Farley shut his eyes and had to look away. He obviously wanted to say something but was compelled to keep quiet. "I'm getting a drink," he announced and walked away.

"You do that," Gilda hissed after him then looked back at Raina and maintained her sinister smile. "It was nice talking to you, Raina."

"Wish I could say the same," Raina scoffed then smirked. "Bipolar bitch."

As Raina turned and walked away, she could hear Gilda huff at the comment.

Chapter *17*
The Devil Had Blue Eyes

Raina approached the portable bar after her awkward encounter with Gilda Nixon and paused near Farley, who already had his drink in his hand. Farley cast a look at her and immediately frowned.

"I'm so sorry," he announced timidly. "I really am. Gilda's been under some--" Farley hesitated then shook his head. "There's no excuse. She's a bitch. Again; sorry."

He hurried away before his wife caught them talking again and would assume they were having an affair. Raina rolled her eyes then saw Dane standing behind the portable bar staring at her with question in his eyes. He obviously wanted to know what had happened. Nole had been standing at the opposite end of the bar and moved closer to Raina with a drink. He clearly had a few too many already.

"Raina, don't you look lovely this evening," Nole announced while giving her a quick and lustful once-over.

She didn't even look at him while gritting her teeth. "I swear, Nole," Raina snarled. "You hit on me, and I'm going straight to my father."

He frowned and collected his drink with a little added vigor. "What's with you women tonight?" Nole demanded then walked away.

Dane stood behind the bar and chuckled at the entire situation after having witnessed both incidents.

She glared at him seeing little humor at the situation. "Something funny?"

"It's nice being on the other side of your charming personality," Dane announced while grinning.

"Yeah, well," she announced defensively. "You may be next, so watch yourself."

"You can't intimidate me," he announced while grinning. "You defended my honor against Callie's insults. I'll never let you live that one down."

"That was nothing personal," she informed him with little interest. "I just seized the opportunity to lash out at the lovely bride-to-be."

"Be snarky if you must," Dane remarked. "But I know the truth." His smile mocked her. "You secretly like me."

She groaned and rolled her eyes. "Please don't let that get around," Raina muttered then eyed him behind the bar. "Why are you bartending instead of Levi? I thought he was always designated bartender at these small gatherings."

"Yes, he usually is, but he's currently a little too wasted at the moment," Dane informed her. "I thought I'd take over and keep him out of trouble."

"I see." She eyed him suspiciously. "Are you sticking around for the nuptials tomorrow?" she asked while cleverly raising her brows. "Or are you vacating the scene promptly at nine?"

"No, out of respect for Mr. Steele, the staff all agreed we'd stick around for the wedding," Dane informed her. "Titus said he was going to some club later on in the evening. I think the rest of us are just hanging out." He eyed her and smiled daringly. "I'm thinking about going totally wild and staying up to nearly ten o'clock."

"Hmm," she cooed while eyeing him. "Don't do anything too crazy there, Dane."

Dane casually leaned on the bar closer to her. "Oh, I am. Just between us," he announced while lowering his voice and shifting looks around to make sure no one was around to overhear their conversation.

With anticipation, Raina leaned closer to hear what he was about to confess.

"I'm actually reading a novel by an author who's still living," Dane announced and maintained a serious look then nodded. "It's going to be a wild night."

Raina had a hard time controlling her laughter. "Oh, you bad boy!"

Dane straightened and appeared more serious. "Those days are long gone," he informed her. "No more soaping windows and toilet papering trees for me. I'm trying to clean up my bad boy image."

"Too bad," she teased while grinning. "I was going to suggest you come as my date. It's a passive-aggressive thing. I can't imagine anything that would piss off my wicked stepmother more."

Dane stood rigid a moment at the comment then managed a smile. "As tempting as that sounds, it would also piss off my current employer, and I'm not ready to live in a cardboard box just yet."

"I suppose it would also go against my promise not to ruin their wedding," Raina admitted with defeat.

"Oh, you don't need to worry about that," Dane informed her. "I think the bride's sister will handle that task nicely on her own."

Both glanced at the couple bumping and grinding on the makeshift dance floor.

Raina shook her head disapprovingly. "They may find that style of dance a bit awkward to Beethoven's sixth."

Dane chuckled then indicated the couple with a curious look. "Is that really the new trend in dancing?"

"I wouldn't know," Raina replied with a defeated sigh. "I haven't actually danced since--" She hesitated and considered the comment then raised her brows. "Let's just say it's been a while."

"Being I haven't seen my twenties in a few years, I'd say I'm more out of practice than you are," Dane announced. "I can't even remember the last time I danced." He then indicated the couple practically dry humping on the dance floor. "And it certainly wasn't like that."

"Yeah, me either," she replied. "Jenna has a few good moves on her, and Miller isn't half bad. I'm sure between the two of them they could give me a few pointers if I were really interested."

"I caught the chauffeur convention dancing out behind the garage one time," Dane informed her. "They tried to teach me a few moves." He rolled his eyes and groaned. "What a disaster."

"Show me," Raina insisted while grinning wanting to see his impressive moves.

"No, I'd be too embarrassed," he replied.

She looked around, made certain no one was watching, and then looked back at him. "It's just us," she announced then insisted. "Come on. Show me."

Dane groaned with embarrassment. He took a step away from the bar, placed his hands out in front of him, and did the swinging snake hips. Raina stared at him with some surprise and gawked over the bar. His dance moves were more than impressive. They were a bit of a turn-on. Dane abruptly stopped and laughed at himself. She raised a skeptical brow and met his gaze.

"Whelp," she announced and returned to her seat. "Even the butler is a better dancer than me."

"I feel silly," he replied while appearing embarrassed.

"You have nothing to feel silly about," she insisted. "The chauffeurs taught you well. You should probably go back and learn the rest of the dance."

He rolled his eyes while hiding his grin and waved her off. Did he honestly think his moves weren't that good?

"What else don't I know about you?" Raina asked.

"I don't know," he replied while eyeing her. "What *do* you know about me?"

"Not much, I suppose," she replied and shrugged. "Other than being a clean freak, the others don't gossip much about you."

"Probably because I'm a private person," he informed her. "I don't give them anything to gossip about."

"You read a lot of boring books, and you know everything that goes on around the house," she informed him. "That's as much as I know."

"Guilty on both charges."

As she stared into his blue eyes a moment, she allowed an inappropriate thought or two cross her mind. She tensed then shifted uncomfortably.

"It's way past my bedtime," she finally announced. "Maybe my inner demons will let me get a few hours' sleep tonight for a change."

Dane smiled and poured her a shot of tequila. "This might help."

Raina laughed and drank the shot. She made a face then stood. "Oh, that's foul."

"Sorry, Levi drank all the good stuff," Dane teased. "Might I make a suggestion?"

"Sure."

"Check out the gym in the basement tomorrow," he announced. "Get rid of some of that aggression before the wedding. You'll feel a lot better."

She eyed him with a curious look. "Is that what you do?"

"I find scrubbing the kitchen floor by hand a great outlet, but that's probably just me," he teased.

"I promise; that *is* just you," she informed him while laughing. "Goodnight, Dane."

"Goodnight," he announced then hesitated. "Raina."

Raina eyed him having never heard him call her by her first name before. She smiled then left.

Chapter *18*

The Beginning of the End

Raina and Jenna entered the basement gym early the following morning. The home gym was the size of a tennis court and contained almost every piece of exercise equipment imaginable. There were two televisions on opposite sides of the room, which allowed those on the elliptical machines to watch one television while those working with weights to watch another. There was a small bar in the front corner, which had some counter seating for after the workout. A door in the back led to the steam room. It was still early, and they had plenty of time after breakfast before they even needed to think about getting ready for the wedding. Both women laughed as they entered the gym.

"I'm telling you," Jenna announced. "I know some amazing ball flattening kicks."

"You're awful," Raina laughed.

"You said you took self-defense classes all four years in college," Jenna announced. "I'd think you'd be quite good at them by now."

"I'll admit," Raina announced. "Those classes and the kicks came in handy the one time I needed them."

Jenna tensed slightly, appeared uncomfortable, and eyed her friend knowing exactly what time she was referencing. "You got in a few good shots, huh?"

Raina drew a deep breath and trembled. "Yeah, a few," she remarked then hesitated. "Although not nearly as good as Dane's shot." She held her arms up in a pretend shotgun and pulled the trigger.

"Those bastards got what they deserved," Jenna announced proudly then looked around the gym.

Jenna marveled at the amazing workout room Otto created in the basement. Both stopped when they saw Elana and Keefe already using the punching bag located in the far corner overtop of the mats.

"Looks like we'll have to wait our turn," Jenna remarked and smirked knowingly. "I guess everyone has some pent-up aggression today."

They approached the back corner containing the punching bag and stood alongside Elana, who watched Keefe repeatedly punch the bag. He then karate kicked the bag, giving it a tremendous jolt.

Jenna raised her brows. "Your boyfriend is pretty impressive."

Elana glanced at them and grinned with childlike fascination. "Keefe is into MMA fighting," she announced. "He's top in his class."

They watched Keefe punch and kick the bag with surprising force and moderately decent technique. His muscle mass slowed him down a little, but what he lacked in speed and agility, he made up for with sheer power.

"He's good," Raina muttered.

Keefe struck the bag with a series of punches and kicks while grunting loudly from overexerting himself in order to impress the women. Raina glanced alongside her and was nearly startled to see Dane standing next to her. He somehow managed to sneak up on them without even trying. Dane watched Keefe's impressive moves with little reaction and appeared almost bored.

"Is it me, or did the room suddenly fill with testosterone?" Dane remarked dryly.

"Knowing fancy moves doesn't automatically make a man good in an intense situation," Raina remarked to the butler without looking at him then drew a deep, apprehensive breath. "That requires a cool, level head."

Dane eyed her suspiciously while cocking his head. "Was that some sort of compliment?" Dane asked and hid his smile.

She avoided looking at him and tensed after realizing she'd actually made the comment aloud. "More like ramblings from someone deprived of sleep."

Keefe spun into a roundhouse kick and struck the bag so hard it rattled. Jenna and Raina raised their brows at the aggressive move.

"Show off," Dane scoffed while frowning then left the basement gym.

§

The wedding crew busily set up chairs and decorations between the terrace and the gazebo. Hanson chased the workers around while yelling for them to be careful around the lawn and his flowerbeds. Jimmy Love chased Hanson around while screaming and attempting to shoo him away. The flamboyant wedding planner wore a bold red, rhinestone infested suede jacket, a white satin shirt, simple black dress pants, and red dress shoes drenched in red rhinestones to match his jacket. He could be seen coming halfway across the garden.

The house was flooded with caterers and wait staff prepping for the reception to be held in the ballroom and on the outside terrace. Dozens of caterers stormed the kitchen and buzzed around in a frenzy of organized chaos. Levi hustled out of their path only to get in the way of more caterers. As pans crashed, Levi dodged them. Jimmy Love ran into the kitchen after the caterers carrying pans and trays. He shouted orders in a high-pitched yowl that only the local dogs could possibly hear. Despite the frenzy of activity, Dane leaned against the main counter with mild disinterest and casually sipped his morning coffee in his favorite mug.

As Levi attempted to keep out of traffic, Jimmy Love turned his attention on the plus-sized cook and swatted him with a dishtowel while chasing him from the kitchen. For some reason, Levi felt threatened by the rhinestone-studded wedding planner and obeyed him. Callie appeared from the back stairs in a lavish, white satin robe. She dodged several caterers while rushing for Jimmy Love, who was amazingly easy to spot in his flashy jacket among the caterers dressed in black pants and white shirts.

"Jimmy Love," she cried out in panic. "Where's my maid-of-honor!"

He spun around when he heard her and threw his hands in the air. "Relax, pooky!" His hands frantically waved in the air like some crazy prayer to the gods. "Jimmy Love is all over it, girl!" He touched his earpiece while raising the attached microphone to his mouth. "What's my twenty on the maid-of-honor?" His hands gestured wildly. "Find my maid-of-honor!" He hesitated a moment while listening to his associate on the other end then looked at the frantic bride. "I have my second in command on it. You just go back upstairs and work on your lips, honey."

Jimmy Love dramatically shooed her up the stairs then looked around and appeared to notice Dane standing around with little purpose. Jimmy Love erratically snapped his fingers to Dane across the chaotic kitchen. Dane stared at him with bewilderment. Jimmy Love nodded and motioned him over with a demanding look. Dane smirked almost deviously and motioned him over with a beckoning finger. Jimmy Love appeared irritated and again motioned him over with a hand wave and more conviction. Dane sneered his disapproval and responded with the same motion. Jimmy Love rolled his eyes and fought his way across the sea of caterers to Dane relaxing with his back against the main counter.

"You're in charge around here, aren't you, darling?" Jimmy Love asked although it seemed more like a statement than a question.

"That's the subject of some debate," Dane replied with little emotion and cleverly raised his brows. "What can I do for you, J.L?"

Jimmy Love eyed him with surprise then yowled excitedly. "J.L. Pet names. I love that! Do me a huge favor, honey, and keep our happy bride-to-be *happy* until we locate the MOH."

"You've picked the wrong man for the job," Dane replied with disinterest. "The lady of the house and I don't exactly get along. I assure you; my mere presence will make her *very* unhappy."

"Honey, no one gets along with a bride on her wedding day," Jimmy Love announced and placed a hand dramatically to his forehead. "I sometimes wonder how I maintain my sanity." He again touched his earpiece to someone buzzing in his ear. "You found my MOH? Super-fabulous! Send her right on up to the bride's room. I do not want that girl stressing out. She scares me!" He lowered the microphone and eyed Dane. "You're off the hook, gorgeous." He then looked him over and gave an approving grin. "Until later tonight, that is."

Dane's expression dropped, and he immediately straightened.

Jimmy Love looked him over and dramatically groaned with approval. "Oh, lordy," he exploded. "We're going to have one hell of an evening!" His expression suddenly dropped as he caught a glimpse of a caterer carrying a tray then chased after her while squealing in a shrill voice. "Girl, you are not serving that!"

§

Moments from show time, the garden and terrace were filled with more than two hundred well-dressed guests already making use of the portable bar and hired bartenders. Titus stood alongside Hanson not far from the garden and attempted to keep him calm. Hanson was ready to scream at each of the guests for the divots they were making in his precious lawn. Women with high heels sinking into the turf seemed to be his main focus. Each time a piece of paper fell to the grass, he prepared to lunge. Titus finally got Hanson to join him by the garage, which was far enough from the action to keep the groundskeeper sane.

§

Within the house, Otto paced the flower-filled grand hallway while watching the massive staircase, also cascading with flowers. The nervous groom-to-be looked particularly handsome in his expensive, black tuxedo with a white vest. Dane approached and offered a pleasant smile.

"You look very handsome, Sir," Dane announced.

Otto eyed him but was so tense that he couldn't seem to accept the compliment. "Do I look nervous?" he asked while fidgeting.

"No, not at all," Dane easily lied.

"You're a terrible liar, Dane," Otto remarked then fidgeted with his white rose boutonniere. He glanced at Dane. "Did you dismiss the staff?"

"Yes, Sir," Dane replied. "Everything seems to have come together. You can probably relax now."

"I'm getting married in twenty minutes," Otto announced and shifted now that he was unable to pace with Dane in front of him. "How can I possibly relax?"

"I can pull the Ferrari around front at a moment's notice," Dane announced calmly. "Just give the word."

Otto glared at Dane then chuckled. "No, I don't think that will be necessary, but thank you anyway," he announced taking the comment as a joke. He looked around and again fidgeted. "I haven't seen Raina all morning and neither has Miller. She didn't run out, did she?"

"I don't believe so," Dane replied. "Have you looked in the library?"

"Of course. I looked there first," Otto announced then hesitated while staring at the butler. "You are staying for the wedding, aren't you?"

"Of course, Sir."

"I appreciate that," Otto announced then fidgeted and placed his hand on Dane's shoulder. "I know how close you were to Brenda--"

"She was an amazing lady, Mr. Steele," Dane informed him. "Your decision to marry Ms. Burton is in no way a reflection upon your feelings for your late wife. I'm sure your son knows that too."

Otto stared at the butler with some surprise then managed a tiny laugh. "Your ability to read people is truly frightening, Dane," he remarked before resuming his nervousness. "Before you join the others, would you find Raina? I'd like to see her before we begin. I'm afraid she may be feeling a little left out. You know; with Miller being my best man and no role for her."

"I'm sure you're worrying over nothing," Dane insisted, "but I'll find her for you."

"Thanks, Dane," Otto announced with relief. "You're a good man."

"Don't let that get around," Dane announced and offered a teasing grin. "It'll ruin my bad reputation."

Chapter *19*

Cutting it Close

Raina stood on the mat in the gym before the punching bag wearing an old pair of frumpy shorts and a black tank top. She aggressively kicked and punched the bag with precision and brute force. Jenna leaned against the nearby wall with her arms folded across her chest and watched her friend assault the bag. Jenna was dressed for the wedding wearing a sexy yet elegant red dress and high heels. She watched her friend and appeared almost bored.

"Less than twenty minutes until show time," Jenna informed her, having been on a countdown for the last thirty minutes. "Care to wrap this up?"

"Got a hot date I don't know about?" Raina scoffed and again kicked the bag while gritting her teeth. "Getting together with Nole, perhaps?"

"I do have a hot date, but it's certainly not Nole," Jenna informed her

Raina hesitated and turned to eye her friend with some surprise. "When did this happen?"

"Last night," Jenna replied and grinned. "Miller asked me to be his date."

"You're kidding?" Raina gasped then laughed. "I'm impressed." She turned and kicked the bag. "Your plan to annoy him into dating you actually worked."

"That wasn't my plan," Jenna scoffed while rolling her eyes. "Your brother is almost as emotionally shut off as you are. He thinks he's being my knight in shining armor. Saving me from Nole's clutches. I assure you; he doesn't believe it's a date."

"And when do you intend to tell Miller it actually is a date?" Raina teased while looking over her shoulder at her friend.

"I'm hoping he picks up on my body language on the dance floor," Jenna replied then shrugged without care. "If shameless sultry dancing doesn't bring him around, I'll probably have to give up."

Raina turned to face her friend with a concerned look. "No, don't do that. He'll eventually come around," Raina insisted then offered a tiny smile. "I'd like to see you two get together. It's just--it's difficult enough losing the woman you love, but losing her like that. It's not something anyone should have to go through."

"Your father seemed to handle it rather well," Jenna muttered.

"Yes, he thinks he's in love with Callie," Raina announced then frowned with disgust. "Personally, I think he's masking his hurt by fulfilling his sexual needs with a woman half his age. If he wasn't in such a hurry to marry her, he'd probably realize it."

"Yes," Dane announced from across the gym. "Callie has that effect on men."

Both looked back at Dane, who casually stood near the doorway past the stairs. He had his hands in his pockets while watching them.

"Jesus," Jenna scoffed and straightened. "He's like a cat sneaking around."

"Yeah, Levi wants to get him a collar with a bell on it," Raina teased then resumed kicking and punching the bag with a little more aggression.

"You do know what time it is, right?" Dane asked while crossing the gym and approaching them.

She didn't bother looking at him. "It's either the bag or Callie's face, Dane," Raina announced and again kicked the bag. "Think about it."

"Do I get to vote?" Dane asked.

Raina smiled but didn't let him see it.

"Okay, it's officially ten minutes until show time," Jenna announced while straightening. "I'm heading upstairs." She eyed Dane and smirked. "She's your headache now."

"She's been my headache for years," Dane replied with humor.

Jenna laughed then walked across the gym, her high heels clomping against the floor before reaching the stairs. Dane approached and took Jenna's spot. He leaned his back against the wall and mimicked Jenna's pose, folding his arms across his chest. Raina didn't want to admit he was a bit distracting. She hated that he looked so handsome in his suit.

"Your father wants to see you before he makes the biggest mistake of his life," Dane informed her. "The least you can do is give him that. You're not even dressed yet."

Raina groaned and finally turned toward him. "Put you in a red dress and high heels, and you could pass for Jenna," she huffed.

"I haven't got the legs to pull off that look," Dane replied simply.

Raina approached the nearby bench and snatched her black dress that had been draped across it. Dane eyed the careless handling of the expensive evening dress.

"You're seriously wearing a black dress to your father's wedding?" he demanded.

"I'm in mourning," she scoffed then eyed him impatiently. "I'm also pressed for time, so you'll probably want to turn around."

Dane appeared bewildered then watched as she removed her tank top to reveal her black bra. He was slightly stunned and quickly turned his back to her. She slipped into the dress and out of her shorts. Dane turned his head and was nearly hit in the face with her sweaty gym shorts. He glanced back to see she was already in the dress. Raina slipped into her strapless, high heels then held up her hair and turned her back to him.

"Zip me?"

Dane hesitated, took a step toward her, and zipped her dress. He paused while standing over her shoulder just close enough to make her uncomfortable.

"What a lovely fragrance you're wearing," he announced a little too close to her ear so that she could almost feel his breath on her neck. "Ode d' sweaty gym shorts."

She turned and glared at him despite his cheap grin. "Cut me some slack," Raina huffed. "We can't all fall out of bed looking pretty like you."

Raina effortlessly twisted her long hair into an upward twist then secured it with two metal hair sticks resembling small daggers.

Dane gave her a quick once-over and appeared surprised. "That took you less than a minute," he remarked with astonishment. "What do you women do for the other fifty-nine minutes?"

"Laugh at you guys for waiting on us."

She removed a tube of lipstick from her cleavage, hastily applied it, and then looked around for something to blot it. Raina turned to Dane and quickly kissed him on the cheek, leaving a reddish brown lipstick print on his face.

"See," she announced then grinned. "Guys are good for something after all."

He frowned while removing his handkerchief and wiped the lipstick from his face. "You're slowly working your way back to intolerable."

"Be civil, Dane," she announced, flashed a devious smile, and raised her brows suggestively, "or I'll give your private number to Jimmy Love."

Dane suddenly glared at her. She laughed then linked onto his arm and walked with him for the stairs.

§

Dane escorted Raina down the grand hallway to join Otto, who was relieved when he saw her. As they approached, her father watched them with a strange but curious look. A smile crossed his face at some inside joke. Dane handed Raina off to her father, gave a polite nod, and then headed back to the kitchen. Otto hugged Raina.

"I was worried you decided to blow off the wedding," her father teased.

"I wouldn't do that, Dad," she insisted.

Miller hurried toward them from the kitchen area dressed in his black tuxedo with a baby blue and white plaid vest. He looked dashing in his rented tuxedo.

"Your bride is coming down those stairs in five minutes," Miller announced while pointing at the grand stairs. "You need to be in the gazebo now."

"I'm coming," Otto replied then looked at Raina and smiled. "I just wanted my daughter to walk me down the aisle."

Raina smiled warmly and nodded. "I'd be honored, Dad," she announced.

Otto linked onto her arm and extended his hand. "Lead the way, my dear."

§

The large crowd was seated before the gazebo on either side of the white aisle runner covering the stone walkway. Raina walked Otto down the aisle with Miller following then took her seat in the front with Jenna as the men proceeded up the steps and into the gazebo. A man in a kilt was playing the bagpipes. The tune changed to signal the beginning of the wedding. A moment passed before Tia and Olivia proceeded down the aisle wearing their matching, strapless, baby blue, satin dresses. The dresses were form-fitting, hugging the women's curves and revealed more than enough cleavage.

Each bridesmaid wore a hair clip with white and light blue flowers and sprigs of baby's breath. Each carried a cascading bouquet containing white roses and carnations in varying shades of blue. Elana appeared next wearing the same dress as the bridesmaids, except her hairpiece was larger than what the others wore. The man playing the bagpipe changed the song to the Wedding March. Everyone stood and turned. Keefe, looking more than handsome in his rented black tuxedo similar to the groomsmen, walked Callie down the aisle.

Callie looked stunning in a floor-length, white silk wedding gown with more glitter and lace than a fairy tale princess. Her dress was also strapless to match her bridesmaids. She wore a lavish tiara that sparkled like a thousand diamonds and probably cost almost as much. A stunning diamond and emerald necklace drew the right amount of attention to the beautiful bride. The necklace contained one large emerald and three smaller emeralds on each side with small diamonds between each.

Raina stared at the necklace as her mouth fell open and suddenly clutched Jenna to keep from falling. Raina then looked at Miller in the gazebo. He saw the necklace and looked back at Raina with the same stunned look. Miller glared at Callie as she continued down the aisle. His expression hardened to silent rage. Raina watched her stepbrother and waited for the explosion, but it didn't come. She couldn't believe Callie was wearing Brenda's necklace!

Chapter 20
Show Time!

The elegant wedding ceremony had over two hundred guests witnessing the union. The staff stood behind the half wall on the terrace not far from the kitchen and watched with matching frowns of displeasure. Titus shook his head with disgust while Levi patted his shoulder and spoke softly. Sloan rolled her eyes and alternated between shaking her head and chewing her fingernails. Hanson snuck drinks from a flask when he thought no one was looking. Dane stood rigid with his hands in his pockets and an emotionless expression on his face, although it was made clear, he didn't approve either.

As the happy couple exchanged rings, Miller's eyes remained glued on the expensive emerald necklace around Callie's neck. Raina sat rigid in her front-row seat and nervously watched Miller's seething hatred as it seemed to boil over. That he remained silent was nothing short of a miracle. Jenna sat alongside Raina in the front row and seemed more interested in watching the expressions of her friends rather than the wedding. She couldn't figure out the problem and now wasn't the time to ask.

"If there's anyone here who thinks this couple should not be wed, let him speak now or forever hold his peace," the minister announced.

There was an awkward silence. Raina closely watched Miller in silent horror, hoping he didn't 'speak now'. Miller finally looked away from Callie and met Raina's gaze. They exchanged verbal glares as if having a silent conversation with their eyes and facial expressions.

"Then by the grace of God, I now pronounce you husband and wife," the minister proudly continued. "You may kiss your bride."

Otto and Callie kissed warmly but passionately and received some applause. Raina sank in her chair and appeared emotionally drained. She was certain her father was making the biggest mistake of his life, but she vowed to stay out of it. Now that it was over, she wondered if she'd regret that decision for the rest of *her* life. Otto and Callie walked down the aisle and were showered with birdseed by their friends and business associates. As the crowd dispersed, Raina barely made it to her feet when Miller grabbed her arm and pulled her into the gazebo with him. She nearly tripped up the steps in heels she wasn't used to wearing anymore. He roughly spun her to face him, startling her. She was almost convinced he was mad at her.

"What the hell was that?" Miller bellowed. "Was that my mother's necklace? It was, wasn't it?"

"Miller, calm down."

"Did you give it to her?" he demanded.

Raina stared at him with shock and horror. "What? No, of course not," she cried out defensively. "Dad didn't give me your mother's jewelry. I told him to give it to you. I assumed you had it."

"That son-of-a-bitch," Miller lashed out. "He gave my mother's jewelry to that little whore!"

Raina fidgeted and nervously looked around with concern, hoping his voice hadn't carried. Thankfully, the guests were already out of earshot. Jenna was the only one who remained close enough to the gazebo to hear their conversation.

"You can't say anything tonight, Miller," Raina insisted as her eyes pleaded with him to calm down. "I'll talk to Dad in the morning."

"Bullshit!"

Her brother appeared ready to explode and could barely stand still. Every muscle in his body seemed to be twitching. He was a ticking time bomb.

"You're not going to cause a scene at their reception," Raina scolded while glaring at him. "We're taking the high road on this. You promised."

He shot a look at Raina that frightened her. "That was before I found out *your* father gave that bitch my mother's jewelry," Miller lashed out and flung his arms in the air. "All bets are off, Raina."

"It's probably a misunderstanding," Raina attempted to explain, although she couldn't understand how that was possible. "He probably let her borrow the necklace for the wedding. I'll get it all straightened out in the morning." Her eyes again turned demanding even though he refused to look at her. "You're not going to cause a scene. You need to get yourself a drink and calm down." Raina looked back at Jenna. "Get Miller a drink. I'll detain him here."

Jenna nodded and hurried for the portable bar, maneuvering past the sea of men waiting for drinks. She grabbed a drink out of one of the man's hands and hurried back to the gazebo. She handed Raina the glass of scotch.

"Here."

Chapter 21

The Love Train

The ballroom was set up for the ritzy reception with buffet tables, ice sculptures, and flower arrangements scattered throughout the elegant party room. More than a dozen caterers carried trays of appetizers and glasses of champagne. There were two, large portable bars with four hired bartenders mixing drinks for the guests. An orchestra dressed in formal wear played classical music while the guests danced the waltz. Raina pretended to mingle with the crowd while holding her untouched champagne as a mere prop but had zero interest in sharing in the joyous occasion. She watched everyone and everything as if it were a social experiment rather than a party.

The happy couple mingled with their guests and appeared to have a good time. If there was one thing Otto was good at it was entertaining people, especially considering most of the guests were his friends and colleagues. Unfortunately, Otto's ability to entertain the masses came in second at this particular celebration. Jimmy Love stole the show and drew in a crowd of women with his animated conversations. He had everyone cheering him on while dancing with all the gorgeous, single women, a few married ones, and even some of the wealthiest pompous men. He had everyone laughing. He then started a conga line despite the classical music and made train-whistling sounds.

"Everyone on board the 'love train'," Jimmy Love cried out and 'woot wooted' while pulling his imaginary train horn to gain attention.

Tia and Olivia were the first to file in behind the flashy wedding planner as they worked their way through the ballroom collecting more people for their train. With each 'woot woot' from Jimmy Love, those behind him chimed in after him. It was a remarkable sight. As their train passed the Nixon's, Farley gave them a 'woot woot' only to receive a glare from Gilda. On the less joyous side to the special occasion was Gilda Nixon, who attempted to keep her husband from having any fun at the reception.

It was possible she was already cranky that her husband had been a groomsman paired up with Tia while Gilda was sidelined. Gilda wore a rather elegant green evening dress that readily revealed some cleavage. The slit up the left leg also gave a rare glimpse of her long legs. Monitoring her husband while successfully avoiding any interaction with her maid, Elana, made for a full-time job at the reception. Despite a changing perception in society, Gilda Nixon was old school and didn't believe employers should socialize with their servants in social settings.

Raina guessed her father was still a member of that club as well, since despite his close relationship with the staff even they weren't invited to attend the reception. It was possible he was concerned what his country club buddies would think about his staff mingling as guests at his wedding. Raina assumed Callie would want them there since they were part of her life as well. Of course, it was possible Callie was the reason they weren't invited, considering her relationship with the entire staff had been on shaky ground even before she became the lady of the house.

If Raina were to have a big wedding, she already decided that the staff would all be invited. They had been a major part of her life growing up, and 'class' stigmas wouldn't dictate her feelings on the matter.

"Here comes the 'love train'," Jimmy Love cried out as the ever-growing conga line weaved in and out of the socializing masses.

Despite some of the stuffy guests attending the party, everyone seemed entertained by Jimmy Love's antics. As the 'love train' made its way through the crowd a second time, Tia and Olivia pulled humored guests into the conga line. When they saw Farley enjoying the 'train', the two gorgeous women pulled him into the train with them. He mildly protested, but they were more persistent than his protests and successfully got him involved. As Farley 'woot wooted' around the room in the train between the two attractive women, Gilda silently seethed. Farley was going to pay for having a good time, Raina was almost certain.

Once the 'love train' had dispersed, much to everyone's sadness, Gilda started in with her husband for participating, particularly with attractive women involved. Although her scathing words were kept low enough that others couldn't hear them, it was easy to see she was angered by his behavior with the attractive women. Or was she just mad that he was having fun? After listening to her berate him for nearly ten minutes, without so much as defending his actions, he went to the bar for another drink. Raina shook her head and wondered how he tolerated the woman. She again felt sorry for Farley and was surprised he hadn't killed his wife years ago.

"There's an unhealthy relationship," Raina remarked to herself since she wasn't socializing with anyone at the moment.

Raina looked around the room for something new to entertain herself. After disembarking the 'love train', Elana and Keefe resumed their attempt at socializing with the stuffy crowd. They drew plenty of attention to themselves with their loud, inappropriate conversations with the mostly reserved, wealthy guests. Raina wondered if the couple lacked social skills or just wanted to make the other guests uncomfortable. She wanted to give them credit for trying, but at the same time, Raina wasn't entirely convinced Keefe and Elana weren't purposely causing a scene to amuse themselves.

When Keefe and Elana had enough social interaction, they returned to the dance floor. Despite the orchestra playing classical music, they danced to their own beat. Some inappropriate bumping and grinding on the dance floor was enough to create a little tension among the well-bred, refined guests. Raina was now almost certain they were seeking attention and wanted to cause a scene.

While finding a secluded corner to remain safely detached from the festivities, Raina scanned the room to see how her friend was doing with Miller. She spotted them on the dance floor. Jenna and Miller danced to the slow song, but instead of enjoying their dance, they appeared to be in a heated discussion. Despite that Miller was well on his way to being drunk, he didn't appear any more relaxed. Jenna officially had her hands full attempting to keep him calm and quiet. Jenna had volunteered to keep him stable, but Raina knew they'd eventually have to remove him from the wedding reception in order to preserve the *happy* occasion.

"You're damned right I'm angry," Miller announced to Jenna while they slow danced.

Jenna attempted to keep his attention focused on her rather than the murderous looks he kept shooting at the blushing bride. Jenna finally took his chin in her hand and turned his head to keep his eyes on her.

"Hey," she remarked firmly. "I know you're angry, but this isn't the time or place for a confrontation. Think about your father."

"I know," Miller sulked and refrained from shooting looks around the crowded ballroom. "I've just never been this angry before." He hesitated then frowned. "Well, after the murders I was pretty angry. Despite everything she was dealing with, Raina somehow kept me going."

"Funny, she says the same thing about you," Jenna informed him with a serious expression.

Miller drew a deep breath and attempted to keep himself calm. "I don't know why everyone is so weirded out by our relationship," he remarked. "Why does everyone assume there has to be something going on between us? I've never thought about her as anything but my sister."

"Your relationship battles most people because you're so close," Jenna offered. "I've witnessed it firsthand, and I've only seen two people who have a special bond that's anything but sexual."

"After the murders, we desperately clung to each other," he remarked then eyed Jenna. "Emotionally, I mean. Despite how strong she seemed, she was a complete train wreck, but she kept it all bottled inside. Me?" Miller chuckled for the first time. "I was a raging bull. The hostility and anger was eating me alive." He again focused his attention on Callie across the room, his eyes never leaving the emerald necklace. "I just want to kill the little bitch."

Jenna poked him in the chest. He yelped and looked back at her with surprise.

She glared into his eyes. "That's enough of that talk," Jenna insisted. "This is your father's wedding day. It's his moment, and you won't ruin that for him." She drew a deep breath and remained serious. "If it'll make you happy, I'll punch her in the face tomorrow."

Miller managed a laugh and gave her a small hug while they danced. "I believe you would too," he remarked then sighed and met her gaze with a more serious one. "No promises, but I'll do my best."

"It's a start."

Across the ballroom, Raina remained on the sidelines rather than actually participate in the festivities. Socializing was the last thing on her mind. She just wanted to get drunk and forget this day ever happened. Unfortunately, getting drunk really wasn't an option at the moment, since Jenna would need all the help she could get with Miller, who spent almost as much time at the bar as poor Farley. The wait staff brought in by the caterers consisted of many attractive women and several dashing men. One of the attractive servers went out of her way to greet Raina with a tray of meaty little pastries.

Raina politely declined. Her stomach couldn't handle food after it had been tied in knots since she first saw Callie wearing Brenda's necklace. As the attractive server made her way through the crowded room, Nole was in hot pursuit. Unfortunately for the woman, he wasn't interested in her tray of pastries. By the speed the female server traveled, she knew it too.

"Jesus, Nole," Raina scoffed under her breath while watching him and shook her head in disapproval. "He really needs to be neutered."

Raina glanced toward the kitchen entrance and saw Levi and Sloan disappear back into the kitchen before they were caught gawking. They were obviously stealing peeks at the reception they weren't invited to attend. Raina eyed the ballroom filled with guests, considered her options, and then headed for the kitchen entrance.

Chapter 22
The Other Side of the Door

Raina entered the kitchen amid a flood of caterers heading to and from the ballroom with trays of expensive treats. Despite the commotion, Levi and Sloan stood with Titus and Hanson at a back counter. They either had confiscated a tray of food or had been given one by the caterers. Although they enjoyed the food, the mood among the staff was solemn and depressing. Raina approached the four as they nibbled on hors d'oeuvres.

"God, I'm so bored," Raina announced and leaned on the counter near them.

"The real party is out back by the garage," Sloan informed her while smiling slyly. "The chauffeurs are having an epic poker game."

Raina eyed Titus. "Not your scene?"

"I'm not in the mood," Titus muttered and sounded as if he were drunk, although he hadn't been drinking since he planned on leaving for a nightclub in the city within the hour.

"Never mind him," Sloan announced. "He's sulking over Callie."

"I'm over Callie, I'll have you know," Titus launched with irritation. "She's turned into the wicked witch of the west. I think most of us will be looking for jobs before the honeymoon is over."

"Not me. If Dane stays, I stay," Levi replied. "He can handle Callie, I'm sure of it."

"I don't understand how he can be so casual about it," Hanson remarked while doing a good job of covering his own drunken condition. "He dated Callie too. She tossed him over just like the rest of us. Why isn't he pissed?"

"He was handpicked by Mr. Steele," Levi informed them. "Even Raina couldn't get him into trouble, and she's the boss's daughter."

"Handpicked?" Raina asked hearing that for the first time. "Why's that?"

"I don't know," Levi replied while shrugging. "I overheard a conversation between Mr. Steele and Mrs. Steele back when they hired Dane. Your father said something about 'owing him that much'."

Hanson appeared irritated in his drunken condition and glared at Levi. "What the hell does that even mean?" he demanded.

"I'm not sure," Levi replied defensively. "I wasn't exactly involved in the conversation."

"More like listening through keyholes," Sloan muttered then eyed Raina. "What's with Miller? He looks pissed about something, and I'm guessing it's more than just the whole wedding thing."

"Of course he's pissed," Titus snapped. "His father just remarried."

"Callie was wearing his mother's jewelry," Raina reluctantly offered. "I'm sure it's a misunderstanding."

"I thought I recognized that necklace," Sloan gasped as her eyes widened. "Where did she get it?"

Raina stared at her with surprise. "You didn't give it to her?"

"No, of course not," Sloan replied. "The late Mrs. Steele's things were stored in the attic when Callie moved into the new master bedroom. The jewelry box went into the attic along with the rest of her things. I assumed Mr. Steele put her more expensive jewelry in the safe. He must have given her the necklace to wear."

"Borrow, perhaps," Levi corrected. "I don't think Mr. Steele would give Callie his deceased wife's jewelry. He was saving it for Raina."

"I told him to give it to Miller. It was his mother's jewelry," Raina informed him. She drew a deep breath and tensed. "I know you guys are off duty, but if Miller gets out of hand, can I count on you to help intervene?"

"Absolutely," Hanson announced without hesitation, although he wouldn't be in any condition to do much of anything soon.

"Judging by his current condition, I'm guessing he's going to be out cold in a few hours anyway," Titus remarked with little emotion.

"I appreciate your help," Raina announced then groaned. "I should probably go back in there and at least give the appearance of having a good time. I mean it's--" She consulted her watch. "Oh, God. It's not even seven o'clock?" Raina groaned with disgust then looked at Titus. "What's the buy-in for this poker game?"

"Hang around," Sloan announced while grinning. "Things usually get more interesting as the night goes on and people get sloppy drunk."

"Wrong crowd," Raina corrected. "Dad's friends and colleagues don't get sloppy drunk and create scenes. Miller's the only one I'm worried about." She reconsidered the comment. "Although, I'm sure Elana and Keefe will do something mortifying."

"You're on the wrong side of the door, Raina," Sloan informed her. "Nothing happens out *there*. The bad boys bring it back here." A cheap grin crossed Sloan's face. "At some point, there's going to be at least one wild fling happening somewhere in this house. Only the boring ones take it to the bedrooms."

"The fun ones pick one of the empty downstairs rooms," Levi informed her while grinning. "We see and hear it all working behind the scenes."

"And the wild ones take it outside," Hanson remarked with a cheap grin. "I'll patrol the grounds and report back with the first outdoor affair."

Hanson stole a few pastries for his patrol duty and left the kitchen through the back door. Raina looked at the others with her mouth hanging open.

"Are you serious?" she gasped with surprise. "Guests at our parties do that sort of thing?" She pointed toward the ballroom door. "Those pompous, spoiled rich people?"

"All the time, Raina," Sloan informed her. "Especially with the caterers. I'm sure Nole is working the room as we speak. He's usually the prime suspect when we hear moaning through closed doors."

Raina shook her head and hid her smile. "You guys seriously need to find better hobbies."

§

It was a little after eight o'clock that night, and the reception was still going strong within the ballroom. On the terrace just outside the glass ballroom doors, Jenna stood alongside Miller, who leaned on the half wall while staring out at the nearly dark garden. There were still several lights on in the backyard lighting up the pool and gazebo area, but the rest was dark. Miller appeared quiet and sedate. He barely spoke, which could have been from excessive alcohol. Raina stepped onto the terrace through the ballroom doors, eyed her brother's turned back, and then exchanged looks with Jenna.

"Don't worry. He's fine," Jenna answered her friend's silent question.

Miller didn't bother looking back and responded, "He's drunk."

Raina approached and gently rubbed Miller's shoulder from behind. "Why don't you turn in?" she delicately insisted. "You'll feel like shit in the morning, but at least this day will be over."

Miller straightened then glanced at both women. His eyes were glossed over, and he could barely stand on his own.

"I think I'm going to take a walk," he informed them in a sedate tone.

"I don't know if that's--" Jenna attempted to intervene, concerned for his welfare.

Raina placed a hand on Jenna's shoulder and gave her a reassuring look. "It's okay, Jenna," she replied gently. "He's going to see Alicia."

"Oh," Jenna replied and shifted uncomfortably.

Miller stumbled from the terrace and headed into the garden with his hands in his pockets. He walked along the path that would eventually take him to the family crypt.

Jenna watched him walk away until he disappeared into the darkness of the garden. She then frowned and cast a look at Raina.

"Not exactly the first date I was hoping for," Jenna remarked.

"It's been a rough day for him," Raina informed her. "He probably feels as if his mother is being replaced, which is how I felt when my father married his mother." She drew a deep breath and held it a moment. "I hope to God my father didn't give Callie Brenda's jewelry. As much as he loves my father, he may not forgive him for disrespecting his mother that way."

"I'm starting to think having a crush on your brother isn't in anyone's best interest," Jenna remarked with defeat and folded her arms insecurely across her chest. "His love and devotion for his dead fiancé is endearing and what I love most about him, but it's also what's going to keep him from ever having another relationship again."

"I'm sorry, Jenna," Raina announced with a sigh. "I was hopeful, but I did try to warn you." She smiled and nudged her friend. "Why don't we go back inside and dance or something?"

"I'm not in the mood, and that's not the sort of music someone my age dances to," Jenna remarked then frowned. "No, I think I'm going to take a walk in the garden." She hesitated and raised her brows. "And I actually mean a walk in the garden."

"Okay, but avoid the garage," Raina warned her. "I hear the chauffeurs are gambling out back." She shook her head with disapproval. "I've played poker with them before. They're ruthless."

Jenna managed a humored smile.

"I'm going to bed," Raina informed her with a bored sigh. "I'll see you in the morning."

"Yeah, I won't be too far behind you, I'm afraid," Jenna replied with a slight laugh. "This has got to be the worst party I've been to in my life."

"Yeah," Raina sighed. "Welcome to the world of the rich and pompous."

"You can keep it," Jenna teased then managed a tiny smile. "Goodnight."

Chapter 23

Tequila Sunrise

Raina approached the library and didn't seem too surprised to find the light on. Most of the rooms were left dark during the party to keep the guests from wandering around the mansion. If left to their own devices, guests would leave dirty glasses in every corner of the house. Raina entered and paused within the doorway when she saw Dane sitting on the window seat with an open book on his lap. He stared out the window at the front grounds of the dimly lit estate.

"I think you're in my seat," Raina teased while casually leaning against the doorframe with her arms folded across her chest.

Dane snapped out of his own little world and looked at her. She had apparently surprised him. He chuckled in his throat while eyeing her.

"I can't believe you stayed at the party this long," Dane announced while grinning. "Looks like I lost fifty dollars." He frowned and shook his head with disappointment. "Your father's going to expect me to pay up too."

Raina rolled her eyes then smiled. It was almost as funny as shameful that her own father was in on the outrageous bets among the staff.

"I guess I know you better than you know me," Raina announced.

He gave her a baffled look. "Oh?"

"I knew you'd be here," she informed him.

"Sure you did," Dane announced then laughed at her expense.

Raina grinned and revealed a bottle of tequila and two shot glasses hidden within her folded arms. "I thought you could use a drink."

Dane stood and stared at her with surprise. "Where did you get that?" he asked.

"The game room bar," she replied.

She grinned as she approached and set the shot glasses on the library desk. He eyed her suspiciously.

"I locked the cabinet," Dane informed her.

"I know where you hide the key."

Dane laughed and took the bottle from her. He uncapped it and filled the first shot glass then cast a suspicious look at her as he filled the second glass.

"If we're drinking to the happy couple, I respectfully decline," he announced.

"I *disrespectfully* decline drinking to the happy couple," she announced while grinning. "Insert a colorful expletive of your choice here."

He laughed and handed her one of the shot glasses then took the other for himself.

She raised her glass and mocked him with her smile. "We could drink to your month of freedom before your life sentence to Callie?"

"You're cruel," he muttered.

They clinked glasses and drank their shots. Dane immediately refilled their glasses.

"Did I miss anything exciting?" Dane asked.

"At one of these parties?" she boldly announced and rolled her eyes. "Be serious."

Both drank their second shots. Raina grimaced from the foul tasting booze while Dane eyed the bottle and smiled his approval.

"You stole the good stuff," he announced.

"Still tastes like shit to me," she muttered.

"I noticed some attractive young men attending the wedding," Dane remarked then eyed her. "None asked you to dance?"

"No, I'm unapproachable," she replied and extended her empty glass to him for a refill.

Dane chuckled in response and refilled her glass. "You said it; I didn't."

"You're not exactly a people person yourself, Dane," she quipped and drank another shot.

He cast a glare at her. "Did you come here to argue with me or to get drunk?" Dane demanded while holding up the bottle.

She held up her empty glass while nearly choking from the last shot and frowned. "The latter."

"Okay then--"

Dane refilled both their glasses. Raina approached the window seat, made herself comfortable with her legs stretched across the seat, and stared outside while playing with her glass. The first few shots were already starting to hit her.

"She's going to break his heart, isn't she?" Raina whispered almost to herself.

"Undoubtedly."

Dane set the bottle and his glass on the window ledge. He moved her legs and joined her on the broad window seat on the opposite end while facing her. Raina groaned with defeat and placed her legs across his lap, barely aware he was there.

"Why didn't you warn him?" she asked without taking her eyes off the outside world beyond the window.

"I did warn him," Dane muttered.

She looked at him with surprise. Dane didn't bother looking back at her. Instead, he casually removed her strapless shoes and dropped them to the floor with a clatter.

"He told me under no uncertain terms to mind my own business," he replied with a defeated sigh and began massaging her bare feet.

She continued to stare at him with surprise by his response not even aware he was massaging her feet. "He knew you two dated, right?"

"That's probably why he didn't take my warning seriously," Dane replied with little emotion. "I'm sure her side of the story was far better than mine."

"You dated for three weeks," Raina muttered and snorted a laugh. "It has to be a pretty short story."

"We went out a couple of times; she used me, and then dumped me. End of story," he replied while meeting her gaze. "Short enough?"

Raina shrugged and leaned her head back against the wall. "I'm sure you got what you wanted from her," she informed him.

"I thought she was a nice girl. I treated her like a nice girl. I didn't even make a play for first base," Dane remarked then raised his brows while smirking. He took a break from massaging her feet, held up his shot glass, and raised a daring brow. "I'm officially the only man in this house who hasn't slept with the shrew."

As he drank his tequila, Raina stared at him with surprise by the comment. She couldn't believe he hadn't slept with Callie. She felt her respect level for the butler take a sharp upward turn. A humored smile crossed her face.

"I wouldn't say you're not the only man in the house," she informed him without hesitation. "Miller didn't sleep with her either."

He cast a sharp look at her and refilled his glass. "I challenge that."

"Be serious," she scoffed.

"Miller was here one weekend the summer after she was hired," Dane informed her. "She was supposed to go out with her sister but ended up staying home instead. Miller and I were the only ones home that night. I swear I heard some pretty wild sounds of passion coming from Callie's room, and since he was the only other person in the house--"

"Then she snuck someone else into the house," Raina insisted and drank her shot. She again made a face from the taste. "If he'd slept with her, he would have told me. In fact, he would have told our father, because that would have been the one deal breaker that could have stopped the wedding."

"Unless she blackmailed your brother," Dane suggested while casting a look at her.

"He didn't sleep with her, and stop suggesting he did," Raina snapped hotly then frowned. "I know my brother. Drop it."

"Someone needs a few more shots," Dane muttered and sharply eyed her.

Raina frowned and held out her glass. Dane laughed and refilled her glass. She eyed the handsome butler and felt sympathetic. She knew he wasn't as innocent as he looked, but despite their sorted past, she was certain his heart was in the right place.

"I'm sorry you didn't get anything out of the whole ordeal," she remarked gently, attempting to smooth over her unfounded outburst. The alcohol was starting to hit her hard. "I guess you were completely off base with that good girl theory, huh?"

"Just a little," he replied and drank the contents from his glass then immediately poured another. "It bothered me initially, but I'm glad it never went that far."

She stared at him with surprise. "Really?" Raina didn't even think that was possible.

He resumed massaging her feet and avoided looking at her. "It lessened her hold on me," Dane replied with little emotion. "She has her claws so deep into Titus; he still runs when she snaps her fingers."

"Are you trying to tell me you're emotionally attached to all the women you've ever slept with?" she asked and had to keep from giggling.

Raina was pretty sure she was quickly passing buzzed into inebriated. The room was starting to spin, and she swore the shadows were dancing on the walls.

"You make my prowling days sound grander than what they were," he teased then grinned. "Contrary to what you seem to think, I'm not quite the stud you believe me to be." He chuckled in his throat sounding almost drunk himself. "I was a lanky teenage bookworm. Honestly, girls scared me. Sadly, adulthood hasn't treated me much better. When I was younger, being polite and quiet got me used quite a bit." He considered the comment and smiled slyly. "I suppose my fears weren't unfounded. Girls *are* scary."

Raina giggled while staring at him. "Bullshit," she announced now feeling the full effects of the alcohol. "I think you're just a hopeless romantic."

"I've been called worse."

Chapter 24
Double Down

Dane and Raina laughed at each other as they still sat on the library window seat together and again emptied their shot glasses. They'd lost track on how many that had been, but both were feeling the full effects of the tequila now. Raina refilled their glasses then eyed the worm at the bottom of the bottle. She grimaced and set the bottle down. Raina groaned and again leaned her head against the wall.

"This is the best I've felt since I got here," she remarked while feeling relaxed for the first time.

"That's because you're buzzed," Dane announced while snickering.

She laughed and held up her shot glass. "I'm way past buzzed," Raina announced. "I'm somewhere between wasted and what the fuck."

Dane was amused by the comment and chuckled in his throat. They again clinked glasses and drained the contents. Raina eyed him and finally realized he was massaging her feet.

"*That* may have something to do with it too," she teased and indicated his hands on her feet.

"I have a mild foot fetish," he teased.

She giggled and refilled both their shot glasses. Raina eyed him while enjoying her foot massage then seemed to realize her free foot was snug against his crotch. She was almost certain he was aware of her foot's location, but if he didn't care, neither did she. Raina made fists with her toes against his crotch and could instantly tell he was enjoying the foot massage more than she was. Despite that he didn't look at her, a mildly devious grin crossed his face, which told her he'd been aware of her foot's location the entire time. Despite her drunken condition, she realized she needed to end his foot fetish fantasy before things went too far. Especially since she seemed to be the instigator. Raina looked at him and smiled drunkenly.

"I want to dance."

He gave her a strange look and disapprovingly shook his head. "I don't know that you should go back to the party in your condition," Dane responded, reluctant to release her feet on his lap. "You're obviously drunk because I see two of you."

She stared at him a moment then laughed uncontrollably at his comment. He laughed with her, although it was obvious he no longer knew why. Surprisingly, while drunk, he seemed his usual straight self except when he spoke, his words made less sense. That in itself was funny.

"I'm fine, you're the one who's drunk," Raina insisted while controlling her laughter. She grinned and waved him off. "I certainly didn't mean I want to go back to that sideshow of a reception." She stared at him across the window seat and smiled while taking in an eyeful of him. "I want to dance with you. Show me your moves, Gene Kelly."

Dane grinned, downed his shot of tequila, and then pulled her to her feet. She fell against him and laughed at herself. He attempted to hold her up without falling over himself and appeared equally humored. Dane attempted to collect himself and maintain his balance. He was able to pull off a steady stance despite his drunken condition. They listened to the music from the orchestra coming from the ballroom and danced the waltz.

Despite their drunkenness, they danced flawlessly together. Raina wouldn't admit it, but she was feeling a little dizzy as they twirled around the marble library floor. Dane gracefully dipped her back then pulled her back up and into his arms, holding her a little closer. Both were having difficulty maintaining their balance now. She giggled with delight and clung to him as they now danced slow and close in order to hold each other up.

"I liked that last part," Raina giggled. "Made my head spin."

"I'd like to take credit for that," Dane teased, "but it's probably the tequila."

She looked into his eyes while clinging to him as they slow danced. Raina admired his handsome face and didn't bother hiding her smile for once. A sly smile crossed her face as she said whatever she felt like saying.

"I was hoping to dance with you tonight," she informed him.

"You were?" he asked with some surprise.

She lightly played with the lapel of his expensive uniform. She'd wanted to run her hands along his suit as long as she could remember and seemed to be making up for lost time. It felt exhilarating finally being able to touch him and not think about it.

"Growing up," she informed him, "I used to fantasize about the perfect man." She grinned while studying him then met his gaze. "You're the perfect man."

He snorted a laugh and could barely control his grin. "I highly doubt that," Dane informed her and groaned. "You're so far off base; you're in the wrong ballpark."

She stared at him a moment then laughed. "I have no idea what you just said."

Dane laughed with her and shook his head. "I honestly don't even know what we were talking about."

Raina continued to caress his jacket and enjoyed running her hands along his chest. She hadn't even stopped to think about his hands caressing her waist and the small of her back.

"I'm comfortable around you," she informed him then met his gaze with less confidence. Her smile faded as she tensed. "I've been a little distrusting of, well, anyone since--"

She couldn't bring herself to speak about the murders and what happened that night.

Dane's expression turned serious to join hers. "I understand," he replied gently.

"You're the only one who could," she announced timidly and felt the tears swell in her eyes. "Anytime I try to talk about it to Miller; he shuts down emotionally. I feel like I have to keep it bottled up because no one can possibly understand what I went through that night." She raised her brows while staring into his eyes. "Except you, because you went through it too."

Dane tensed while they slow danced. "I'll gladly discuss what happened that night with you, but that's going to require a lot more shots," he informed her. "This day has been bad enough."

She smiled warmly and continued to run her free hand along his suit. "You're absolutely right," she announced and again turned playful while her hand caressed him. "We've both suffered enough for one day. I just want to enjoy our dance and then drink myself stupid."

Dane drew a sharp breath, held it a moment, and then offered a mildly strange grin. "As tempting as that sounds, I think we've had too much already," he informed her.

She stared into his eyes a moment and raised a curious brow. "It's definitely possible you've had too much," Raina remarked. "Is that your hand on my ass?"

Dane considered the question then chuckled with enthusiasm. "I believe so, but considering where your hand is, I thought it'd be okay."

Raina looked down and realized her hand was lovingly caressing his crotch, which he'd obviously been enjoying by the reception she received. She lifted her eyes and met his gaze without removing her hand.

"I question your style of dancing," she announced skeptically. "You should probably stop taking lessons from the chauffeurs."

"Were we dancing?" he asked in all seriousness. "I don't remember that."

"God, you are so wasted," she scoffed then laughed while pulling away from him, although he was reluctant to release her.

She stumbled for the window seat, snatched the bottle of tequila, and took a swig directly from the bottle. "If we're going to continue this conversation, I need to be drunk."

"You are drunk," he corrected while laughing.

"Not drunk enough," she remarked then stumbled toward him.

Raina didn't stop in time, collided with him, and caught onto him to keep from falling. Dane held her against him while attempting to keep his balance and knocked her against the library table. She clung to him and laughed despite being pinned between him and the desk. Fortunately, she didn't drop the bottle and laughed for no reason. She wasn't even aware that Dane was kissing her neck while keeping her pinned to the desk. Somehow, she'd managed to wrap her right leg around his hip and buttocks while clinging to him with her entire body. She tapped his shoulder with the tequila bottle. He pulled away just far enough to meet her humored grin as she waved the bottle.

"Drink up."

He accepted the bottle while chuckling. "You're the boss," he announced and took a swig.

"That would be a first coming from you," she teased then giggled while clinging to him as her hand freely traveled his body.

Dane just about spit out the tequila from the comment then laughed with her. He was about to set the bottle on the desk behind her when his expression dropped. Raina eyed the partially empty bottle of tequila as well and suddenly grimaced. The worm was gone.

Chapter 25

The Return of Bridezilla

There were fewer than fifty guests still remaining at the reception a little after midnight. The orchestra had nearly finished packing up their equipment, and the caterers were collecting dirty dishes and cleaning up the last of the food from the buffet table. Otto and several well-dressed men loudly debated business while a few of the other guests hung out at the bar and joked around with them. Despite his friend's drunken condition, Otto managed to remain sober for his wedding night. Tia approached Otto and his friends. She appeared exhausted and a little lost.

"Have any of you seen Jimmy Love or Olivia?" Tia asked while glancing around the quickly emptying ballroom.

"Not in a while," Otto remarked to the lovely young woman. "The last time I saw Jimmy Love, he was chasing after one of the caterers arguing about the cake top. He could be in the kitchen. Olivia might be in the powder room down the hall."

"I tried the bathroom," Tia pouted then frowned. "I hope they didn't go to bed without telling me."

The group of men at the bar gave her a strange look, but she didn't seem to notice.

Tia offered a polite smile and pointed to the kitchen. "I'll check the kitchen for them," she announced then turned and walked away.

Otto and his friends exchanged bewildered looks, considered the comment, and then shook their heads while holding back their snickers.

"No, that can't be what she meant," one of the men announced.

Despite that they laughed, none of the men seemed convinced it wasn't exactly how it sounded. The men brushed it off and resumed their assassination of one another's characters, finding it fun to berate their friends to their faces. Otto laughed with his business associates and finally waved his hands at their drunken antics since they no longer seemed to make sense.

"Okay, enough," Otto announced. "This is my wedding night, and I have better things to do than argue business with a bunch of lushes." He grinned almost deviously. "Now, if you'll excuse me, I must find my bride and retire for the evening." He waved them away. "Go home."

They laughed, waved him off, and headed for the bar with the remaining crowd. Even though the bartenders had left at midnight, the bar remained open with one of his friends playing bartender. There was no telling how long some of his friends and business associates would hang around. Since most had limousines waiting for them, they could stay and drink as long as they liked. Otto left the ballroom and headed down the grand hallway in search of his bride, who wanted to show her friends some new antiques in the lounge that she'd found on their last trip abroad. Otto walked along the hallway and stopped to see Levi and Sloan outside the closed library door attempting to listen through the thick wood.

He eyed them suspiciously. "What are you two still doing up?"

Both waved their hands without looking back and shushed him. Neither was aware they were shushing their boss, and they didn't seem to care either.

Otto appeared surprised then offended as he approached his staff listening by the door. "What are you doing?" he now demanded.

Despite now knowing it was their boss behind them, they remained glued to the door. It was obvious they knew he wouldn't be upset by their behavior.

"Someone's getting it on in the library," Sloan whispered without taking her ear from the door.

"Oh?" he asked then smirked, joining in on the fun. "Are we taking bets on who it is?"

"It has to be Nole," Levi insisted in a whisper. "He was flirting with a few of the caterers an hour ago in the kitchen, and no one's seen him since."

"Thirty bucks says it's the redhead," Otto announced while grinning.

"I'm going with the blonde," Levi remarked.

"I think it's Jimmy Love," Sloan interjected.

Otto and Levi gave her surprised looks. She shrugged without explaining herself. Otto waved them away from the door. Several guests had been passing by and stopped with curious looks regarding the three standing outside the closed library door.

"So let's find out," Otto announced while grinning like a schoolboy and opened the door.

As Otto stood in the library doorway, his expression immediately dropped. Nole had Otto's blushing bride bent forward over the library desk. Callie's wedding dress was pulled up over her backside, and Nole's pants were around his ankles as he grunted while banging against her from behind. When they heard the door creak, Nole jumped away from Callie and hastily pulled up his pants while Callie screamed and pulled her dress down. They were too late since everyone had already seen everything there was to see. Levi and Sloan stared past Otto with their mouths hanging open. Several guests stood behind them, strained to look into the room as well, and gasped at what they had witnessed.

§

Otto stormed through the grand hallway toward the kitchen with Callie attempting to chase after him as she fumbled with her bulky dress. Her white lacy panties hung from her left ankle. She hadn't taken the time to pull them up after she was caught in a compromising position with Otto's best friend. The stunned guests watched the bride chasing after her angry groom with her white panties flopping around her foot. Levi and Sloan followed at a safe distance then paused to see the underwear discarded on the floor.

"Otto, wait, let me explain!" she cried out in panic as she ran after him.

He suddenly stopped and turned to face her with an explosive look on his face. "Explain? Explain what?" he cried out in anger and rage. "You were fucking my best friend at our wedding reception! How can there possibly be anything to explain?"

She stared at him a moment and was unable to speak. Otto turned and stormed into the kitchen. The kitchen door struck Jimmy Love and tossed him into one of the caterers, who had been carrying the top of the wedding cake. The cake top splattered on Jimmy Love's rhinestone-studded jacket and expensive, white satin shirt while the caterer fell backward onto the floor. Jimmy Love stared at the icing covering him and appeared almost paralyzed at the mess on his clothes. He then watched Otto storm across the kitchen. Several caterers who were still buzzing around leaped out of the angry groom's path. Jimmy Love grimaced and shook cake from his jacket while muttering colorful curse words. Nole stormed through the door after Otto and cast Jimmy Love forward. He slipped in the mangled cake by his feet and fell on top of the caterer who had fallen to the floor. Jimmy Love screamed as shrill as the female caterer had.

"Otto, listen to me," Nole called after him.

Otto ignored him, grabbed his car keys from the pegboard located alongside the back kitchen door, and stormed out of the house. Nole hurried after him. Levi and Sloan entered the kitchen and looked at the mess. Jimmy Love sat on the floor alongside the caterer and pouted. Levi grimaced and hurried Sloan past them.

§

Jenna played poker on the hood of one of the stretch limos alongside the garage with the four remaining limo drivers. They used one of the driver's jackets placed on top of the hood to keep from scratching the expensive limousine. Jenna puffed on a cigar alongside the men and drank booze from the flask being passed around while they bet on their current hand. Once the last man in the game called, Jenna grinned and set down her winning hand containing all four aces. There was a loud round of groans followed by laughs from the four neatly dressed chauffeurs.

"I'm afraid this isn't your lucky night, boys," Jenna announced while chuckling through the cigar clenched in her teeth.

As she collected the change and bills from the pot on the limo hood, Otto stormed past them. All four men jumped with surprise and pretended to be doing something other than gambling. Jenna stared with surprise, immediately picking up on the groom's emotional state. The drivers realized he wasn't interested in their game or what they were doing to pass the time. Otto opened the first bay door on the eight-car garage to reveal the black Ferrari. Nole soon appeared and hurried past the limo drivers after Otto.

"Otto, listen to me--"

Nole caught up with Otto just short of the first garage door. Otto turned and punched Nole in the mouth, knocking him onto his backside in the driveway. All four chauffeurs gasped with surprise and watched the explosive scene with anticipation of a fight. Otto stormed into the first bay, started the Ferrari, and burned out in reverse. One of the chauffeurs pulled Nole from the driveway to avoid the speeding sports car as it backed out. The Ferrari whirled around, burned out on the pavement, and rocketed down the driveway past the mansion. Jenna, the four chauffeurs, and Nole watched him speed away.

"What the hell was that all about?" Jenna gasped and watched as the car disappeared out of sight.

Nole roughly pulled away from the chauffeur who had assisted him. He then straightened his jacket and hurried back for the house.

Chapter 26
WTF?

Eight o'clock Sunday morning. Raina slept peacefully beneath the covers on the bed while curled on her side. She woke to sunlight poking through the sliver of an opening in the curtains. She groaned and felt her head pounding. As she attempted to move, she felt some resistance. Raina looked down at her naked body and saw a man's arm clinging to her abdomen. She then realized that the man's naked body was pressing snug against her from behind. For a moment, she was paralyzed with fear and realization that she'd done something unthinkable, but she couldn't even remember where she last was and whose company she'd kept. As her head pounded in rhythm with her heart, Raina again looked at the man's arm and recognized the expensive watch on his wrist.

"Oh, my God," she cried out as she pulled away and sat up in the bed.

She immediately regretted the action while clutching her pounding head as she held the sheets to her naked body. Dane jumped with alarm and looked around his bedroom in the staff wing.

"What? What happened?" he gasped then clutched his head as well and groaned with pain as he fell back onto the bed, revealing his naked body to where the covers just reached his hips.

There was a brief moment where neither moved and held their pounding heads. Dane slowly lowered his hand and looked at the disheveled woman sitting in the bed alongside him where he lay. His expression dropped, and he groaned, again covering his eyes with his hand.

"Ah, hell--"

Raina looked around the spinning room with disorientation while holding her aching head. Once the room stopped spinning, she looked back at Dane and his partially naked body. Although she took in a sweeping gaze of his excessively toned body with the perfect amount of chest hair, she couldn't bear looking at him knowing what they'd done. He peeked out between his fingers, eyed her, again groaned, and looked away.

"Oh, God," he gasped now unable to look at her.

"Tell me nothing happened," she gasped while clutching the sheets to her naked body.

Despite not remembering anything from last night, she knew waking up with no clothes alongside a naked man almost certainly meant something happened.

"I am so sorry, Raina," he timidly announced.

"I'm drawing a blank after the foot massage," she informed him while having a difficult time looking at him even though his eyes were covered. "Maybe nothing happened."

She couldn't believe she actually suggested waking up naked together was possibly all a misunderstanding. When she briefly looked at him, she could see the thin sheet clinging to his naked body. Obviously, something had happened!

Dane kept his eyes covered and shook his head with shame. "Oh, I am *so* sorry."

"You remember?" she gasped and cast a quick glance at him, although she still couldn't look at him.

Dane groaned in response with his hand over his face, which told her more than she needed to know.

"I don't want to know the details," she groaned in response then looked around the room for her clothes as her anxiety increased. "I have to get out of here before someone finds me here."

Despite that he didn't get up, Dane removed his hand from beneath the covers. Raina looked back at him. His head was turned away while extending her black panties toward her. She snatched her panties from him with some hostility and slipped them on while remaining under the covers. She scanned the room for her clothes and saw her dress on the floor not far from the bed. She tugged on the covers to keep them over her while reaching to the floor for her dress. Raina didn't even care that she couldn't find her bra. She slipped into her dress while managing to keep herself covered then sprang from the bed to pull it the rest of the way down. As she frantically attempted to zip the back, Dane grimaced and peeked at her.

"I'm really sorry, Raina."

She glared at him while struggling with her zipper. "Stop saying that," she launched as her cheeks reddened. "It's freaking me out!"

Dane was about to get up when he pulled back the covers and hesitated as if suddenly remembering he was naked. Despite her embarrassment, Raina had to sneak another peek at him. His body was more athletic and muscular than she had ever imagined. His suit hid it well. She also noticed several glaring scars along his upper torso, shoulders, and arms. He certainly had more scars than the average man, particularly someone considered refined. Dane pulled the sheet back up to his waist and scanned the room for his briefs, which was Raina's cue to dash into the bathroom.

§

Nine o'clock Sunday morning. Sloan and Jenna sat the island counter in the kitchen while Levi and Dane stood on the opposite end near the main counter. They were seemingly engrossed in gossip hour. It was almost shocking how quiet the mansion was considering the circus just ten hours earlier. Raina appeared on the back stairs and paused at the bottom, unnoticed by the staff and Jenna whispering at the island counter. Raina remained out of sight by the back stairs and allowed her eyes to fall upon Dane. She still couldn't remember much beyond the foot massage in the library. She recalled some slow dancing, but it was all pretty hazy.

As she studied him, her heart skipped a beat. Although she hated admitting it, she'd had intimate thoughts about Dane from the first day they'd met even in spite of their attempts to berate each other. A small part of her wondered what she missed. Did she enjoy it? Was he passionate? Maybe she was lucky she didn't remember any of it. She certainly wasn't going to ask him for the details. Her thoughts strayed as she studied the handsome butler. Her curiosity was killing her, but her disappointment in herself trumped that curiosity. She approached the island counter from the back stairs and avoided looking at Dane.

"You're kidding," Jenna gasped and couldn't tear her eyes away from Levi.

Raina stared at the others as if she'd walked in on something monumental. For a brief moment, she was concerned it had to do with her irresponsible night with Dane.

"What's happening?" Raina asked as her heart pounded with concern.

Jenna looked at Raina with a shocked expression. "I can't believe what I'm hearing."

Raina felt panic sweep through her and glanced at Dane, who appeared unusually tense. He hadn't told anyone about their drunken fling, had he? Dane caught her look and fidgeted.

"Your father walked in on Callie and Nole," Dane gently informed her.

"Walked in on them?" Raina asked with confusion. "What do you mean?"

"Doing the nasty right there in the library," Levi informed her with less tact than Dane had used.

Raina's eyes widened with shock and near horror as she stared at Levi then looked at Dane and Sloan, who obviously knew something about what had happened.

"Levi and I were standing right next to your father when he caught them in the act," Sloan informed her. Her eyes widened as she shook her head. "I'm still in shock over it. I can't imagine what your poor father felt when he saw that. Not to mention there were about ten other guests who'd seen it as well. Naturally, your father stormed out."

"I was hanging out at the garage around midnight last night," Jenna informed her friend. "I saw your father punch

Nole then take off in the Ferrari. I didn't know what had actually happened until just now."

"We didn't want to say anything in front of the caterers," Sloan remarked and shook her head. "We felt terrible for Mr. Steele."

"I'd better check on my father," Raina gasped as clear thinking returned.

"He hasn't come back yet," Levi announced. "The Ferrari is still gone."

Raina stared at the others with alarm. "Someone should look for him, don't you think?"

"When we saw he wasn't back this morning, we sent Titus out to look for him," Sloan informed her while appearing sympathetic. "I'm sure he's okay." She then glared at Dane. "When all hell breaks loose, that would be the one time you decide to sleep in."

Dane eyed her with surprise and fidgeted. "I wasn't the only one drinking last night," he snapped at her while attempting to hide his embarrassment.

Raina tensed not wanting the others to drag Dane's drunken evening into the current situation. She impatiently eyed Levi and Sloan.

"Has anyone seen Miller this morning?" Raina asked with concern.

"He's probably still sleeping off his drunken stupor," Sloan replied then shook her head. "I certainly didn't want to disturb him with this."

"I feel so bad for my father," Raina remarked while sinking into a mild depression.

"I'll never forget that image as long as I live," Levi announced as he stared at nothing and his eyes widened. "I mean, they were doing it right there on the library desk. All I saw was her wedding dress and his bare bottom thumping like a jackrabbit."

"Levi!" Dane scolded and gave him a stunned look at the vulgar comment.

"It's not his fault, Dane," Sloan interrupted. "It's burned in my mind too. Poor Mr. Steele. We should get Callie out of the house before he returns. He's liable to kill her. I know I would if I were him."

"Is her sister still here?" Dane asked while attempting to regain his composure.

"Yeah, they're sleeping it off in the crimson room," Sloan replied. "I don't know if she heard what happened. I think she and Keefe turned in early last night."

"Okay, Sloan," Dane announced taking command of the situation. "I want you to check on Callie. If she's sleeping, wake her. I don't care how you do it, but you have to convince her to leave with her sister. I'll talk to Mr. Steele when he returns and gauge his state of mind. We'll make sure he's completely calm before we let him see her." He turned his attention to the cook. "Levi, go to the sister's room and explain the situation. Make sure Elana takes Callie away from here until we're sure there won't be a problem."

"I should wake Miller," Raina announced then hurried for the back stairs.

Jenna followed Raina while Sloan and Levi brought up the rear.

Chapter 27

Gunnysacks and Cement Shoes

Jenna fidgeted while standing in the second floor hallway outside Miller's partially open bedroom door. Raina could be heard talking to her brother, who sounded half-asleep and hungover.

"Son-of-a-bitch!" Miller cried out then stormed into the hallway while slipping into his tuxedo shirt. He still wore his tuxedo pants, possibly having passed out while getting undressed. He stood in his bare feet while hastily buttoning his shirt as Raina hurried after him with his shoes. He spun to face Raina, stopping her.

"I told you we should stop that unholy union," he cried out and snatched his shoes from her. "No, you insisted we take the high road!"

Elana entered the hallway with Levi, who had told her what happened last night.

"We think it's best to get Callie out of the house just until we're sure Mr. Steele is behaving rationally," Levi attempted to explain to the bedraggled woman, who was obviously hungover herself.

"Behaving rationally?" Miller exploded while glaring at Levi. "His bride was fucking another man on their *wedding* night! Why the hell should he be rational?" Miller's look turned even more hostile while he gestured erratically in a fit of rage. "He needs to throw that slut to the curb; preferably from the second-story window!"

"I'm sure she has a reasonable explanation," Elana announced seeming alarmed by Miller's call to violence with his outburst. "We haven't heard her side of it. And don't call my sister a slut!"

"Reasonable explanation?" Miller continued his tirade. "There isn't a 'her' side. She was caught in the act. She's guilty!" He stood rigid and glared at Elana. "What's her side? She felt sorry for poor Nole because he never got to fuck a bride?"

Elana lunged for Miller with anger. "I've had just about enough of you!"

Jenna caught the irate woman and kept her from reaching Miller. Miller didn't help the situation by continuing his rant. Judging by the color of his face, he was about to escalate further.

"Good, because after my father annuls his marriage to your whore of a sister, we won't have to see you ever again," Miller launched back.

"No one said they're getting a divorce," Elana proclaimed while wiggling free from Jenna's hold and attempted to compose herself.

"Are you insane?" Miller cried out while almost laughing psychotically. "She screwed another man on their *wedding* night! Do you honestly think he's going to stay married to the little tramp?"

Keefe appeared in the hallway wearing only his pants, displaying his broad, muscular chest. "What the hell is going on out here?" he demanded.

Miller glared at the much larger man then looked back at Elana. "Collect your sister and get the hell out of this house," he shouted.

"Will someone tell me what is going on?" Keefe again demanded while looking mildly intimidating.

"This house belongs to my sister and her husband; not you," Elana shouted back. "We'll leave when Otto and Callie tell us to and not before!"

Sloan entered the hallway from the master bedroom and seemed a little bewildered.

Elana saw the maid and hurried toward her. "I want to talk to my sister."

"She's not in her room," Sloan remarked while looking puzzled. "Their bed wasn't slept in."

Miller snorted a sarcastic laugh. "She probably left with Nole."

"Her wedding dress isn't in there either," Sloan reported with some confusion. "She didn't bother to change, so she must have left last night right after the fight."

"Maybe Otto came back, and they went someplace private to talk," Elana suggested.

"I doubt that. Someone would have noticed the Ferrari returning," Raina insisted then eyed the others. "She must have left with someone else. She may have thought what we were thinking and decided to stay away from my father until he's had sufficient time to cool off."

"Well, I'm not leaving until I hear from my sister," Elana huffed then folded her arms across her chest in a mild temper tantrum before spinning on her heels and storming back into her room.

Keefe seemed surprised at how quickly she darted away and hurried after her into the room. He slammed the door shut behind him despite still being moderately clueless about what had happened.

"There's no way Dad took her for a ride to talk," Miller insisted and cleverly raised his brows. "Unless it was with a shotgun, gunnysack, and cement shoes."

Raina looked at her brother with surprise. "That's a horrible thing to say, Miller," she scolded.

"Yeah, but everyone was thinking it," Jenna muttered in response.

Raina groaned at her friend then looked at Sloan. "Can you search the empty bedrooms? Maybe she wanted to avoid my father and found an empty room," she announced. "I'll help Levi search the staff wing rooms."

§

After a brief search of the few unoccupied bedrooms on the second floor, Sloan knocked on Tia's bedroom door. It was still early to be waking the guests, but Tia and Olivia were Callie's friends, so she may have sought them out. When the bedroom door opened to reveal Jimmy Love, Sloan was briefly set back.

"Oh, uh, hey," Sloan announced while staring at the slightly disheveled wedding planner in a flashy, satin oriental robe that only made it to his thighs. "I'm sorry to bother you. I thought this was Tia's bedroom."

"You got the right room, girl," he announced then flashed a smile as he left the bedroom.

Sloan looked after him and watched him sashay across the hallway for his own bedroom. He headed into his own room without looking back. Sloan looked back to the open bedroom door and saw Tia approach the doorway. She wore her own satin robe that clung to her excessively wet body. She smiled and offered a tense laugh while running her fingers through her wet hair.

"This isn't how it looks," Tia announced and attempted to close her robe over her wet body.

Sloan held her hands up in the air, hid her grin, and shook her head. "I'm not here to judge you," she announced, although it was obvious her mind was reeling at what she'd possibly just witnessed.

"We, uh, well," Tia fumbled then seemed to give up, appeared embarrassed, and smiled at the maid. "Is there something you needed?"

"I was wondering if Callie spent the night with either you or Olivia," Sloan announced then pointed to the nearby door. "Maybe I should check with Olivia."

"You mean Jimmy Love was telling the truth?" Tia gasped. "He said he heard some gossip that Callie was caught in the library with that creepy guy from the party. Otto's friend."

"Yeah, that actually happened," Sloan reported then held her breath. "I assume you haven't seen her since."

"No," Tia replied as her eyes widened with concern. "You can't find her?"

"We're still looking," Sloan replied. "I'm sure she's around somewhere. We want to get her out of the house before Mr. Steele returns, so he's properly cooled before they see each other. I'll ask Olivia."

"Ask Olivia what?" Olivia asked and appeared in the doorway behind Tia.

Sloan was momentarily stunned as she stared at Olivia, who wore a sexy nightgown. She then looked down the hall to Jimmy Love's bedroom before looking back at the two young women.

"She's obviously not here," Sloan announced and gently cleared her throat while fumbling over herself. "I'll check with the other guests."

The two women noticed the way Sloan fidgeted while staring at them, exchanged looks, and then eyed the maid as they laughed nervously.

"No, no," Olivia announced while appearing embarrassed at the situation. "You have the wrong idea. This isn't how it looks."

"Yeah, there was this monster spider in the bathroom," Tia attempted to explain.

Sloan offered a smile and held up her hand. "Honestly," she announced. "I'm just the maid. You don't have to explain anything to me."

§

Raina and Levi searched the staff wing bedrooms for Callie. Naturally, they started with Callie's old bedroom then worked their way through the vacant bedrooms. There were ten decent sized junior suites in the staff wing, although only three were currently occupied. The eight-car garage had two large, one-bedroom apartments built above it, which Hanson occupied one while Titus had the other. The staff wing suites weren't nearly as impressive and all had the same general layout as Dane's bedroom. Each had a small living area within the bedroom and their own private baths. Raina and Levi checked the seven empty rooms as well but didn't find Callie in any of them. If she hadn't been in her old bedroom, it was doubtful she'd use one of the vacant ones. She'd undoubtedly go someplace familiar.

"She must have gone home with one of the other guests," Raina reluctantly remarked as they headed toward the end of the staff wing. She then glanced at Levi. "When did you see her last?"

"The last time I saw Callie, she was chasing after Otto with her panties hanging from her white, satin shoes," Levi announced with little emotion.

Raina cast a look at him. "That's a colorful image you just painted," she remarked.

He eyed her and raised his brows. "I'll never forget that entire scene," Levi informed her. "I mean, Nole's ass was about as white as Callie's wedding dress. He was like a jackrabbit going to town." His eyes widened, and his hands were gesturing wildly. "It looked like he was humping a huge, white marshmallow. There was so much wedding dress and this lily-white, man's ass in the middle of it."

Raina stared at him with astonishment. "Can you stop?" she gasped, stunned by the details she didn't want to hear.

Levi didn't even look at her as he seemed to relive some horrifying trauma. "Nole's pants were around his ankles," he continued dramatically. "There was this loud slapping sound as he went at her while grunting like a demonic pig."

She held her hand up in the air and turned her head away. "Levi, please!"

"I can't help it," Levi announced in his defense while becoming animated. "I walked in on my sister and her boyfriend once, and it scarred me for life!" He shook his head as they approached the employee's lounge at the end of the hall. "To this day, I can't date women my own size. I just keep seeing my sister with her toothpick of a boyfriend flattened like roadkill beneath her."

Raina groaned, paused outside the employee's lounge, and spun to face Levi. "Not one more word about anyone getting it on," she threatened.

He nodded sympathetically and pretended to zip his lips. They entered the employee's lounge, which consisted of a small kitchen and a living room with a large screen television. The living room looked like a cyclone had gone through. There were papers, take-out boxes, and soda cans everywhere. Oddly enough, the kitchen was spotless.

Raina shook her head. "Well, this looks like your room," she muttered. "Doesn't Dane complain?"

"Dane and Sloan don't come back here much," Levi informed her. "Sloan is either in her room or on the little patio out back. Dane spends most of his free time in his room or in the library."

Raina shook her head and looked back into the staff wing corridor. "That's the entire staff wing," she remarked. "She must have gone home with someone else."

"They're going to get divorced, right?" Levi asked and seemed almost enthusiastic.

She eyed him with some surprise to his candor. "I'd assume so."

"I feel bad for your father after seeing them doing the nasty in the library," Levi remarked. "But I'm glad she'll be out of our lives. She may have been a terrible maid, but she was an even worse lady of the house. She treated Dane like complete crap. I mean, you were mean toward him back in the day, but she was a total ogre. Honestly, I don't know how he could take it from her day in and day out like that without killing her."

Raina shifted uncomfortably as they headed back down the hall toward the main house and the kitchen. "I'm surprised Dane didn't kill me back then," she remarked while reflecting back. "We got into some pretty nasty fights."

"Honestly, I think he just enjoyed tormenting you," Levi informed her. "When you'd come home from college, he'd have Titus pick up yellow roses for your room. He even read your books while you were away."

"Really?" Raina asked then eyed Levi with some surprise. "I thought he didn't read any books by authors who weren't dead."

"Yeah, well, about that. Don't ever say I said anything," Levi announced. "But he's not nearly as refined as he'd like everyone to think he is."

"Huh?" she remarked then sank into thought. "That's interesting."

"I saw him without his shirt once," Levi continued. "He has a shitload of scars. I don't know what happened to him, but he must have gotten into quite a few scrapes."

Raina reflected back to that morning when she saw him barely covered by the bedsheet. He did have several glaring scars.

"One time, after Callie dumped him for Hanson, Hanson started shit with Dane," Levi informed her. "Dane got in Hanson's face and ripped him a new one. The language! I learned a few new colorful phrases that day."

Raina sank into thought then muttered, "How many men could pull a knife from their own leg?" She shivered at the thought.

Levi glanced at her with a bewildered look. "What's that?"

She looked back at him, managed a smile, and shook her head. "Nothing."

Chapter 28

The Happy Couple

It was noon, and no one at the mansion had heard from either Otto or Callie. Dane was on the portable kitchen phone while Levi and Sloan stood around him and listened to the conversation. Miller, Jenna, and Raina hurried into the kitchen through the main door as Dane hung up the phone. They approached the staff near the counter.

"We saw the Ferrari pull up," Miller announced. "It's heading for the garage."

"Yes, I've just been told. That was Titus on the phone," Dane informed them. "Mr. Steele appears to be alone in the Ferrari. Callie isn't with him."

Thundering footfalls were heard on the back stairs, indicating someone was running down them. Elana and Keefe entered the kitchen and looked around with concern.

"We saw the Ferrari pull up. Is she with him?" Elana demanded.

"Titus didn't think so," Dane reported.

Miller was about to head for the outer kitchen door when it opened to reveal a disheveled looking Otto still in his tuxedo from the wedding. Everyone stared at him uncertain what to say. He saw their looks, frowned with exhaustion, and headed for the back stairs.

"I know, I shouldn't have taken off like that," Otto informed them. "You can take turns yelling at me after I shower."

"Where's Callie?" Elana demanded, stopping Otto in his tracks.

Otto turned before the stairs and looked at her with surprise by the question. Anger quickly replaced his surprise. "I don't really care," he announced then looked at Dane and attempted to regain his composure. "Could I get some coffee upstairs?"

"Certainly, Sir."

"I'll take it up," Miller immediately volunteered. "My father and I need some time alone."

Elana wasn't about to let it go, and she didn't care what sort of mood Otto was in. "So you haven't seen Callie since last night?" she again demanded and kept him from heading up the stairs.

"No, and I suspect that's a good thing," Otto snapped back while glaring at her. "Wasn't she in the 'honeymoon suite' with Nole or maybe one of my other friends?"

Elana became irritated and attempted to hide her embarrassment.

"She's not in the house," Raina gently informed him.

"Good," Otto scoffed. "Saves me the trouble of throwing her out." He then smirked at Elana. "Try Nole's bed." Otto headed up the stairs without another word.

Elana turned to face the others with a look of rage. "So that's it?" she blurted out. "No one cares that something could have happened to her last night?"

There was an odd silence from the others. Miller smirked and shrugged, which infuriated Elana even more.

Raina turned to Dane and released a sigh. "Why don't you call Nole's house?" she suggested. "Maybe she did leave with him."

Dane nodded and picked up the phone.

Raina then looked at Sloan. "Would you check the other guest bedrooms? I don't care if you have to wake the others. Maybe she bunked with someone else." Raina then looked back at Elana. "You could call some of her other friends from the reception. Maybe she went home with one of them."

Elana nodded while removing her cell phone and motioned for Keefe to follow her. They headed out the back kitchen door for the terrace.

Raina then turned to Levi. "Can you call Titus and Hanson at the garage and ask them to check the grounds for Callie?" she suggested. "Jenna and I will search this level, Miller can take the attic, and Levi and Dane can search the basement."

"Not me," Miller announced with little concern. "I'm taking coffee to Dad. He needs me." His eyes then narrowed. "Callie can go to hell."

As Miller headed for the coffeepot, Dane hung up the phone.

"Mr. Oaks isn't answering," Dane informed Raina. "Should I send Titus to his house?"

"Yes, that's a good idea," Raina replied then frowned. "I think it's possible she's with him, which could be why he's not answering."

"I'll search the basement by myself," Dane informed her. "Levi can take the attic, but I suspect she more than likely got drunk and passed out somewhere on the grounds."

"If that's the case, she shouldn't be too hard to spot in her wedding dress," Raina muttered.

§

An hour later, Raina and Jenna walked onto the terrace after having searched the entire first floor of the mansion. Neither had any luck locating the missing bride. They looked toward the garage and saw Titus and Hanson as the two men headed toward the house.

"Nole insisted she wasn't at his house, and he hadn't seen her since last night," Titus informed her. "I actually believe him. He looked hungover. I suspect he was drinking half the night."

"I checked the garden, the entire garage area, my workshop, the lawn equipment shed, and the pool house," Hanson informed her. "Did you want me to scour the rest of the estate beyond the garden?"

"No, I don't think she'd have wandered as far as the family crypt or into the woods especially in her wedding dress," Raina informed him. "Let's wait for the others to report in. Maybe they found her in one of the guestrooms or at one of her friend's houses."

The others soon joined them on the terrace as well and shook their heads indicating they didn't have any luck locating the missing bride either.

"She didn't leave with any of the people she knew from the reception," Elana insisted while insecurely folding her arms across her chest.

"I checked with the other overnight guests, and they hadn't seen her since last night either," Sloan announced. "We could try some of the other guests who were still here at the time. One of them could have offered her a ride to a hotel or to stay with them until things cooled down."

"I can't imagine her leaving with any of Otto's friends or business associates," Keefe insisted. "I'm sure she would have come to our room first and woke us. If not to our room, she would have gone to Tia and Olivia's rooms."

"She wouldn't have gotten far on foot," Sloan informed them. "She was wearing a wedding dress."

"None of the cars are missing," Titus reported.

"I could call the local cab companies," Dane suggested.

"Why would she call for a cab?" Keefe demanded in anger. "She would have come to us first. My car is here. She knew that."

"Are we sure we've searched everywhere?" Dane asked and appeared curious. "If she didn't leave with someone she knew, and didn't ask for comfort from someone still here, I think we should assume she got drunk and passed out somewhere on the estate grounds."

"That's what I would have done," Raina announced.

"That's what most of us did," Jenna muttered.

"I'll walk the estate grounds up to the woods," Raina reluctantly announced with a defeated sigh. "Maybe she did go that far."

"I'll go with you," Dane immediately volunteered.

Raina tensed at the thought of being alone with Dane. "I should probably take Hanson," she remarked. "My father might need you."

Dane gave her a strange look then frowned and nodded. Raina joined Hanson and left the terrace. Jenna hurried after them.

Chapter 29
Third Time's a Charm

The elegant, marble family crypt was nearly fifty yards beyond the sprawling gardens and offered privacy as well as a quiet atmosphere. Hanson was careful to keep the area surrounding the crypt as tidy as the rest of the yard and even had some flowers planted around the marble building. Weeping willow trees surrounded the small clearing containing the crypt. Beyond the crypt was vast woodland that extended for miles. Raina and Jenna followed the gardener toward the family crypt, which was their first stop. If Callie had passed out somewhere, she'd be easily spotted in her white wedding dress. Since there wasn't any sign of her, the family crypt seemed like the most logical place to start before heading past the weeping willow trees and into the woods, where Callie was less likely to have ventured.

"Honestly, Raina," Hanson announced and shook his head while looking around. "You can't possibly think Callie wandered out this far in her wedding dress. She's not the outdoorsy type to begin with, so I doubt she'd come out here in her emotional state."

"We looked everywhere," Raina informed him with noted defeat in her tone. "She didn't just disappear. She must have gone somewhere." She then eyed him as they continued their trek toward the family crypt. "You dated her for a few months, didn't you?"

"A few months?" he scoffed and snorted a laugh. "Try two years."

"That long, huh?" Raina remarked. "You probably know her better than the rest of us. Where do you think she would have gone after being caught like that?"

Hanson laughed and appeared almost humored by the question or possibly the whole situation. "I suppose she'd be looking for someplace to sulk," he reported then mocked Raina with a grin. "Can you blame her? When she arrived here, she made it her mission to sleep with every man who could advance her position. She couldn't make it work with Dane, because, well, he's Dane, and I was just mildly entertaining until Titus came along." He shook his head and frowned. "I can't believe I actually thought about asking her to marry me. Thank God Titus came along and saved me from making that mistake."

"She dated Titus for quite some time, didn't she?" Raina asked.

"You mean after she stole him from Sloan? Yeah, close to a year, I think," Hanson replied then waved her off. "Despite what Titus may think, I don't think she ever loved him either. If you ask me; she had her sights set on your father from the moment he became available."

"Was it that obvious?" Raina asked.

"Absolutely," he proclaimed. "She just had to wait until the time was right to make her move. She made herself emotionally available when he was grieving and then ramped it up a notch or two close to a year after Brenda's death." Hanson frowned while reflecting back. "We found out she was officially dating your father only a few weeks after she broke it off with Titus. Titus and I agree that they'd probably been seeing each other unofficially before that."

"I guess Titus was pissed about their relationship, huh?" Raina muttered.

"More like heartbroken," Hanson replied and shook his head while frowning. "When she dumped me for Titus, I handled it much better."

"Are you saying you're more forgiving toward Callie than Titus had been?" she lightly teased while raising her brows in question.

"No, I'm saying Titus couldn't exactly punch your father in the face," Hanson announced then laughed. "Titus and I got into one hell of a brawl when Callie left me for him. We messed each other's faces up so badly, both of us had to wear sunglasses for a week to keep your father from seeing our black and blue eyes." He grinned and laughed. "Every morning for an entire week, Sloan would do my 'makeup' to conceal the bruises on my face."

She stared at him with some surprise by the comment. "I can't believe you and Titus got into a brawl like that," Raina remarked.

"Callie brings out the worst in men," Hanson announced with little emotion.

As they continued toward the crypt in a moment of silence, Jenna looked around the property and marveled at the sheer size of the estate grounds.

"So your father owns all this land?" Jenna asked while looking around.

"The estate is nearly one hundred acres," Raina informed her. "There's a path through the woods that eventually comes out to a pond. Miller and I spent many summers swimming there."

"I heard my predecessor was official lifeguard," Hanson remarked.

"He kept us from drowning; not that we needed a lifeguard," Raina teased.

Jenna eyed the crypt as they approached. "So that's where Miller goes to think?"

"Yeah, that's where Alicia and his mother were laid to rest," Raina informed her then held her breath. "My mother too."

Jenna looked around and rubbed her chilled arms despite the warm morning. "It's creepy out here," she muttered. "What's with all the weeping willow trees?"

"My mother loved them," Raina replied. "There were four out here in the beginning. My father plants one every year since her death."

"By himself," Hanson added. "He refuses any help from me. It's his ritual."

"Are we actually going inside the crypt to look for her?" Jenna asked while eyeing the creepy building now in front of them.

"It's not locked," Raina informed her. "We probably should."

"I'll pass. Knock yourselves out," Jenna remarked then looked around outside the crypt while grimacing. "I'll wait out here."

Raina and Hanson headed for the crypt door and easily pushed it open. Jenna walked around the clearing and looked at the full, drooping weeping willow trees surrounding the small building. As she passed the crypt, she heard one of the branches creak. A gentle breeze blew the drooping limbs, giving them an even creepier appearance. Something white swayed from one of the trees just behind the crypt. Jenna looked at the nearby tree. Callie, still in her wedding dress and tiara, hung by her neck from one of the tree branches. Jenna stared with horror and held back her scream.

"Holy Christ! Raina!" she cried out hysterically. "Hanson! Come quick!"

Raina and Hanson ran from the crypt and around back to join Jenna where she stood nearly paralyzed with fear. Both stopped when they saw Callie hanging from the tree not more than ten feet from them. A small bench was toppled beneath her white stocking feet, and her unblemished, white high heels lay on the ground beneath her. Callie's body gently swayed in the breeze. Her eyes remained open as if staring at them, but they knew she was dead by the color of her face. Raina took a step toward the dead woman. Jenna caught her arm and stopped her with a vice-like grip.

Hanson removed his cell phone from his pocket and was already attempting to call the police despite his trembling hands. Raina stared with horror at the young bride as she gently swayed from the tree. Raina then saw a folded wedding program between her diamond tennis bracelet and her wrist. The temptation to remove it was strong, but Raina resisted not wanting to disturb anything before the police arrived. Undoubtedly, it was a suicide note. She forced herself to look at Callie's face, almost unable to identify the woman after hanging for nearly twelve hours. Raina allowed her eyes to stray to Callie's neck. The emerald necklace was gone!

Chapter *30*

About Last Night

Otto sat on the lounge sofa while holding his head. It was difficult to tell if he was hungover, distraught, or both. The staff and overnight wedding guests had gathered in the lounge as well and seemed to stare with blank expressions of surprise and possible shock. A police detective entered the lounge, causing everyone to either jump up or look at him. Detective Payne was in his early to mid-fifties. Despite his age, he was in amazing physical shape. He was by no means a handsome man, but he did have a full head of mostly gray hair but few wrinkles. He wasn't a tall or muscular man and seemed average in many ways. The detective approached Otto and extended the wedding program now within a plastic bag.

"We found this suicide note on the back of a wedding program tucked under her diamond bracelet," the detective announced. "It's written to you, Mr. Steele. Can you verify that it's your wife's handwriting?"

Otto eyed the note on the program but didn't take time to read it. "It looks like her handwriting," he replied in a sedate tone.

Elana jumped from her chair and practically lunged for the detective. "I would know," she announced.

The detective handed her the wedding program in the clear evidence envelope.

Elana took a moment to read the suicide note then frowned and nodded. "Yeah, that's her handwriting."

She returned the wedding program to the detective and started to sob. Keefe sprang to her side and collected her in his arms, holding her.

"Your statements match her state of mind at the time she wrote the note," Detective Payne announced. "She was distraught with guilt over what happened last night, so she took her life. Naturally, there will be an autopsy, but I'm convinced it was suicide." He hesitated and drew a deep breath. "My sympathies to the family."

§

That evening, Raina sat on the window seat within the library and stared out the window while holding her knees to her chest. She didn't even pretend to be reading. There was a light tap on the open door, but she didn't bother looking or responding. Miller entered the library, approached the window seat, and sat by her feet.

"I can't believe Dad said that twit and her boyfriend could stay the night," Miller scoffed.

"He was being nice," Raina muttered without looking at him. "Callie's dead. Try to show some sympathy."

"Sorry, I don't have any," Miller announced with little emotion. "She cheated on him on their wedding night, got caught, and couldn't live with losing her new, cushy lifestyle." He stared at her even though she didn't look at him. "Why should I feel sorry that she killed herself?"

Raina sat up straight, held her breath a moment, and finally looked at Miller. "When we found her hanging from that tree, I noticed your mother's necklace was missing," she gently informed him.

His eyes widened with surprise. "What?"

"While Hanson and I waited behind the crypt for the police, I looked around the ground beneath her body," Raina added. "It wasn't there."

"So?" he scoffed. "It's probably in her room."

"I looked there too," Raina informed him while sighing. "It wasn't on the dresser or in her jewelry box, although, I did find a lot of your mother's jewelry in with Callie's jewelry."

Miller stared at her a moment then stiffened. "It was suicide, Raina," he announced. "Don't go making this into something it isn't."

"I'm not suggesting someone killed her for her jewelry," Raina remarked. "She was still wearing her diamond tennis bracelet and engagement ring. I'm just curious about what happened to the necklace." She hesitated while staring at him. "I'm wondering if someone found her out there earlier and removed it."

Miller's mouth fell open with surprise. "You mean me?" He shook his head. "No, Raina, I didn't take the necklace. It's rightfully mine. I'd have no reason to take it off her corpse," he insisted. "Maybe she lost it on her way out to the crypt. Maybe it fell off during her romp with Nole." Miller then became angry. "Hell, maybe Nole stole it."

"I suppose as long as her death is determined to be suicide, it's probably just a coincidence," Raina replied.

"Exactly," he announced then attempted to relax but noted her expression. "You have that look. Something else has you bugged."

She shifted uncomfortably. "It's just--" Raina tensed and stared at Miller. "I just keep thinking about her white satin shoes and her white stocking feet."

"What about them?" he asked not understanding the significance.

"They were white," she gently replied.

"Weren't they supposed to be white?" he remarked.

"Hanson was throwing a fit during the wedding with the women's heels sinking into the soft lawn and creating divots," Raina explained. "The heels of Callie's shoes didn't have any dirt or grass stains on them. That indicates she didn't walk on the grass. During the wedding, she was walking on the white aisle runner over the stone walkway to the gazebo."

"So?" Miller remarked and shrugged. "She took her shoes off when she walked out to the crypt."

Raina sighed and nodded. "Yes, she could have," she replied. "But then her white stockings would have had grass stains on them, but they didn't."

"Stop it," he insisted with annoyance. "It was ruled suicide. Don't do this."

She again nodded, although she couldn't stop her mind from straying to the unblemished shoes and white stockings.

"I'm going to bed," Miller informed her. "It's been a long day already. You going up?"

"No, I'd rather sit here and try not to think about any of this," she replied.

Miller patted her leg and left.

§

Raina entered the empty, quiet kitchen a little after midnight and turned on the kettle for tea. She barely heard the staff wing door. When she turned, she saw Dane approach the island counter. He was still dressed, indicating he hadn't gone to bed yet, which was unusual for him considering what time he would need to get up to start his morning routine. Raina fidgeted and avoided looking at him. Despite that she refused to look at him, he stared at her.

"I know it's been a rough day for everyone, but don't you think we should discuss last night?" he asked while seeming tense. "You've been avoiding me all day, and you won't even look at me."

She attempted to look at him but couldn't do it. There were too many rampant emotions, and she couldn't control them.

"What's there to discuss? We were both drunk out of our minds," she replied while attempting to make it sound as if it wasn't that big of a deal. "I'm not blaming you." She then glanced at him and raised her brows almost demandingly. "And if you apologize again, I swear to God; I'll throw something at you."

"Fair enough," he replied and leaned his back against the island counter while staring at her even if she couldn't look at him. "Are you mad at me?"

She drew a deep breath then sighed. "I'm mad at both of us," Raina replied. "It's been a rough day, Dane. I just want to have a cup of tea and hide under my covers until morning." She eyed him. "Can you understand that?"

"Yes, I understand," he announced. "Why don't you go upstairs? I'll bring your tea to you."

"No, that's okay," she replied a little too quickly. She didn't want him in her bedroom.

"I wasn't suggesting--"

She groaned and attempted to control her emotions. "I know you mean well," she replied in a timid tone. "It's nothing personal, I swear." Raina hesitated then cast a quick look at him. "It's just when I look at you; I have these horrible images flashing through my mind. It's like a pornographic film playing over and over in my head. With everything that's happened, I can't handle that right now."

"I understand," he replied timidly then returned to the servant's quarters.

Raina groaned and held her head.

Chapter *31*

Nine-tenths of the Law

Early the following morning, Raina stirred beneath the covers on her bed unable to sleep then groaned and stared at the ceiling. She hadn't been able to shake her conversation with Dane from last night. Although she didn't blame him and told him as much, she knew he was feeling guilty about what happened, and she didn't do anything to reassure him that it was truly okay. Raina needed to stop dwelling on their indiscretion and let it go. More importantly, she needed to let Dane know he should let it go. She groaned with disgust at herself, snatched her cell phone from the nightstand, and sorted through her contacts. She was about to press the button for Dane's cell phone then groaned and hastily returned the phone to the nightstand.

Raina got out of bed and paced the room in her shorts and tank top that she typically slept in. She heard the familiar sound of the Ferrari from the distant garage. Raina approached the large window and looked outside. She could see her father's black Ferrari speed away from the garage. By the sounds she heard, it raced down the back road once it was outside the gates. Something had her father riled up early that morning. Raina appeared curious and sat on the window seat. Perhaps he was conflicted with his love and hatred for Callie and was wrestling with both sorrow and relief that she was dead. Raina made herself comfortable on the window seat and rested her head against the wall while sinking into thought.

She allowed brief images of her father's wedding night to creep into her thoughts. She remembered sitting on the window seat in the library with Dane while they drank and he rubbed her feet. She saw images of them dancing in the library, but she couldn't put the rest together. Maybe it was for the best that she didn't remember their one-night-stand. Perhaps that would make it easier to erase it from her memory, yet she somehow felt cheated. He was able to remember their sexual encounter, but she couldn't. It was almost unfair. She couldn't even remember their first kiss. Raina considered the comment then thought back to her stepmother's funeral.

During a moment of grief, they kissed. Technically, that was their first kiss, so she did actually remember it. A strange feeling stirred inside her as memories of her years of feuding with Dane flashed through her mind. Raina jumped off the window seat, crawled across her bed, and again picked up her cell phone. She was about to press Dane's number when she heard a clunk from the master bedroom next door. She looked at the wall separating her bedroom from the master bedroom and felt concern.

Horrible memories returned to her from that awful night. She jumped off the bed and headed for her bedroom door. Raina walked along the hallway and approached the new master bedroom. She peered inside through the partially open door and heard someone moving around. She pushed open the door. Elana removed the jewelry from Callie's jewelry box and placed it into a bag on the bed. Keefe routed through the dresser drawers looking for something. Raina stared with horror then pressed the button on her cell phone without putting it to her ear.

"What the hell are you doing in my father's bedroom?" Raina suddenly demanded.

Keefe and Elana looked at her with surprise then turned arrogant.

"Otto said I could have Callie's things," Elana boldly announced.

"Sure, and that's why you waited until he left to take them," Raina snapped. "I don't know what he told you, but I'm sure he didn't say you could take the jewelry. Especially since some of that jewelry isn't hers."

"I don't know what you're talking about, but you can take this up with your father when he gets back," Elana launched. "I'm entitled to my sister's belongings, and I'm taking them. Now go away and leave me alone."

"If you attempt to leave this house with that jewelry, I'm calling the police," Raina informed her and turned angry.

"You call the police," Elana snapped. "I'm within my rights to take my sister's things!"

Elana shut her bag and pushed past Raina to leave the room. When Raina attempted to stop her, Keefe shoved her out of the way. Dane appeared in the doorway with his hands respectfully behind his back and blocked Elana's path.

"Get out of my way, butler!" Elana snarled.

"Gladly, just as soon as you set the bags down," Dane announced.

Keefe pushed past Elana and poked Dane in the chest. "We don't take orders from you, jerk off."

"Maybe you'd care to take this up with my friend--" Dane removed the shotgun from behind his back and held it to his side while aimed at Keefe. "Remington."

Keefe jumped back with surprise, stared at the shotgun, and then looked at Elana. "He wouldn't, would he?"

Elana stared at the shotgun with alarm. "I don't know," she nearly choked on her words. "I'd heard he shot that one intruder."

"Yeah, made a real mess of my room," Raina casually announced. "Buckshot and guts everywhere."

Elana and Keefe dropped their bags and stared at the shotgun while almost paralyzed with fear. Dane smirked, raised the shotgun barrel to his shoulder, and stood aside. He politely indicated the doorway, allowing them to pass. Both scurried from the room. Raina exhaled with relief then looked at the shotgun he held and shook her head.

"Honestly, I was little worried you might pull the trigger," she announced and laughed nervously.

Dane smiled and pulled the trigger. Raina jumped as the shotgun clicked. Nothing happened.

He offered a sly smile. "I didn't have time to load it," Dane teased.

She stared at him with disbelief and near horror. "You're kind of scary, Dane."

He shrugged while grinning. "I'd like to believe it's part of my charm."

"Sure, if you consider being a psychopath charming," she muttered.

He eyed her with surprise. "What? You don't?"

She stared at him a moment almost stunned by the response then noted his innocent look and laughed.

Chapter 32

What a Payne

Elana and Keefe sat on one of the lounge sofas with untouched cups of coffee on the table before them. Both appeared to sulk that they hadn't been able to leave with Callie's possessions. Raina sat in an oversized chair near the fireplace with a bored look while Miller leaned in the doorway with his arms across his chest and a scowl on his face. He appeared to be guarding the doorway in case the couple attempted to remove anything else from the house before Otto returned. The Ferrari was heard pulling up to the front of the mansion, which was unusual, but it seemed Otto was in a hurry to return after the phone call he'd received. Raina sighed with relief and immediately straightened.

"Good, now you can see I was telling the truth," Elana announced and sat forward on the sofa. "I had permission to take her things. They're rightfully mine."

Only a moment passed before Otto stormed into the room, nearly knocking Miller over, and glared at Elana. "What the hell do you think you were doing?" he demanded with rage in his eyes.

Elana turned defensive. "You said I could have her things," she cried out showing her own anger. "She was my sister!"

"I said you could have her clothes and shoes," Otto launched back then glared at her. "You know damned well that didn't include the jewelry. The fact that you waited until I left to collect her things proves you knew that."

"She was my sister," she again insisted. "Her things belong to me!"

"No, she was my wife," Otto reminded her. "I'm the surviving spouse. I paid for her jewelry; therefore it remains part of my estate."

"Her jewelry belongs to me!"

"Obviously, you understand nothing about marital property," Otto snarled.

"And half of that jewelry belonged to my mother," Miller chimed in with his own hostility boiling over. "Neither Callie nor you had legal claim to any of that!"

Otto looked at Miller with surprise. "Your mother's jewelry?" he demanded. "What are you talking about?"

"Callie was wearing my mother's necklace at the wedding," Miller snapped back and glared at his stepfather. "Don't pretend you didn't notice. You bought it for her on your wedding day. I found almost all my mother's jewelry in Callie's jewelry box!"

"How did it get there?" Otto demanded then looked at Elana for an explanation.

"You gave it to her," Miller snarled back at his stepfather.

Otto looked back at Miller with surprise. "No, Miller. I never gave it to Callie. I offered it to Raina after Brenda died, but she said you should have it," he remarked. "You told me you didn't want it, so I put it away thinking you'd want it later after you were married." He shook his head defensively. "I swear I didn't give your mother's jewelry to Callie. I would never have done that."

"Then Callie stole it," Miller snapped.

Elana sprang to her feet with anger. "Callie wasn't a thief!"

"We're not arguing about this now or ever again," Otto growled then glared at Elana. "I'll have Callie's clothing packed and sent to you." He turned to Miller. "You, me, and Raina will go through the jewelry in Callie's room and remove everything that belonged to your mother. You can either put it in my safe or take it with you."

Miller fidgeted and attempted to relax. "Thank you," he replied almost timidly.

"That's not fair," Elana proclaimed.

"Nothing about the last two days has been fair," Otto snarled back at her. "You don't like it? Go talk to an attorney. Let him tell you that you're shit out of luck. Now, if you don't mind, I think it's time you left." His look turned demanding. "Please don't ever return."

Elana scoffed and made a motion to Keefe, who stood and joined her as the doorbell rang. Dane appeared in the grand hallway almost out of nowhere to answer the door. It was apparent he'd been standing nearby listening to their entire conversation, evident by the tiny smile on his face.

"This isn't over," Elana warned Otto in a threatening tone. "I'm suing you for wrongful death. It's your fault she killed herself!"

"It was her own actions that caused her to take her life," Otto snarled back then sneered at her. "Good luck in court with that one."

Dane stood in the doorway with Detective Payne standing alongside him and watched the exchange.

"Is this a bad time?" the detective asked.

Dane gently cleared his throat. "Detective Payne, Sir," he announced a little late.

Otto glared at the butler. "Yes, I see him, Dane."

Dane quickly disappeared into the grand hallway. All eyes were now on the detective.

"Sorry to intrude in your grief, but we got the results back from the autopsy on your wife, Mr. Steele," Detective Payne announced and raised his brows. "She was struck on the back of the head before being hanged."

They all stared at him in silent surprise.

"What?" Otto gasped. "Couldn't that have happened when she hanged herself?"

"The medical examiner says no," the detective replied. "Calculating the height of the branch and the stool, your wife wouldn't have been able to hang herself. I'm afraid she was murdered."

Elana suddenly turned to Otto and pointed her finger at him. "It was you," she cried out. "You're the only one with enough motive to want her dead!"

"Okay, let's not point fingers," the detective announced. "The time of death is estimated between midnight and two in the morning. I'm going to need a list of everyone who was still at the house between those hours."

"I'm sure the staff can help with that list. They know everything that goes on around here," Otto informed him. "Dane and Levi should be in the kitchen."

"After I get that list, I'll want to discuss your alibi first, Mr. Steele," Detective Payne informed him.

Otto nodded and frowned. "I understand."

Chapter *33*

The Butler Did It

Raina stood within the hallway before the kitchen door while alternating wringing her hands together and running her fingers through her hair. She could hear Levi and Dane talking to the detective through the door, and it sent every nerve in her body on edge. Everyone on the staff hated Callie and would be prime suspects second only to her father and Miller. She debated entering the kitchen or minding her own business until the detective decided to question her. Raina groaned and felt compelled to join them in the kitchen. As she entered, she saw Detective Payne standing by the counter with Levi, Sloan, and Dane. As the detective talked to them, Levi wrote names on a paper. Raina eased her way closer to the counter while attempting to look casual.

"The Nixon's stayed over that night and were present," Sloan added.

Levi wrote their names on the paper then pointed his pen at her. "Nole left right after Mr. Steele decked him."

"No, he came back inside to talk to Callie," Sloan informed him, "but he couldn't find her, so he went into the ballroom for a drink."

"Other overnight guests were her sister and her boyfriend, that wedding planner guy--"

"Jimmy Love," Sloan remarked. "Oh, and her friends Tia and Olivia."

"Titus?" Levi asked.

"No, he went out to some nightclub in the city," Sloan offered. "He left a little after seven o'clock. I don't think he returned until after two."

"Our time frame is midnight until two," the detective informed them. "Put him down."

Levi scribbled Titus' name on the list and handed it to the detective. "That should be everyone including the guest's chauffeurs."

"Thank you," Detective Payne replied then eyed the list. He returned his attention back to the staff. "It's been brought to my attention that the deceased was once on staff and there was some hostility toward her new position in the house." He eyed those within the kitchen. "So while I'm here, can the three of you tell me your whereabouts between midnight and two in the morning?"

"Here, cleaning the kitchen," Sloan admitted. "There was wedding cake everywhere. We couldn't let Dane see the state of the place."

"Both of you?" the detective asked while pointing his pen at them.

"And half a dozen caterers," Sloan replied.

Levi nodded in agreement.

Detective Payne then eyed Dane. "What about you?" he asked. "I'm told you dated the victim a few years ago. Where were you last night?"

"I was in my room sometime before eleven," Dane informed him. "I had been hitting the tequila pretty hard and must have passed out because I didn't hear any of the commotion in the kitchen."

"So you were alone?" Detective Payne asked with a curious look.

"Yes, Sir," Dane replied without flinching.

Raina fidgeted, cursed herself, and stepped forward. "Don't lie to protect my reputation, Dane," she announced then looked at the detective and held her composure. "Dane wasn't alone, Detective Payne. He and I got drunk and spent the night together in his room."

Levi and Sloan shifted looks of shock and disbelief between them. Their mouths hung open, but neither appeared able to speak.

Detective Payne eyed Dane, who fidgeted and nervously rubbed the back of his neck. "Is that true?" the detective asked. "Were you together?"

Dane frowned and avoided looking at the detective or Raina. "I'd rather not answer that question," he remarked with embarrassment.

"I'll take that as 'yes'," the detective muttered, jotted something in his notebook, and then looked at Raina. "And you're willing to testify under oath that you were together the entire time between midnight and two?"

Raina frowned and nodded. Levi and Sloan attempted to hide their dirty smirks. They were enjoying the news a little too much. Dane glared at them with a threatening look, which caused them to scurry out of the kitchen.

"Thanks for the list," the detective announced. "If I have any more questions, I'll let you know."

As the detective left the kitchen, Dane looked at Raina and frowned. "I'm not a suspect, and neither are you," Dane insisted. "Why did you admit to that?"

"You used to date Callie," she replied. "He knew that. I'm not going to let you come under suspicion when you have a perfectly good alibi."

"I appreciate what you did for me, Raina," Dane announced. "I hope you don't regret that admission when it gets around the entire house."

"Do you really think Sloan is that big of a gossip?" Raina demanded.

"Not Sloan," he insisted with a defeated sigh. "Levi's our gossip queen."

"I did the right thing, and I don't regret it," she announced then fidgeted and attempted to look into his eyes. "I also had time to think about what happened between us the other night, and I feel it's important that you know that I'm okay with it."

He stared at her with surprise by the admission. "You are?" Dane asked while studying her. "I was positive you would hate me forever."

Despite having a difficult time looking him in the eyes, she forced herself to meet his gaze. "I knew a lot of girls in college who lost their virginity to ill-mannered, drunken frat boys with lousy reputations," she informed him then drew a deep breath and held it a moment while staring into his blue eyes. "I wanted my first time to be with someone special." She offered a weak, tiny smile. "Who's more special than the man who saved my life?"

Dane's expression dropped at her words as he stared at her. "Did you just say your first time?" he asked with surprise and some anxiety. "Are you telling me--?"

"Yes," Raina replied without hesitation and nodded. "You were my first."

Dane turned away from her, leaned on the counter, and groaned while holding his head with remorse.

"It's okay--really."

Dane straightened and sighed. "It's not okay. Not only did I sleep with my boss's daughter, but I slept with my boss's *virgin* daughter," he announced and shamefully shook his head. "You have no idea how horrible I feel."

"We were both silly drunk," she reminded him. "You shouldn't feel guilty about what happened."

He avoided looking at her and again rubbed the back of his neck. "I'll have to disagree with you on that," Dane remarked then shifted uncomfortably while staring at her. "I feel guilty because--" He groaned and looked away. "Because, honestly, I enjoyed it."

Raina stared at him with surprise by his candor.

He caught her look then groaned and turned away. "You wouldn't understand," Dane muttered more to himself. "It's a guy thing."

"Why would I mind that you enjoyed it?" she demanded. "Were you supposed to hate it?"

"Doesn't that make me morally reprehensible?" he asked while glancing at her. "I shouldn't enjoy something that's done nothing but make you uncomfortable. I'm a perfect gentleman with someone like Callie, who was my girlfriend at the time, yet I disrespect an actual lady, who also happens to be my boss's daughter. I preached to you about protecting your reputation, and then I'm the one who does the most damage to it. Doesn't that make me a horrible person and a bit of a hypocrite?"

"Of course not," she insisted then fidgeted slightly and offered a tense smile. "I'd probably be insulted if you *didn't* enjoy it."

Dane managed a tiny laugh while attempting to relax. "I'm glad we were finally able to get this out in the open," he announced. "I've been torturing myself mercilessly since that morning. I don't think I could live with myself if I set us back two years."

"You don't need to worry about that, I promise." Raina fidgeted while studying him. "I really need to ask," she announced then hesitated. "Did *I* enjoy it?"

He seemed surprised by the question. "You still don't remember any of it?"

She shook her head. "No, nothing," Raina replied and immediately countered on her comment. "And I don't want to hear the details either. I'm not ready for that. Just a vague answer will do."

"Fair enough," he replied then considered the question and offered a timid smile. "Let's just go with you were mildly to moderately uninhibited and pleasantly pleased."

She stared at him unable to respond then shook her head. "I'm starting to think you made up the entire thing," she announced. "That sounds nothing like me."

"Allow me to disagree respectfully," he teased and flashed a smile.

She glared at him then shifted uncomfortably. "Okay, now I'm starting to hate you again."

"Too soon to joke about it?" he asked while grinning. "You did say you were okay with it, and I'm pretty sure virgins can't fake orgasms."

She glared her annoyance then smirked. "Oh, you want to play? Fine," she scoffed. "Virgins also don't need to use birth control."

Dane's expression dropped as he thought about the comment.

Raina smiled deviously and nodded. "Yeah, you just think about that for the next few weeks," she announced then spun on her heels, headed across the kitchen, and left through the hallway entrance. When she reached the other side of the door, she cringed and nervously ran her fingers through her hair. "Crap. I need to find a calendar."

Chapter 34
Everyone's Got One

Detective Payne had returned to the lounge a little while later to ask those remaining a few questions about the night of Callie's death just to get an idea of who was where and with whom. Dane entered the lounge a short while later with a rolling cart containing assorted beverages, pastries, and a pitcher of martinis. Otto gave Dane a suspicious look as if wondering what he was up to by rolling out the party cart.

"So we have Sloan and Levi in the kitchen along with half a dozen caterers," Detective Payne announced. "Jenna was playing poker with the four remaining chauffeurs until one in the morning before turning in for the night." He then looked at Miller. "Miller passed out in his room sometime between ten and midnight. Mr. Steele left in the Ferrari after confronting his wife, and Nole Oaks left shortly after the confrontation." He then looked at Callie's sister. "Elana and Keefe were in their room just before midnight where they admitted they clearly were *not* sleeping."

Elana nodded while Keefe grinned in response.

Detective Payne glanced at Raina. "And Raina was with the butler in his room," he announced, "where they were watching a movie and fell asleep."

Raina glanced at Dane, who smirked while pouring drinks. Raina didn't know how Dane managed it, but he somehow got the detective to leave out their drunken escapades. Perhaps the detective felt sorry for Dane and didn't want to see him get in trouble with his employer. What they did in his room didn't need to be shared with the others as long as Detective Payne was satisfied with their alibi.

"I have each of your statements, so that should cover it for now," the detective announced. "I'll just need to talk to the chauffeur and gardener then I can interview those who'd already left but were present at the house between midnight and two." He shut his notebook. "I'll let you know if I need any more information."

"Dane will contact Titus and Hanson and have them meet you in the kitchen," Otto announced. "Save you a trip to the garage."

"I appreciate that."

Dane left the lounge with Detective Payne. Once the others left the lounge, Raina's father held her back and eyed her suspiciously.

"You were in Dane's room watching a movie together?" Otto asked with a strange look on his face.

She tensed slightly to his question but attempted to keep from revealing her anxiety. Raina managed to shrug and offered a tiny smile.

"He mentioned he was going to his room to watch a movie," she replied. "I know he has unusual taste in movies, but I thought it might be an interesting change of pace." She raised a clever brow. "Do you have a problem with us watching a movie together?"

"No," Otto replied. "Not at all. It's just the two of you hated each other two years ago, and now you're watching movies together in his bedroom." He shrugged. "It's just surprising, I suppose."

"We discussed why our feud ended," she again reminded him.

"You're right," Otto replied while smiling more naturally. He then tilted his head and appeared curious. "What movie did you watch?"

She felt as if her father were testing her. Raina hesitated only a moment then laughed. "Damned if I remember the name of it. Some British flick with a bunch of boring people I couldn't understand doing things that didn't make any sense."

Her father chuckled at her answer. "Yeah, that sounds about right."

Raina made a mental note to seek out Dane and give him a heads up in case her father asked him what movie they'd watched. Surely, he could come up with a movie based on her lame description.

§

Titus and Hanson sat at the island counter while Detective Payne stood off to the side and jotted notes in his book. Both men drank coffee while Dane and Levi prepared lunch at the main counter behind them.

Detective Payne eyed Titus. "So you left around seven o'clock for the city and didn't return until approximately two in the morning."

"Yes, that's correct," Titus replied then grinned. "I have half a dozen women who can vouch for me. I made a lasting impression on quite a few lovely ladies."

"I'm sure they'd willingly vouch for you," Detective Payne replied with little emotion if not jealousy. "Unfortunately, you were still back in time to be considered a suspect."

Titus' expression dropped at the detective's admission.

Detective Payne eyed Hanson. "And you were in the garden cleaning up from the wedding until after midnight?" he asked. "So you must have seen Mr. Steele take his car from the garage."

"No, I saw him heading toward the garage with Nole following him then I heard a commotion," Hanson replied. "A few minutes later, I saw the Ferrari drive away. I couldn't see the garage from the garden."

"I'm aware that both of you had at one time dated the deceased, but neither of you are currently under suspicion," the detective informed them. "I'm just getting a timeline of events together."

"If you want a good suspect, you should question the wedding planner, Jimmy Love," Titus informed him.

"I heard he's a real character," the detective replied then eyed Titus with some surprise. "Why would you think this Jimmy Love had motive?"

"I heard Callie and Jimmy Love having a heated argument a few hours before the wedding," Titus informed him. "I didn't think that guy was capable of that sort of hostility, especially since he prides himself on calming the bride, but they nearly went at it."

"Anyone have a picture of this guy?" the detective asked with interest.

"I should have one on my cell phone," Titus replied and removed his phone.

He skimmed through the photos on his phone while Detective Payne watched over his shoulder. There were several pictures of excessively attractive women taken at the nightclub, presumably from Saturday night. He finally came to the ones from the wedding.

"Hold up," Detective pain announced and pointed his pen at the phone. "Enlarge that picture."

The detective had indicated the picture of Callie walking down the aisle. Once Titus enlarged it, Detective Payne indicated the emerald necklace she wore.

"That's some necklace she's wearing," the detective remarked.

"Yeah, she always had a thing for emeralds," Titus insisted with little emotion.

"She wasn't wearing it when we found her body," the detective announced.

Titus shrugged with little interest. "Maybe she took it off upstairs."

"I find that unusual considering she was still wearing her one-karat engagement ring and a diamond tennis bracelet," the detective remarked. "Why would she take time to remove a necklace of lesser value?"

"If you knew Callie, you'd know why there's no understanding her behavior," Titus replied.

§

Sloan arranged place settings in the dining room for lunch. Since the detective was still hanging around and the others were reluctant to leave, they had additional guests for lunch. Dane hurried into the dining room and approached Sloan.

"Did that detective ask you about the necklace Callie was wearing at the wedding?" Dane asked with concern.

"Yeah, he wanted to know if it was in her room," Sloan announced while straightening. "I told him I hadn't seen it. We looked through her jewelry, but it wasn't there. It's possible Elana got her hands on it when they were rummaging through Callie's things." She stared at Dane with concern. "You don't suppose he thinks someone killed her for that necklace, do you?"

"It was rather valuable," Dane replied. "But it doesn't make sense that they'd steal the necklace and leave behind her engagement ring and tennis bracelet." He studied her a moment. "Was she wearing it when Mr. Steele caught her and Mr. Oaks together?"

"Oh, yes," Sloan gasped as her eyes widened. "I remember seeing it when she ran after him. It was very eye-catching."

"So she either lost it outside, or someone took it from her," Dane announced. "A lot of the guests who were still here heard what happened and knew she'd be alone that night. It's the perfect setup for a jewelry snatch. Perhaps things didn't go according to plan."

"Maybe she wasn't supposed to see the thief, and he killed her so she couldn't identify him," Sloan suggested.

"Let's hope that's the case," Dane muttered while looking preoccupied.

"Why?" she asked with concern. "Are you thinking something else?"

"The scenario where Mr. Steele is the best suspect," Dane muttered.

"I know he was mad, but he'd never kill her," Sloan insisted.

"That doesn't mean he won't be found guilty," Dane replied. "I need you to search the master bedroom and all the guestrooms for that necklace. I'll ask Hanson to scour the grounds between the terrace and the crypt. I'll search the library and any other rooms I suspect she may have passed through after the incident in the library."

"There's something you seem to be forgetting," Sloan announced before he could leave the dining room.

"No, I'm not forgetting Miller," Dane replied. "I'll take responsibility for searching his room." He hesitated while staring at her. "You didn't mention him to the detective, did you?"

"You mean the daggers in his eyes when he saw her in his mother's necklace?" Sloan asked then shook her head. "No, I didn't say anything. That's not to say someone else won't mention it though."

"Finding that necklace is priority one after lunch," he informed her. "If you find it, notify me immediately."

Chapter *35*
Honor Thy Father

Raina hurried into the kitchen, nearly plowing down the revolving door, with a look of paranoia on her face. She approached Miller, who hung out at the island counter with Dane and Levi and startled all three men.

"Did I just see Detective Payne leaving with Dad?" Raina exploded.

"Yeah, he took Dad away," Miller informed her while frowning.

"He didn't take him," Dane corrected while seemingly calm. "He asked him to accompany him to the station for some additional questioning."

"He wasn't allowed to refuse," Miller announced while glaring at the butler. "In my book, that's the same as *taking* him."

"There's no reason for panic just yet," Dane insisted. "He's not being charged; just questioned."

"Then after they question him, they'll charge him," Raina protested and shook her head with concern. "He needs a lawyer."

"I already have a call into his lawyer," Miller informed her.

"That woman was trouble the moment she slithered through that door," Levi muttered with disgust. "Why did Mr. Steele hire her anyway?"

"Mr. Nixon asked him to hire her," Dane replied. "Mrs. Nixon insisted he fire her."

"Yeah, because Callie was having an affair with Mr. Nixon and she found out about it," Levi proclaimed. "Pawn her off on us instead."

"God, she's dead, and she's still causing problems around here," Miller scoffed.

"You people are cold," Raina scolded while eyeing the three men with disgust. "I wasn't exactly fond of her, but she didn't deserve to be murdered."

Miller raised his brows and eyed her. "You don't know that."

Levi and Dane simultaneously tensed and minded their own business. Raina stared at her stepbrother with surprise. She then eyed Dane and Levi, who offered nothing and pretended they weren't even listening.

"Wow," Raina announced then indicated Miller. "Him I get." She glared at Dane and Levi. "But you two? Absolutely heartless." She stormed from the kitchen, hitting the door with enough force to strike the doorstopper.

Levi looked at Dane and sulked. "She thinks I'm heartless," he pouted. "That hurts."

"Never mind her," Miller scoffed and waved him off. "She needs to get laid."

"Yeah, Dane," Levi teased and looked at Dane while grinning. "You should probably get on that."

Dane suddenly glared at Levi. Miller appeared surprised by the comment and gave them each a strange look.

"What the hell is that supposed to mean?" Miller demanded.

§

Titus had been keeping busy that afternoon by washing and waxing the cars outside the eight-car garage. He had his jacket off and his sleeves rolled up just beyond his elbows, displaying his muscular lower arms. Jenna, Raina, and Miller approached the garage and noted several cars parked outside. Titus had finished wiping down the Bentley when he saw the three approach.

"I'm sorry," Titus announced while eyeing them. "Did I miss the call for a car? I would have brought yours out-front for you."

"No, we're fine, Titus," Miller announced. "The walk helped cool some of us down."

"I'm fine," Raina snarled at her brother.

Titus hid his smile and walked away. It was obvious he didn't want to get between the feuding stepsiblings.

"I can't wait to get away from this place for a while," Jenna announced.

"A ride to the police station isn't going to be very exciting," Miller informed her. "Dad's lawyer said they're not charging him with anything, but I'd like to stop by the station anyway."

"Enjoy your boring trip to the police station," Raina announced. "Jenna and I have other plans."

He eyed her suspiciously. "What are you up to?" he demanded.

"I want to visit Farley Nixon at the country club," Raina boldly announced. "I'd like to talk to him when his wife isn't around."

"I don't know what you're hoping to learn," Miller remarked with a sigh, "but if you want to waste your time, be my guest."

"The Nixon's knew Callie better than anyone at our place," Rainer reminded him. "If Farley was having an affair with her, he probably knew her the best."

"And where will that get us?" Miller demanded.

"I don't know, but it beats sitting around waiting for them to pin her murder on our father," Raina insisted. "It's my time to waste."

"The country club is on the opposite side of town from the police station," Miller reminded her. "We'll need to take two cars." He considered his options. "I suppose I could borrow one of Dad's cars."

He was about to approach the garage door when Titus appeared from the first bay.

"I'll drive the ladies," Titus informed Miller. "It's a beautiful day, and I'd love to get my mind off all this, well, you know."

Miller eyed Raina and shrugged. "Do you want Titus to take you to the country club? I could take your car," he announced. "It'll make things much easier."

"Can we take the limo?" Jenna asked sounding a little giddy.

"Yeah, sure," Raina replied.

"I'll meet you at the club for drinks," Miller informed them.

"See you there in an hour or so," Raina replied then eyed Titus.

He smiled charmingly and extended his hand toward the freshly washed limousine.

§

While riding in the back of the limousine, Jenna admired the luxury of a first-class lifestyle. She finally figured out how to work the radio and fiddled with it. Raina couldn't take watching her friend play with all the buttons like a kindergartner and moved to the backward facing seat near the front. She opened the glass partition to reveal Titus in the driver's seat. She caught a glimpse of his profile and realized his eyes were slightly glossy almost as if he'd been fighting back tears.

"Are you okay, Titus?" she asked with concern.

"I'm fine," replied. "Allergies."

She knew that wasn't true and felt sorry for the guy. He was obviously hurting from everything that had happened over the last few months.

"I know you dated Callie for nearly a year," Raina announced gently. "It's understandable if you're upset by her death."

"I know how everyone felt about her," Titus remarked. "I mean, I sort of hated her a little myself, but no one seems to care that she's dead. It just bothers me that her death brings so much joy to others."

"It does seem that way, I suppose," she replied with a soft sigh. "Maybe once the police have her killer we can have a memorial or something for her. Perhaps invite her friends and sister." She eyed him sympathetically through the rearview mirror. "It's tough to have closure when there hasn't even been a proper funeral."

"That would be a nice gesture, but I doubt anyone from the house will want to attend," Titus replied while looking back at her through the mirror. "The staff all hated her, especially Dane."

"Why especially Dane?" Raina questioned with surprise. "I thought they only dated briefly. I heard they were never really that close either."

"There's a reason why they only dated a few weeks and why she never slept with him," Titus announced then tensed. "Maybe I shouldn't say."

"And maybe you should," Raina replied.

"It can't get back that I said anything, because lord knows I have my own skeletons in my closet," the chauffeur informed her.

"I won't tell anyone what I heard from you," Raina reassured him then watched one of the windows raise and lower while Jenna giggled.

"When we were first dating," Titus offered, "Callie told me the reason she ended it with Dane was that she discovered something about his past--something *disturbing*."

"Disturbing?"

"That's the word she used."

"What was it?" Raina asked now curious. Disturbing was a concerning word choice.

"She didn't elaborate, and I didn't press her," he replied. "All I know is she said she found a locked box in his room. She opened it and found something disturbing about his past." He shook his head. "Whatever it was, it was enough for her to abruptly end it. She started dating Hanson shortly after that. I know Dane thought she was just using him, but there was more to it than that. She told me she only dated Hanson because she wanted protection from Dane."

"Protection from Dane?" Raina asked with surprise. "She thought he'd hurt her?"

"She seemed to think so," he replied. "Whenever I questioned her about her relationship with Dane, she'd distract me with sex."

Raina sank into thought and wondered what Callie had discovered in the mysterious locked box she'd found in Dane's room. What could she possibly have found that was disturbing and made her fear for her life? If it was something so incriminating, why hadn't she gone to the police? It didn't make sense.

Chapter 36
Cheaters, Liars, and Thieves

Raina and Jenna sat with Farley Nixon at a private corner booth in the quiet country club lounge. Each had drinks on the table before them. The lounge had an old, gentleman's club feel to it. Rich dark wood, dim lighting, intimate booths, and a large antique bar. Despite the large windows, wooden mini-blinds kept out most of the natural light. Many of the tables were intimate booths allowing seclusion and privacy. Farley remained tense and shifted uncomfortably several times while already working on his second drink.

"If my wife knew we were discussing Callie, she'd kill me," he informed them and looked around the lounge as if expecting someone to be eavesdropping on their conversation.

"Why's that?" Jenna asked.

"The worst kept secret in town," he replied and nervously leaned on the table. "You must have heard that Callie and I had an affair several years back. That Detective Payne seemed to zero in on it rather quickly and questioned me about it extensively."

"If your wife already knows, why would she be upset that we're discussing Callie?" Raina asked.

"Gilda is crazy jealous. Literally crazy," Farley informed her then took a large swallow from his glass. "My wife found

out about our affair and wanted me to dismiss her immediately."
His eyes widened dramatically with fear. "You don't just fire
the woman you're having an affair with. They tend to take that
personally."

"So you convinced my father to hire her instead of firing
her," Raina muttered then made a face. "So I have you to
thank for that little gift that just keeps giving."

"I'll admit, I didn't tell your father the whole truth about
her dismissal," Farley replied uncomfortably. "I told him Gilda
was going through one of her jealous fits of rage and accused me
of sleeping with Callie. I told him she insisted I fire her or
she'd divorce me." He fiddled with his drink. "That's all true,
except her accusation was more than an accusation. It's not as
if it mattered at the time. Your father was completely devoted
to Brenda. Their marriage wasn't in any danger by pawning off
Callie onto him."

Raina shook her head with disappointment. "Didn't you
think to tell my father about your relationship when you found
out he was dating her?"

"I wanted to, but he seemed happy," Farley explained. "I
mean, she made me happy too. Why shouldn't he be happy,
right?"

"Can't argue with that," Jenna muttered then eyed the
nervous man. "How did your wife find out?"

"Someone found out about our affair and secretly recorded
us together," he explained.

"One of the staff?" Jenna asked while staring at him with
surprise.

"Doubtful. The video was shot from outside the window,"
Farley explained. "If I didn't pay them for their silence, they
were going to send the video to my wife." He frowned and
shook his head. "At the time, Callie tried to convince me to
come clean with Gilda and not pay the blackmail, but I couldn't
let my wife see that video, so I paid them. I paid on several
occasions. My wife caught me paying the blackmail money, and
that's how she found out about the affair." He reconsidered the
comment. "Well, she strongly suspected. Naturally, since my
wife knew, I decided to stop paying the blackmail money and
dismiss Callie. It would get both the blackmailer and my wife

off my back. Once my wife knew, the blackmailer had nothing more to hold over me, so he left me alone."

"Who do you think killed Callie?" Raina asked while leaning across the table.

"Under the circumstances, I'd say your father did it, but I know him too well," Farley insisted. "He's more of a 'get your lawyer involved than take justice into your own hands' kind of guy." Farley shook his head. "And that hanging business? I can't imagine him ever doing something like that. It's a little too grand, you know, over-the-top. A lover seeking revenge wouldn't fake a suicide in that manner. He'd slip pills into her drink. That's how you kill your lover."

Raina and Jenna stared at the man across from them a moment and raised their brows as if coming to the same conclusion.

"Sounds like you've given that some thought," Jenna muttered.

"I think most married men do," he replied with little concern and sipped his drink.

Neither woman moved for a moment then pushed their drinks away.

§

It was almost dinnertime, and the staff was busy setting the dining room table. Raina appeared on the back stairs, glanced around the empty kitchen, and listened a moment. She could hear the familiar voices coming from the nearby dining room. Raina seized her opportunity and hurried through the servant's wing doorway. Dane kept the house running on a tight schedule, so she knew how long they'd be out of the kitchen. It was a small window, but she felt she had to risk it. Raina hurried down the staff wing corridor and entered Dane's room. She quietly shut the door behind her and began a quick search of the room. She looked under the bed, frowned, and then checked the closet.

Dane's suits hung neatly and almost perfectly spaced. She marveled at the neatness of his closet and shook her head. He was more of a prima donna about his clothes than most women. She then looked at the shelf above the suits and saw the black, fireproof locked box. Titus had been right about there being a locked box. Raina removed the slightly heavy box no bigger than a shoebox and set it on the floor. Thankfully, it was a key lock. She removed a paper clip and worked on the lock. It took some time, but it finally sprang open. She hesitated a moment before opening the box.

To her surprise, she saw a large amount of cash, several legal papers, a 9mm semiautomatic, and three envelopes. She opened the thicker envelope to reveal several military medals and stared bewildered at them. She opened another thick envelope to reveal several passports. Raina looked at each passport with horror. Dane's photo was on each one with different names and addresses all issued before being hired by her father.

"What the hell--?"

Who was he? James Bond? Raina studied them briefly then placed them back inside the envelope. She opened the last envelope, which was the thinnest. There were several newspaper articles referencing jewelry heists in different countries. One of the articles had a photo from a fancy gala of some sort, although she couldn't read it since it was in Italian. She stared at the picture a moment then became alarmed. To her surprise, she saw Dane standing in the background looking like an aristocrat holding a champagne glass. There was no mistaking he was a guest at that particular party and not a servant. She glanced over the dates of the articles then looked back at the passports.

"Oh, hell no."

She heard faint voices in the servant's corridor. Raina stuffed everything back into the box and hurriedly replaced it to the shelf in the closet. When she heard someone in the hallway closer to Dane's room, she looked around for somewhere to hide. Raina darted into the bathroom and hid behind the door, although that would do her little good if Dane found her there. Another door within the hallway opened and then closed a moment later. It seemed as if she were in the clear. Raina slowly emerged from the bathroom and approached the bedroom door. She listened a moment then heard the servant's wing door open and close. She sighed with relief before slipping out of the room.

Raina hurried down the staff wing corridor toward the kitchen and paused before the door. She listened by the door but didn't hear anyone. Raina gently opened the door and peered into the kitchen. Luckily, it was empty. She hurried through the doorway then heard voices by the dining room door. Her heart was now pounding. Raina bolted for the refrigerator and opened it. Levi entered the kitchen as she removed a bottle of water.

"Raina, you're just in time," Levi announced cheerfully. "Dane was about to announce dinner to the others in the lounge."

"Lucky for me; my timing is amazing," she announced while grinning.

Chapter *37*

No One's Above Suspicion

Raina sat on her bed later that evening and typed into the search bar on her laptop. She consulted a paper that she had scribbled the names she remembered from the passports and typed them into an internet search. None of the names produced any results, which was mildly infuriating. She groaned with defeat then contemplated her next course of action. She typed 'jewelry thefts, Italy' and glanced through the results. She picked one from six years ago, before Dane's employment with her father. The same article from the newspaper in the locked box envelope appeared on the screen. She studied the picture and clicked to translate the article from Italian to English. She studied the screen with great interest while reading the article aloud.

"Over a million dollars in jewelry was stolen from the duke's penthouse suite during a formal party at the famous downtown hotel," she read softly aloud. Raina stared at the picture with Dane in the background and shook her head with disbelief. "I can't believe it."

She couldn't get past the disappearance of Brenda's emerald necklace with the coincidence that Dane was a potential jewel thief in his former life. The necklace theft made little sense either way. If the murder was the result of theft, why did the thief leave behind Callie's diamond tennis bracelet and one-karat diamond engagement ring? Taking the obvious theft out of the equation, the murder pointed back at Miller. He was the only one who'd be interested in his mother's necklace and not the other, more expensive jewelry. But, by his own admission, the necklace belonged to him, so he had no reason to steal it. Raina groaned and held her aching head.

§

Otto sat at his desk in the study and stared at his computer, but he was obviously somewhere else. The study was old school with antique furniture, dark wood, and a refined, gentlemanly appeal. Her father's desk was the showpiece of the room, befitting of a man of great wealth. The small desk lamp and the glow of the computer dimly lighted the room. There was a knock on the open door bringing him out of his mild trance. Otto looked up as Raina entered and approached his desk.

"Are you okay?" she asked with concern for his emotional state.

"Yeah, I'm fine," her father replied and attempted a smile, although it was obviously fake. "It's been a rough couple of days."

"I know," she replied gently. "It's late. Why don't you go to bed?"

"Oh, Raina, if only I could," he announced with a depressed sigh and leaned back in his chair while rubbing his eyes. "There aren't enough sleeping pills in the world to put me to sleep tonight."

"I'm sorry to hear," she replied and sat on the edge of the expensive desk facing him. "I know you won't approve, but do you suppose I could look at the employee files?"

"I suppose I don't really care," he teased back and forced a humored smile, "but I would like to know why you're interested."

"Let's just say I don't have faith in Detective Payne," she informed him. "I've been poking around in Callie's past a little, and I'm looking for that shred of evidence that might point to someone other than you for Detective Payne to sink his claws into."

"You're right, I don't approve, but there's no harm in you looking at the employee files," her father remarked. "Dane takes care of that. He keeps all that stuff in the computer somewhere. You can ask him for them."

"Oh," she replied with disappointment. "I, uh, didn't know you relied that heavily on him."

"He's far more organized than I'll ever be," Otto reluctantly admitted.

"It's late," she announced. "I'll bother him in the morning."

"I'm sure he's still puttering around the kitchen," he assured her. "I doubt he'd mind."

"It can wait," she announced then managed a smile. "Goodnight, Dad."

"Goodnight, Raina."

§

Miller stood on the back terrace and leaned on the half wall while staring out to the dimly lit garden and possibly beyond it to the crypt. Jenna stepped out of the mansion through the dining room doors and approached him. She sat on the half wall near him and attempted to gauge his emotions.

"You seemed quiet at dinner," she remarked while studying him. "I thought you'd be in a better mood with Callie out of the picture."

"I was initially, but now I'm starting to feel guilty about it," he informed her and frowned. "I liked it better when it was suicide." He shifted uncomfortably and cast a look at her. "Raina's right, Callie didn't deserve to be murdered. Her indiscretions at the reception would have been sufficient cause to remove her from our lives forever."

"I know it's none of my business," Jenna gently announced then grimaced at the question she felt she had to ask. "But did you and Callie have a fling at one time?"

Miller straightened and stared at her with surprise. "What? Me and Callie?" he gasped as his eyes widened with something resembling horror. "You must be kidding."

"It's a valid question," Jenna insisted in her own defense. "She seemed to enslave most of the men in the house with her feminine wiles. Why not you?" She shifted uncomfortably. "I mean, you were young and single when they hired her. Things happen, don't they?"

"Yes, things happen, but not with her," he announced proudly then eyed her. "No, I never slept with Callie." Miller fidgeted and frowned almost reluctant to continue. "I was too busy chasing Sloan around the house."

"Really?" Jenna asked with surprise then attempted a smile although hiding her jealousy, which seemed to be obvious to everyone but Miller. "Did you ever catch her?"

"A couple of times," he admitted with a chuckle then shifted uncomfortably. "She'd only been working here maybe a year. It was really just a casual thing." Miller hesitated then managed a smile. "Well, for her."

"You had feelings for her?" Jenna pressed and easily hid her jealousy.

"Yeah," he announced while smiling. "I thought I was in love. Completely freaked her out. We got into a blowout, and that ended that. Six months later, I met Alicia. Ironically, Sloan wanted to pick up where we'd left off, but I was already in love with Alicia. Sloan didn't handle it very well, but she got over it when Titus came along. She fell hard for him. Even though she won't admit it; I think she still loves him." He sank into another world. "When Callie stole him from her, I felt terrible for her. I knew how she felt about him. She took it very badly. Callie and Sloan were at each other's throats after that."

"And Sloan never came back your way?" Jenna considered her words wisely. "After Alicia?"

"There hasn't been anyone since Alicia," he confided then drifted out and stared across the estate toward the crypt. "I sometimes wonder if there ever will be."

Jenna fidgeted slightly but managed a smile. "Then it's a sad day for women."

Miller seemed surprised by the comment and eyed her. She met his gaze then slid off the half wall, kissed him on the cheek, and smiled warmly.

"Goodnight."

He watched her with a dumbfounded look as she headed inside.

Chapter *38*

Butler with No Name

Despite it being five o'clock the following morning, Raina was already up. She had shaken herself out of bed half an hour earlier, wanting to make certain she was the first one up within the house. She needed privacy in order to access her father's computer without the early rising staff, namely Dane, knowing what she was up to. She sat behind the computer in the study and searched through files with growing frustration. It seemed as if the employee files she required were password protected. Raina groaned and leaned back in the chair.

"You're up early," Dane announced.

Raina opened her eyes with surprise to his voice and looked at the butler standing in the study doorway. She attempted to relax and appear calm.

"Yeah, I couldn't sleep," she easily lied. "My father needs a new computer. This one is slow."

"It's not that old," Dane replied and crossed the room to the desk. "What are you trying to do?"

She tapped a key, backing off the password protected employee file screen as he rounded the desk and looked at the monitor. He stood uncomfortably close to her and pressed a button. He was so close to her; she could smell the familiar scent of his soap and the insanely appealing aftershave he wore.

The password page reappeared causing her to fidget slightly, knowing she'd been caught.

"There's your problem," Dane announced and straightened. "You need a password to access employee records. I suppose your father forgot to mention that when he told you to see me to access those files."

"I didn't see a point to disturbing you, and I was bored," she again lied.

Dane leaned across her, typed in the required password, pulled up the employee files for her and then raised an arrogant brow while uncomfortably close to her.

"I'm disappointed that you feel the need to lie to me," he announced with little emotion while staring into her eyes only inches from his. "I assume that means you're suddenly suspicious of me."

For a moment, she stared helplessly into his blue eyes. He then straightened and gave her a disapproving look. "You do remember that you were with me at the time of Callie's murder."

"I never said I didn't trust you," she insisted, although that was a lie as well. "I just didn't want you getting the wrong idea."

"Oh, well, I'm glad to hear," he replied, but it was clear he didn't believe her. "I'll leave you to your investigation. I hope you find what you're looking for."

Dane left the study shutting the door behind him to allow her some privacy. Raina frowned and felt guilty for being suspicious of him. The contents of the locked box once again entered her thoughts. How could she trust him after what she'd seen? Who was Dane? She straightened with renewed determination to find out and clicked on Dane's employee file. To her surprise and horror, his file was empty. Her father obviously told Dane she wanted access to the employee files. Had Dane purposely deleted his file? Or was it always empty? Raina stared at the empty file folder on the screen and remained deep in thought.

§

Before breakfast, Otto sat on the back terrace with a cup of coffee in his hand. He stared out at the garden and remained deep in thought as he had the night before in the study. Raina walked onto the terrace and stared at the silent man. She felt sorry for her father. His world had been shattered almost beyond repair, and her concerns about Dane wouldn't help him any. With Callie's murder looming over their heads, she wasn't sure she could keep her suspicions from her father. Sure, she had spent a drunken night with Dane, but she didn't remember any of it. Was it possible Dane planned the whole thing? With a little creative thinking, it was even possible Dane drugged her, planted her in his room, and slipped away to murder Callie. Waking up naked alongside Dane in his bed and his assurance that they had a drunken fling would be enough to secure his alibi. She couldn't deny or confirm anything from that night.

Raina pushed her thoughts aside and approached her father. First things first. She needed to find out about Dane's mysterious employment. She needed to know who the man posing as their butler really was. Raina approached her father interrupting his self-loathing.

"Morning, Dad," she announced and attempted to sound cheerful for his sake.

Otto looked back and smiled when he saw her. "Good morning, darling," he announced in an equally cheerful tone. "Would you like Dane to bring you some tea?"

"No, I'm good, thanks," she replied while joining him at the small, round table. "I was looking through the employee files this morning."

"Was Dane helpful?"

"Uh, yes," she replied then fidgeted. "Actually, I was curious about that. Were you aware that he doesn't have an application on file? It seemed--odd."

Her father shifted and appeared uncomfortable, which surprised her. "Oh," he announced gently and cleared his throat. "Well, he came highly recommended. I didn't feel the need to bother with all that paperwork."

His words were almost startling. He sounded nothing like her businessman father. That wasn't the way he conducted his profitable businesses. What was this strange hold Dane had over her father? It was time to get it into the open.

"Since the day Dane walked through that door you've been defending him," Raina boldly announced now unable to control her concern. "It's as if he can't do any wrong, and now I'd like to know why."

"I don't feel it's my place to discuss this with you, Raina," Otto delicately replied.

She stared at him with surprise. Once again, he was defending Dane, and it made no sense. "What?" she gasped then stared at him demandingly. "What the hell are you keeping from me? What do you know about him that you're not willing to tell?"

Her father stared at her a long moment as if debating how to respond. Otto groaned and shook his head. "I hate being put between you and Dane, but you're not going to let this go, are you?"

"No," she announced defensively. "A woman's been murdered, and I need to know who I can trust."

He studied her a moment then shifted uncomfortably. "Is there more between you two than just a drunken one-night-stand?" Otto asked with an almost painful bluntness.

Raina felt her heart pound in her chest as she stared at the look in her father's eyes. "You don't believe we were just watching a movie that night?" she asked and kept from twitching.

Otto raised his brows almost demandingly. "Give me some credit, Raina," he remarked and snorted a laugh. "I've been around. I know sexual tension when I see it. Maybe you can hide your emotions from me, but Dane is afraid to even look at you in my presence."

"You've never been that good at reading people before," Raina remarked with a skeptical look. "When did you get that good at it?"

"Probably around the time Dane mentioned you two watched a Mel Brooks movie in his room on Saturday night," Otto casually replied.

Raina felt her heart drop as she stared at her father. She couldn't hide it. She knew he saw the stunned look on her face. Dane only read old, dead authors, but he told her father they were watching hardcore comedy. It made no sense. Her father's expression softened.

"It's okay, Raina," he announced. "I don't judge you and Miller when it comes to your personal lives. I'm the last one to judge anyone."

"To answer your question," Raina boldly announced. "It was just a drunken mistake, no one is to blame, and we've agreed to get past it."

"Since you were honest with me, I should be honest with you and tell you what you want to know about Dane," Otto announced then drew a deep, tense breath. "Do you remember our old butler, Dawson?"

Raina shook her head and remained stumped. "Who the hell is this Dawson?" she demanded. "Why is it everyone knows this guy but me?"

"Well, you were only six when he died," he announced in her defense.

"Dad, I remember a lot of things from back then," she informed him. "I just can't remember a butler named Dawson."

"You used to call him DawDaw," Otto offered.

She stared at him with a stunned realization. "DawDaw?" Raina gasped. "He was my grandfather."

"No, Raina," her father corrected. "DawDaw was not your grandfather. He was our butler."

"But he'd have tea parties with me," she insisted. "He'd take me to the park. We'd go for ice cream."

"Yes, he did all that, but he wasn't your grandfather," Otto informed her.

Raina stared at him in disbelief and shook her head. "Wow," she muttered. "I guess NaNa wasn't really my grandmother either."

"No, she was your nanny," Otto informed her.

She eyed him suspiciously. "Are you really my father?" Raina demanded. "Because my life suddenly doesn't make any sense."

Otto laughed while grinning. "Yes, I'm your real father." He then sank into thought. "Although, you never know. Your mother did have a thing for Elvis."

She groaned. "Don't even joke."

Her father took a deep breath then turned serious. "Back to Dawson," he continued and fidgeted. "He was Dane's grandfather."

Raina stared at her father with disbelief. "Miller said Dawson's grandson lived here for a few months before the accident."

"Yes, that boy was Dane."

Horror crossed Raina's face. "Levi said Dawson was driving the Ferrari," she announced. "Dawson died in the crash with my mother."

"Yes. Dane only lived here six months before his grandfather was killed," her father informed her. "At fifteen years old, he'd lost everyone he'd ever cared about. I had every intention of taking him in, but I guess he felt abandoned and ran away." Otto drew a deep breath while staring at her. "I didn't see him again until six years ago when I ran into him at the country club looking for work. Despite the name change, I knew who he was. We talked for over an hour, and I hired him on the spot."

Raina shook her head in disbelief. "My God, his grandfather was Dawson," she gasped. "That's so sad." She gave her father a curious look. "So what was he doing all those years?"

"As harsh as you may think this sounds, it was a condition of his employment that I didn't discuss his past with anyone," her father informed her. "I'm sorry, Raina. My judgment will have to be good enough for you."

"So you trust him unquestionably?"

"More than that," he announced and raised his brows. "I trust him with *your* life. And considering he nearly died saving you, I'd think you would too."

Her thoughts strayed to the night Dane saved her life while nearly sacrificing his. She remembered it vividly. Too vividly. He deserved her trust, but she couldn't get the newspaper articles from her mind.

"Perhaps neither of us has enough facts to make that assumption," she gently informed him and shifted uncomfortably. "I should see if Jenna is up yet."

Raina headed back into the house and entered through the kitchen. Dane stood near the back stairs while watching her with a hard to read expression.

"Did you find out what you wanted to know?" he asked with a curious look.

"Why does it seem as if you're always somewhere nearby to overhear private conversations?" she asked and felt her distrusting pang return.

"Only when I suspect they're about me," he readily offered then turned and headed into the servant's wing.

Chapter *39*

The Payne Is Back

Raina sat on the window seat within her bedroom that evening with her closed book on her lap. She stared out the window into the darkness while off in another world watching it rain. Her thoughts strayed to her mother, and the night she died. Every time it rained, she thought about her mother. There was a soft tap on her partially open door. She didn't bother looking at the door since she knew who it was. Miller entered wearing fashionable, club-ready clothes and a bold grin on his face. He saw Raina dressed in her frumpy shorts and worn sweatshirt and immediately frowned.

"You're not dressed," he protested.

"I don't feel like going out," she replied with little enthusiasm and leaned her head against the wall. "I just want to sit here and be depressed."

"Save that crap for the memorial service tomorrow night," Miller announced then considered the comment and shook his head with disgust. "I can't believe Dad is hosting a memorial in Callie's memory."

"Maybe he's forgiven her, considering she was murdered," Raina remarked.

"You're like a broken record," Miller scoffed then pouted. "What am I supposed to do tonight? I need to get out of here before I go crazy."

"I'm sure Jenna still wants to go. She loves to dance--even with you," she teased. "Take her; have fun."

"Maybe I will," he sneered.

"I said you should."

Miller groaned with annoyance. "Fine, I'll take Jenna, but if she throws herself at me, it'll be your fault when I sleep with her."

Raina managed a smile and laughed. "I'll want to hear all about it in the morning," she teased.

"You're intolerable this time of month," Miller remarked and shook his head.

"It's not PMS, Miller."

"No, worse," Miller replied while glaring at her. "It's every time it rains."

"Rain depresses me," she replied almost timidly while drifting off into her own world.

Miller tensed and realized what was bothering her. "Oh, the night your mother--" he began then silenced. "I wasn't thinking. I'm sorry."

Raina frowned and looked back out the window. "Drive carefully, okay?"

"Don't worry; I will," he replied with a little more sympathy. "They aren't calling for enough rain to flood the bridge across the driveway, so we shouldn't have any trouble getting home tonight."

She eyed him suspiciously. "Does that still happen?" Raina demanded then shook her head displaying her irritation. "With all Dad's money, you'd think he'd have found a way to prevent that from happening."

"The stream overflows once every five years," Miller responded. "So we're inconvenienced for a few days every few years. I don't see the point to him spending all that money for a three-day problem every five years."

Raina frowned and looked back out the window. "I hate rain," she again muttered.

Miller nodded and sighed. "Yes, I know," he replied. "I'll see you in the morning."

Raina didn't bother looking away from the window as her brother left the room.

§

After breakfast the following morning, the doorbell rang.

Dane headed up the foyer steps, approached the front door, and opened it to reveal Detective Payne, who was joined by several police officers.

"Good morning, Detective Payne," Dane politely announced then eyed the half dozen officers joining him. "Are you here for someone in particular?"

Detective Payne handed him an official-looking folded paper. "This is a warrant to search the estate."

"On what grounds?" Dane asked with some surprise but didn't bother looking at the document.

"An anonymous tip that we might find something Callie's killer doesn't want us to find," the detective replied without revealing too many details about his visit.

"Vague and mysterious," Dane replied with a hint of humor. "It's nice to know you're on top of things, Detective Payne."

Detective Payne gave Dane a strange look then sneered with annoyance. "Would you mind gathering everyone in the lounge while my men search the premises?"

"Actually, I would mind," Dane announced while smirking and cocked his head to the side, "but since your judge outranks me, I suppose I must."

Dane headed for the grand staircase with one of the officers following him. He glared at the officer on his heels then shook his head at the lack of trust.

§

Dane appeared on the back kitchen stairs moments later with his police escort. He entered the kitchen to find Raina sitting at the island counter with a cup of tea before her. She eyed the officer following Dane.

"I don't mean to alarm you, Dane," she announced with a skeptical yet serious look on her face, "but it's possible you're being tailed."

"This is Officer Binky," Dane informed her.

"That's Bickley," the officer corrected in an annoyed tone.

"He also has no sense of humor," Dane informed her. "I'm one wisecrack away from being arrested for obstruction of justice."

"Hmm," Raina remarked while grinning, "then I should probably get out while I can."

"We're asking that everyone in the house assemble in the lounge while we search the mansion," Officer Bickley informed her.

"Oh?" she asked with surprise. "What are you looking for?"

"Something vague and mysterious," Dane informed her while grinning.

"That's your last warning, butler," the officer snarled and glared at him.

Dane was about to speak when Raina sprang to her feet and placed her hand over his mouth. She smiled sweetly at the officer.

"You'll have to forgive him," she announced with some humor. "He hasn't had his morning coffee yet. He can be mildly cranky."

She removed her hand from his mouth. Dane glared at her without humor. She took his hand in hers, lacing her fingers between his, and pulled him toward the main kitchen door. Dane suspiciously eyed the way she held his hand but didn't comment.

"I'll keep him detained in the game room," Raina informed the officer then grinned playfully. "Maybe a few mimosas will improve his attitude."

"Yeah, you do that," Officer Bickley muttered under his breath.

Dane and Bickley exchanged glares as Raina led the butler from the kitchen. She didn't know what had happened between the two, but they were acting like a couple of junkyard dogs ready to get into a fight.

Chapter 40

Raging Hormones

Everyone within the house gathered in the game room so Detective Payne could keep an eye on them. He obviously wanted to make sure someone having something to hide didn't get a chance to sneak off and remove incriminating evidence. Miller seemed to be in a good mood despite the early hour as he mixed mimosas for everyone including the staff. He leaned closer to his stepfather, who was seated at the bar alongside Levi, and cast a glare at Payne standing guard at the doorway entrance.

"What's he looking for anyway?" Miller finally asked.

"Who knows," Otto remarked with little interest and sipped his mimosa.

"Anonymous tips are never good," Levi informed them with concern. "I've seen enough detective shows to know the tipster is usually the killer, and he's planted something incriminating on whoever he's trying to frame. Mark my word; the police are going to find something that one of us has in our possession that we've never seen before." His eyes suddenly widened with horror. "God, my room is so cluttered, anyone could have planted anything in there without my knowledge."

Dane stood nearby and eyed Levi without emotion. "If I were you, I'd be more worried about the piles of dirty clothing," he muttered.

Levi considered the comment and grimaced.

"You're certainly in a foul mood today," Otto announced while eyeing Dane. "Someone track mud through your kitchen?"

Dane sneered at his employer. "Women trouble," he scoffed.

Levi noted the tension between the boss and the butler. He grimaced, sank down in his chair, and pretended he wasn't there.

Otto returned the glare, and his eyes narrowed as he easily caught the hidden meaning. "We will not go back to the way things used to be," he scoffed with annoyance. "I don't care what the two of you have to do to achieve it, but I want peace and harmony in this house."

Officer Bickley entered the game room and approached Detective Payne. They talked a moment quietly, catching everyone's attention. Detective Payne looked at Dane.

"Dane, we found a locked box in your quarters," the detective announced. "Do you have the key?"

"Yes, Detective," Dane replied and straightened. "I'll unlock it for you."

As Dane approached them, Raina sprang to her feet and followed him to the doorway. Detective Payne eyed her. She returned the look with little concern to whatever he was thinking.

"I'm coming along," she announced boldly. "Someone has to keep him from making offensive wisecracks."

§

The fireproof locked box sat on Dane's bed with another officer standing over it. Dane removed a key from the bottom of a small, wooden jewelry box and handed it to Detective

Payne.   As the detective unlocked the box, Raina glanced at Dane's profile and watched for a response.   Considering she knew what the box contained, she was surprised that he watched with little to no expression.   It was amazing how calm he seemed.   She then saw him twitch as the box was opened. Officer Bickley stared into the box, appeared stunned, and removed a stack of old, girly magazines.   Detective Payne stared at the decade-old magazines with astonishment.

"You're kidding," the detective cried out.

All eyes were now on Dane with shared surprise.

Dane shrugged and showed little reaction.   "We all have our vices, Detective."

Miller appeared in the doorway, saw the officer with the old girly magazines in his hand, and chuckled in his throat. "You've caught him, Detective Payne," Miller announced while turning almost giddy.   "Arrest that pervert!"

Detective Payne glared at Miller, who continued to chuckle as if witness to some inside joke.

"If you think that's shocking, wait until you look in Sloan's underwear drawer," Miller announced while barely containing his humor.   "She has a shocking collection of things that vibrate.   In many colors and sizes too."

Miller left the room while laughing at the detective's expense.   Both officers and Detective Payne left Dane's room with embarrassment and disgust.   Dane approached the bed, picked up the magazines, and leafed through them.   He dropped them in the box, shut it, and looked back at Raina, who casually leaned against the nightstand near him.

She raised her brows almost demandingly and hid her grin. "What sort of man locks his porn in a fireproof box?"

"A very private one," he scoffed.

Raina chuckled and left the room.   Dane stared after her then reluctantly followed.

§

Raina sat reclined on the window seat within the library and stared out the large window with her head resting against the wall. She watched the parade of police vehicles leave the estate after their wasted afternoon. Dane entered the library and shut the door behind him, which he rarely did. Raina didn't bother looking at him and hid her smile.

"I guess Detective Payne didn't find anything worthwhile, huh?" she remarked.

Dane crossed the library, stood over her with a demanding look, and didn't respond. She glanced up at him, studied his stern expression, and grinned.

"You're welcome," she announced.

"You're lucky you weren't caught," he scolded with some hostility.

She made a face and waved him off. "I saw them coming a mile away," Raina announced then hid her smile. "I was already coming down the back stairs before they were heading up the front steps." She eyed him. "Incidentally, a kindergartener could pick that lock."

"And what if they had found what you removed?" he asked with a disapproving stare. "Then what?"

"Then I'm guessing you'd be locked up and questioned extensively," she replied. A humored smile crossed her face. "Trust me, they were never going to find your secret stash where I hid it," she informed him.

"Don't be so sure," he announced. "They search washing machines and vacuum cleaner bags. Anyplace you can hide something; they'll think to look."

"I'm far more clever than that," she insisted while smiling deviously.

"Where are my things?" he almost demanded.

She stood despite that he didn't move, forcing her to stand only inches from him. Raina stared into his blue eyes while maintaining her grin.

"Wouldn't you like to know?" she teased.

As she attempted to move past him, he stepped into her path and stared her down.

"I'm serious, Raina," he growled. "This isn't funny, and it isn't a game."

"And if I refuse?" she questioned while raising a curious brow as she stared into his eyes only inches from hers. "What then?"

He stared back at her then tensed and drew a deep breath. "I'll ask nicely," he gently replied with noted defeat.

She smiled and led him from the library.

Chapter 41

Gut Instincts

Raina led Dane into the kitchen, causing him to glance around suspiciously. She paused by the island counter, grinned slyly, and felt beneath it. A panel popped open within the wooden base under the cabinet revealing a small compartment. Raina removed a pillowcase from the compartment and dumped the contents on the counter. The gun, multiple passports, a stack of money, and envelopes fell to the counter. Dane frowned with some irritation and possible embarrassment and hastily returned the items to the pillowcase.

"Miller used to hide his cigarettes and girly magazines from our father in there," she informed him. "Those were his magazines they found in your locked box. I'm assuming he recognized them, which would explain why he found it so funny."

Dane shook his head while glaring at her. "Why did you risk removing incriminating evidence?" he demanded and frowned. "You could have gotten into a lot of trouble if you had been caught."

She stared at him a moment then sighed. "Yesterday you asked me if I found out everything I wanted to know," she reminded him. "Well, I did. I realized I trust you with my life, and that's going to have to be good enough for now."

Raina shrugged. "I can't confirm without a shadow of a doubt that you never left the bedroom the night Callie was killed, but I believe you when you say you didn't."

He stared at her a long moment with a strange look. "Considering what you found in that box, I'm surprised you could possibly have that much faith in me."

"You mean all those medals and accommodations of a highly decorated war hero?" she remarked.

"Are you so sure they're mine?" he asked with a curious glance. "After all, I have five different passports. What makes you think I didn't steal them?"

"Eventually I'll ask for an explanation," she informed him. "But for now, I think someone is trying to frame you for Callie's murder."

"What makes you think that?" he asked with surprise. "I've admitted those passports are mine. I'm pretty damned suspicious."

Raina removed the emerald and diamond necklace from her cleavage and held it up. Dane stared at the necklace with surprise and near horror.

"Where did you find--?" His eyes suddenly widened. "Was that in my box?"

"Yes, oddly enough, considering it wasn't there yesterday," she informed him. "Someone planted this with your secret stash to incriminate you."

"That would have been enough evidence to fry me," he insisted.

She added it to the pillowcase containing his goodies. Dane appeared curious and again dumped the bag onto the counter. He sorted through the envelopes, removed the thinner of the three, and opened it revealing the newspaper articles.

"What the hell--?" he asked with surprise and stared at the articles.

Her expression dropped. "Those aren't yours?" she asked with surprise.

"No, I wouldn't keep something like this," he insisted. "It's an admission of guilt. Whoever put that necklace in my box must have put this in there too."

"No, that was there yesterday," she informed him.

He looked at her with surprise. "It was?"

"When's the last time you were in that box?" Raina asked while studying him.

"I haven't opened that box in over five years," he informed her. "I don't need to be reminded of my past." He shoved everything back in the pillowcase, placed it in the compartment, and then looked at her. "What made you look in there in the first place? How did you even find that box?"

"Titus told me Callie dumped you when she found something disturbing in a locked box in your room," Raina informed him.

"I don't remember Callie ever having been in my room," he informed her. "I can't imagine why she'd have gone through my things."

"Do you think Titus lied about that?"

"If he did, it was so he could frame me for Callie's murder, which means he either believes I killed her or he did and is looking for a scapegoat," Dane remarked.

"So he feeds me that information about something 'disturbing' in your locked box thinking I'd go to the police," she announced. "When that didn't happen, he calls in an anonymous tip." She shook her head. "If that's the case, he's going to be pissed that the police didn't find any evidence against you."

"I can't imagine Titus having a grudge toward me," Dane remarked with surprise. "I didn't take Callie from him. He didn't even take Callie from me. She dated Hanson between us."

"Maybe she did look in your locked box and told him she'd found something," Raina suggested. "Perhaps that information just made you a convenient scapegoat. He had good motive to kill her."

"Unfortunately, he's not the only one," Dane remarked. "To know her was to hate her, it seems."

"And all the suspects will be here tomorrow night for her memorial," Raina reminded him.

"That was the idea."

She stared at him with surprise. "My father organized the whole thing?" Raina asked.

"Unknowingly."

She stared at him a moment then gasped. "You?"

Dane shrugged. "Well, a man needs a hobby," he casually replied.

"You do realize if we get the suspects riled up, they're going to probe into our alibi as well," she reminded him. "It's going to come out that we spent the night together."

"You have such little faith in me," Dane announced. "I already have a contingency plan in place for that."

"Really?"

"I intend to tell them I was drunk and you seduced me," he announced with little emotion then walked away.

Raina stared after him with a look of shock then turned angry. "Now wait just one damned minute!"

He cast a look back at her as she followed him and grinned slyly. "I also intend to tell your father that you're carrying my baby," Dane teased. "I hear shotgun weddings in the fall are quite beautiful."

She gasped with horror. He laughed as she chased after him.

Chapter 42

A Bitch to Remember

The following evening, around five o'clock, over two dozen guests along with the mansion staff attended a memorial service in the game room for Callie. Although the staff despised Callie, it was a chance to attend a party rather than serve one, so they willingly attended. Levi tended bar and had been serving himself along with the guests. He made his famous martinis that had everyone raving and coming back for more. He could barely keep up with the demand of more than thirty people filling the game room. Tia, Olivia, Jimmy Love, and the Nixon's attended along with Otto's former best friend, Nole. There was a combined effort to keep Nole and Otto from getting within twenty feet of each other. Elana and Keefe naturally attended, especially since they knew it would annoy the Nixon's, who once again had to attend a party alongside their hired help.

Once the party was underway, everyone seemed to be indulging in excessive amounts of alcohol. None of the guests brought their own limousines since a handful would be spending the night and Titus would take a few of the guests home. Titus, Hanson, and Sloan hung out at the bar with Miller and Jenna. Levi poured a martini for Sloan and pushed it across the bar toward her. She declined with a wave of her hand.

"None, for me. Thanks," Sloan announced and received looks from the rest of the staff. She gave them a baffled look. "What? I can't pass on alcohol? Do you guys think I'm an alcoholic or something?"

Titus, Hanson, and Levi made faces and muttered teasingly under their breath almost in unison. She glared at the three men with disbelief and shook her head.

"I'm not the party girl I used to be," Sloan insisted. "I'm taking my nursing schooling seriously."

"I didn't know you were going to school to be a nurse," Jenna announced with interest.

"She's been going to nursing school forever," Titus offered while sipping his soda.

"It's not easy holding down a full-time job and going to school," Levi remarked while wiping the counter of spilled martinis. "I can't imagine all the loans you'll have to pay back."

Miller grinned and chuckled into his glass while sipping his martini. "I hope not," he remarked with humor. "Considering my mother's estate is still footing the bills."

There was a strange silence as everyone looked at Miller. Sloan's mouth fell open with surprise.

"What?" she gasped.

Miller looked around the bar and seemed surprised by the looks he was receiving. He then eyed Sloan. "You knew that, didn't you?"

"The nursing school said I was awarded a scholarship," she announced with astonishment. "No one ever said the late Mrs. Steele was paying for it."

Miller groaned then muttered, "I've got a big mouth."

"Your mother was paying my way through nursing school?" Sloan pressed.

He sighed and reluctantly nodded. "Yeah, she wanted to see you achieve your dream," Miller remarked then frowned. "She never had the chance to go to college. She liked doing things like that."

Levi shifted uncomfortably behind the bar. "Well, now I don't feel so bad. Mr. Steele paid for my two months of culinary school in Tuscany," Levi admitted. "He paid for the entire trip."

"He bought me that piece of land just on the edge of town," Hanson announced. "I hope to have my house completed by the time I retire."

Titus frowned then groaned, although he seemed uncomfortable. "He bought my Corvette for me," he reluctantly offered. "Here I thought he just liked me more than the rest of you."

"Can I get a job here?" Jenna chimed in.

"I'm guessing he must have done something for Dane over the years," Hanson remarked.

Everyone except Miller simultaneously looked across the room at Dane, who played pool with Raina, although they didn't seem in any hurry to finish their game.

"What do you give the guy who saved your daughter's life?" Levi remarked.

"The beach house in the Virgin Islands," Miller muttered.

All eyes were suddenly on him. He glanced at the others then chuckled.

"I'm just kidding," Miller teased then appeared somewhat serious. "Although, after the murders, my father did send Dane to the beach house for a few weeks while he recovered from his injuries. Six months later, Raina and I wanted to spend some time at the beach, and my father said he sold that house."

"What an amazing coincidence," Jenna remarked.

"I guess Mr. Steele shot down Dane's first choice reward," Sloan announced then grinned.

"What was his first choice?" Titus asked with great interest.

"Raina," Levi teased.

"Okay," Miller announced while glaring at the others. "We're not doing this. That's my sister, so we won't be discussing anyone's sexual fantasies involving her."

"Come on, Miller," Sloan announced while grinning. "Do you actually believe that bullshit alibi that Raina and Dane were watching a movie in his room the night Callie was murdered?"

He stared at her with a strange look. "Raina and I always watch movies together," Miller insisted. "As people love to point out, we're not blood relation, but we've watched movies in my bed, and nothing has ever happened. Why shouldn't I believe her?"

"Because Detective Payne was respecting their privacy," Levi announced.

Sloan smiled and giggled. "Raina told the detective they were drunk and spent the night together," she remarked and cleverly raised her brows. "With the way Dane attempted to deny it, you know shit happened."

Miller stared at them a moment with surprise then looked at Jenna alongside him. "Did she confide this to you?" he suddenly demanded.

Jenna held her hands in the air and turned defensive. "She didn't say anything to me about it," she announced. "I did, however, see her slipping into her room Sunday morning still wearing her dress from the party." Jenna considered the comment and nodded. "I recognized the walk of shame. Considering they couldn't even look at each other for a full twenty-four hours tells me something happened."

"Yeah," Titus remarked while laughing. "He's afraid if he looks at her someone might see how *happy* he is when she's around."

"Again," Miller scoffed. "That's my sister."

"She's *not* your sister," Hanson lectured then grinned. "And don't tell me you've never gotten hot and bothered by her either."

Miller groaned and rolled his eyes. "I'm going to be violently ill."

"Are we really having this discussion?" Sloan demanded and eyed those around her. "Can we show a little respect for Raina and Dane, the man who could make our lives miserable for his own amusement?"

"Well, we could discuss the 'boner dance' Titus does when he looks at you," Hanson teased.

Titus appeared embarrassed and caught the look he received from the others. He glared at Hanson. "Why the hell would you even say something like that?"

"Oh, please," Levi groaned then casually refilled everyone's martini glasses. "You've wanted to get back into Sloan's pants ever since you got out of them."

Sloan looked at Titus with some surprise. He made a face while avoiding looking at her and waved off Levi.

"He's delusional," Titus remarked then glared at the cook. "And I'm going to hit him later."

Despite not commenting, Sloan seemed to consider what she had just heard. Elana and Keefe finally joined the others at the large bar after successfully annoying the Nixon's.

"I can't believe Detective Payne searched the entire mansion and only found a stack of girly magazines," Elana announced with some surprise.

"What kind of place is this?" Keefe demanded. "Not even a single joint?"

"What did you think he'd find?" Jenna prodded.

"I don't know," Elana remarked with irritation. "Maybe something that would point to whoever in this house killed my sister."

"And what makes you think it was someone in this house?" Miller demanded. "Did you call in that bogus tip to the police hoping they'd find something?"

"Of course not," Elana cried out. "The police already know who killed her; they just can't make an arrest without proof."

"Oh, and who's that, Elana?" Miller launched hotly.

"I don't need to tell you, Miller," Elana snarled. "You know damned well who wanted her dead."

The Nixon's had been standing nearby listening to the conversation. Gilda seemed unusually irate while Farley attempted to hold her back to keep her from approaching those at the bar. Gilda broke free from his hold and approached Elana.

"You also know exactly what sort of woman your sister was, Elana," Gilda cried out.

"Please, Gilda," Farley begged in a docile tone. "Don't cause a scene."

"No, Farley, it's about time I spoke up," Gilda launched then spun to face Elana. "Your sister was a conniving, blackmailing whore. Just because I couldn't prove she was the one blackmailing my husband, that doesn't mean I don't know she was the one." Gilda's eyes narrowed with hatred and anger. "Yes, I'm also surprised the police didn't find anything. I'm sure she kept that blackmail video, and if they had found it, it would prove what she really was once and for all."

"You can't talk about my sister like that," Elana shot back while jumping from her seat at the bar.

"I most certainly can," Gilda snarled back. "Your services are no longer required at our home. Perhaps you can seek employment here and wiggle your way into Otto's bed the same way your sister had!"

Elana was about to respond when Farley pulled Gilda away from them. Elana attempted to bolt after them, but Keefe held her back and attempted to calm her as well. Half the room was now staring at them.

"Someone was blackmailing Farley with a sex video of him and Callie?" Miller gasped with surprise.

"That's not true," Elana shot out. "If it were, Callie would have told me about it. She would never have allowed something like that to circulate."

"Suppose there was this blackmail sex tape," Jenna suggested. "Is it possible the blackmailer was using it to extort money from her to keep it from Otto?"

"There was no tape," Elana again proclaimed. "Gilda just made that up as an excuse to fire Callie for her relationship with Farley."

"You think she may have been meeting the blackmailer by the crypt when she was murdered?" Keefe asked Jenna.

"Keefe, there was no tape," Elana insisted while becoming further agitated with the entire conversation. "Callie would have confided in me if there was. No one was blackmailing her."

"It sounds like a pretty damned good motive," Miller interjected. "She refuses to pay, they scuffle, and he hits her on the head. Not wanting it to look like murder, he stages her suicide."

Tia and Olivia approached the bar and seemed interested in Miller's comment.

"I overheard Callie talking to someone on her cell phone about some video," Olivia offered. "We were out for a girls' night a few months ago. I don't know who she was talking to, but she sounded upset."

"You don't know who she was talking to?" Jenna asked with a curious look.

"I have no idea," Olivia announced then looked at Tia in silent question.

Tia shook her head. "She didn't offer," Callie's friend remarked, "and we didn't ask." Tia looked at Elana. "You were with us. Did you overhear that conversation?"

"I don't remember her having a conversation about a sex tape," Elana insisted while becoming angry. "If something like that happened, she'd tell me about it. I think you're mistaken about what you think you overheard."

"No," Olivia insisted. "She definitely said something about a video and being concerned about it." She then looked at Tia and snapped her fingers. "She was talking to a man. Remember, she said something to the caller that he should find out who it was and beat him up."

"Yeah," Tia agreed. "It would be odd to tell another woman to beat up some guy. That's usually something you'd tell another man to do."

"She had to be talking to Otto," Elana insisted and shook her head. "Who else would Callie have been talking to? She was out with us so that just leaves Otto."

"I don't think it was Otto," Olivia insisted. "She hung up on him without saying goodbye. I don't think I've ever heard her talk to Otto that way on the phone."

Elana sank into thought then cast a look at Keefe. He shrugged and shook his head. She looked back at those around the bar with more insistence.

"I'm telling you," Elana again insisted. "There was no blackmail tape. Callie would have told me if someone had been blackmailing her with a sex tape."

They heard a commotion across the room. Jimmy Love stood between Otto and Nole, who were violently shouting at each other.

"This place is like a soap opera," Levi muttered.

"I admit I had an affair with Callie," Nole cried out to Otto while pushing against Jimmy Love. "You could never handle a woman like that!"

"Low blow," Jimmy Love scolded in a high-pitched screech.

"Everyone here knows you killed her in a fit of jealous rage," Nole shouted in anger.

"You were supposed to be my friend," Otto shot back. "You betrayed me, you bastard!"

"Boys, boys," Jimmy Love attempted to calm the men who were about to crush him while standing between them. "Not that I don't love a good testosterone-fueled, ass whooping, but this is a memorial, remember?"

Titus and Hanson ran across the room and pulled Otto and Nole away from each other. Both men fought against their captors then attempted to relax. Otto finally pulled away from Titus and headed for the bar.

Jimmy Love gave Titus a quick once-over. "Hmm, you must work out."

Titus rolled his eyes and walked away.

Jimmy Love pointed and called after him, "That was a compliment, honey!"

Chapter 43

Keep Your Enemies Closer

Only an hour later, the memorial service continued to unravel with raw emotions and accusations flying. Raina and Dane pretended to play pool while keeping an eye on the others. Raina wore a simple black dress that revealed a little too much cleavage and plenty of leg. Under the circumstances, it seemed like the perfect dress to wear to Callie's memorial. Dane and Raina spent more time leaning on their pool sticks than actually playing the game.

"You learn a lot when you step onto the sidelines," Raina remarked and eyed the show in progress.

"One of the joys of being a servant," Dane informed her. "People forget you're there. They tend to speak freely around the staff as if they're invisible."

Raina gave him a quick once-over then raised a demanding brow. "You never practiced your invisibility technique around me," she insisted. "I'm pretty sure it was quite the opposite. You were always annoyingly present."

Dane chuckled as he glanced at her before finally returning to the pool table to make his shot. "That's because I was being a prick and wanted to get on your nerves."

"You succeeded," she teased while admiring the sexy butler make the tricky shot. "I heard our drunken antics already got around the whole house."

Dane missed the shot then frowned while straightening. He appeared tense. "Which included your father," he remarked with a groan. "Ironically, he's acting as if nothing happened. I'm worried he may kill me in my sleep."

"He brought it up the other day. He's not getting involved in my personal life," she remarked then shook her head while suspiciously eyeing him. "You really can do no wrong in his eyes, can you?"

Dane seemed surprised by the admission. "Huh, he actually said that? I guess I can do no wrong," he remarked then added a humored grin as she leaned over to make her next shot.

Raina wasn't positive, but she swore he was checking out her backside as she leaned over the pool table.

"You'd think a drunken one-nighter with his daughter would be enough to push him over the edge," Dane casually remarked as if purposely attempting to get a rise out of her.

She straightened and eyed him without making her shot. "Aren't we being bold tonight?" Raina remarked while raising her brows. The fact that he felt comfortable enough to joke about it told her he'd come to terms with what had happened. "He knows you have a colorful past, but does he know you were a jewel thief?"

He eyed her sharply and moved around the table to face her. "Now who's being bold?" Dane remarked then shrugged with less interest. "He knows I was involved in illegal activity. I doubt he knows the specifics." He gave her a sly once-over. "You're the first person who's ever actually called me on it."

"Unfortunately the killer knows too," she informed him and again leaned over the pool table, finally making her shot. She straightened and glanced at him. He turned away a little too quickly, almost confirming he'd been eyeing her cleavage while bent over the table. His embarrassment was cute. "Must have taken quite a bit of research to find all those articles on you."

"Some weren't me," he insisted. "I've never even been to some of those countries."

Raina studied him a moment and felt she needed to pry. "Why did you do it?"

"After eight years in the military, I was discharged only to discover I had no skills," he confessed. "I was only qualified to be a security guard or professional hitman, so I went a different route. I had the skills to slip in and out of secure locations, so I put that to good use." He considered the comment and shrugged. "I enjoyed the thrill more than anything. After a few years, I grew tired of living out of a suitcase and longed for something more stable."

"You mean you ran out of money," she teased while grinning.

"No, I retired with over five million dollars in my pocket," he replied.

Her expression dropped as she stared at him with surprise. "You're kidding."

"When I gave up that lifestyle, I gave up the money I gained from it. Well, most of it," he informed her. "I gave it to a children's hospital. They even named their new wing after me."

"Bullshit."

He raised his brows in question and stared back at her. "Would I lie?"

"Hmm. Good question," she remarked then eyed him suspiciously while hiding her grin. "Is your name really Dane Kingston?"

"Daniel Dawson Kingston," he informed her. "My team gave me the nickname Dane."

"Why Dane?"

"Great Dane," he replied simply. "You know, like Marmaduke."

"Why did they call you Great Dane?" she asked and leaned on her pool stick while standing alongside him.

"I couldn't tell you," he replied. "I certainly wasn't the biggest dog in my platoon."

Raina studied him a moment with a strange smile on her face. He noted her look, appeared curious by it, and had to smile back.

"What's that smile about?" Dane asked.

"I just can't imagine you dirty and sweaty," she remarked with a laugh.

He stared into her eyes a moment and offered a tiny, playful grin. "Trust me, you don't know the half of it," he announced with a chuckle.

She stared back at him and attempted to understand his hidden meaning. As she stared into his eyes, she couldn't deny her incredible curiosity and intrigue in the handsome man. It was bad enough she was attracted to the quiet, serious man she'd come to know over the years, but his former life as a soldier and a jewel thief intensified those feelings. Throw in a little-added mystery, and she had a hard time resisting the urge to throw herself at him. He was no longer the butler; he'd spontaneously combusted into James Bond.

§

Half of the guests attending the memorial had left by eight o'clock that night, which left the guests who would be spending the night. There were also two couples Titus would be driving home a little later. If the weather forecast was correct, a tropical storm would reach them later that night. It promised to be a big one. Jenna and Miller hung out by the pool table and appeared to be having a good time together despite that neither was drunk. It was possible Jenna was hustling Miller at a game of pool. Miller missed another shot and straightened while cursing.

"I'm completely off my game tonight," he announced with disgust.

"I think you're just not as good as you boasted," Jenna teased and easily made her next shot and won the game. She turned toward Miller, grinned, and held out her hand.

He frowned and slapped a ten-dollar bill into her palm. She gleefully placed it down the cleavage of her shirt, catching Miller's attention before he quickly looked away.

"Want a rematch?" she asked while raising a sly brow.

"Not tonight," he remarked. "I think this entire memorial party is throwing me off." Miller looked around and frowned. "It just feels so fake. Only about four people here even liked her."

"Yeah, she certainly knew how to alienate herself with just about everyone, didn't she?" Jenna muttered while leaning her back against the pool table as she scanned the room. "I can't imagine going through life making it my mission to piss off everyone."

"Well, for you it comes naturally," Miller remarked and flashed a sly grin.

Jenna glared at him and raised her brow. "You're not funny, Miller."

"I disagree," he teased. "You and Raina would be bored to tears if I didn't go out with you to nightclubs."

"You got me there," she replied and straightened. "Raina doesn't really like dancing."

Miller eyed her with some surprise. "So why is it we're always going out to clubs?"

"Because I like to dance," Jenna insisted.

"No, you like to scope out the guys," Miller corrected while giving her a daring once-over. "I swear; you flirt with every man there."

Jenna drew a deep breath and spun to face him. "Yeah, because the idiot I want doesn't even know I exist," she announced boldly. "If he did, I wouldn't have to spend quite so much time trying to make him jealous."

Miller stared at her a moment as if putting her words and hostility together. "Wait," he announced with a strange look. "Are you talking about me?"

She groaned with defeat and looked away. "I'm just wasting my time chasing a man who'll always be in love with someone else."

He continued to stare at her as if he'd finally figured it out. "Jenna, I, uh--" He fumbled over himself. "Maybe we should talk about this."

Jenna met his gaze and shook her head. "I'd rather not," she replied then kissed him quickly on the lips.

When she pulled away, he stared at her with surprise and seemed unable to react for a moment.

"I, uh, need a drink," he announced and hastily walked away.

Jenna watched Miller cross the room, bypassing the bar, and leave the game room. She groaned and cursed herself under her breath.

"Great," she muttered. "Nice going, Jenna."

Just across the room, Tia approached the bar where a moderately drunken Levi served martinis to Olivia, Hanson, and

Jimmy Love. She sat at the bar and indicated Titus and Sloan across the room.

"Why didn't someone warn me that the cute chauffeur was dating the maid, Sloan?" Tia huffed while shooting glares at those sitting at the bar.

Hanson and Levi stared at her with some surprise then eyed Titus and Sloan, who stood near the game room doorway. They appeared to be arguing. Both looked back at the attractive woman.

"They're not dating," Hanson informed her. "What makes you think they're dating?"

"Elana said he was single," Tia remarked and shook her head. "I thought I'd start a conversation with him, but Sloan came over and got all weird. Next thing I know; they're fighting. Sounds like a couple to me."

Hanson and Levi exchanged bewildered looks then simultaneously shook their heads.

"There's no universe where Sloan would ever take Titus back," Levi announced a little louder than intended and caught the attention of those at the bar.

"Why's that?" Jimmy Love asked while leaning his chin on the back of his dainty hand.

Levi drunkenly shirked back and stared at the flashy man. "Because they used to date, and he broke her heart when he dumped her for Callie," he announced.

"The breakup of the century," Hanson muttered into his martini then took a sip. "By the time she could finally tolerate being in the same room with him, Callie dumped him. For some reason, that started a whole new round of anger and accusations."

"I've been there, honey," Jimmy Love announced while straightening and sipped his martini.

"The last few months, they've graduated back to being in the same room together without fighting," Hanson added then shook his head. "Callie really fucked things up for them. Sloan and Titus were great together."

The cook laughed in response then grinned at the gardener. "You're only saying that because Callie dumped you for Titus," Levi announced a little too loudly in his drunken tone.

"Maybe," Hanson muttered.

Tia and Olivia seemed uncomfortable by the conversation since the group was talking trash about their friend, whose memorial they were supposedly attending. Jimmy Love put his hand up as a blinder to the women and attempted to signal Hanson to cut the conversation in front of Callie's friends.

"As much as I hate to admit it," Olivia announced with a sigh. "Callie was a heartless bitch at times."

Tia nodded in agreement. "She slept with my boyfriend," her friend remarked.

"She slept with everyone's boyfriend," Olivia scoffed. "We've been friends such a long time; I just sort of overlooked her flaws."

"I've had my share of bridezillas," Jimmy Love announced then waved his hand dramatically, "but that girl was the worst! She made me raise my voice." He eyed those at the bar. "I've *never* yelled at a bride before. Not even the one who accused me of sleeping with her groom-to-be."

"Did you?" Levi asked with a sly, drunken smile as he leaned heavily on the bar.

Jimmy Love eyed Levi and raised his brows. "Honey, I never kiss and tell."

When they looked back, Sloan stormed from the game room. Titus appeared annoyed and defeated before running after her.

"Well," Hanson announced with a sigh. "They're either going to kiss and make-up or one of them won't be alive in the morning."

Chapter 44
The Lady Is a Tramp

Otto and Farley sipped their martinis and talked near the large screen television while Gilda stood nearby with her drink and appeared bored. It was around eight-thirty, and the party was still going strong despite that half the guests had gone home for the night.

"Come golfing with me next weekend," Farley insisted to Otto despite Gilda rolling her eyes at the mention of golf. "You should get out and do something to get your mind off everything that's happened."

"Well, you aren't wrong about that," Otto muttered then eyed Farley and grinned. "Yeah, sure. Golf sounds better than my original plan of sinking into my work and making everyone in the boardroom miserable."

Gilda finally walked away seeming unable to handle country club or golf stories. Otto waited until Gilda was out of earshot and nodded after Farley's wife.

"Is it me or is Gilda a little on the cranky side these days?" Otto remarked.

Farley waved off his wife now that she couldn't hear them. "Just the usual with her, I'm afraid," he announced then frowned. "She's so jealous over me; she actually accused Raina of flirting with me."

Otto stared at him with surprise. "You're kidding?" he remarked then shook his head. "That must have gone over well with Raina."

Farley suddenly grinned and held back his laugh. "Raina called her a bitch," he announced and attempted to contain his smile.

Otto chuckled and nodded. "Yeah, that sounds like Raina," he teased.

"If I hadn't been so embarrassed at the time, I would have enjoyed it more," Farley remarked and laughed. He then indicated Raina, who hung out with the butler at one of the pub tables. "What's with her and the butler? They seem awfully chummy lately."

Otto waved them off. "I stopped questioning their love-hate relationship," he announced without care. "At least they're not at each other's throats."

"Do you think she's dating the butler?" Farley asked with some surprise.

Otto shrugged almost disinterested. "I don't know, and I don't care," he casually replied.

"What if it's something more serious?" Farley asked. "Do you really want your daughter marrying the butler?"

Otto eyed Farley and raised his brow. "You and I are the last people to judge others for that sort of thing," he announced with a look that made Farley uncomfortable.

"You knew, huh?"

"My staff loves to gossip," Otto informed him. "And they don't mind including me. I accepted Callie despite knowing why you pawned her off on me."

Farley fidgeted. "Sorry about that," he announced timidly. "Gilda wanted me to fire Callie, but it wasn't that easy."

"I understand," Otto replied then managed a smile. "Despite how poorly things turned out, I don't have any hard feelings about it."

Nole approached them after overhearing their conversation. "So you'll forgive him but not me?" Nole demanded.

Otto immediately turned and glared at Nole. "That happened before I was with her," Otto launched then glared at his former friend. "You didn't just fuck Callie on my wedding day; you fucked me too!"

"She never loved you anyway," Nole scoffed. "I did you a favor."

Their arguing rapidly escalated, alerting the others at the party.

"You did me a favor?" Otto demanded then laughed. "How noble of you, Nole!"

"I wasn't the only one she was screwing behind your back," Nole launched.

Farley was quick to back away, wanting no part of the current topic or the two men in a heated face-off. Dane and Raina quickly interceded.

"What the hell is that supposed to mean?" Otto launched in anger.

"Just what it sounds like," Nole shouted back. "Callie slept with just about every man in this room, and I don't mean before you two were engaged!"

Everyone looked at Nole with surprise when they heard the comment. The men eyed each other in silent question to the accusation almost as if wondering which of them he was referencing. Raina guided her father away from the situation, but Nole wasn't as easily deterred and resisted Dane's attempt to lure him away. Nole punched Dane in the mouth, surprising everyone, then bolted for Otto and Raina, who had their backs to him. Before Nole could reach them, Dane grabbed Nole by the arm and stopped him. Nole spun around and threw his fist for Dane's face. Dane blocked the punch then grabbed his wrist and twisted his arm behind his back, driving Nole to his knees. Nole cried out and appeared paralyzed with pain. Dane held his wrist while barely exerting himself and showed little emotion.

There were several gasps from around the room. As Raina watched the scene that had unfolded, she saw flashes of the night her stepmother was killed. She relived the entire scene from the moment Dane showed up with his shotgun. Her heart pounded as she reflected upon his amazing fighting skills and how he violently took down the second killer. She returned to reality and stared at the unfolding scene before them. Dane eyed the man he held immobile on his knees.

"Do you intend to play nice, or do I dislocate your shoulder?" Dane announced almost calmly.

"I was just leaving," Nole snarled from his vulnerable position.

The butler released his wrist and took a step back. Nole clutched his shoulder in agony and slowly straightened while glaring at Dane.

Dane politely extended his hand toward the hallway. "This way, Mr. Oaks."

Everyone watched Dane follow Nole to the game room doorway. As Dane passed Jimmy Love at the bar, he smiled and slipped a napkin into Dane's jacket pocket then winked at him. Dane gave him a bewildered stare then continued from the room after Nole.

§

Half an hour later. It was a little before nine o'clock that evening, everyone remaining at the mansion had intended to spend the night, which was roughly seven additional guests. Titus had left to take the last of the guests home, so he'd be gone an hour or longer. Sloan and Keefe seemed to have vanished, but they could have been in the kitchen with Hanson, who had offered to get more shrimp cocktail for the party. Dane seemed to be missing ever since he escorted Nole from the game room leaving Raina at the bar with the others.

Otto had finally calmed down and accepted Farley's challenge to a game of pool. They had a friendly wager going, which made the game more interesting. Gilda hung around one of the pub tables and remained bored. She could have easily left the party and gone to bed, but it was obvious she wanted to keep an eye on her husband and make sure he behaved. Tia and Olivia, who were both pleasantly drunk, stumbled their way over to the pool table and watched the game that seemed to be heating up between the two friends.

"Who's winning?" Tia giggled while watching the men play their game.

Otto had just enough martinis in him to enjoy the gorgeous woman smiling at him. He returned the smile and straightened.

"Actually," he announced cheerfully. "I'm mopping the floor with this loser."

Both women giggled, which only encouraged Otto's harmless flirting with the drunken women. Had he been sober, he probably would have thought better of flirting with Callie's friends.

"Fact check," Farley boldly announced and glared at his friend. "The game is tied so far, and this loser may be mopping the floor with you, you old bastard."

The women giggled drunkenly at the horseplay between the older men. Otto seemed to be in a good mood for the first time since his wedding day went sideways. If it took a little harmless flirting from two lovely, young women to achieve that then so be it. As the two women whispered to each other while giggling, Otto stepped up his harmless flirting. He was about to approach the lovely ladies when Gilda suddenly stepped in and glared at the drunken women.

"What's wrong with you two?" Gilda snarled, alerting Farley to his wife's attack on the young women. "Can't find any men your own age? They're old enough to be your fathers!"

Otto stared at Farley's wife as she verbally attacked the poor women, who instantly frowned and scurried away. When Gilda turned, she nearly collided with Otto.

"What the hell is your problem?" Otto lashed out while glaring at Gilda.

"I saw them flirting with my husband," she snarled in anger.

"No," Otto snapped back. "They were flirting with *me*, and *I* was enjoying it! You may feel entitled to ruin your husband's life, but you have no right to interfere in mine." He pointed across the room. "You either find someone else to harass or go to your room. Either way, stay the hell away from me!"

Gilda huffed and looked at her husband for him to defend her against Otto. Farley looked away, avoiding getting involved, although he was having a tough time hiding his grin.

"Are you going to let him talk to me that way?" she demanded.

"Leave him alone too," Otto shouted in anger.

Gilda glared at her husband, who still didn't look at her or comment, huffed, and then crossed the room where she flopped into a chair away from everyone else. Farley cast a look at Otto and could barely contain his grin. Otto indicated the pool table with some annoyance.

"It's your shot," Otto snapped.

"Actually, it's your shot," Farley teased.

Otto waved him off and attempted to concentrate on his pool game while muttering under his breath.

Chapter 45
It's About to Get Real

Jenna left the kitchen and walked onto the well-lit patio. She approached the half wall and partially sat on it while staring at the dimly lit garden. She sighed with defeat then looked at the darkened crypt in the distance. Her frown said it all. She couldn't possibly compete with Miller's true love, the woman savagely torn from his arms. It was his passion for his dead fiancé that attracted Jenna most, but it was that same passion that would keep him from ever seeking another. Jenna wasn't surprised when she saw Miller on the path in the garden heading back toward the mansion from the crypt. Earlier, she'd frightened him off, and he retreated to the woman he loved as she'd seen him do numerous times during their visit.

As Miller got close to the house, he spotted Jenna on the patio and fidgeted while placing his hands in his pockets. He reached the patio and seemed unable to look at Jenna as he paused near her. She moved off the wall and debated going back into the house to avoid a discussion with Miller. He leaned his back against the half wall and finally met her gaze.

"I know I shouldn't have left you like that when things got a little too real back there," Miller gently informed her.

Jenna folded her arms across her chest and shivered from the damp night air. She managed a slight shrug and pretended it didn't bother her.

"I understand," she remarked and attempted a smile. "I should have known better. You aren't ready, and I should never have thrown that on you the way I did."

Miller stared at her with surprise. "No, it's not your fault," he insisted and saw her shiver. He removed his jacket and placed it over her shoulders, now standing closer to her. "I'll admit; I've been emotionally and even sexually disengaged from women since Alicia's death. Losing her like that was a lot to process, and it involved a lot of guilt."

He backed away from her, leaned against the half wall, and looked down. Miller drew a deep, shaken breath.

"I was at a nightclub having a good time with my friends while my mother and the woman I loved were being brutally murdered," he announced then looked up to meet her gaze with tears in his eyes. "If that sort of guilt wasn't bad enough, I have to live every day knowing that Raina, who nearly died with them, secretly blames herself when it should all be on me."

"It wasn't your fault you weren't there," Jenna insisted while staring at him. "You couldn't have predicted something like that. Every day we do things that could affect our lives. You can't blame yourself for something you couldn't foresee or control."

"I know," he replied timidly, wiped the tears from his eyes, and attempted a tiny smile. "I stood over Alicia's casket two years ago and vowed I'd never love another woman."

Jenna nodded with understanding.

Miller drew a deep breath and straightened. "Tonight, I stood before her and begged her to forgive me for not being able to keep that promise."

She stared at him with surprise and seemed uncertain if she actually understood what he was saying.

"I know she'd be happy for me," Miller announced then offered a tiny smile. "Especially knowing she was a friend of Raina's."

Jenna appeared relieved and smiled more naturally. "Someone who'd keep you in line."

"That too," he teased then took her hands in his and stared affectionately into her eyes. "I'd like to be officially your problem."

Jenna grinned and laughed. "I accept," she teased.

Miller pulled her into his arms and touched her face. He hesitated a moment while staring into her eyes and then kissed her warmly but passionately on the lips. Jenna immediately returned the kiss. As their kiss heated up, Miller broke it off and smiled almost timidly.

"I'm out of practice at anything remotely intimate," he nervously admitted then fidgeted. "Are you okay with taking things slow?"

She laughed and patted his chest. "I've been waiting for you more than a year," Jenna informed him. "I think I can wait a few more weeks."

"Weeks?" Miller gasped while staring at her with near horror. "I never said anything about weeks. I didn't mean *that* slow."

"Let's go back to the party, have a little fun, and just let things happen at their own pace," she announced.

"That sounds good," Miller agreed and walked toward the kitchen door with her. "I mean; a few days or a week at most. Not weeks."

§

Raina sat at the bar with Jimmy Love while he talked to the drunken Levi. The robust cook practically lay on the bar in an attempt to hold himself up while engaging the flashy man in conversation.

"I don't know how you do it," Levi announced with heavily slurred speech. "How do you get all those women to fall all over you? What am I doing wrong?"

"Darling, you have personality, you just need to project that personality," Jimmy Love announced with animated enthusiasm. "I'm an open book, that's why everyone wants to be next to me. You need to set your personality free, baby!"

"And then I'll get women?"

"Would I steer you wrong?" Jimmy Love proclaimed while gazing at the drunken cook. "Look here, I have another wedding this coming Saturday, and I could use someone like you--" He gave him a quick once-over. "Without the excessive alcohol. One evening with me, and you'll have women falling all over you."

Raina rested her chin on her fist and watched the exchange with bewilderment. She couldn't deny that Jimmy Love was single-handedly the most mysterious and interesting man she'd ever met.

"I have to ask," she finally announced to the flamboyant man. "What's your deal? Are you into men or women?" Raina fidgeted realizing she'd actually asked the question aloud.

Jimmy Love looked at her and squealed with delight. "Honey, I love *everyone*! Makes no difference to me. Fat, skinny, black, white, green, purple. I love them all! All people are beautiful!"

Raina straightened and smiled. "Okay then."

As Dane entered the game room, Jimmy Love gave him a firm once-over. "And I'm really liking that one," he announced. "So proper yet devilish. Hmm, hmm. Have mercy."

"Jimmy Love," Raina announced firmly and stared into his eyes while smirking. "If you want that one, you'll need to fight me, and I promise you, I'm not as nice as I look."

Jimmy Love cried out with enthusiasm. "You go, girl! Far be it for me to come between a woman and her man!" He then eyed her with a serious look. "Unless you're into threesomes. Because I can get into that."

She laughed and patted his flashy rhinestone jacket. "Not in this lifetime, Jimmy Love."

Raina left the bar and approached Dane.

"You've been gone over half an hour," she remarked. "Did you drive Nole home?"

"No, I just showed him to the door," Dane explained. "I heard a commotion in the kitchen, so I went to check on it. There was a situation between Hanson and Titus I had to referee."

"They were fighting?" she asked with surprise.

"No, arm wrestling," Dane explained. "I made twenty bucks with my bet on Hanson."

"Hanson beat Titus at arm wrestling?" she gasped.

"Hanson is stronger than most people realize," Dane informed her.

"Wasn't Titus supposed to be driving some of the guests home tonight?" Raina asked. "What was he still doing in the kitchen?"

"He was on his way to the garage to pull the limousine around front for the guests," Dane informed her. "Since the ladies were using the hallway powder room, he had time to slack off."

Raina glanced at her watch then looked around the room containing the remaining drunks. It didn't seem as if the frat party would be winding down anytime soon. Hanson finally returned to the game room and joined Levi and Jimmy Love at the bar as Levi was about to make a fresh pitcher of martinis.

Raina looked back at Dane. "I think I'm going to get a cup of tea and turn in early," she informed him. "This party is turning into land of the wasted."

"I was thinking about turning in soon myself," Dane informed her. "That tea sounds good. I'll walk you to the kitchen."

Chapter 46

Affir du Cœur

Raina and Dane entered the now empty kitchen a little after nine o'clock that night. Sounds from the party in the game room could be heard across the entire mansion and even in the kitchen. Dane put on the kettle for their tea while Raina removed two mugs from the cupboard. She placed Dane's favorite mug on the counter, which made him smile. The large, black mug contained a revolver with the words, 'Don't talk to me until I've had my coffee'. Raina leaned against the counter and watched Dane as he collected the tea bags, sugar, and creamer. As she watched him, she thought back to their drunken encounter. Although she didn't remember any details, she remembered waking up the next morning in his arms. She was reminded how his naked body felt pressed against her from behind.

She remembered catching a glimpse of him with the sheet barely covering his naked body and wished she could go back to that moment. Despite her somewhat dramatic reaction at the time, she couldn't stop thinking about what must have happened. That she couldn't even remember kissing him was enough to make her insane. Raina desperately wanted to remember her first time. She wanted to remember every touch. As she returned to reality, Raina realized Dane was staring at her with a bewildered look and a strange smile. She turned defensive and raised her brows in question.

"What?"

"You were staring at me--" he responded then smirked and approached the kettle. "With bedroom eyes."

"I was not," she immediately countered then blushed because she'd been called out and attempted to look anywhere but at him.

He shrugged it off while maintaining his grin as he poured hot water into each of their mugs. "It's okay," he announced. "I get that a lot."

She glared at him through squinting eyes conveying her 'be for real' look.

He caught her stare and laughed. "I'm very popular with women over sixty," Dane teased and focused on their tea. "I'm told I smell good."

Raina stared at him only a moment before fidgeting. "Who initiated?"

Dane looked at her, surprised by the question. "Excuse me?"

"In the library the night of my father's wedding," she announced with more confidence. "Who initiated?"

He turned to face her and cocked his head. "So now we're discussing it?"

She glared at him and waited for an answer.

Dane shifted uncomfortably. "I don't remember who initiated," he replied. "Some of the details are fuzzy."

"So you initiated," she replied matter-of-factly.

"How do you get that from 'I don't remember'?" Dane asked.

"Because you're protecting yourself," she replied while grinning. "You want the moral high ground."

"Do you honestly think I'd do that?" he scoffed then shook his head while turning away.

She studied him a moment longer, noting his slightly tense attitude, and his inability to look at her. The realization then hit her. "No, you wouldn't do that," Raina announced with conviction. "You'd lie to protect my feelings. I initiated."

He avoided looking at her. "Why would I care to protect your feelings?" Dane cast a look at her and smirked. "It's my mission to torment you, remember?"

She leaned against the counter and watched him. "What did I do to initiate?"

Dane groaned and avoided looking at her. "I thought you didn't want details."

"I changed my mind," she replied.

"Some of the details are fuzzy," he reluctantly announced while turning to face her. "I remember we were drinking and laughing at God knows what. I had enough sense to know I should get you to your room before you passed out, and you agreed to let me walk you to your room. We barely made it to the library door, and you went full-blown sex kitten on me." He drew a deep breath then shook his head. "Honestly, I have no idea how we got to my room, but I pretty much remember everything that happened from the moment the door closed."

Raina strained to remember any of it, but nothing came to her. She shook her head. "I don't understand what possessed me to jump on you like that," she remarked then tilted her head with a look of frustration. "Are you sure you're not leaving something out?"

"No," he replied. "I just took your hand and walked you to the library door."

She tensed while staring at him after hearing the last remark.

"You turned oddly serious and very quiet," he informed her. "I remember wondering if you were ready to pass out. That's when you went wild."

She was silent a moment while staring at him then fidgeted. "Do you remember when we were upstairs in my bedroom just before the ambulance arrived?" she asked.

He seemed surprised by the question. "It's forever burned into my mind," Dane replied. "Why do you ask?"

"After I stopped your bleeding, I almost went into shock," she remarked.

"Yes, I remember."

"You put your jacket on me to keep me warm," she reminded him.

"I remember that too."

She stared into his eyes. "Then you held my hand," Raina gently informed him. "You held my hand and didn't let go until I lost it on the porch when I saw Miller."

"I remember that very well," he replied.

Raina took his hand in hers and stared at his hand in silence. Feeling his hand brought about every memory from that horrible night. Once the bad memories faded, she only remembered one. Dane comforted her when she needed it most. She drew a deep breath and met his gaze.

"I loved you for that," she announced softly.

He stared back at her as if uncertain how to respond. "I loved you long *before* that."

Raina stared into his eyes only a moment before placing her hands to his face and kissed him warmly but quickly turned aggressive. Dane slipped his arms around her waist, immediately pulled her against him, and returned the aggressive kiss. Pent-up passion simultaneously exploded from both as they kissed and groped each other without concern that someone might walk in at any moment. Dane pulled her leg up to his hip and just about knocked her against the island counter while pressing against her as she attempted to slip him out of his jacket. He ran his hand firmly along her leg clinging to his hip and caressed her thigh beneath her dress, eagerly working his way up her leg. There was no reservation, and the once refined butler had completely vanished.

As he pinned her to the island counter, she wrapped her other leg around his hip while clinging to him, giving him unrestricted access. He pressed against her while groaning then pulled his mouth from hers and kissed her neck toward her exposed cleavage. Raina groaned in response to his hips grinding against hers, penetrating her thin dress. Despite being sober, her head was spinning. For a brief moment, she didn't even care if he took her right there. They heard someone in the hallway and immediately jumped apart while panting from the intense moment. Raina stared into his eyes as he attempted to compose himself, but it was obvious he was beyond composure.

"Your room," she gasped while still panting from the heat of the moment.

Dane grabbed her hand without comment and pulled her to the staff wing doorway. They heard someone within the staff wing beyond the door. Dane immediately changed direction and pulled her up the back stairs, making a course change for her room instead.

Chapter 47
Bed Sheet Bingo

Dane and Raina were entwined beneath the covers in the dim lighting within Raina's bedroom. He held her hands in his while pinning them against the mattress near her head. He warmly kissed her neck while he lovingly and slowly thrust his hips against her. She kept her legs locked around his waist allowing him unobstructed and uninhibited access to her body as her heels gently caressed his naked buttocks. He finally released her hands, allowing her to eagerly caress his chest as his hands slipped beneath her buttocks. Every memory from their first drunken encounter came rushing back to her as he affectionately made love to her. As he gently lifted her hips upward, the new sensation nearly drove her out of her mind as her body quivered against his.

When she gasped loudly in response, his thrusts became more aggressive causing her to cry out in ecstasy. As he bucked against her, she clung to his neck in an effort to keep from hitting the headboard, which seemed much closer now. With a final thrust and a groan that followed, Dane collapsed against her for a brief moment. He finally lifted his head as he panted heavily and met her gaze with a pleased grin then chuckled lightly.

"I tried to be a gentleman," he gasped out of breath while gently caressing her face. "I'm afraid I may have failed. I hope I wasn't too aggressive."

She kissed him warmly on the lips while caressing his chest and then smiled in response. "You didn't fail," Raina announced. "You were perfect."

Dane grinned, moved off her, and collapsed to the bed while attempting to catch his breath. He then pulled her into his arms and held her against him. She could feel his heart pounding against her hand. Both were pleasantly mussed and moderately exhausted. He held her affectionately and kissed her forehead and face several times.

"If I knew it was that much fun, I would have seduced you years ago," she teased.

Dane chuckled and clung to her. "Shamefully, I would have let you."

She lifted her head and met his gaze. "Really?"

"Come on, Raina," he announced while grinning. "You were just as hot then as you are now. And six years ago, my hormones were in overdrive."

"Six years ago, you were in love with Callie," she reminded him.

"No, six years ago I wanted to go out with Callie, but I wanted you first--and more," he informed her.

Raina stared at him with a surprised look. "I can't believe you thought of me that way," she remarked. "I honestly thought you hated me."

"Sometimes I did," he admitted then sighed and caressed her shoulder while staring at the ceiling. "Mostly I just wanted you." He cast a sly look at her and grinned.

"Ironically, I was attracted to you too," she announced then frowned. "Until you spontaneously combusted into my father." She returned her head to his chest. "It's funny, once in the middle of one of our annual character assassinations, I nearly kissed you."

"Four years ago over Christmas break?"

Raina again lifted her head and stared at him with surprise that he knew the time. "Yeah, that's the one," she replied then laughed. "I don't know--just something in your eyes made me want to kiss you."

"Maybe because I was thinking the same thing," he teased. "You probably saw the lust in my eyes. Two years ago in the library *that* night was particularly hard on me. That tank top you were wearing was practically see-through and drove me out of my mind."

She eyed him with surprise and smiled. "The one that you told me to cover up?" she asked then laughed. "So that's it, huh? You weren't so much offended as you were turned on."

"Oh, the fantasies going through my mind," he announced then groaned and cast a sideways look at her in his arms. "I came so close to kissing you."

Raina sighed deeply and grinned. "I probably would have kissed you back," she responded.

He groaned at the thought then clung to her and nuzzled her in his arms. "Is it ridiculous to think there could be something more between us?"

"You mean like more frequent visits and you sneaking into my bedroom?"

"You know what I mean," Dane announced then frowned. "Am I just being Callie?"

"You want a real relationship?"

"I've wanted a real relationship my entire life," he informed her. "Everyone I ever cared about either died or ran out on me." He groaned. "God, I am Callie. I'm so damaged; I don't deserve a relationship with someone like you." He sank into his own thoughts. "For eight years as a soldier, I shot whomever my superior officer told me to, watched half my buddies die for reasons I still don't understand, and spent several years stealing millions in jewels from wealthy men, not unlike your father." He frowned and shook his head. "I preach morals and honesty when I'm the least moral and honest person I've ever known. Once, seven years ago, I was so many different people, I almost forgot my real name. I'm the guy I'd threaten you to stay away from."

"Hmm, way to sell yourself there, Dane," she remarked. "Have you stolen anything in the last six years since you've turned your life around?"

"No, of course not," he insisted. "Well, I took a pen from the bank once, but I'm pretty sure they don't mind."

"Have you been dishonest to benefit yourself?"

"To benefit myself?" he asked while casting a glance at her. "No, but I did withhold circumstantial information from Detective Payne to protect your father and brother."

"I did that too," Raina informed him. "I think there are two options for our situation. Option one. We secretly carry on a fling when I come to visit once or twice a year until one of us finds a permanent relationship. Or option two. We start a relationship like a normal couple and deal with my father's criticism." She cast a look at him. "I prefer option two, but I'm okay with whatever makes you comfortable."

"Of course I want option two, but even if I could convince myself I'm worthy, how would that work?" he asked and attempted to look at her. "You live five hours away. I work twelve-hour days, six days a week."

"I suppose I'd have to give up my apartment with Miller and move back here," she replied.

He stared at her with surprise. "Would you actually do that?"

Raina shrugged then smiled. "It's a perk to being the daughter of a millionaire," she teased.

"You should probably think about it before making a decision," he informed her. "You'll be the one receiving flack for dating the servant."

"You're right. I should give it some serious thought," she replied then considered the comment and smiled. "Okay, I thought about it. I'll move back. Of course, that means Miller will also be moving back."

"I'm sure your father will hate having his children living back at home with him," Dane laughed. "It's going to be so crowded around here."

Raina laughed softly and clung to him. He returned the embrace and shut his eyes.

"This is the best I've felt in a long time," he announced then sighed with content. "I may not even yell at anyone tomorrow."

The outside light that had kept her room dimly lit suddenly went out. Both looked around with surprise. The digital alarm clock was out as well.

"Isn't there supposed to be a tropical storm approaching?" she asked with concern while pulling away from him. "I overheard Titus say he wanted to be back before the storm reached our area."

"No, that storm won't reach us for a few hours. Besides, the backup generator should have kicked on by now," he announced then groaned and sat up. "I should probably check on that. We don't want the drunks fumbling around in the dark."

Dane got out of her bed and slipped into his discarded clothes on the floor. She sat up in bed while holding the sheet to her naked body and watched him fumble with his clothes through the glow of the moonlight shining into her bedroom.

"Are you worried?" she asked with concern.

"Unexplained power outages always worry me," he announced. "Call it my former life in crime suspicions. If you want to keep someone from seeing something, you cut the power. It causes disorientation and chaos."

"I should come with you."

"There's no reason to drag you out of bed," Dane insisted while slipping into his shirt then raised his brows. "It just means more work for me getting you out of your clothes again."

She smirked at the comment. "I sympathize with you," Raina muttered, "but I'm coming along."

Chapter 48

Chickens with Their Heads Cut Off

Raina stood alongside Dane in the basement with a flashlight aimed at the massive generator. She'd seldom seen Dane without his jacket and tie, which he'd left back in her room so they could get to the generator in less time. Raina had dressed quickly as well, wearing her frumpy shorts and sweatshirt rather than slipping back into her dress. Dane looked over the generator and appeared bewildered. The generator should have turned on automatically when the power went out, but it didn't seem to be working. Dane pressed a button. The generator came to life without hesitation, and a few emergency lights came on within the basement.

She eyed him with a curious stare. "What was wrong with it?"

He stared at the enormous generator while frowning. "It was switched off," he informed her then looked around with noted concern.

Raina was becoming alarmed by his strange silence and look of deep thought. "Should we be concerned?"

"No, not just yet," he replied and came back to life. Dane looked at her and attempted a reassuring smile. "Let's check on the others just to be safe."

Although he didn't say it, she was convinced he was hiding his concerns regarding their unusual situation. He took her hand securely in his and led her toward the basement stairs not far from the kitchen. What should have been a romantic gesture felt oddly like a security measure. She sensed he was more worried than he let on. As they entered the grand hallway from the basement, Raina noted how quiet the house suddenly seemed. The backup generator provided enough light to give the grand hallway a creepy feel.

As they walked past several dark rooms, Raina couldn't help but shiver while keeping close to Dane, who still clung to her hand. They approached the game room where they had left the party nearly an hour earlier. Dane and Raina entered the dimly lit game room but discovered the room was empty. The dirty glasses, beer bottles, and empty plates remained littered around the room. They exchanged puzzled looks.

"Where did everyone go?" she asked in a soft tone while nervously looking around.

Dane still didn't release her hand. Although he seemed calm, she could feel his hand tensing against hers. "I don't know."

"It's only a little after ten o'clock," she reminded him. "Do you honestly think everyone went to bed?"

"No, I don't. It's early. I'd think most of the guests should still be up," Dane informed her. "Let's take a quick look around."

He led her from the game room, keeping her close behind him as they entered the hallway. Dane paused and looked down the hall to the foyer. The front door was partially open. He pulled her behind him as he hurried for the foyer. She clung to his hand and had to jog to keep up with his fast gait. He headed up the foyer steps and pulled the door open. They looked outside at the dark driveway and the parked cars near the fountain.

"It doesn't look as if anyone had left," Dane announced more to himself then looked around. "I wonder why the front door was open."

Raina noted one of the familiar expensive cars and nudged Dane while indicating the car. "Isn't that Nole's car?" she asked with surprise. "I thought he left."

"I only saw him to the door," Dane replied while staring at Nole's car while in thought. "I'll admit; I didn't actually watch him drive away." He stared at Nole's car a moment longer then looked at Raina. "Let's find the others."

§

After a quick search of the first floor common rooms, Dane and Raina entered the dimly lit kitchen a few minutes later. They startled Levi, who was sitting at the kitchen table working on eating an entire plate of leftover appetizers. It was uncertain whether their sudden appearance startled him or the fact that he was caught binge snacking, which he often did after a night of excessive drinking.

"You scared me, Dane," Levi announced with a mouthful of food.

With how drunk the cook appeared, it was surprising he was still conscious. Dane remained suspicious and looked around the eerily silent kitchen.

"Where is everyone?" Dane asked.

"Sloan went with Titus to take some of the guests home, so he'd have company on the return trip, and Mr. Steele was going to his study," Levi informed him. "I'm not sure what happened to the others. I vaguely remember someone offering to show Jimmy Love the Rolls in the garage. Before I knew it, I was alone in the game room, so I came in here to, uh, clean up a little. I think the power went out."

"Good observation," Dane muttered. "We didn't find anyone in any of the common areas."

"I guess they all went to the garage with Jimmy Love," Levi remarked.

"We're running on the backup generator," Dane reminded him. "There won't be any power out there. They'll be fumbling around in the dark."

"Do you want me to go out there with a flashlight and make sure they're all right?" Levi asked.

"If you don't mind," Dane replied and again looked around while deep in thought. "I'm a little concerned that Nole never left. There's no telling what he's up to. Mr. Steele may need our assistance."

"Yeah, sure," Levi announced and stood with some unsteadiness. He grabbed a flashlight and headed out the back kitchen door.

Raina turned toward Dane with a concerned look on her face. "I'm worried about my father, Dane," she announced. "There's no telling what Nole might do. I mean, what if Nole had killed Callie?"

"I'm sure he's fine," Dane assured her. "But we'll check the master bedroom. He'd been drinking quite a bit. Maybe he went to sleep it off."

They headed for the back stairs and nearly collided with Sloan entering through the back kitchen door.

"What's going on?" Sloan demanded. "Levi said you were worried because Nole's car is still here. All the outside lights are out. Are we on the backup generator?"

"Yes, the power's out," Dane replied. "Did you see anyone on your way inside?"

"No, just Levi," she replied.

"Where's Titus?" Dane asked.

"He saw one of the garage bay doors open and went to close it," she announced. "Levi said you asked him to check the garage for some of the guests. Is something wrong?"

"No, I just want to do a quick headcount," Dane informed her. "We'll check the guestrooms and the master bedroom and see who's accounted for."

§

Raina entered the dimly lit second floor hallway from the master bedroom and joined Dane and Sloan as they approached from the opposite end.

"No one is answering in any of the occupied rooms," Sloan announced.

"Miller didn't answer either," Dane reported.

"My father isn't in his room," Raina informed them and met Dane's gaze with her own concerned one. "I'm getting worried, Dane."

"There's no cause for alarm yet," he replied. "We still don't know who went to the garage. We'll check with Levi. Maybe everyone went out there. Your father is proud of that Rolls. He probably went out with them. They could just be fumbling around in the dark with the power out."

As they approached the back stairs, Dane took Raina's hand and led the way down the mostly dark, narrow staircase to the kitchen. They entered the kitchen from the back stairs and looked around, but there was no sign of Levi. Dane appeared frustrated as he approached the side cupboard. He removed two flashlights and handed one to Sloan.

"Sloan, would you check the staff quarters for Levi?" he asked.

Sloan nodded while accepting the flashlight and entered the staff wing through the kitchen door. Not all the areas would be well lit, and he didn't want her fumbling around in the dark by herself.

Dane fiddled with his flashlight while deep in thought. He finally looked at Raina with a strange seriousness. "I need you to wait here," he announced. "I'm going to the garage and see what's going on."

"By yourself?" she asked with concern.

"Someone needs to wait here for Sloan," he reminded her. "I don't want her left alone in the house."

The outer kitchen door opened, startling both. Titus entered the kitchen and received bewildered looks from Dane and Raina.

"Where's Levi?" Dane asked.

"I wouldn't know. I haven't seen him," Titus announced. "I just got back from dropping off some of the guests. What's with the power?"

"Sloan said she went with you," Dane insisted while appearing mildly suspicious. "She's been back fifteen minutes now."

"Yeah, I know. I went to check on the open garage door," Titus announced and again looked around. "It was totally dark in there. I was afraid someone was trying to steal the Rolls. What happened to the power?"

"Your guess is as good as mine," Dane replied. "Levi said Hanson was showing Jimmy Love Mr. Steele's classic Rolls. They weren't out there?"

"No, no one was out there."

"Not even Levi?" Raina asked with concern now feeling her anxiety rising.

"It was pitch-black out there. I had my flashlight, but I didn't see anyone," Titus informed them. "I'm sure I would have seen the glimmer of Jimmy Love's bold outfit by the glow of my flashlight had he been out there."

Raina turned to Dane with concern. "Dane, I'm really getting worried now."

Dane didn't respond to her concerns and instead focused his attention on Titus. "I want you to find Sloan in the staff wing in case Levi came back inside," he firmly instructed. "I don't want the two of you out of each other's sight. Raina and I are going to the garage and look for Levi and the others."

"Maybe we should call the police," Raina suggested while nervously fidgeting.

"It's just a power outage," Titus informed her making light of her concerns. "The last thing we need is the police crawling around here again."

"Why does that make me even more nervous?" Raina muttered.

"There's no reason to get all worked up," Titus again announced.

"I'm getting a bad feeling too, Titus," Dane insisted. "Just stay with Sloan. If Raina and I don't return in fifteen minutes, I want you to call the police."

"And tell them what?" he demanded. "It's a power outage. Why are you wigging out?"

"Because unexplained power outages and mischief often travel together," Dane snapped.

Titus shook his head. "You're one weird dude, Dane," he scoffed.

"Fifteen minutes, Titus," Dane commanded while glaring at him and pointing a warning finger. "Find Sloan. Don't leave her out of your sight."

Dane captured Raina's hand and pulled her close to his side. Titus eyed the way Dane held Raina's hand as if he feared letting her go.

Titus appeared concerned for the first time and nodded. "Yeah, okay," he replied and headed for the staff wing as Dane led Raina out the back kitchen door. Titus hurried along the dimly lit corridor. "Sloan," he called out. "Sloan, where are you?"

All the doors to the staff rooms were closed except Dane's door near the end of the corridor. Sloan didn't respond. Typically, the staff kept their bedroom doors closed, and the vacant rooms were kept locked. Titus hurried to the only open door and peered into Dane's dark room. Sloan lay face down on the floor with the lit flashlight not far from her outstretched hand.

"Sloan," Titus gasped and ran into the room.

As he fell to his knees alongside her, the bedroom door shut behind him. Titus spun on his knee toward the closed door in the nearly dark room and reached for the flashlight.

§

Dane held Raina's hand as he led her across the dark patio and along the walkway toward the dark garage. Raina clung to Dane's hand and looked around. There was just enough light to see the garage from the house, but she wondered why he didn't use the flashlight he carried in his free hand. Once they reached the garage, Dane turned on his flashlight and checked the bay doors. They were all closed and locked. Everything appeared eerily silent. They approached the limo parked outside the garage where Titus had left it. He opened the back door of the limousine, briefly glanced inside, and then shut the door. He looked back at Raina as she nervously wrung her fingers together while scanning the area surrounding the garage.

"This is starting to feel like some horror movie," she insisted. "Everyone from the party mysteriously vanishes. It's never a good sign."

Dane drew a deep breath while looking around the silent garage area. "Okay, it's time to call the police," he announced a little too quickly.

Chapter 49

What the Hell?

Dane and Raina entered the empty kitchen and looked around with bewilderment. They weren't out back long, but Titus should have found Sloan and returned to the kitchen by the time they got back.

"I thought you told Titus to wait here for us," Raina remarked while nervously looking around.

"Yeah, I did," he muttered.

"Should we check the staff wing?" she gasped with concern while squeezing his hand.

"No."

Dane pulled her to the island counter, keeping her only inches from him, and opened the secret compartment. He removed his service pistol from the pillowcase, checked the magazine, cocked it, and handed it to her. She uncertainly took the gun and stared at it with surprise. He shut the compartment and grabbed the phone. His look was concerned as he set the phone back down without completing his call.

"It's dead, isn't it?" she gasped.

Dane felt for his jacket and realized he wasn't wearing it. He looked at Raina. "I left my jacket upstairs," he announced. "Do you have your cell phone on you?"

"I rarely keep it on me when I'm in the house," she replied.

Dane pulled her from the kitchen toward the hallway door. They left the kitchen and hurried along the grand hall and toward the foyer. Once they reached the front door, he pressed the security code into the panel, setting the alarm, and then opened the door. Lights on the panel flashed. Within seconds, the alarm wailed within the house. He then opened the foyer closet door and removed a baseball bat, keeping it clutched in his right hand. Dane pulled Raina into his arms and held her close to him while listening to the alarm wail and flash. Raina clung to the gun and looked around.

"Where is everyone?" she demanded with concern. "Why aren't they reacting to the alarm?"

Dane nervously looked around as well. "Because they can't."

She looked back at him with horror in her eyes. "What?" Raina gasped.

Dane clung to her hand and pulled her down the hall for the game room. He looked inside before pulling her in behind him. They approached the bar containing several empty and partially full glasses. Dane picked up several glasses and smelled each, leaving Raina puzzled.

"What is it?" she asked not understanding.

"Nothing," he replied and set the glass down. "That's a good thing."

"How's that a good thing?"

"That means it probably wasn't poison," he informed her as he looked around.

Raina stared at him and held back her gasp. She wasn't sure what he was implying, but it frightened her. Dane checked the martini pitcher and studied it. A white film coated the bottom.

"What's that?" Raina asked with concern.

"I'm guessing sedatives," he replied and then looked around the game room while the alarm continued to wail.

"So we're not being paranoid?" she demanded and felt her entire body tense.

"Maybe you're not, but I sure as hell am," he announced. "We'll wait for the police by the front door."

He pulled her from the game room and back to the foyer where they waited by the front door as the alarm continued to wail throughout the house. They barely heard a thump from upstairs over the wailing alarm. Both looked to the ceiling with concern.

"Wait here," he announced. "The police should be here soon. I'm going to see who's up there."

He attempted to release her hand, but she refused to let go of him.

"Are you insane?" she gasped. "First Levi disappears then Sloan and Titus. Now you want to go off on your own and investigate a strange noise. Have you ever seen a horror movie? You're not going up there without me."

Dane eyed the gun in her hand, considered her comment, and nodded. "Okay, you cover me."

Raina held the gun with more conviction and nodded. Dane clutched his baseball bat and led her toward the stairs. She kept watch behind them with her back to the wall as they headed up the stairs. Once they reached the landing, Dane released her hand and held the bat in both hands. He quietly walked along the hallway with Raina behind him while clutching his shirt in her free hand. She kept her back to the wall and held the gun close to her chest while darting looks around the dimly lit hall. The alarm continued to wail, which didn't settle her nerves any. It was loud enough to keep her from hearing anyone moving around. Dane opened the master bedroom door and peered inside but didn't see anything. He moved to Raina's room and looked inside. They still didn't find anything.

They crossed the hall to Jenna's bedroom. He opened the door and peered inside the mostly dark room. Dane suddenly darted into the room startling Raina, who lost her grip on his shirt. Raina entered the room behind him and saw him hurry for the bed. He turned on the bedside light, which was on the emergency outlet, brightening the room. Raina let out a sharp gasp when she saw Jenna lying naked beneath the covers. Dane checked her pulse and appeared relieved.

"She's alive."

As he moved from the bedside, Raina lunged for the bed and sat on the edge. She nudged her friend gently at first then with added vigor.

"Jenna! Jenna, can you hear me?" she cried out with concern.

"I'll get a cold cloth from the bathroom," Dane announced. "Stay here."

Dane hurried into the bathroom and turned on the light. Miller lay on the floor wearing only his boxer shorts. Dane knelt alongside Miller and nudged him.

"Miller? Come on, wake up," he announced then looked out the door to the bedroom. "Raina, Miller's on the bathroom floor. He's out cold as well."

Raina remained on the edge of the bed while attempting to wake Jenna and looked toward the bathroom. "Is he okay?" she called back.

"I think so," Dane responded from the bathroom.

Raina tapped Jenna's face with a little added vigor. Jenna groaned and opened her eyes. Raina heard shouting from downstairs followed by thundering footfalls on the steps. Raina slipped Dane's gun under the pillow then attempted to keep Jenna awake.

"Jenna, are you okay?" she asked.

Jenna again opened her eyes and looked at Raina with bewilderment then looked around the room. "What the hell happened?"

"You tell me," Raina replied.

"I don't know," she gasped and felt the sheet over her naked body. "Miller and I were--" She suddenly gasped with horror and nearly shot up in bed. "Miller!"

Jenna clutched her head, swayed slightly, and collapsed back onto the bed with a groan.

"He's okay," Raina insisted and handed her Miller's discarded shirt. "Dane found him on the bathroom floor."

As Jenna struggled to sit up with Raina's assistance, they could hear the police calling from the hallway.

"In here!" Raina called out then helped her friend slip into Miller's shirt.

Raina buttoned the shirt for her. Jenna shook her head with some disorientation almost unaware that Raina helped dress her.

"I don't know what happened. Miller and I were just kind of fooling around. When things started heating up, I suddenly felt dizzy. I didn't even have that much to drink," she announced while holding her head. "Miller went into the bathroom to get me a cold washrag, and that's all I remember."

Raina heard the police officer now calling from the second floor hallway.

"In here," Raina called back.

The police officer appeared in the doorway with his weapon drawn and scanned the room. He saw them and lowered his gun.

"Is everyone okay?" the officer asked. "Is there an intruder?"

"We were having a party," she informed the police officer. "Someone must have spiked the martinis. My friend and brother passed out up here, but we can't find the others. The cook, maid, and chauffeur were attempting to locate the others, and then they disappeared."

Dane appeared from the bathroom with a disoriented Miller leaning heavily on his shoulder. Dane helped him to the bed where he collapsed with a groan. Jenna collapsed alongside him and held his head to her chest.

"Someone cut the power and the phone lines an hour ago," Dane informed the officer. "We're on the backup generator. We can't find the others. At least eleven people are unaccounted for."

"I'll contact my partner downstairs," the officer announced. "We'll search the estate for the others." He then spoke into his hand radio and hurried from the room.

"Why don't you see if you can get them dressed?" Dane announced then drew a deep breath. "I'm going to check the other rooms."

Raina gave him a concerned look. "Maybe you shouldn't go off on your own."

Dane tensed and appeared to be holding something back. "I think the alarm and the police presence ended whatever happened here."

She stared at him with a strange look. "You think something happened, don't you?"

"I don't know what happened here," Dane insisted, "but I don't think someone drugged the entire house just for a cruel prank. Wait here for me."

Raina nodded and watched him leave the room.   Jenna struggled to sit up and looked at her friend.

"What happened?" Jenna asked with concern.

Raina held her breath a moment.   "I'm afraid we're about to find out."

Chapter *50*
Gut Feeling

Raina sat on the coffee table in the lounge across from Miller and Jenna, who still appeared slightly groggy. Gilda and Farley Nixon sat in the far corner of the room attempting to stay awake. Dane had found the couple passed out in their bedroom after the police had arrived. It was now after eleven o'clock, and the power remained out leaving just the backup generator to power various lights and other appliances. The limited lighting would hamper the search for the remaining missing guests. Dane, now properly dressed, entered the lounge with Jimmy Love dramatically draped over his shoulder. Hanson, Tia, and Olivia followed with the same look of disorientation. Everyone collapsed into chairs with exhausted looks. Dane attempted to place Jimmy Love in an oversized chair, but he was reluctant to release Dane.

"You're such a comfort in my hour of need," Jimmy Love announced while clinging to the butler.

"It was just a sedative," Dane muttered. "I think you'll live."

Dane finally shook him off his shoulder. Jimmy Love fell into the chair with a bounce and a delighted squeal.

"Oh, you're so dominating," Jimmy Love cried out. "I love that in a man."

Dane ignored him and approached Raina, who watched him with a concerned look on her face. She was hoping he had an update on the others.

"One of the officers is still trying to wake Levi in the Rolls Royce bay," Dane informed her. "It would appear as if he drank the sedated martinis after the others. They said he's fine just out cold."

"No word on my father yet?" she asked while nervously wrenching her fingers together.

"No, not yet," he replied. "I'm going back out to help look."

She made a motion to follow him. He stopped her with a stern look.

"You should stay here with the others," he announced. "I'll let you know when we find your father."

As Dane turned, the second officer helped Sloan and Titus into the lounge. Both held dishtowels to their heads. Dane and Raina appeared alarmed when they saw blood on Titus' dishtowel.

"What happened, Sloan?" Raina gasped.

"I was checking the bedrooms like Dane told me," she insisted. "Dane's bedroom door was open, so I went to check it out. When I entered his room, the door shut behind me. I turned, and that's all I remember until I woke up with an officer standing over me, and Titus was on the floor alongside me."

"Of course," Dane deducted. "The two of you took some of the guests home in the limousine. The martinis must have been drugged after you'd left."

"I wasn't drinking martinis," Titus insisted. "I only had a couple of beers since I needed to drive some of the guests home."

"I didn't have any alcohol tonight," Sloan announced. "Levi was making another pitcher of martinis when I left."

"Anyone else still missing?" the officer asked.

"My father," Raina quickly announced.

"Possibly three guests," Dane informed him. "I'll help you look."

Dane left with the second officer. Sloan sat on one of the sofas alongside Titus. He smiled sympathetically and brushed her blonde hair matted with blood from her face. Sloan returned the smile and sank against him as he held her.

"I should help look for my father," Raina announced while fidgeting.

Raina stood and hurried for the archway. She nearly collided with the first officer guiding Elana and Keefe into the room. Elana wore Keefe's shirt over her otherwise naked body.

"I found these two passed out in the gazebo," he announced.

Jimmy Love eyed the couple. "What happened to your clothes, honey?"

Elana shook her head with disorientation. "I'm not sure," she muttered while remaining unsteady.

"They were both, uh, in the buff," the officer reported. "We were lucky to find what clothes we did."

Elana managed a soft laugh. "Some party, huh?"

"It's best if everyone waits here for now," the officer informed them while gesturing with his hands. "We'd like the paramedics to check you out first. No one's in any condition to be up and about until the drugs completely wear off. Just relax and take it easy for a little while longer."

Elana and Keefe sat on the nearby loveseat and clung to each other. As the officer left the room, Raina paced and glanced at those seated around her. All appeared exceedingly groggy and disoriented. She thought about Dane's earlier comment. Why had everyone been drugged? Whoever drugged them didn't want any witnesses to something. Alarm swept over her, and she ran from the room. Miller watched her, appeared concerned, and attempted to stand. He fell back onto the sofa with a groan. Raina ran along the grand hallway and hurried into the kitchen. A paramedic tended to Levi, who sat at the table with his head resting on it.

"Oh, I feel like crap," Levi moaned.

Dane entered the kitchen with the second officer. "We haven't checked the basement or the attic yet," he informed the police officer.

Raina ran to Dane, grabbed his arm, and pulled on him. "I had a terrible thought," she cried out. "Come on!"

She pulled him toward the back kitchen door. Dane hurried after her with the second officer following on their heels.

§

Dane hurried alongside Raina while holding her hand as they approached the crypt. He seemed to know what she was thinking and was slightly apprehensive. The officer was only steps behind them.

"Why would he come out this far?" the officer called out to them while attempting to keep up.

"He wouldn't on his own," Raina responded with increasing concern.

As they hurried past the crypt, they heard a tree branch creaking. Dane suddenly grabbed Raina and pushed her into the officer.

"Keep her here!"

The officer held Raina despite his confusion. She fought the officer's grip, pulled away, and ran after Dane. The officer ran after her. Dane suddenly stopped past the crypt with a look of horror on his face. He spun and attempted to grab Raina before she could see it. She darted away from him before he could grab her and looked at the tree. In the dim lighting, she saw the outline of a bound, naked man hanging from the very same tree as Callie had. His innards lay on a pile below his bound ankles as his body swayed. Dane grabbed Raina and attempted to turn her away as she screamed. The officer ran past them and shined his flashlight on the hanging man. To their surprise, it was Nole.

Chapter 51

Not Again!

It was just before midnight and an hour after they'd found Nole gutted and hanging from the tree behind the crypt. Detective Payne and several officers were tending to the investigation at the back edge of the estate. Raina sat at the island counter in the kitchen wearing Dane's jacket and trembled while he clung to her. The second officer stood near them and attempted to drink coffee with trembling hands. He was equally traumatized by what he'd seen.

"I've never seen anything like that before," the officer admitted while shaking his head repeatedly. "Ten years on the force." He eyed Dane while maintaining his disbelief. "Who'd do that to a man?"

"It takes a special brand of sociopath to gut a man, I assure you," Dane informed him.

"I've never seen anything that--that violent before," the officer continued while staring at Dane. "How can you be so calm?"

"I lived through similar nightmares before. I guess I'm immune now," Dane replied then nodded to the officer's coffee cup. "Drink your coffee, Officer. You appear to be going into shock."

The officer obediently sipped his coffee and stared blankly at the countertop. Dane handed Raina her cup of tea then placed his arm around her and attempted to help keep her warm. She looked at him as he held her.

"I'm worried about my father," she announced, unable to think about anything else.

"I know," Dane replied. "Detective Payne is here with four more officers. They'll find your father. I'm sure he's fine."

"You're sure because you think he did it, don't you?" she asked timidly.

"No, I don't," Dane announced with certainty and rubbed her arms to keep her warm. "Your father isn't capable of doing that to another human being, particularly someone who was once his best friend."

"Who would be capable of doing something like that?" Raina then asked.

"Most likely a psychopath with hunting experience," Dane informed her. "Judging by what I saw, there was little to no hesitation. Our killer drugged everyone in the house, shut off the power along with the backup generator, and executed Nole methodically and with great forethought."

The officer looked up from his coffee and stared at them with surprise. Another officer entered the kitchen through the main door with Otto, who appeared unsteady and disoriented. Raina jumped from her chair, ran to her father, and hugged him.

"Dad, I was so worried when we couldn't find you," she cried out.

"I'm fine, just a little groggy," he informed her then appeared curious. "What the hell happened?"

"Just about everyone had been drugged with the martinis," she replied. "Where were you?"

"We found him out cold in the hall closet," the officer alongside him replied.

"The hall closet?" Dane asked with surprise.

"I don't know how I got there," Otto insisted. "I was heading into my study. The next thing I know, I'm waking up in the hall closet with a police officer standing over me." He stared at them and remained puzzled. "Levi made those martinis. Certainly, they don't suspect he had anything--"

"Nole's dead," Dane informed him.

Otto stared at Dane with shock and surprise. "What?" he gasped. "How? When?"

"Over an hour ago," Dane replied. "He was hanging from the tree behind the crypt."

"That's impossible," Otto insisted. "He left hours ago. You showed him out."

"I didn't exactly watch him leave," Dane informed him. "He must have come back inside."

Detective Payne entered the kitchen with another police officer at his side. He looked around then focused his attention on Otto.

"I'm afraid I'll need to take you in for questioning, Mr. Steele," Detective Payne announced.

Otto groaned with annoyance. "I didn't kill him," he snarled. "I was unconscious in the hall closet. Someone drugged me and put me there."

"Everyone knows you hated Nole Oaks," the detective announced. "You caught him having sex with your bride on your wedding night. The manner in which he was killed was violent, like a revenge killing. The fact that he was hanging from the same tree as your wife tells me it was symbolic." Detective Payne studied him a moment. "Considering that criteria, you're my best suspect. Now, do you come along willingly, or must I place you under arrest."

"That won't be necessary. I'll go along willingly," Otto reluctantly replied then cast a look at Dane. "Call my lawyer. Put him on retainer."

Dane frowned and nodded. Raina hugged her father then pulled back as they led him away. The officer at the table left with them as well. Once they were alone, she turned to Dane with some hostility.

"He didn't do it, Dane," she insisted.

"I know."

"They're going to pin it on him," she remarked fighting her concern and anger. "It looks bad for him."

"Yes, I know."

"What are we going to do?" she demanded while her frustration elevated.

"Put his lawyer on retainer," Dane candidly admitted with a sigh.

"That's it?" she launched with surprise.

"What do you want to do, Raina?"

Dane headed for the staff wing door and passed through it. She hurried after him, following him down the hallway with concern and annoyance.

"I don't know," she announced. "Something. Anything but sit around."

"Do you think we should illegally search the suspects' homes?" Dane demanded. "Should we risk being arrested for breaking and entering on the hopes we might actually find something?"

Raina followed him with her arms across her chest and disgust on her face. "Well, I--"

"Even if we knew what we were looking for, it's probably locked in some safe," he continued with little emotion then cast a glance at her as they approached his room. "Do you know how to crack a safe? Disarm a security system?"

"No, but--"

Dane stopped by his bedroom door and turned toward her with a serious look on his face. "Well, you're in luck," he announced simply, "because I do."

Raina followed Dane into his room and shut the door behind them. She watched as he approached his closet, removed a suit bag, and hung it on the door. When he opened the bag, there were several neatly pressed military uniforms. He removed a black outfit from the back and looked at it while frowning.

"I thought you were out of my life forever," he muttered to the uniform.

"What sort of uniform is that?" she asked with a strange look on her face.

"That, my dear, is a tactical combat outfit," he teased and offered a playful grin. "Or as I prefer to call it; my stalking outfit."

"Like Batman?"

He eyed her and raised a brow. "More like Zorro," Dane replied then muttered. "If Zorro stole from the rich and kept it for himself."

Raina ran her finger over several sewn spots. "What happened here?" she asked. "Someone not so crazy about you breaking into his house?"

"Uh, that was a little disagreement in Iraq," he informed her. "Got me ten stitches, a purple heart, and my first stolen helicopter."

"You mean that was from your military days?" she asked with surprise then suddenly eyed him. "Wait, your first stolen helicopter? How many did you steal?"

"Six, I think," he replied. "Although I did blow up a few dozen." Dane shook his head while frowning. "Such a shame too. I like helicopters."

"You were a pilot?"

"Oh, God, no," he casually replied. "They'd never let me fly a helicopter."

"I thought you said you stole them," she remarked and eyed him suspiciously. "You certainly didn't put them in your pocket."

"No, but I never actually landed one successfully," he informed her. "I sort of crashed them. Six stolen, six crashed." He thought back reflectively and smiled. "I miss flying."

He tossed the outfit onto the bed and removed his shirt. She eyed the familiar scars on his arms, chest, side, and back. She remembered them well from earlier that evening. Seeing the sewn material on his uniform told her how he acquired his scars.

"You've seen quite a bit of action, haven't you?" she asked while studying his upper body.

"More than I care to remember," he informed her then sank into his own world. "We lost a lot of good men--good friends. I always managed to walk away even with a few extra holes in me and down a pint of blood or two." He offered a tiny, strange laugh. "When we went on dangerous missions, my commander would tell the new guy; 'if the mission takes a crap, stand behind Great Dane'."

Raina appeared to sink into thought and remembered her father telling her the same thing once. She finally looked at him and smiled.

"Why'd they say that?"

"I suppose because I'm tough to kill, and I always have a plan," he informed her then raised his brows along with a sly grin. "Even if it sometimes involves methodically crashing a helicopter."

Raina stared at him, studied his boyish grin only a moment, and then threw her arms around his neck, kissing him passionately and aggressively. Dane appeared slightly surprised but returned the kiss without hesitation and lowered her to the bed.

Chapter *52*

Murder Makes the Heart Grow Fonder

Dane was dressed in his black, combat outfit while Raina lay naked on the bed beneath the covers. She looked pleasantly rumpled but contented while watching him. Despite their quick yet particularly satisfying romp, Raina still felt an overwhelming urge to pounce on the handsome, mysterious butler. He traded in his suave, distinguished gentleman's suit for a rugged warrior's uniform, and it made her want him more.

"Is there something you want me to do while you're off prowling?" she asked while raising her brows seductively.

"I wouldn't mind if you waited in bed for me," he teased while grinning.

"I could wait in my private Jacuzzi," she replied with her own sly smile.

"Even better."

Raina then turned serious as concern overtook her playful mood. "How long do you think you'll be gone?" she asked while shifting nervously.

"A couple of hours."

"Hmm, I might be a little pruney by then if I waited in the hot tub," she remarked. "Is there something else I could do instead?"

"No, just don't let anyone know what I'm up to," he replied.

"I don't even know what you're up to," she remarked while studying him. "Are you going in blind, or do you actually have a plan?"

"I told you, I always have a plan," he announced while grinning. "When framing me for Callie's murder backfired, our killer went out of his way to make your father look guilty. That makes me suspicious." He raised his brows while eyeing her. "Why attempt to frame me at all? Why not just go for your father in the first place?"

"So you know what you're looking for?" she asked with surprise.

"Yes, but I'm not sure it's tied into the killings," he insisted while considering the question. "Where I find it will tell me if it's connected."

"Can you give me a little more information than that?" she asked.

"You should ask yourself how the killer knew about my past, and why he wanted to frame me," Dane informed her. "If you can come up with those answers, you'll be able to figure it all out."

"How do you intend to leave the house undetected?" she asked with a curious look. "Everyone will see the car headlights and start asking questions."

"I won't turn on the lights until I'm in the tree-lined portion of the driveway," he replied while grinning.

"Taillights?" she asked.

"Keep the others away from the lounge windows," he teased.

Dane kissed her quickly on the lips, offered a sly grin, and left the room. She watched him leave, considered his comment, and was instantly bewildered.

§

Nearly two hours later. It was a little before two in the morning, and the parade of police and emergency vehicles had left moments before the storm had reached them. Everyone was still gathered in the lounge after their ordeal. Those who had been drugged drank tea while the effects of the sedation slowly wore off. The news of Nole's violent death had everyone on edge, although none had been told the gruesome specifics about the killing just that he was found hanged behind the crypt. The tropical storm had finally made its way up the east coast and reached them. It had started raining nearly an hour earlier, and it wasn't supposed to stop for a couple of days.

Raina appeared tense while listening to the rain outside and periodically glancing at the grandfather clock. She hated the thought of Dane driving in the rain along the dark back roads. A slight shiver ran down her spine as her worst fears played out in her mind. She couldn't let the pouring rain and thoughts of her mother's car accident distract her even if it was making her insane. Raina then looked at Sloan and Titus on the sofa. Despite that a paramedic had looked everyone over, Sloan fussed over Titus' temple laceration. He appeared to enjoy the attention she offered, while she seemed more comforting than just any nurse. Raina couldn't be positive, but she suspected the maid and chauffeur had finally forgiven the past. She guessed murder makes the heart grow fonder.

"Are you sure you don't want to go to the hospital?" Raina asked Titus and Sloan despite that the paramedics did a nice job on their bruises and lacerations.

"No, I hate hospitals," Titus insisted and made a face. "Full of sick people."

"The paramedic said he didn't need stitches," Sloan announced. "I don't think either of us has a concussion." She tensed then offered a smile at Titus. "I think I'm going to bed. I've had enough of this day."

"What a horrible party," Keefe groaned from across the room where he sat alongside Elana.

"I think I'm ready for bed too," Elana remarked while still seeming slightly groggy. "Booze and sedatives are a bad combination."

Keefe tensed and gently caressed Elana's bare leg, since she was still only wearing his oversized button shirt. "Are you sure you want to stay here tonight?" he asked and offered a sympathetic look. "Maybe we should run away from this place as fast as we can."

"Neither of us is in any condition to drive," Elana reminded him. With a scowl on her face, she then indicated the Nixon's, who remained mostly quiet in the corner of the room. "We can't exactly get a ride with them either. They're in the same condition as we are."

"Yeah, you're right. That storm is already pounding the crap out of us. We don't want to get caught in that either," Keefe remarked then shook his head and eyed his girlfriend. "As soon as the sun is up, though, we're out of here. This place is cursed or something."

Raina considered the comment and felt a cold chill run down her spine. She wondered if his assessment was right.

"Where's Dane?" Miller finally asked while looking around. "I haven't seen him in a while."

"I think he was tidying the kitchen last I saw him," Raina announced and refrained from looking nervous. "Apparently, cleaning relaxes him."

"Maybe I should check on Dad at the police station," Miller announced with a groan.

"He'll be fine," Raina insisted, not wanting Miller venturing off after his ordeal. "His lawyer was on his way there when I spoke to him. You need to take it easy tonight. You're in no condition to be driving in this weather."

Miller reluctantly nodded in agreement then cast a quick glance at Jenna. She smiled a little too sweetly and took his hand. He returned the smile and looked at Raina.

"As long as you're sure," he announced. "I'm going to bed." Miller then eyed Jenna and hid his tiny smile. "I'll walk you to your room."

Sloan groaned and rolled her eyes. "Oh, please," she announced loud enough for the others to hear. "Everyone here knows you're hooking up."

Miller and Jenna shifted uncomfortably but didn't bother hiding their grins.

"I should see if Dane needs any help cleaning up before I pass out for the night," Levi announced with little enthusiasm at the thought.

"I'm sure he can manage," Raina announced while fidgeting. She didn't need him realizing Dane wasn't in the kitchen and commenting on it in front of the others. "You should rest too."

Raina saw Tia and Olivia fussing over Jimmy Love, which reminded her that he was in the room. It was possibly the quietest she'd ever seen the flashy man. Despite how many martinis Tia and Olivia must have had, Raina thought it was interesting that they weren't in nearly as bad shape as the others were. Thankfully, Gilda was silent for a change. Her poor husband, who had to be feeling pretty lousy himself, doted on her despite his own misery. His efforts to make her feel better were punished by the hateful looks she gave him. Hanson couldn't even stay awake. He'd been asleep in one of the corner chairs for the last two hours. Raina again looked at the grandfather clock then saw Dane appear in the doorway, now changed back into his butler uniform. Raina was surprised but relieved to see him.

"Miss Steele, you and your brother will be happy to know I found evidence that will clear your father and point to the real killer," he announced proudly.

Miller appeared surprised and sprang to his feet. He immediately regretted his sudden movements and clutched his head. "You have?" he gasped then seemed relieved. "That's great. Who's the killer?"

"I don't have sufficient evidence to announce that just yet, but I think once I have a look at this, I'll know." Dane held up a flash drive on a decorative keychain.

Everyone stared with curious looks at the flash drive he held. Raina cast looks at the others within the room and attempted to gauge their reactions, but they revealed nothing. They all seemed equally curious and did little to draw suspicion on themselves.

"I'll get with the two of you in the morning after I've had a chance to look at it," Dane informed them. "If that'll be all, I'll be turning in now."

"Uh, yes, of course," Raina announced. "Goodnight, Dane."

Dane left the lounge as everyone stared after him. Once he was gone, everyone seemed to tense simultaneously, making them all appear guilty.

Chapter 53

Busted!

Dane sat behind the computer in the study a little after two in the morning. By the male and female moans coming from the monitor, it sounded as if he were watching a low-budget porn movie. The study door quietly opened. Dane didn't bother looking up since he was expecting the visitor.

"I'm glad you got my invitation, Elana," Dane announced with little emotion and pressed a button on the keyboard. The sounds from the video stopped.

Elana stood in the doorway to the study and frowned then shut the door behind her. "What invitation?"

"You know damned well where I found this flash drive, and I'm sure you recognized the keychain as your own," he informed her. "This flash drive contains all the dirt you've been using to blackmail people of influence around town." He eyed her with surprise. "Were you actually blackmailing your own sister, or was Callie in on it with you?"

"I don't know what you're talking about," she scoffed while folding her arms across her chest.

"You can deny it all you want, but we both know it was you," Dane insisted. "You videotaped Callie with Mr. Nixon then used the video to extort money from him. I assume you made a decent amount of money off it, but then Mrs. Nixon found out about the affair, fired Callie, and ended your gravy train." He raised a curious brow. "So what happened? Did you attempt to blackmail your own sister after she married Mr. Steele? Did you threaten to show him the video if she didn't pay you hush money?" His eyes narrowed while staring at her. "I think she refused, and in a fit of rage, you hit her on the head. You couldn't have her telling anyone, or it might get back to the other people you were blackmailing, and then you'd go to jail." He considered the comment and grinned. "Or worse."

"I certainly didn't kill my sister," she scoffed while glaring at him. "Go to the police with that flash drive. You can't prove I blackmailed anyone."

"I don't have to prove anything," he replied with little concern. "I just need to open my big mouth. The accusation will be enough." Dane's eyes widened in false horror. "Imagine if all those people you've been blackmailing find out it's been you all along--" He shook his head then smiled deviously. "I wouldn't want to be you when they found out, and I doubt they'd be interested in whether or not there was any proof."

There was a tense moment of silence between them as they exchanged glares across the desk. Elana sneered at him and sat on the edge of the desk facing him.

"Callie knew her affair with Farley wasn't going to end in him divorcing his wife, so we came up with the blackmailing scheme together," Elana informed him. "Callie realized it would require her involvement in a sex tape, but she knew it would be worth it in the end. Besides, if we played our cards right, Farley would be the only one seeing that video anyway." Elana managed a tiny laugh. "Callie even played the martyr going as far as to tell Farley not to pay the blackmailer. That way he'd never suspect either of our involvement." She stared at him and shifted uncomfortably. "Well, considering you haven't gone to the police, I assume you want something," she huffed. "Some sort of deal?"

"You're absolutely right," Dane informed her. "I want half of your take."

Elana gritted her teeth but seemed to have little choice if she didn't want the rumor coming out. "Fine, but then you stay the hell out of my way."

"Of course," Dane announced while grinning slyly. "I wouldn't want to prevent you from making us money, now would I?" He leaned back in his chair and raised a skeptical brow. "Oh, and by the way, you'll have to try harder the next time you try to frame me for murder. Planting that necklace and those old articles in my locked box was pretty stupid."

She could have attempted to deny the accusation, but she was more curious than anything else. "What did you do with the necklace?" Elana asked with some annoyance.

"I thought you said you didn't murder your sister?" Dane remarked while eyeing her cleverly. "You practically admitted to taking the necklace to frame me."

"I know what you're thinking," she insisted. "But you're wrong." Elana drew a deep breath and shifted on the corner of the desk. "After she screwed up things with Otto by fucking Nole, she came to me for help. The necklace was a down payment."

"Down payment on what?"

She rolled her eyes and groaned. "Keefe and I were going to help her extract money from Otto." She raised her brows. "One way or another." Elana adamantly shook her head. "But I didn't kill my sister. She was alive when I left her in the gazebo around twelve thirty." She frowned and again studied him. "So what did you do with the necklace?"

"Let's just say I intend to use it to get Mr. Steele off of a murder charge," he informed her. "Unlike you, I know how to frame a person and get away with it."

"Why would you want to get Otto off the murder charges?" she demanded. "If he takes the fall, the police stop their investigation."

"Oh, I have bigger plans," Dane informed her. "A little grooming and some prodding, I can arrange it, so you'll be the next Mrs. Steele." He grinned slyly and chuckled in his throat. "And that would be far more profitable for both of us, don't you agree?"

"I don't think Keefe would be too keen on the idea," she informed him.

"You don't need Keefe anymore," he informed her. "With my brains and Mr. Steele's wealth, you and I can have everything. It's perfect."

She considered his ingenious plan then laughed. "I like the way you think," Elana announced while grinning. "I knew you weren't actually retired. You were waiting for the right moment to strike, weren't you?"

"I have my faults," Dane informed her. "If you had me to guide you from the very beginning, you wouldn't have had to use Callie as a go-between to Mr. Steele's money. It could have been you all along. Lucky for you I don't hold a grudge against you for trying to have me killed."

"When did I try to have you killed?" she asked with surprise.

"When you hired those men to kill Brenda Steele two years ago," Dane informed her. "That was the plan, wasn't it? Kill Mrs. Steele and frame me? That's why you planted those old articles in my locked box. It was supposed to look like I killed her and she fatally wounded me during the attack. Your first mistake was hiring outside help. Your second mistake was not anticipating Miller and Raina's early arrival. I guess I really screwed your plans that night, didn't I?"

She stared at him with surprise and shook her head. "You've got that all wrong," Elana insisted as her eyes widened. "I never killed anyone. I'll admit; the death of Otto's wife was a stroke of luck for Callie, but I certainly wouldn't condone killing anyone."

"Oh?"

"Our original plan to dig up dirt on Otto was almost screwed when Callie started admiring Brenda's jewelry," Elana admitted. "Callie always had a thing for emeralds. Brenda caught her in her jewelry box, but when she didn't take the necklace, she decided to confront Callie without involving you. I guess Brenda knew you would immediately fire her. I think Brenda felt sorry for Callie, and since she didn't actually steal the necklace, she decided to give her another chance." Elana added a tiny laugh. "Callie was concerned you would find out and fire her anyway, that's when we had Keefe dig up dirt on your past. Callie planted those articles in your locked box as an insurance policy. You know; in case you became meddlesome."

"I was the wild card, huh?" he teased, mocking his past.

"Sure, Callie found your locked box shortly after she arrived here. I guess she was hoping to steal something of value then changed her mind," Elana informed him. "Those passports you were hiding were worth more than the money you had hidden, but you can't con a conman." She managed a tiny laugh. "Naturally, she let me in on what she'd found but blackmailing you wouldn't be worth the trouble you'd bring. I told her to leave you alone and stay as far away from you as possible. When Callie was murdered, I just wanted the investigation ended, and you had the most incriminating past to make that happen."

"Yes, lucky me," he muttered.

"After Brenda's death, Callie, Keefe, and I plotted and planned a way to move my sister from maid to lady of the house," Elana explained then laughed. "With Raina and Miller out of the house, it made her seduction of Otto that much easier. She just needed to keep you from finding out until Otto was already head-over-heels for her and could keep you in check."

"And you were right to assume that," he announced. "Had I caught her coming on to Mr. Steele, I would have fired her on the spot." He hesitated and studied her. "I guess things didn't work out for either of you in the end, huh?"

"Actually, everything was going according to plan," Elana corrected him. "I intended to blackmail her with her very own videos after she was married to Otto, but then she had to go and fuck it up, literally, by doing Nole on her wedding day." She frowned and shook her head with distaste. "I don't know what she saw in him. I guess he was good in bed--and over a desk. It was obvious Otto would divorce her. It was all going to be over before it even began. When the police ruled her death murder, I had to find a scapegoat. Who better than the butler with evidence already in his locked box from two years ago. It seemed perfect."

"I suppose it did seem perfect," Dane announced then shrugged. "I guess I'm just too sneaky for my own good. Try to remember that."

"There is one minor problem standing between you and me cleaning out old Otto," Elana informed him.

"You mean Keefe?"

"I mean, he's a lot of fun, but he's not the brightest guy," she insisted then shrugged. "Other than flexing his muscles, he doesn't bring much to the party. Know what I mean?" She smiled almost seductively at Dane. "With you as my new partner, we don't need him, and we wouldn't want to share all Otto's money with him."

"Are you saying you'd like to 'terminate' your relationship with him?" Dane asked.

Elana laughed then smiled. "You really are smart, aren't you?" She shook her head. "I want nothing to do with killing anyone, but I'm sure you could find a way to pin the murders on him. That would be enough to remove him from the picture. You're smart, right?"

"I'm grossly underestimated," he announced then grinned. "I hear and see everything in this house, and no one notices me. Let me worry about Keefe. You just go upstairs and act naturally. I'll have a foolproof plan by morning."

She stood and eyed him while grinning. "Callie had no idea what she was giving up with you," Elana announced and gave him a quick once-over. "After we have all Otto's money, maybe you and I could be more than partners."

"Concentrate on Otto," he informed her and showed little reaction to her seduction scene. "You need to succeed where Callie failed. We don't need another repeat of that wedding night."

"You're right. Just keep that in mind," she announced while grinning. "See you in the morning."

As Elana left the study, Dane leaned back in the chair and stared at the open doorway while deep in thought. Only a few minutes passed before Raina entered the study and shut the door behind her. She leaned against the door with her arms across her chest and a cold look on her face.

"I think I'm going to be sick," she muttered.

"You and me both," he announced while frowning.

"Please tell me she confessed to everything and you got it all on video," Raina remarked and finally straightened.

Dane casually removed an expensive tie clip and held it up. "It's all right here on my little spycam," he announced then frowned and tossed it across the desk. He groaned with defeat and rubbed his eyes. "She didn't kill anyone."

Raina stared at him with surprise then turned angry while approaching the desk. "She's lying."

"No," he replied with a defeated sigh. "She confessed to blackmailing just about everyone and even how she tried to frame me for her sister's murder. Unfortunately, I believe her when she says she didn't kill anyone."

She looked at him with concern. "Aren't you afraid she'll tell the police about your past?" Raina asked. "It would look very bad for you if Detective Payne learns you were a jewel thief."

"She has no proof," Dane reminded her. "I was trained to cover my tracks and vanish without a trace. Detective Payne can dig all he wants; he'll never find anything to link me to those thefts. According to my real passport, I haven't even left the country since my discharge from the service. She has more to lose by turning me in. I've got the goods on her blackmail operation."

Raina sat on the edge of the desk and held her head. "At least you're in the clear," she scoffed then straightened. "Unfortunately, that still leaves my father and Miller back on the prime suspect list."

Dane stood, approached her, and pulled her into his arms. She clung to him while resting her head on his shoulders and gently smoothed his suit jacket.

"We'll figure out a way to clear them," he insisted softly in her ear. "I promise you; neither of them will be framed for murder. I just need time to connect the dots." He sighed and pulled back to look into her eyes and offered a reassuring smile. "Between the two of us, we can figure this out."

She stared into his eyes a long, silent moment. "I don't want to be alone tonight," Raina said almost timidly.

Dane smiled while staring into her eyes. "I'll be up in ten minutes with tea," he announced and gently touched her face.

He kissed her warmly but passionately then hesitated and opened the desk drawer. He removed his semiautomatic and handed it to her. She stared at it a moment with some confusion.

"I want you to keep this on you, for protection," he informed her.

"Are you sure?" she asked. "Shouldn't you keep it on you?"

"No, I have my shotgun," he replied then grinned. "And I suspect we'll be spending a lot of time together, so it's best you keep it on you."

She smiled timidly and accepted the gun. Raina placed the gun down the back of her pants and covered the handle with her shirt. Dane walked her to the study door where they parted ways. Raina headed for the main stairs while Dane headed for the kitchen. Raina paused by the banister at the bottom of the grand stairs and looked down the hall toward the kitchen. Dane paused near the kitchen door at the opposite end and stared back at her while smiling. He blew her a kiss then danced backward through the kitchen door without taking his eyes off her. Raina laughed and headed up the stairs.

Chapter 54
Raina Days and Mondays

Early the following morning. Dane woke in Raina's bed and reached alongside him to find her spot vacant. It was five o'clock in the morning and only three hours after they'd gone to bed. It was at least half an hour until sunrise, but by the sounds of the pouring rain that had continued throughout the night, there wouldn't be any sun. Dane looked across the room and noticed the bathroom door was open and the area beyond it remained dark. Dane turned over in bed and scanned the room. Raina sat on the window seat with her head against the wall and stared into the darkness at the pouring rain. She was miles away in her own thoughts. Dane sat up in bed and scratched his mildly mussed hair.

"Did you get any sleep last night?" he asked.

She didn't look at him, and her expression didn't change as she pulled her knees to her chest. "Not really," Raina gently replied.

"Are you worried about your father being questioned by the police?" he pressed.

"A little," she replied then shifted uncomfortably. "I hate the rain."

"I'm not particularly fond of it either," he announced then lay on his side facing her while propped on his elbow. "If there's a moment in time that shapes and defines who you are for the rest of your life, mine was the night my grandfather died."

Raina looked at him as the words left his mouth and felt her heart sink. They stared into each other's eyes across the dimly lit room a long moment without comment.

Dane shifted beneath the covers then managed a tiny smile. "Your father told you, didn't he?"

"Yeah," she replied softly. "I dragged it out of him." Raina shifted uncomfortably while studying him. "Why did you run away?"

"Don't you remember what you were like at fifteen?" he teased then frowned. "I'd lost my entire family over the course of a few years. I was angry at the world. I heard your father talking to child services. I knew he wanted me to stay, but I didn't want anyone feeling sorry for me. I didn't want the burden of caring about anyone again."

Raina moved off the window seat and joined him on the bed. She crawled under the covers with him and snuggled against him then met his gaze.

"Where did you go?" she asked delicately. "You were only fifteen."

"I went home," he replied and offered a tiny smile. "My parent's home had been left abandoned. A rickety, old farmhouse in the middle of nowhere. Yes, I'm a farmer's son. I planted corn, milked the cows, and shoveled shit."

She managed a tiny laugh trying to imagine him working on a farm. Her look turned serious. "How were you able to survive on your own in the middle of nowhere?" Raina asked with surprise.

"There were still some crops growing. I planted some of my own as well, and my friends would bring me things," he replied then shrugged while frowning. "Other things I'd steal. A year or so later, my friend's brother talked about joining the military. I wanted to find a new life, so I followed him."

Raina stared at him a moment then skeptically raised her brows. "You couldn't have been eighteen."

He chuckled and shook his head. "No, I was two months from turning seventeen at the time. I didn't have a driver's license or a birth certificate. The recruiter was nice enough to take my word and that of my friend's brother that I was eighteen." Dane frowned. "He died during our first tour in Iraq."

She again felt her heart sink. "You really did lose everything you ever cared about."

Dane offered a strange smile. "You asked why they called me 'Great Dane'," he remarked then raised his brows. "Every unit has that one man willing to sacrifice himself above all others. He's usually the man with nothing else to lose. He doesn't worry that he might die, because he has nothing left to live for."

She stared at him, feeling the horror, but she understood. "You had a death wish," Raina replied softly.

"There are two types of soldiers who get medals for bravery," he informed her while raising his brows. "Those who are brave and those who are stupid." He grinned almost proudly. "I'm the latter."

"I doubt that," she affectionately replied and caressed his chest. She then stared at him with concern. "You don't still have a death wish, do you?"

He eyed her with surprise, grinned, and chuckled in his throat. "Hell, no." Dane then considered the comment. "Although, you might be disappointed to learn that only changed when I came to work for your father and stepmother. I finally had a family." He hesitated and raised his brows. "Not that I didn't have a family in the military, but constantly being vigilant in keeping them alive during life-and-death situations only intensified the risk-taking."

Raina kissed him affectionately on the lips then touched his face while staring into his eyes. "I realize I wasn't the nicest person toward you back then," she informed him. "But despite what you thought, I never tried to get you fired. Maybe after our first clash, but I actually enjoyed fighting with you." She made a face. "Miller *never* argued with me. It was quite annoying."

Dane laughed and pulled her against him while nuzzling her. "Not that I didn't enjoy our uncivilized behavior toward each other, but I prefer holding your naked body to mine."

She gently caressed his shoulders and chest while staring into his eyes. "As strange as it sounds; the pouring rain makes me want you more."

He grinned and brushed his lips past hers. "It is rather romantic."

Dane kissed her warmly but passionately. She immediately returned the kiss with a little more aggression. Dane groaned, flipped her onto her back, and positioned himself on top of her while kissing her.

§

Just before sunup, Miller thundered down the grand stairs in his bare feet. He had hastily pulled on a pair of pants and was attempting to slip into a white, button shirt on his way down the stairs. He jumped the last few steps and ran to the foyer, scaling the few steps before reaching the double doors. He unlocked and threw open the door. A man walked past the fountain toward the front patio while braving the pouring rain and violent wind.

"Dad," Miller cried out and stepped onto the patio beneath the covered porch.

Otto had his hands in his pockets and was in no particular hurry up the outer steps. He was already soaked. He groaned as he approached Miller, who eyed him with surprise.

"Why didn't you call for someone to pick you up at the police station?" Miller demanded. "Did your lawyer drop you off at the bottom of the driveway? What the hell--?"

"He had no choice," Otto replied and stepped into the foyer while dripping wet.

Miller entered and closed the door behind them. "Why's that?"

"The bridge is completely flooded," Otto explained with little patience. "In case you hadn't noticed, it's pouring like a bastard out there."

"Completely flooded?" Miller asked. "Impassable?"

"That's what completely flooded means, Miller," Otto grumbled.

"The house phones are down, but why didn't you call our cell phones?" Miller demanded. "We could have met you at the bottom of the lane. My God, that's a quarter of a mile trek up the driveway."

Otto glared demandingly at him. "I did call. I called Titus, Levi, and Dane," he announced with impatience. "No one answered." He shook his head while frowning. "Everyone still doped from the earlier drugging? I get Levi not hearing the phone. He can't hear anything over his own snoring, but why didn't Titus answer? Why isn't Dane picking up his cell phone?"

Miller tensed and rubbed the back of his neck. "I'm guessing Titus turned his off," Miller remarked then fidgeted. "Dane probably left his phone in his jacket pocket on vibrate again."

Otto glared at Miller through squinting eyes. "Dane's never forgotten his phone in his jacket pocket," he remarked. "And he can hear that thing vibrate a mile away in the middle of the night--even above Levi's snoring."

"Maybe he's in the shower. He's usually in the kitchen by six," Miller informed him. "You can yell at him after you've showered and changed into some dry clothes." He then turned enthusiastic. "Why don't I tell him to bring you an Irish decaf coffee to your room?"

Otto stared at Miller a moment as if attempting to read his expression then waved him off. "Yeah, you do that," he muttered and sloshed his way up the stairs.

Miller cringed then headed down the hallway for the kitchen. Once he was past the stairs, he ran for the kitchen.

§

Miller silently ran up the back kitchen stairs and paused at the top of the second floor. He peered down the corridor and saw Otto enter his master bedroom. Once the door shut, Miller ran quietly down the hallway and stopped outside Raina's bedroom door. He tapped lightly on the door but feared knocking too loud or others would hear. When there was no response, Miller felt his pockets and removed his credit card. He slipped it between the door and the frame near the doorknob and easily sprang the lock. Miller opened the door and saw a mass moving beneath the sheets along with soft male and female moans. Miller ran his fingers through his hair while fidgeting and cleared his throat. Dane leaped off Raina, rolled across the mattress, and nearly fell from the bed. Raina pulled the sheet across her naked body and gasped with horror while looking at the door. She stared at her stepbrother with shock, which was quickly replaced with anger.

"Damn it, Miller," she cried out in a harsh whisper.

Dane attempted to hide under the sheets, partially hidden by the now sitting woman.

"I'm sorry," he announced while fidgeting. "Really sorry, but Dad's home." Miller shifted from foot-to-foot while looking anywhere but at the bed. "The bridge is out. He's soaked from the walk and pissed that Dane didn't answer his cell phone, which is why he had to walk the entire way to the house."

"Son-of-a-bitch," Dane muttered just loud enough for Raina to hear.

"Wonderful," she huffed with little emotion while glaring at her brother. "That's fucking fantastic. Exactly why are you bothering me?"

"Because he's going to come looking for Dane, and I don't think you want Dad finding him naked in your bed," Miller announced matter-of-factly.

"Give it up, Raina," Dane muttered and poked his head out from beneath the covers. "He obviously knows."

"Considering your bed is against our connecting wall," Miller announced sarcastically, "yeah, I know." He shifted uncomfortably. "So get lover boy dressed and out of your room before Dad gets out of the shower."

Miller left the room and quietly closed the door behind him. He turned and saw his father leaning against the wall a few feet away with his arms folded across his soaked body. Miller jumped with surprise but refrained from gasping.

"Did Dane give an ETA on the Irish coffee?" Otto scoffed while raising his brows.

"I, uh, well--"

Otto rolled his eyes and straightened. "Relax, Miller," he muttered. "I know more about what goes on around here than most people think. Those two are good for each other. Once they stopped fighting, it was only a matter of time before they figured it out." He then frowned. "Tell him to shower first, because if he smells like sex, I'll have to kill him."

Otto casually turned and headed back to his room on the opposite side of Raina's room. Miller stared after his stepfather and exhaled.

Chapter 55

Butler Knows Best

Raina entered the dimly lit kitchen from the back stairs an hour before breakfast and looked around. Despite having fixed the power issue from the night before, they were again operating on the backup generator. The generator only allowed for a few lights and specific outlets to remain on, making the kitchen unusually dark. This time the power was knocked out from the storm, and they'd have to wait it out. They had been unable to fix whatever had been done to the landline phone. The storm continued to rage outside the windows, leaving the morning dark as night. The staff had collected around the island counter with their morning coffee and discussed the emergency plan for getting through the storm. Raina remained by the bottom of the stairs and watched Dane take charge of the situation and hand out instructions to the rest of the staff. She enjoyed 'Dane in charge'. His commanding and authoritative presence was a complete turn-on.

She didn't want to interrupt their meeting. Despite that the backup generator would mean that those inside the house would be quite comfortable, Dane was treating it like a matter of national security. He took his job seriously, and the staff's job was to ensure that their employers and the houseguests were comfortable. His last statement resonated with her, and she now understood the seriousness of what should have been a mundane situation. They had a house full of guests, but more importantly, one of them was possibly the man or woman who gutted Nole!

Raina saw a metal box on the counter that she'd seen before in the bottom cupboard. Having never been curious about it, she never opened it. Dane opened the box and set a dozen miniature hand radios on the counter then removed just as many hand-sized flashlights. The staff began checking each one to ensure they all worked properly. Raina made her way closer to the counter now and eyed the staff. Despite her presence, Dane continued with his meeting.

"Apart from the staff, there are eleven guests," Dane informed them. "That means we'll all need to pull together to ensure their comfort and safety." He looked at Levi. "How many kerosene lanterns do we have?"

"Ten, I believe," Levi informed him. "But they're in the basement storeroom. We also have a few dozen candles down there as well."

"We should be okay until this evening," Dane announced. "After breakfast, you and Hanson can secure the lanterns and candles from the basement. We'll need them set up in the common rooms for additional light later tonight." He eyed the staff. "We're going to play this safe. Everyone gets a partner. Levi and Hanson will be team one, and Titus and Sloan will be team two."

"Leaves you one short of a team," Sloan informed him.

"I'll be tending to the family," Dane remarked matter-of-factly. "With Mr. Steele's permission, I want to seal off the unused rooms thereby keeping the guests in a few, select common rooms."

"You sound a bit paranoid there," Hanson informed Dane.

"I am paranoid," Dane informed the gardener. "We're not only dealing with a storm and limited resources with the backup generator, but someone in this house may be a killer."

The staff suddenly grasped the seriousness of their situation and shifted looks among themselves.

"The phones have been down since last night," Sloan announced with concern.

"I haven't been able to get a signal on my cell phone either," Titus reported. "That must mean the cell towers are down or overloaded from the storm."

"And now you understand why I'm paranoid," Dane informed them. "I don't have to remind you that just last night someone drugged almost everyone in the house while they murdered a man. For all intents and purposes, we have to assume the killer is still in the house."

"And we're completely cut off," Hanson muttered with a horrifying realization.

"Additionally, the backup battery for the alarm system was drained last night," Dane informed them. "So we don't even have that to back us up in an emergency."

"What's the situation with the driveway?" Hanson then asked. "Is it passable?"

"Early this morning, Mr. Steele managed to cross the bridge in waist deep water," Dane informed them. "Miller took a quick drive down there less than an hour ago, and the water is now above the bridge walls. The stream is a raging river and impassable by car or on foot. At its current speed, anyone attempting to cross would be pulled away." He eyed the staff. "We're stranded here for at least twenty-four hours *after* the rain stops with zero communication with the outside world."

"Even hiking the woods would be too dangerous," Hanson informed them. "The stream on the other side of the property is probably just as bad. Even if we made it that far, there's no one living anywhere nearby in that direction."

"That's why we're going to stay put and ride it out," Dane informed them. "I already spoke to Mr. Steele, and he's going to suggest that his guests stick together as much as possible, particularly toward evening." He straightened proudly. "Team one and two will each have a walkie-talkie, and I'll have one. This will allow us to communicate with one another. Otto and Miller Steele will each have one as well. The remaining seven will be distributed among the guests once Mr. Steele has them paired."

"I don't get one?" Raina finally announced, interrupting their meeting.

Dane didn't even bother looking at her. "You don't need one," he replied.

"Seems a little sexist," she remarked. "Seeing how my father and brother each have their own."

Dane cast a look at her but didn't comment. She wasn't sure what his look meant.

Sloan smiled with a slightly mocking stare and patted Raina's shoulder. "I think you've just been paired up with Dane, dear," she announced and held back her giggle.

Raina eyed Sloan, wondering what she was suggesting and how much she actually knew. Dane then eyed her and raised his brows. His look told her all she needed to know. Raina shifted uncomfortably and eyed the remaining staff. Levi, Hanson, and Titus were now hiding their smirks. She cast a look at Dane.

"Wow," Raina announced while shaking her head in disbelief. "I guess you lose points for that discretion you pride yourself on."

"Don't blame his discretion," Levi informed her. "He's as tight-lipped as always. When I ran into him in the kitchen early this morning, he was still in the same suit he wore yesterday." The cook then raised his brows. "And he wasn't shower-fresh either."

"Besides," Titus announced while grinning. "When a man who's been sexually deprived for years has a full night of 'anything goes', he's not nearly as big of a dick to his co-workers."

"Okay," Dane snarled and glared at the others. "Enough already. Show a little respect and an ounce of class. Now everyone has a job to do, so let's get started." He spun his hand in the air. "Let's get breakfast rolling. The guests will be getting up soon."

Levi had Hanson's help with breakfast while Sloan had Titus help her stack dishes on the rolling cart to prepare the dining room table. Raina approached Dane, who seemed tense and moderately embarrassed.

"I'm really sorry, Raina," he announced delicately. "Levi was already in the kitchen when I slipped down the back stairs. I knew he was a gossip, but I didn't know he was quite so observant."

"It's okay," Raina replied and offered a warm smile. "I don't care that they know. Now that my father knows, it's easier having it out in the open anyway."

"You don't mind that people know you're sneaking around with the hired help?" he asked timidly.

"Mind?" she asked then laughed and patted his chest. "I'm proud of that little fact."

Dane groaned then looked over his shoulder at Levi and Hanson, who were busily working on breakfast and lightly arguing as usual. He looked back at Raina and leaned closer to her.

"I have to remain professional in front of the rest of the staff," he informed her in a soft tone then grinned. "But don't think for a moment I won't ravish you the first moment we're alone together."

Raina smiled and laughed. "Oh, I'm counting on it," she cooed then played with his tie while giving him a devious and seductive once-over. "I'm also accepting that as a challenge. If you thought I tormented you with our arguments, just wait. Our new relationship is going to be a lot more fun."

Raina winked and ran her hand firmly past his crotch as she walked past him and left the kitchen. Dane shut his eyes and held back his groan of pleasure.

"I knew it," he muttered to himself. "This whole thing was a six-year revenge plot in the making."

"Did you say something?" Levi asked, shaking Dane from his fantasy.

Dane looked back at the two men at the counter then snatched a walkie-talkie. "I told the girl not to go off on her own, but she never listens," he announced. "I'd better make sure she arrives safely with the others."

He hurried from the kitchen after Raina. Levi rolled his eyes and shook his head while Hanson stared after the butler with bewilderment.

"Was that code for a quickie?" Hanson asked Levi.

"Yeah, I think so," Levi remarked then shrugged. "If it makes him less of a prick, I'm all for it."

§

Dane hurried with a determined, serious walk down the nearly dark grand hallway after Raina. She looked back and saw the serious look on his face.

"Is something wrong?" she asked while grinning almost mockingly.

He shook his head while frowning. "I told you not to go off on your own," Dane snapped while taking her arm, surprising her. He hurried her into the library then shut and locked the door behind them. Only a few minutes later, Miller and Jenna walked down the grand hallway toward the kitchen and heard a strange thumping sound from the closed library door. Miller stopped Jenna and listened a moment by the closed door. His brows knitted in confusion. He attempted to open the door but discovered it was locked. The thumping sound stopped. Miller eyed Jenna with bewilderment then tapped on the door.

"Hey, is someone in there?" he announced.

The door unlocked and was opened, revealing Dane. He stepped out and closed the door behind him then eyed Miller with a serious look. "Ah, there you are," Dane announced. "We have a walkie-talkie and flashlight for you in the kitchen. I'll get them for you."

Miller watched as Dane walked down the hall toward the kitchen without emotion then shrugged and followed him. Jenna paused before the closed library door and pushed it open. Raina sat on the window seat with a book in her hand and appeared to be watching the rain outside the window. Jenna entered the library and approached her friend.

"Just hanging out, huh?" Jenna asked and paused before Raina.

She looked at her friend and smiled while attempting to control her heavy breathing. "Yeah, not much else to do," Raina replied.

"There's plenty to do on a rainy day with the power out," Jenna informed her. She then picked up the book from Raina's hand, turned it the correct direction, and returned it while grinning. "But I'm guessing you already know that."

Raina groaned while hiding her smile then laughed. "He's such a little devil," she remarked.

"Hit and run, huh?" Jenna teased while grinning.

"Is that what the kids are calling it," Raina asked with a laugh.

"Yeah, and I'm guessing he's mastered it. Maybe he could teach that move to Miller," Jenna announced then sighed. "I'm afraid he has a lot to learn. He's a little too reserved to play it fast and loose."

"Miller is more of a 'play by the rules' kind of guy," Raina teased.

"I'm going to need to put in a lot of overtime teaching him the art of ignoring those rules," Jenna remarked. "Sloan told me of at least ten places around the estate practically designed with quickies in mind."

"Really?" Raina asked with surprise then sat forward while eagerly eyeing her friend. "Where?"

Chapter *56*
Seriously? It's Still Raining?

As the rainy afternoon progressed into a stormy evening, the mansion guests were becoming restless. Drinking turned into the number one pastime, as they would be stranded for another night. The staff remained in the game room along with the guests and the homeowners. Otto, Miller, Raina, and Jenna refused to drink any alcohol despite their frayed nerves. The staff remained sober as well. Even Levi was no longer interested in drinking. After being drugged the night before, it was understandable, which was why Raina didn't understand why their guests were interested in drinking. It wasn't as if there was much to do as the house got increasingly darker with only the emergency power running, so it seemed like the only thing they could do.

Titus suggested a game of Texas Hold'em to help pass the time. Otto eagerly accepted the poker invitation, which took place at the felt-topped table in the corner of the game room. While Titus, Hanson, Otto, Miller, Levi, and Jimmy Love prepared for a marathon game of poker, Keefe and Elana seemed to be having a falling out of sorts near the bar. Dane, who was currently playing bartender, didn't seem too surprised by the rising tension between the couple. The Nixon's, who were also at the bar, attempted to mind their own business, but Gilda was secretly smiling at the feuding couple.

"What the hell has gotten into you?" Keefe demanded while glaring at Elana.

"What's gotten into me?" she demanded with surprise then pointed an accusing finger at him. "You're the one acting like a first-rate jerk."

"Oh, I get it," Keefe launched as he stood. "There's someone else, isn't there?"

Elana rolled her eyes even though she couldn't meet his gaze. "Oh, please."

Keefe's eyes widened, and he pointed an accusing finger at her. "There is," he cried out then looked around the room. "Since you just turned into a complete bitch in the last twenty-four hours that must mean it's someone here in this house."

"That's ridiculous," she protested then shook her head while sneering at him. "You know what? I don't care where you sleep tonight, but it's not going to be in my room. Find another bed."

"That's fine with me," Keefe shouted back and leaped up from his bar stool. He took a moment to cool off then approached the sitting area where Sloan played a board game with Raina and Jenna. Keefe attempted to control his temper. "Sloan, is there another room I can have for tonight?"

"Yes, of course," Sloan informed him. "You can have the last room on the left near the kitchen stairs. First room on the right, if you're going up the back stairs."

"Thanks," he replied with a depressed sigh then eyed the poker game.

Otto had observed the entire scene. He shook his head and motioned Keefe to join their game. Keefe gratefully accepted the invitation to play poker. Once Keefe had left the bar, Elana exchanged looks with Dane, who poured her another drink. She frowned and thanked him. She was about to sip her drink when she caught the humored look on Gilda's face. Elana slammed her glass down and glared at Gilda.

"What the hell is your problem?" Elana cried out. "Do you think that's funny?"

"A little," Gilda teased then giggled while sipping her martini.

"Ladies," Dane announced in a stern tone. "Anyone fighting won't be served."

Gilda and Elana both frowned and minded their own business. Farley expressed his gratitude to Dane with a thankful look.

Raina, Jenna, and Sloan continued to work their way through a stack of old board games in order to entertain themselves while remaining sober. Although it seemed random, the staff and homeowners were strategically placed around the room to keep an eye on the others. There was an excellent chance one of them was a killer. Raina didn't care what Elana told Dane; she was still convinced she had something to do with the murders. While around the guests, Raina and Dane were careful to disassociate themselves from each other. Dane was sticking close to Elana, who believed they were conspiring against Keefe. Elana believed Dane intended to frame Keefe for the murders and rid them of him so they could team up. Raina hated the idea, but she trusted Dane's judgment.

§

Two hours later, the poker game was still going strong. The men were joking around and having a good time trashing one another. They received several looks from Sloan, Raina, and Jenna as their conversations became vile and distasteful. Jenna frowned and shook her head.

"Men, huh?" Sloan remarked with a tiny laugh. She was obviously enjoying her newly budding relationship with her old flame judging by the way that she kept sneaking peeks at Titus.

Raina eyed her friend and offered a sympathetic look. "If their trash talk is bothering you, Jenna, I could ask them to tone it down."

"No," Jenna announced with a sigh. "I'm bummed because I'm not playing with them."

Sloan and Raina exchanged surprised looks then laughed at the comment.

"No one's stopping you from joining them," Raina insisted while laughing. "Go play poker, if you want."

"No," Jenna replied with a defeated sigh then eyed Raina. "I'll sit this one out. I don't know that it will help my newly found relationship with Miller if I beat him at pool *and* kick his ass at poker."

"Oh, you need to play it cool," Sloan announced and shook her head while keeping a straight face. "You need to stroke a man's ego in the beginning of a relationship." She then smirked. "You don't snip his balls and crush his dreams until after you're married."

Jenna and Raina looked at Sloan. All three laughed at the comment. The three women were alerted to an altercation and raised voices at the bar. Elana and Gilda were screaming at each other and just about crushing poor Farley, who was seated between the two drunken women. Dane leaped over the bar, grabbed Elana around the waist, and held her back while practically pulling her claws from Farley as she attempted to reach Gilda. Dane pulled Elana away from the bar while she kicked and screamed like a wild woman.

Everyone within the game room heard Elana screaming, "You bitch!"

"Settle down," Dane announced without releasing Elana then eyed both women. "The bar is officially closed to the two of you."

"Fine," Gilda scoffed in a drunken tone. She snatched her drink then glared at her husband. "Finish your drink. We're going to our room."

Farley frowned but obediently did as he was told. Both finished their drinks in a few swallows. As Gilda stumbled toward the game room door, Farley followed with less enthusiasm. Elana stopped struggling against Dane's arms and relaxed, allowing him to release her. As she turned with some unsteadiness to face him, he shook his head with disapproval.

Elana smiled sweetly and moved a little closer to him. "Now that the shrew is gone," she announced. "How about another drink?"

His look didn't soften any at the drunken woman. "I wasn't kidding," Dane informed her with little emotion. "You've had enough."

She huffed with annoyance then looked around the room. Everyone had returned to what they were doing and pretended they hadn't been watching the incident. Elana looked back at Dane.

"Great," she scoffed while leaning heavily on the bar to hold herself up. "What am I supposed to do the rest of the night?"

"There's an intense game of Monopoly being played over there," Dane announced and indicated the three women. "Maybe you can get in on that action."

Elana rolled her eyes and groaned. "I'd rather go to bed," she huffed then eyed Dane and smiled almost slyly. "No one is supposed to go anywhere alone. Will you walk me to my room?"

Dane reluctantly nodded and left the game room with Elana, who was just about falling down drunk. She clung to his arm while giggling and flirting. Although secretly opposing it, Raina watched while Dane escorted the drunken woman from the room. Raina received stares from Sloan and Jenna from around the coffee table where they played their board games. She frowned and attempted to get back into the game.

"Whose turn was it?" Raina asked, no longer interested in the game.

"I believe it was yours," Sloan announced.

"Did you want to go along with them in case Dane needs assistance with her?" Jenna asked.

Raina shook her head despite being uncomfortable. "No," she replied. "He'll be fine. We agreed to maintain a low profile around the guests."

She couldn't admit to them that Dane was working an angle with Elana and needed some time alone with her. She also couldn't deny it made her a little jealous even if there was no reason to be. Raina wasn't the only one not happy about Dane escorting the drunken woman to her room. Keefe sat at the poker table with the guys and silently seethed. It was possible he thought Elana was dumping him for Dane. Essentially, Elana was doing just that but not in the way Keefe may have been thinking.

Dane returned to the game room almost forty minutes later, which seemed a little longer than necessary. Raina couldn't help feeling a little concerned that Elana attempted to seduce Dane in her drunken condition. Despite that it was entirely possible the woman came on to him, she was convinced Dane couldn't be seduced by someone like Elana. She was certain his feelings for her were true. Raina just wished she could dismiss the jealous pang in the pit of her stomach. Dane returned to the bar and picked up the dirty glasses when he caught Raina's glance across the room. He offered a tiny, secret smile then placed his hand to his heart and pointed at her. Raina hid her smile and resumed her game.

Chapter *57*

Things That Go Bump in the Night

Miller and Jenna walked with Raina along the second floor corridor toward her room just before midnight. Miller was issued a kerosene lantern to help brighten the mostly dark hallway despite the sporadic, emergency lights along the hallway. Normally, the emergency lights would be sufficient, but with the concern that someone in the house was a killer, the lamp allowed them to see all around them. They paused before Raina's bedroom door.

"I should check your room and make sure it's safe," Miller announced.

"I'm sure it's fine, Miller," Raina insisted then watched as he entered her room with the kerosene lamp. "Just about everyone is downstairs playing poker."

He ignored her and searched her room, checking the closet, bathroom, and under the bed. Raina stood with Jenna in the doorway and watched him search the room. Both women had their arms folded across their chests and shook their heads in unison.

"This takes me back to when he used to look under my bed for monsters," Raina remarked.

Jenna laughed and watched Miller make a spectacle of himself with his search. "That sounds sweet," Jenna remarked. "The big brother looking for monsters under his little sister's bed. I'll bet you two were cute together as children."

Raina frowned while watching Miller on his hands and knees looking beneath her bed. She sighed deeply. "Actually, I was referring to last week," she informed her friend.

Jenna eyed her with surprise.

"He's been more than a little paranoid since Alicia's murder," Raina informed her. "When we get home, he'll search the apartment for intruders, and he'll do another sweep before either of us goes to bed. If he hears any unusual sounds in the middle of the night, he searches the house with a baseball bat in his hands." She shook her head and watched her brother. "My bedroom door doesn't even close right after all the times he's broken it down when I'd awaken from a bad dream."

"Great," Jenna muttered. "It should be a fun night the first time I sleepwalk in front of him."

Miller returned to them and smiled proudly. "All clear," he announced then looked concerned. "Are you sure you'll be okay in your room by yourself tonight?"

"You don't have to worry," Raina informed him then smiled slyly. "I won't be alone for long."

§

The poker game was still going on strong after midnight and would possibly continue for another hour or more. None of the men seemed tired, and the game was the perfect distraction for them. Levi was knocked out first. He joined Sloan on the sofa, and helped her with a crossword puzzle. Dane continued to play bartender to Tia and Olivia, who watched the poker game from a distance and appeared bored.

"How long is that game going to last?" Tia finally asked while playing with her drink.

"Judging by the stacks of chips," Dane announced and raised his brows. "It could be a couple of hours."

Both women groaned.

"Jimmy Love promised he'd walk us to our rooms," Olivia pouted and was no longer interested in drinking.

"I'll walk you to your rooms," Dane informed them.

They glanced at Dane and offered polite smiles despite their uncomfortable looks.

"No offense, Dane," Olivia announced while hiding her smile. "But we'd rather wait for Jimmy Love."

He was puzzled by the comment despite the 'no offense' part. Both women giggled at the look they received.

Tia leaned across the bar and smiled at the butler. "Jimmy Love gives us foot massages," she informed him.

Dane eyed them a moment as if debating what that was code for. Both women again giggled.

"Actual foot massages," Olivia offered. "He has some sort of bizarre foot fetish and really gets into it."

"He does guys feet too," Tia informed him with a serious look. "In case you're interested."

Dane tensed then shifted. "Uh, thanks," he replied. "I'm good."

When Titus was knocked out of the poker game, there was a roar of laughter from the rest of the players. Titus grumbled and groaned but finally laughed about it. Levi and Sloan were quick to spring from the sofa and return to the staff quarters with Titus. Despite Titus having his own apartment above the garage, he chose to stay with Sloan in the staff wing so that they wouldn't be isolated in his apartment away from the house. Levi's room was only steps across the hall from Sloan's room, so he wouldn't technically be alone either. Once they had left the game room, it was just Otto, Hanson, Keefe, and Jimmy Love in the poker game.

The poker game ended a little after one o'clock in the morning. Hanson headed for the staff wing, where he'd be staying in one of the vacant rooms as an additional security measure. Since the game had broken up, Dane went with Hanson to the staff wing. Otto, Keefe, Jimmy Love, and the two ladies went upstairs together with another kerosene lamp to guide their way. Once they reached the second floor corridor, Keefe headed for his newly assigned room at the end of the hall and Otto headed for the master bedroom. Both men hesitated when they saw Jimmy Love follow the two women into Tia's bedroom. Jimmy Love paused in the doorway, looked back at both men on opposite ends of the corridor, grinned, and kicked his leg up in the air before dramatically entering the room behind the women. Keefe and Otto exchanged looks from opposite ends of the hall, shook their heads in unison, and then entered their respective rooms.

§

Thirty minutes later, Dane appeared on the back stairs and silently headed down the dimly lit corridor with his flashlight in his hand but kept it off. He approached Raina's room and was about to open the door when he heard a door gently shut. Dane hesitated and looked down the dark hallway. He didn't see anyone coming out of their rooms, and it didn't appear as if any of the doors had opened. He stared a moment at Otto's bedroom door just down the hall from Raina's room. When no one came out, he opened Raina's door and slipped into her dimly lit room. He silently shut the door behind him and flipped the lock into place. As he turned, Raina moved onto her elbow while half propped up beneath the covers and smiled at him. She was wearing a sexy nightgown he hadn't seen before.

"You're late," she teased.

He removed his jacket and tossed it onto the nearby chair as he approached the bed. He grinned as he crawled onto the bed with her without undressing.

"I had to wait for your father to go to bed before I even considered sneaking up here," he announced.

"He's aware of the game we're playing," she insisted while raising her brows. "Remember this morning?"

He hovered over her, affectionately kissed her, and then pulled back while smiling. "I know," Dane replied. "But I feel weird following you to your room in front of him."

She caressed his chest while he half-lay on top of her. "You'll have to get over that," Raina insisted. "I want our relationship out in the open."

"Me too. It's just, well," Dane replied with a little less conviction and appeared withdrawn, "I'm afraid I seek your father's approval a little more than you do."

"He approves," she replied then smiled affectionately. "You're fine."

"I'll feel better when he and I discuss it and get it into the open," Dane informed her then ran his hand along the sexy nightgown she wore. "Is this new? Where did you get it?"

"I borrowed it from Sloan," she cooed.

"I like it," he announced then kissed her warmly but passionately.

Chapter 58

Don't Get Jimmy Love's Boxers in a Bunch

Early the following morning before what should have been sunrise, a woman's shrill scream woke Raina and Dane. Dane jumped away from Raina and leaped from the bed, looking around with disorientation. The woman's scream was heard again alerting them to danger. Dane pulled on his pants and ran for the bedroom door while Raina slipped into Dane's discarded dress shirt. She hurried after him as he entered the second floor corridor. Everyone ran into the hallway to discover Jimmy Love screaming like a hysterical woman in the middle of the corridor. For a moment, everyone was confused then saw him pointing at the floor. A man's blood-covered fingers were sticking out from the gap beneath the door.

Dane moved Jimmy Love aside and promptly pounded on the door, but there was no response. He attempted to open the door, but it was locked from the inside.

"That's Elana's room," Raina announced with concern then eyed Dane, who patted down his pants pockets while searching for something to pick the lock.

"She's in front of the door," Miller informed him. "You can't break it down or you'll hit her with the door."

"The Nixon's room has the connecting bathroom," Otto insisted then pointed down the hall.

"Those aren't Elana's fingers," Jenna announced with alarm. "That's a man's hand."

The rest of the guests were filtering into the hallway as Dane ran down the hall to the connecting bedroom belonging to Farley and Gilda Nixon. Dane attempted to open the door, but it was also locked. He pounded on the door to wake the Nixon's, but no one responded. Miller pulled a credit card from his pocket and ran to join him by the door. Dane didn't bother waiting for him and shoved his bare shoulder into the door. On the second thrust, the door broke open. Otto hurried behind him with his kerosene lamp to brighten the room. Both paused in the doorway to the Nixon's room to see Gilda peacefully sleeping in her bed despite the door being broken. It seemed odd she didn't wake from the screaming, banging, and crashing door.

Jenna grabbed Miller's flashlight and ran for the bed while Dane, Otto, and Raina headed through the connecting bathroom and into Elana's bedroom. All three stopped as the kerosene lamp brightened the dark bedroom. Elana lay sprawled across the blood-soaked sheets with several gashes and cuts along her naked body. She had an unmistakable stab wound to her abdomen as well as cuts and slashes along her arms appearing to be defensive wounds from the violent attack. The center of the bed was saturated with blood, and there were more spatters along the headboard and on the sheet partially draped over Elana's bare legs. Raina held back her gasp while staring with horror. It was a lot of blood! How was it possible one woman bled that much?

Dane grabbed Otto's arm and spun the kerosene lamp toward the door since they had seen someone's fingers in the space beneath it. Raina looked toward the door as well. Farley lay naked, face down in front of the door. He had several stab wounds on his back indicating he'd attempted to escape the killer but didn't make it far. Oddly enough, there seemed to be little blood surrounding the wounds. Raina thought it seemed strange that his back wasn't covered in blood, but it was still enough to make her gag. Farley's backside was covered with horrible rigor mortis that appeared to have set in. It seemed odd that the blood would pool beneath the skin on his back while he was lying on his stomach.

"Jesus, Farley," Otto gasped then fidgeted while holding back his grief for his friend.

Jenna ran through the bathroom and paused in Elana's bedroom doorway while breathing heavily. "Gilda's dead," she cried out then saw the butchered woman on the bed and let out a quick, shrill scream.

Dane forced Raina and Jenna from Elana's room and through the bathroom into the Nixon's bedroom. Jimmy Love stood in the hall doorway staring at the dead woman in her bed. He appeared to be paralyzed with fear. Otto held his kerosene lamp for a closer look at the dead woman. Gilda appeared to have died more peacefully than her husband and Elana had. She lay dramatically sprawled across the bed in her white, satin nightgown. There were no signs of blood or trauma.

"What the hell is going on around here?" Otto demanded while shaking his head. "I don't understand any of this."

Dane strained to look at the nightstand and saw the bottle of poison. He straightened and ran his fingers through his mussed hair.

"That's insect poison from Hanson's workshop," Dane announced.

Otto looked at him with surprise. "Are you saying she poisoned herself?"

Dane took the kerosene lamp from Otto and approached the bed for a closer look but was careful not to touch anything. There were smeared bloodstains on her nightgown. He shook his head.

"It seems as though Mrs. Nixon caught her husband in bed with Elana and killed them both in a fit of rage," Dane remarked while maintaining his frown.

"I can't say I'm surprised," Otto scoffed and shook his head in anger. "Farley couldn't make a move without her breathing down his neck." He turned angry. "I knew this was going to happen. The woman was insanely jealous."

"We'll have to seal the room until Detective Payne can be contacted," Dane informed him. "Nothing can be touched."

Otto nodded in agreement and scooted everyone from the open doorway. "You heard the man," he announced in a foul mood. "Everyone out. Just--" Otto groaned with frustration. "Just go back to your rooms. The police will straighten this out when we can reach them."

Her father shut the door leaving the three of them in the room. Otto was off in his own world as he stared at the dead woman, silently loathing her.

"Something feels off," Dane remarked while looking around the room and shook his head. "I can't put my finger on it."

Otto suddenly glared at him. "You're damned right something feels off," he launched in anger. "My friend was just killed by his deranged wife in a fit of passion." Otto shook his head. "I don't get it. If Farley was having an affair with Elana, why would he risk getting together with her with his wife only a room away?"

"He did carry on an affair right under her nose with Callie," Raina reminded him. "Maybe he felt confident she wouldn't find out."

"Gilda was rather drunk last night." Dane sank into thought then turned to face Otto. "With your permission," he announced while straightening proudly. "I'd like to take some pictures of the crime scene once there's some daylight."

"As long as you don't touch anything," Otto replied with a defeated sigh. "That's probably a good idea. If it wasn't a murder-suicide, someone could come along and tamper with the evidence. Photos of exactly how it is now would be beneficial."

"Hanson can put a padlock outside the bedroom door since I broke the doorjamb," Dane informed him. "The sooner, the better."

§

Later that morning, Dane used his cell phone to take pictures of both bedrooms, the position of items, and the three dead people. Raina tagged along and documented things in a notebook, so they'd remember them. Sloan stood near Gilda's bedside and stared at the body. She fidgeted then eyed Dane.

"I'm not sure why you wanted me to look at the bodies," Sloan remarked.

"You're one semester away from your registered nursing degree," Dane replied. "If there's something not right with the bodies, you may pick up on it."

Sloan groaned, ran her fingers through her hair, and studied Gilda's body. "Well, there's discoloration around her lips," she replied. "That indicates poisoning. She has some bloodstains on her nightgown, so that puts her at the scene of the murder next door." She then turned and eyed Dane, who still took pictures. "Are you actually going to make me look at the butchered bodies? Raina already told me what they look like. You don't need me to tell you what you already know."

"Humor me," Dane remarked.

Raina stood in the bathroom doorway and stared at the sink. It was easier to see now that there was some light in the rooms. She stared at the bloodied butcher knife from the kitchen in the sink, staining the white porcelain bowl.

"Dane," Raina gasped and looked back. "The murder weapon is in the bathroom sink. She must have dropped it here on her way back through."

Dane entered the bathroom and took several pictures of the weapon in the bloodstained sink. He then peered into the wastepaper can and took another picture. A pair of gardening gloves were in the garbage can. Both contained a large amount of dried blood on them.

"Those are gardening gloves from Hanson's workshop," Dane informed her.

Sloan reluctantly followed them into Elana's bedroom, cringed, and peered at the dead woman on the bed. Sloan gasped and looked away.

"Oh, God--"

"Remember your nurse's training," Dane announced in a calmer tone.

Sloan glared at him. "This has nothing to do with nursing, you idiot," she cried out. "This is a job for a coroner; not a nurse."

Once she calmed down, Sloan again looked at the butchered woman on the bed. She held back her gasp and the urge to throw up.

"Oh, that's a lot of blood," Sloan gasped while holding her stomach then placed her hand on her mouth. "Definitely knife wounds from the butcher knife in the bathroom. Levi is going to freak!" She drew a deep breath and shook her head. "I'm guessing she's been dead for several hours." Sloan peeked at Farley on the floor by the door and cringed. She started to look away then immediately looked back at the dead man with bewilderment. "No, that's not right."

Dane stared at her with a curious look. "What's not right?"

Sloan looked back at the bed then at the dead man across the floor. "Are we supposed to believe he crawled across the floor while attempting to escape his attacker?"

"That's how it appears," Dane informed her. "I'm not seeing much blood on the floor though, and it's been bothering me."

"No kidding," Sloan announced and again shifted her attention from the bed to the dead man on the floor. "He bled out on the bed. He must have another wound not visible to us."

Raina stepped around the body while attempting not to disturb anything. She crouched near the dead man's face and shined her flashlight beneath him. She gasped when she saw the stab wound covered with dried blood on his neck. She straightened and eyed Sloan.

"He's been stabbed in the neck," she announced. "There's blood covering his chest."

Dane looked back at the floor with little blood. "So if he crawled across the floor, there would be blood on the floor," he announced.

"He didn't crawl anywhere," Sloan insisted. "I'm telling you; he bled out on the bed." She then indicated the stab wounds along his back. "Notice how there's little blood on the wounds to his back?"

Dane nodded.

"They didn't bleed because they were inflicted postmortem."

"Postmortem?" Dane asked with surprise. "You mean after he was dead?"

"Someone moved him from the bed, laid him on the floor near the door, and stabbed him repeatedly in the back after he was already dead," she informed them then indicated his back.

"See the bruising on his back? That's blood that pooled there. It pooled there because he'd been on his back for possibly hours after he died."

"Wait," Raina suddenly announced while shaking her head. "Someone stabbed Farley in the neck and left him in the bed dead for several hours. Then what? They came back later, dragged him off the bed, dropped him by the door, and stabbed him repeatedly. Why?"

Dane shut his eyes and groaned. "Because the killer needed an alibi," he muttered then shook his head.

"That doesn't make any sense," Raina informed him. "If he killed them earlier, he still doesn't have an alibi."

"I think I know what happened," Dane informed them. "I want to examine these pictures on the computer where I can enlarge them. We'll need to work out where everyone was last night. Who left the game room at what time." He stared at the two women with concerning looks. "Let's just keep this new information between the three of us. Tell no one; absolutely no one."

Chapter 59

She Loves Me Not

Later that afternoon, Dane stood on the back terrace under the overhang and watched the rain as it finally slowed. Raina hurried to join him on the porch, linked onto his arm, and leaned in close.

"It's gone," she whispered.

Dane looked at her with concern. "It's not where you left it?"

"I looked," she reported and shook her head. "It was under my pillow this morning. I put it in my nightstand drawer under some books when I took my shower and forgot to take it with me. I went back to my room for it an hour later, and it's not there."

"Someone must have realized you were armed," Dane muttered and shook his head.

"Yeah," she scoffed just loud enough for him to hear. "So now the killer has your gun too."

Dane frowned and stared past the garden. Raina watched the slowing rain then realized where he was staring.

"I'm not sure what you're thinking," she informed him, "but I assure you, there's no way anyone can reach the authorities until the water recedes."

"Yes," he replied with a sigh. "I know. I'm hoping the cell phones will be working soon. If we can contact him, Detective Payne can reach us by helicopter."

She watched him stare off while deep in thought then gently cleared her throat, jolting him back into reality. "Sloan and I have that list together. It may not be one hundred percent accurate, but I think we have everyone's whereabouts up until the time we went to bed. You'll have to fill in the rest since you were the last to go to bed."

She removed a folded piece of paper from her pocket and handed it to him. He accepted the paper and stuck it in his pocket without looking at it. He resumed staring across the garden in the rain.

"Care to let me in on your thoughts?" she asked.

"The logical suspect is Keefe," Dane informed her. "He was Elana's blackmail partner, but I'm convinced she was telling the truth when she denied killing anyone. Keefe has a solid alibi for every murder. Particularly disturbing, neither he nor Elana had access to the drugged martinis."

"So if it's not Keefe, who is it?" Raina asked.

Dane frowned and refused to respond. She stared at him a long moment and attempted to read his profile as he stared at the garden. She then realized he wasn't staring at the garden but the crypt beyond it. Raina suddenly shifted and took a step away from him as her expression dropped.

"You don't suspect Miller could possibly--?"

He eyed her and raised his brow. "Why did you immediately go to Miller?" Dane asked.

She fidgeted and was unable to answer. It wasn't that she was unable, but she didn't want to answer him. "I'll admit; Miller has a lot of demons in his head since Alicia's death," Raina announced, "but he didn't kill Callie."

Dane drew a deep breath while staring into her eyes. "Callie was a young woman. Only a few years older than you," he informed her. "It's likely Callie would want children of her own. If your father had more children, the estate would be divided among all of his children after his death. You and Miller would receive smaller shares."

"Which would still be a lot of money," she corrected. "Besides, Miller and I received our trust funds when we each turned twenty-one. We're comfortable."

"You and Miller share an apartment," Dane reminded her. "He doesn't even own a car."

She stared at him with surprise. "Yeah, so what?"

"He received his trust fund when he was twenty-one, a few years earlier than you," Dane remarked then raised his brow. "How much do you suppose is left in his trust fund?"

"I'm not sure what you're getting at, Dane," she scoffed. "Neither of us lives high on the hog. If I have plenty of money left in my trust fund, I'm sure Miller has plenty as well."

"I know you don't want to hear it, Raina," Dane announced, "but Miller has always been an interesting suspect in what's happened around here. His mother was murdered. His girlfriend was murdered. It makes sense that your father marrying Callie hit him a lot harder than it did you. It's entirely possible your father marrying Callie was too much for him, and he just snapped."

"Okay," Raina launched and moved away from him. "You're way off base, and I don't like what you're insinuating. It wasn't Miller. You seem to forget; he was with Jenna last night, and she'll vouch for him."

"I hate to tell you this," Dane announced then drew a deep, tense breath. "I saw Miller leaving the house through the back kitchen door last night after the poker game broke up. I was leaving the staff wing when I saw him leave. I assumed he was just checking on the condition of the bridge."

Raina stared at him a moment and was at a loss for words. She wasn't sure how to defend Miller since she hadn't realized he'd left the house after they'd gone upstairs.

"I'm sure that's all it was," Raina snapped back then glared at him. "And you're one to talk. You had just as much motive and more than enough opportunity. With your questionable past, I'd think you'd tread a little more lightly."

"Are we back to that?" he demanded. "Did you forget? You were with me when Callie was murdered."

"From what little I remember about that night, it's entirely possible you made up that whole story and just used me for an alibi." She placed her hands on her hips and glared demandingly at him. "In fact, you had more than enough time to kill Nole during the time you were supposed to be showing him to the door. You were gone half an hour."

"I told you," he snarled. "I was in the kitchen with Titus and Hanson."

Her eyes then widened with a startling revelation. "You also walked Elana to her room making you the last person to see her alive. You had enough time to kill her, slip through the connecting bathroom to the Nixon's room, and kill them as well. You could have set up the entire thing in the time you were gone from the game room."

"Now you're talking nonsense," he insisted while remaining unusually calm despite the accusations. "I had no motive to kill Elana or the Nixon's."

"No motive?" Raina scoffed. "You have Elana's flash drive with all her blackmail evidence. If you got her out of the way, the entire operation could be yours."

"Think about what you're saying," he snapped while growing further irritated. "You just don't want to admit I could be right about Miller. You know his state of mind. You know he's been unstable since the death of his fiancé."

Raina then considered something and raised her brows. "In fact; with the way you slinked into my bedroom, I'd say you have more motive than Miller. If you were some sort of conman, who's to say you didn't seize the opportunity to off Callie while working your way into my bed?" She stared at him demandingly. "If Miller took the fall for the murders, my father's entire estate would revert to me when he dies." Raina sneered at him. "Even with a prenup, any man marrying me would be set for life."

He stared at her with surprise. "Do you honestly think I'm only after you for your money?"

"I'm starting to wonder," she scoffed. "But we won't have to worry about finding out. I'm through with you, and after I talk to my father, he may feel the same way." Her eyes narrowed while glaring at him. "Just stay the hell away from me."

Raina stormed back into the kitchen and watched Levi, Sloan, and Titus scurry away from the window as if they hadn't been eavesdropping. Raina headed through the main kitchen door and disappeared. Dane entered the kitchen and eyed the staff with annoyance as they stared at him.

"Show's over," he scoffed. "Back to work."

§

Just before dinner, the entire staff, including Hanson and Titus, helped prepare dinner for their captive guests. Titus helped Sloan set the dining room table while Hanson attempted to help Levi and Dane in the kitchen. Miller appeared on the back stairs, stormed through the kitchen, and barely stopped before Dane.

"You," he snarled with anger and pointed demandingly. "In the study."

"Dinner is--"

"Now," Miller snapped, continued through the kitchen, and plowed through the revolving door to the hallway.

Dane received startled looks from Levi and Hanson, who were astonished by Miller's explosive reaction. Dane straightened proudly then left the kitchen and headed for the study. Dane entered the study and eyed Miller, who sat behind the desk as if he owned the place.

"Close the door," Miller ordered.

Dane closed the study door and again eyed the irate man. "Is there a problem?"

Miller leaped up from his chair while glaring at Dane. "You damned well better believe there's a problem," he snarled. "I heard about your little conversation with Raina this afternoon. As a matter of fact, just about everyone in the house heard about it by now. She's upstairs in tears over it."

Dane fidgeted but maintained his proper mannerism. "I'm sorry she's upset," he announced, "but she was the one who ended our relationship." He drew a deep breath. "With all due respect, our relationship isn't a matter that concerns you."

"She's my sister," Miller launched back. "It damned well does concern me. When my father hears about this, and he will, you'll have a lot of explaining to do."

"And that will be between your father and me," Dane informed him. "Until Mr. Steele speaks with me about the matter, I'll be returning to my duties."

"Not so fast," Miller snarled with anger. "What the hell is your endgame here?"

"I don't know what you're talking about," Dane casually replied. "I don't have an endgame."

"Bullshit," Miller snapped. "Before the wedding rehearsal, you stood right there and witnessed legal documents drawn up by my father dividing most of his property and money between Raina and myself. Why would you tell Raina I had reason to kill Callie over monetary gain when you knew damned well he'd already turned everything over to Raina and me?" Miller shook his head. "If he had children with Callie, it'd be of little financial concern to either of us. Why did you purposely pick a fight with her over that?"

Dane stared back and Miller and showed no emotion. "Raina and I aren't suited for each other," he announced with little hesitation. "I don't see a reason to pursue the relationship any further. Letting her end it seemed the compassionate thing to do."

"Why?" Miller demanded. "Because my father asked you to sign a prenup when he found out you were diddling his daughter?"

Dane tensed and held his breath. "That may have had something to do with it."

Miller groaned and shook his head. "You are so full of bullshit," he snapped back. "Do you think my father doesn't talk to me? Earlier this afternoon, he told me about you. Fact; you approached my father less than a year after you started working here and discussed resigning. You told him you were in love with Raina and couldn't handle the guilt. Fact; my father refused your resignation and offered you an alternative. He had you sign a prenup in the event that you ever became involved with Raina that would exclude you from monetary gain. Five years ago, you signed that prenup, and *my* mother witnessed it."

Dane shifted uncomfortably and frowned at Miller's comment.

Miller continued to stare at him with raised brows and a tiny smirk. "Fact; this morning, you asked my father for permission to marry his daughter." He flopped back into his chair. "You know I have no financial motive to murder Callie, and you asked to marry Raina knowing there was no financial gain in it for you. So I ask again, why did you pick that fight with her accusing me of murder?"

Dane stared at Miller and offered nothing.

Miller stared at him a moment then suddenly sat forward with surprise on his face. "That fight wasn't about me," he announced. "You picked that fight with her in hopes that the murderer would hear it. You knew it would get around the entire house. It was a sting!"

The butler frowned and fidgeted. "Will there be anything else, Mr. Steele?"

"Yeah," Miller launched. "I want in. You could use my help catching this bastard."

"Considering it's you the killer will be framing, I'd say you're already in," Dane informed him. "You need to steer clear of this and secure an alibi in case I'm unsuccessful in my mission."

"Unsuccessful?" Miller asked then stared at him with surprise. "You mean killed, don't you?"

"I suspect the killer will come after me and attempt to frame you for it," Dane replied. "Since your alibi is sketchy during last night's murders as well as the others, you'll be easy to frame."

"What are you talking about?" Miller demanded. "Jenna was with me in my bedroom last night."

"You came back downstairs after the poker game had ended," Dane informed him. "I saw you leaving the kitchen when I left the staff wing. It was dark in the kitchen, so you probably didn't see me."

"I wanted to check on the condition of the bridge," Miller informed him. He brushed the comment aside. "You need my help. I'm pretty damned useful."

"No, I don't need your help," Dane replied. "Stay clear of me tonight. If you attempt to get involved, I'll tattle to your new girlfriend, and I'm willing to bet she's not beyond tying you to the bed to keep you out of harm's way."

Dane turned and left the study without permission. Miller sat back in the chair and frowned. He considered the last comment.

"Tied to a bed, huh?" he muttered then grinned. "That could actually be fun."

Chapter 60

Dinner and a Show

The dining room had dozens of candles on the table and along the sideboards creating a romantic dining atmosphere for the remaining guests. The guest list had been greatly reduced after what was being considered a double homicide-suicide perpetrated by Gilda Nixon. Those within the house were becoming anxious and wanted to leave. Despite the anxiety among those remaining, the talented cook treated them to another amazing meal. They were fortunate that the emergency generator powered enough equipment in the kitchen to allow Levi to present wonderful meals during their confinement. Dane and Sloan again helped Levi serve dinner to the homeowners and their guests. While all eight were seated around the table, dinner talk remained grim about the murders and focused on still being stranded.

"How long until the power is typically restored?" Olivia asked while only picking at her meal.

"Has anyone checked on the bridge now that the water has receded?" Keefe then asked while looking at Otto, who sat at the head of the table. "I can't stay in this place. I'll go insane after what happened to Elana."

"It was a bad storm," Otto informed them. "We've lost power for almost a week once. As for the bridge, I've had Titus and Hanson periodically checking on the water level ever since the rain stopped. It could take two or more days for the water levels to drop below the bridge, but that doesn't mean it won't be passable by morning. I told them if they think they can safely cross with Hanson's pickup truck, they should just go for help."

"So we're stuck here another night?" Tia asked although it was more of a statement since everyone already knew the answer.

"I'm afraid so," Otto informed the young woman then managed a smile. "But we've moved the jukebox to one of the emergency outlets in the game room, so you'll have some music tonight."

Jimmy Love managed some fancy dance moves while seated in his chair. "We'll have a little dance-off tonight," he announced to the women in an attempt to cheer them up and lighten the mood. "That always makes the night a little brighter."

"Yeah, maybe," Olivia remarked with less enthusiasm.

Jimmy Love frowned at his inability to cheer up the women. It was possibly a first for him.

"Count me out," Raina muttered. "I'll be in the library reading."

Otto glared at Raina and the irritation clearly displayed on her face. "Just because it looks as if Gilda Nixon was the killer that doesn't mean I'm lifting the 'buddy rule'," he informed his daughter then eyed the others at the table. "I don't want anyone going anywhere alone."

"But you just said--" Jenna attempted to speak but was cut short.

"Dane spoke to me earlier, and he's not entirely convinced Gilda took her own life," Otto informed Jenna. "Better safe than sorry."

"Wait," Tia suddenly announced with concern. "Are you suggesting someone killed all three of them, and we were meant to think Gilda was the killer?"

"That doesn't make any sense," Keefe blurted out. "Gilda had to have killed her husband and Elana. They were found naked and in bed together." He then turned hostile. "I hope you aren't suggesting I killed them in a fit of rage. I had no idea they were hooking up. I thought she was slinking around with the butler."

Dane shot a look of surprise at Keefe then at the eyes suddenly upon him.

"Excuse me?" Dane bellowed.

Jimmy Love pointed accusingly at Keefe. "You, sweetheart, are totally out of line," he announced. "Everyone in this house knows that stud muffin has the hots for that sweet thing." Jimmy Love then pointed at Raina, who covered her eyes and sank in her chair.

"Is that really the topic here?" Miller demanded then glared at Dane. "If you don't think Gilda killed herself that means one of us here could be a killer." Despite having heard Dane's thoughts on the killings earlier, Miller played dumb.

The murmur in the dining room grew louder as accusations were thrown around the table. Otto groaned and tapped his teaspoon against his crystal wineglass silencing everyone.

"Everyone settle down," Otto announced loudly and caught their attention. "It's just one man's speculation and not based on facts. It's not going to kill you to maintain the buddy system for one more night." Otto eyed his daughter. "If you want to read, you can read in the game room with the rest of us."

"That's ridiculous," Raina scoffed. "How am I supposed to read with all that mindless noise? I'm sure there's going to be another marathon poker game tonight."

"Yes, I suspect there will be," her father replied while shifting uncomfortably. "It'll help take our minds off what happened to our friends last night."

Keefe frowned while picking at his food. "I wouldn't mind something to get my mind off what happened to Elana," he remarked.

"Then I'll read in the kitchen with Levi and Sloan," Raina announced.

"No can do," Levi informed her while removing dirty plates from the table. "I'm getting in on the poker game."

Raina eyed Jenna and raised her brows.

Jenna grimaced at her friend. "Sorry, Raina. I'm playing poker with the guys," she announced. "I'm sure Dane won't mind if you hang out in the kitchen with him."

"Pass," Raina muttered.

Dane frowned but didn't comment. Otto suspiciously eyed both. They refused to look at each other.

"You can join us," Jimmy Love announced enthusiastically and indicated Tia and Olivia. "We're going to dance ourselves silly."

"Thanks," Raina replied then frowned. "Again--pass."

"Everyone will remain in the game room tonight," Otto insisted and eyed Raina. "And that means everyone." He then looked around the dining room. "We're also buddying up in the bedrooms as well, so pay attention."

Jimmy Love leaned on the table with his chin in his hand and grinned with anticipation.

"Raina, Miller, Jenna, and I will stay in my room," Otto informed them. "Keefe, Jimmy Love, Dane, and Levi will stay in the silver room."

Jimmy Love straightened and squealed with delight. Dane, Keefe, and Levi all exchanged strange stares.

"Tia, Olivia, and Sloan will stay in the gold room," Otto concluded. "Those are your buddies, so make it work." He eyed those in the dining room. "After dinner, we'll all adjourn to the game room. Dane, Levi, and Sloan will join us after they're finished in the kitchen. That's final."

"Pardon me, Sir," Dane announced and gently cleared his throat. "Hanson brought me his old ham radio, and I think I can get it to work. It's already set up in the kitchen."

"Can you move it to the game room?" Otto asked while eyeing him.

"It's a bit of a fossil," Dane explained. "I'd rather not move it. If I can get it to work, I'll be able to contact the local authorities in town."

Otto groaned and reconsidered his earlier announcement. "Fine," he scoffed then glared at the butler. "But I don't want you in the kitchen alone."

Levi frowned knowing he'd be nominated to stay in the kitchen rather than join in the poker game.

"I'll stay with him," Miller eagerly announced.

Dane immediately frowned.

"One less man for our poker game," Otto muttered then reluctantly sighed. "All right. You can help Dane with the ham radio."

Dane glared his annoyance with Miller.

Chapter *61*

Amateur Night

Once the staff had cleaned up the kitchen after dinner, Levi and Sloan headed for the game room as Miller entered the kitchen. Dane leaned on the island counter with a disgusted look on his face. The old ham radio was set up on the kitchen table and appeared untouched. Miller excitedly clapped his hands together and eyed the fossil of a radio.

"So what can I do to help?" Miller announced.

"You can go back to the game room," Dane snarled.

Miller raised an arrogant brow and grinned. "You heard the boss," he announced cheerfully. "No one goes anywhere alone."

Dane straightened while glaring at Miller. "What the hell is wrong with you, Miller?" he launched. "I told you to stay away from me tonight. I'm convinced the killer wants to frame you for my murder, and you conveniently put us in the same room together. Can you see how insane that is?"

"I see a perfect opportunity to flush him out," Miller insisted.

"And I see the killer getting exactly what he wanted," Dane snapped. "This isn't a game."

Miller took a quick step toward Dane and glared at him with anger and rage in his eyes. "No, you're right. This isn't a game," he launched back. "Two years ago, my girlfriend and mother were brutally murdered, and my sister nearly died trying to save them. If I'd been home, they'd both still be alive today!" He threw his arms around erratically and then pointed accusingly. "Maybe you have some sort of vendetta or superiority complex. I don't know nor do I care. I want fucking revenge!"

"Yes, I know," Dane snarled back while remaining calmer than Miller. "You seem to forget *I* was there. *I'm* the one burdened with guilt because *I'm* the one who couldn't save them."

Miller fidgeted then frowned while attempting to control his hostility. "I'm sorry," he announced and folded his arms across his chest. "I sometimes forget how close you were to my mother."

"Brenda was like a mother to me," Dane informed him. "When I came here, I had no one in my life. She was the first one who reached out to me and treated me with respect. I let her down."

Miller shifted uncomfortably and avoided looking at Dane. "I'm sorry," he gently replied. "She was naturally maternal and loved everyone."

"I understand how you feel, Miller," Dane remarked with a defeated sigh. "But if you're standing in my way, I can't deal with the situation in an effective manner."

"And what manner is that?" Miller demanded.

Dane removed the double-barrel shotgun from beneath the counter and set it on top without taking his eyes off Miller. Miller stared at the shotgun only a moment then met Dane's gaze.

"I don't care what you do once we catch the killer," Miller remarked. "You want to take him out back behind the woodshed and shoot him? I'm fine with that, but I'm staying." He approached the ham radio on the kitchen table and attempted to understand it. "Can we get this thing to work?"

"No, it's a WWII relic," Dane replied and replaced the shotgun beneath the counter. "I needed a reason to be alone to draw out the killer." The butler sighed with defeat. "If you really want to help, you can make sure all the doors in the staff wing are closed then take a lookout position in the doorway." He pointed a warning finger. "But stay hidden. If the killer comes to us, we need a confession first. No one plays the hero."

Miller nodded. "Got it." He approached the staff wing and looked down the hall. "Two doors are opened."

"They weren't before," Dane remarked with some concern. "We'd better check the windows and patio doors. Make sure they're still locked."

Miller nodded and hurried into the staff wing with Dane bringing up the rear. As they approached the staff wing linen closet, Dane became alert.

"Did you hear that?" Dane announced.

Miller looked around and tensed. "What?"

"It came from the linen closet," Dane remarked and indicated the closed door near Miller.

Miller eyed the door, stepped closer to it, and pulled it open. To his surprise, it was just filled with sheets and other linens. Miller relaxed as he turned toward Dane and was about to speak when Dane shoved him into the closet. Miller struck the rack of sheets and attempted to regain his balance.

"What the--?"

Dane slammed and locked the door. "Amateur," the butler scoffed aloud then smirked and returned to the kitchen as Miller pounded on the linen closet door.

§

Raina sat on one of the plush chairs in the corner of the game room with an open book on her lap while dance music blared from the jukebox. She watched Jenna playing poker with Keefe, her father, and Levi. Tia and Olivia danced with Jimmy Love on the makeshift dance floor near the door, which successfully blocked Raina's unsanctioned exit. She frowned as she watched the dancers. Keefe was knocked out of the poker game with a boldly aggressive move that cost him his entire stack of chips. He laughed it off and headed to the self-serve bar for another drink. Raina put her nose back in her book and attempted to take her mind off her game room prison. When she looked up from her book only a moment later, she realized the room was one guest short.

She looked back at the dancing trio and knew she had to make her move. Raina got up from her chair and approached Jimmy Love dancing with the two attractive women. She tapped him on the shoulder. As he leaned closer to hear what she said above the music, she whispered in his ear. He offered a smile to the women and excused himself, leaving the room with Raina. As they entered the hallway together, Raina looked around while Jimmy Love stared at her with a baffled look and full, pouty lips.

"What did you drag me out here for, honey?" he asked while placing his dainty hands on his hips.

She looked at him and motioned him to keep his voice down. "I need to spy on someone in the kitchen," Raina informed him, "and I needed you to be my 'buddy'. My father would have a fit if I wandered off on my own."

He stared at her with some surprise. "And you think *I'm* letting you wander off on your own?" Jimmy Love dramatically wagged his finger at her. "Uh, uh. No way, cutie pie. If you get yourself killed, I'm in trouble with your big, strapping father. I love a good spanking, but that man would put a serious hurting on my fabulous flanks."

Raina hurried to the foyer with Jimmy Love on her heels. She opened the foyer closet door and removed the baseball bat. Jimmy Love saw her with the bat and jumped back a step.

"This is important," she insisted. "You can't tell anyone I left alone."

"Then I'll go with you," he boldly announced.

"You don't understand," she informed him while gripping the bat. "I'm possibly confronting a killer."

"Sugar," he boldly announced and dramatically placed his hand to his chest. "Jimmy Love isn't nearly as sweet as he looks."

She stared at him with disbelief and remembered his girlish scream in the upstairs hallway. Raina sincerely doubted his ability to defend himself against a spider, but he seemed to be giving her little choice.

"Fine," she huffed. "Stay close and keep quiet."

"I'll be as quiet as a church mouse," he announced then waved his hand and lowered his voice. "Jimmy Love got your back, sweet cheeks." He eyed her backside. "And that back is worth dying for. Hmm, hmm."

Raina groaned and motioned him to follow her down the grand hallway. He placed his hands on her shoulders and dramatically tiptoed behind her.

Chapter *62*

Confession Is Good for the Soul

Dane stood over the relic ham radio on the kitchen table and fiddled with it. He listened to the faint thumping of Miller pounding on the linen closet door within the staff wing. With the staff wing door closed, the thumping was barely audible. There was a creak on the back stairs. Dane approached the island counter while pressing his tie clip spycam, walked around the island counter, and picked up his mug of tea. Dane sipped his tea while viewing the back stairs out of the corner of his eye. There was a faint creak from the bottom step.

"Hey, Keefe," Dane announced without bothering to look at the stairs.

Keefe stepped into the kitchen, eyed Dane, and then looked around. "Where's Miller?"

"Locked in a closet," Dane casually replied.

"You were expecting me, huh?" he asked while removing Dane's missing service pistol from the back of his pants and aimed it at the butler.

"Wasn't too difficult to figure out," Dane replied while showing little reaction to his own gun aimed at him. "I'm

359

guessing you knew Elana was fazing you out, so you fazed her out first."

"Her side business was very lucrative," Keefe announced. "I wasn't going to let her dump me when I helped build up that business from nothing."

"Blackmail, right?" Dane remarked then indicated the gun. "You won't be needing that gun. I'm here to negotiate with you. Elana's death changes nothing. You need a partner, and I still want in."

"Is that what calling me out was all about?" Keefe demanded.

"You're a sloppy killer, Keefe," Dane informed him. "I mean seriously? Stabbing a corpse?" He shook his head. "You need my skills and attention to detail more than you realize. Fortunately for you, I'm willing to make you the same deal I made Elana."

"Yeah, I heard the deal you made Elana," Keefe snapped and eyed him. "You wanted to eliminate me."

"Two's company; three's a crowd," Dane replied. "Elana's dead. We're back down to two."

"Okay, you've got me here," Keefe announced and moved closer to the staff wing door. He pushed open the door, cast a look into the empty hallway, and allowed the door to close. "And we're alone thanks to Otto's no one without a buddy bullshit." Keefe approached the main kitchen door and did the same, making certain no one was listening in on their conversation. When he seemed convinced they were alone, he returned to the island counter. "Miller needs to take the fall for the killings."

"I know," Dane announced and raised his brows. "That's why I picked a fight with Raina. I chose when and where very carefully. I needed the entire house to know that I suspected him in order to set him up to take the fall."

"Clever. If I agree to cut you in on the deal, how do we frame him without sacrificing you?" Keefe almost demanded and showed no faith by keeping the gun aimed at him.

Dane chuckled with a sinister look in his eyes. "I'm certainly not going to tell you my plan," he announced and shook his head. "I need some insurance that you won't kill me and steal my idea."

"You'd better give me something," Keefe demanded.

Dane placed his hands on the counter and leaned on it while staring at Keefe across from him. A strange and twisted smile crossed his face. "We're going to kill Daddy Warbucks, and I'm going to marry Little Orphan Annie."

Keefe stared at him with some surprise and straightened. "Okay, you have my attention," he announced and nodded. "I'm willing to listen."

"With Miller on death row for murder, Raina inherits her father's entire fortune," Dane informed him and shrugged. "A year or two from now, when things cool down, Raina has an accident, and everything goes to me. You let me in on your blackmail scheme until we off Raina, and then we split the Steele fortune fifty-fifty. In two years, you and I will be rich beyond our wildest dreams, and we'll never have to see each other again."

"And you think you can pull that off?"

"Why not?" Dane asked with a curious look then grinned. "I'm a bigger conman than you'll ever be, and I've got the patience of a saint."

Keefe seemed to consider everything he'd said then smiled and laughed. "You know what," he announced and lowered the gun. "I actually believe you."

"I'll be honest; I was a little fooled myself. I find it ironic that I believed Elana when she said she had nothing to do with murdering Callie and Nole," Dane remarked. "I guess I was wrong, huh?"

"No, you were right," he announced then grinned. "She had her secrets; I had mine."

"I see. How did the Nixon's fit into all of this? I'm sure they weren't merely collateral damage," Dane remarked. "Call it professional curiosity."

"Oh, the Nixon's." Keefe chuckled. "Now there's an interesting story. I was bartending at the country club when I first met Gilda Nixon. She was insanely jealous over her husband and suspected he was having an affair. I offered to romance Elana to spy on her husband for her," Keefe announced then snorted a laugh. "Ironically, I was getting paid to bang her hot maid. Talk about dream jobs. Imagine my surprise when I discovered old Farley was having an affair with Callie." He leaned against the counter while keeping the gun in his hand. "When I discovered he was being blackmailed with sex tapes of him and Callie, I told Gilda but conveniently left out *who* was blackmailing her husband. I wanted to put that to some good use for myself."

"No big surprise there," Dane remarked. "I would have done the same."

"Great minds, huh?"

"Don't flatter yourself," Dane muttered.

Keefe frowned his disapproval then laughed at the comment. "Gilda confronted Farley on the affair and the blackmail money. Rather than divorce him, she insisted he fire Callie instead," Keefe announced and shook his head while hiding his cheap grin. "When Gilda learned her husband didn't so much fire Callie as pawn her off onto Otto and Brenda Steele, she was furious. It was then that I convinced her that we could siphon her husband's money into a private account for her, but we'd need to be partners." He shook his head and frowned. "I'd grown bored with Elana. She was such a little girl in so many ways, but Gilda--" He laughed. "Gilda was stuck up just enough for me to have a little fun humiliating her in bed. She was so starved for attention, she eagerly agreed. Talk about a woman who'd do anything in bed--"

"So you were stringing along two women at the same time?" Dane remarked then shook his head. "No wonder it didn't work out for you."

"Who said it didn't work out for me?" Keefe snapped then frowned. "It was Callie who attempted to ruin everything. When Brenda suspected Callie wanted to steal her jewelry, Elana and I had to come up with a plan to prevent her twit of a sister from being fired." He shook his head with disgust. "Callie was more trouble than she was worth. Removing Brenda from the equation was our best option, but Callie begged me not to include Elana in our little plan. She'd never go along with murdering someone."

Dane's look hardened although he didn't react. "You were behind that?"

Keefe chuckled and nodded. "I agreed I wouldn't say anything to Elana if Callie agreed to amuse me now and again." He laughed at the thought. "Can you imagine? I was banging three women for months. Talk about your juggling act," he teased. "I set up the whole thing and even planned it that Elana would unwittingly give Callie and me an alibi for the night of the murder. Unfortunately, I didn't know Brenda wouldn't be alone that night. She was supposed to be alone while Otto was out of town on business." He then frowned. "Not everything went according to plan. I did feel bad that my hitmen had to kill Miller's girlfriend, but it sort of worked itself out in the end. The hitmen dying tragically at your hands helped tie up some loose ends."

"I'm grossly underestimated, I suppose," Dane remarked with little emotion.

"Yeah, no kidding. The long con was now within my grasp. I was still blackmailing Callie for sex as well as stringing Gilda Nixon along while systematically fleecing her husband of his wealth," he announced, fell silent a moment, and then turned irritated. "Somewhere along the way, things took an ugly turn. Gilda became jealous and possessive over me and hated that I was still seeing Elana."

"You were bound to lose that little game," Dane informed him.

"Yeah, women, right? I tried to tell her that Elana was just business," Keefe remarked then shifted almost uncomfortably. "I guess I underestimated Gilda's insanely jealous nature. Not only was she jealous of me seeing Elana, but she still hadn't forgiven Callie for having an affair with Farley."

"So you killed all three of your lovers," Dane remarked with surprise and then raised his brows. "Well, that's one way to end a relationship."

Keefe suddenly laughed. "Oh, that's where you're wrong," he announced. "I'll tell you the whole sorted story since we have time."

Chapter *63*

Return of Bridezilla - Part 2: The Blushing Bride

Otto and Callie's wedding day. Ten minutes until 'show time'. Nole hurried across his guestroom and snatched his expensive watch from the nightstand. He slipped into the watch while shaking his head that he'd managed to forget it in the first place. He was about to leave his room, eyed himself in the bureau mirror, and grinned his approval. He reconsidered and then added a quick splash of cologne. As he headed for the bedroom door, he heard the bagpipes and knew he was supposed to be with the rest of the groomsmen in the garden. He heard voices outside his partially open bedroom door and hesitated just inside his room.

Callie stood with Keefe in the second floor hallway where they were waiting to head down the grand staircase. Since she had no other family, she had asked Keefe to give her away. What should have been a cherished moment sounded more like a heated exchange. Nole couldn't help but listen to the couple even if it meant he'd be late to join the other groomsmen. Upon peering out the bedroom door, he saw Keefe pulling the radiant bride against him while his hand caressed her backside through the thick bridal dress. Nole appeared surprised then grabbed his cell phone from his pocket and recorded the little show. He grinned while watching, hoping to catch of glimpse of Callie's large breasts freed from her dress. Callie attempted to pull away.

"Come on, Keefe," she announced with some annoyance. "I'm getting married in ten minutes."

He didn't allow her to pull away and grinned while chuckling. "That doesn't change anything between us," he insisted.

She pushed him away and stared at him with surprise. "It most certainly does," Callie announced while attempting to keep her voice down. "It's over between us. I'm marrying Otto. He's going to be the only man I have sex with."

Keefe stared at her with surprise then turned angry. "If it weren't for me, you wouldn't even be here today," he snapped. "As for us; it's over when I say it's over." He pulled her roughly against him and stared into her eyes. "I can destroy your relationship with a snap of my fingers. You'd better just remember that. You owe me, and I *own* you." He leaned closer to kiss her and grinned slyly. "It's my turn to kiss the bride."

She stopped him and gave him a stern look. "You'll get lipstick all over you," Callie informed him. "We have to be down those stairs in ten minutes."

He opened the master bedroom door and took her by the hand. "Fine," Keefe announced. "Then you can kiss me where no one will notice the lipstick."

Callie groaned with annoyance and reluctantly entered the room with him. Nole hurried into the hallway while still recording with his cell phone. He approached the door that was still partially open, held his cell phone to the small gap, and watched the screen. Callie unzipped Keefe's pants then moved to her knees in front of him. Nole grinned and held back his enthusiasm while recording the couple together.

§

Later during the reception. Callie stood by the large table filled with beautifully wrapped wedding presents and assessed the gifts she and Otto had received. There were so many gifts, Callie was nearly giddy at the sight. The card basket was overflowing with cards and probably monetary gifts. Nole approached Callie while she was alone at the gift table and paused alongside her. She was too busy checking out the gifts to notice him.

"Amazing reception, huh?" Nole announced while standing a little closer than acceptable.

Callie glanced at him and smiled while taking a step back to put some space between them. "Yes," she replied. "Are you enjoying yourself? There are plenty of single women. I hope you asked Tia and Olivia to dance."

"I love weddings," he informed her and again moved closer making her slightly uncomfortable. Nole was notorious for that sort of behavior, so most people overlooked it. "Honestly, I've always wanted to *fuck* a bride."

Callie sharply looked at him and appeared stunned by his words then saw the cheap grin on his face. "Excuse me?" she bellowed while placing her dainty hands on her hips.

Nole held up his cell phone and played the video. Callie stared in horror at the image of her on her knees in her wedding dress performing oral sex on Keefe. She tore her eyes away from the image on the cell phone and stared at Nole with her mouth hanging open, unable to speak.

He grinned with anticipation. "If you don't want Otto to see this little stag film on his wedding day, you'd better meet me in the library in ten minutes," Nole informed her. "We can discuss the price for deleting this from my phone."

She stared at him as her expression dropped then turned angry. "Fine," she snarled.

Nole grinned and left the ballroom. Callie attempted to compose herself, put on a false smile, and approached her groom, who was hanging out with some of his business friends. They seemed to be having a good time drinking and laughing. She affectionately touched Otto's arm and smiled sweetly.

"Darling," she announced catching his attention.

Otto grinned and pulled her into his arms. She patted his chest while maintaining her smile.

"Are you ready to turn in?" he asked. "Just give the word."

"Actually, if it's okay with you, I'm going to the lounge to show some of my friends those antiques we'd bought," she informed him.

"Sure," he announced. "You have a good time with your friends. I'll catch up with you in a half an hour or so for our 'goodbye tour' before turning in."

"I'd like that," she responded then kissed Otto quickly on the lips and left the ballroom.

Chapter *64*

Return of Bridezilla - Part 3: Everyone Loves the Bride

The library door opened, startling the couple grinding over the desk. Callie spun around allowing her wedding dress to fall back into place and stared at Otto, who stood in the library doorway with a look of shock and horror on his face. His anger surfaced, but instead of yelling, he turned and left the library. Callie cast a glare at Nole, who was more interested in zipping his pants with trembling hands. Callie shoved him aside and ran for the library door, chasing after Otto despite her panties caught around her left ankle. Otto stormed through the grand hallway toward the kitchen with Callie attempting to chase after him. The bride fumbled with her bulky dress so that she wouldn't trip over it. Several stunned guests watched the bride chasing after her angry groom. Levi and Sloan pursued them from a safe distance.

"Otto, wait, let me explain!" she cried out in panic as she ran after him.

He suddenly stopped and turned to face her with an explosive look on his face. "Explain? Explain what?" he cried out in anger and rage. "You were fucking my best friend at our wedding reception! How can there possibly be anything to explain?"

She stared at him a moment and was unable to speak. Otto turned and stormed into the kitchen. Callie turned and saw several guests staring at her in complete silence, although their eyes judged her. Nole, now dressed, ran after Otto, attempting to catch up to him. Levi and Sloan exchanged concerned looks and hurried after Nole since it wasn't in his best interest to confront the irate Otto. Callie ran past the remaining guests in the hallway as fast as her white, satin shoes would carry her and bolted into the nearby dining room. She slammed the door behind her then held her head a moment while holding back her sobs. She ran to the house phone on the side table not far from the kitchen entrance, picked it up, and pressed her sister's phone number with a trembling finger.

A giggling, drunken Elana answered the phone. "Yeah?"

"Elana," Callie gasped into the phone while looking nervously around the room. "Where are you?"

"Keefe and I are upstairs in our room," Elana responded from the other end. She giggled. "We're having our own wedding night if you know what I mean."

"I need you to meet me right away," she informed her sister while trembling. "There's been some trouble. Big trouble."

"Where are you?" Elana announced in a more serious tone. "We'll be down in two minutes."

Callie could hear the caterers bustling around in the kitchen. By the sounds of raised voices and Jimmy Love squealing, something must have happened.

"No, I'm in the dining room," she announced. "There's too much commotion in the kitchen." She looked at the glass terrace doors and the dark gazebo in the distance. "Meet me in the gazebo. I can make it out there without anyone seeing me."

"We'll take the main stairs and slip around the side of the house to avoid being seen," Elana informed her. "Give us five minutes."

Callie hung up the table phone and hurried from the dining room through the French doors leading to the terrace. She hurried along the stone walkway while nervously looking around. Hanson was seen darting from the garden and heading for the garage. A commotion coming from the garage was far enough away that no one would hear or see her heading for the gazebo. She hurried into the dark gazebo and sat on the built-in bench. Elana and Keefe appeared within the gazebo only a few minutes later. Both had hastily dressed, indicating they had been engaging in their own wedding festivities before being interrupted. Elana approached her distraught sister as she stood. Callie threw her arms around Elana and hugged her while nearly down to tears.

"What is it?" Elana asked and pulled away.

Callie trembled and began pacing. "Nole had damaging information he intended to share with Otto," she informed them. "He demanded sexual favors for his silence. Otto walked in on us together."

Keefe rolled his eyes and groaned with annoyance almost as if he knew she'd somehow blow it. Elana stared at her sister in disbelief.

"He demanded sexual favors from you on your wedding night?" Elana gasped with horror.

"Why, Callie?" Keefe demanded while glaring at her. "You should have called us right away. What could he possibly have had to warrant such a foolish decision on your behalf?"

Callie glared at Keefe and immediately turned angry. "He secretly videotaped a *private* conversation," she snapped demandingly. "And don't you dare put this on me because you were in the video too."

Her look told Keefe exactly what Nole had caught on video. Keefe frowned and looked away. Elana attempted to calm her sister.

"We can fix this," Elana insisted.

"How?" Callie demanded. "I can't tell him Nole blackmailed me into having sex with him. Nole will simply show him the video and make it even worse." She threw her arms in the air. "It's possible he's already showing him the video."

"Leave that to me," Keefe huffed and looked nervous for the first time. "I'll get his cell phone from him and destroy the video."

"The marriage is over," Callie insisted and shook her head while fiddling with her engagement ring. "All Otto's money is gone. I'll be left with nothing."

"We didn't come this far to leave empty-handed," Keefe announced in anger. "I'll get Otto's money. It's going to take some time, but I can siphon it from his accounts a little at a time without him noticing. By the time his accountants figure out what happened, I'll have moved most of it." He shifted a demanding look at Elana and raised his brows as if silently commanding something from her.

Elana understood the look and returned her attention to Callie then frowned. "This is going to cost you big time, Callie," she announced. "We're not going to bail you out of this for free."

She stared at her sister with surprise. "What do you want from me?" Callie demanded. "All I have access to is my jewelry, and he's going to demand all that back too."

Elana indicated the emerald necklace. "You took that from Brenda's jewelry box in the attic," she insisted. "He won't even realize it's missing. It's worth a small fortune. Consider it a down payment."

Callie frowned, removed the necklace, and reluctantly handed it to Elana. Keefe eyed Elana and indicated the necklace in her hand.

"You'd better find a good place to stash that for now, Elana," he informed her. "I want to work on some damage control with your sister. I'll meet you back in the room in half an hour."

Elana nodded and slipped from the gazebo. She headed around the opposite side of the house away from the garage area and any reception activity, so she wouldn't be seen. Keefe turned to face Callie with a disgusted look and shook his head in annoyance.

"You really are stupid," he snapped in anger.

"Me?" she demanded while glaring at him with an accusing look and took a bold step toward him. "You were the one who insisted we mess around before the wedding. Nole only got that video because of your arrogance."

He wasn't pleased with the tone or the accusation. "Do you want my help or not?" Keefe demanded in anger. "Maybe I'll just go upstairs right now and tell Elana all about how you secured your position as lady of the house."

Callie stared at him with horror then turned angry. "That was all *your* idea," she hissed while keeping her voice down. "You hired those men. You have just as much to lose as I do. I can tell Elana all about your little side deals like blackmailing me to be your little concubine. I'm sure she'd love to hear that."

A strange, twisted smile crossed his face as he stared her down. "Watch yourself, Callie," he snarled. "You don't want to make me angry. Your sexual favors are the only thing keeping me from destroying you."

"Go ahead," she snapped back. "I'll take you down with me."

He chuckled in his throat. "That would be quite an achievement," Keefe announced while grinning. "A police investigation will reveal you and you alone were behind the hit on Brenda Steele. I've covered my tracks far too well. You'll go down alone."

She stared at him with horror. "That's impossible," she gasped.

He shook his head while smiling deviously. "No, that's called framing your partner," Keefe replied mocking her. "You'll continue to do what I say and when I say it. Are we clear?"

Callie stared at him and attempted to read his eyes to see if he was possibly bluffing. She fidgeted then sneered and nodded. "Lucky for you I'm not really in a position to take you on right now," she scoffed while remaining angry. "But I promise; your day will come."

"You can't threaten me," he informed her and chuckled. "It doesn't work that way. I threaten you." He studied her a moment and raised an arrogant brow. "And since your antics cost me a fun-filled evening with your sister, you can make me happy by taking her place."

She rolled her eyes and sneered at him with disgust. "Fine," Callie scoffed.

He grinned and laughed at her. "Come on," Keefe announced playfully. "You have to love the irony. You have sex with Farley to blackmail him then I blackmail you for sex. It's like the circle of life."

She rolled her eyes. "You're not even a little bit funny, Keefe."

"And yet I'm still laughing," he announced with humor.

"You make me sick," she snarled. "Let's just get on with it."

Chapter 65

Return of Bridezilla - Part 4: Swing Low, Sweet Chariot

Gilda walked along the terrace, needing some fresh air and wanting to escape her husband's drunken antics with 'the boys'. The faint sounds of male and female groans were heard coming from the gazebo. Gilda appeared curious and approached the path. As she got closer, she saw Keefe taking liberties with a woman bent over the gazebo bench. Anger and jealousy were clearly seen on her face. She'd just about had enough of Keefe's pretend relationship with Elana. It needed to come to an end, and she no longer cared how. Gilda approached the gazebo, prepared to interrupt their little side quickie, when she saw the white wedding dress bunched against Keefe as he thrust wildly.

Gilda held back her horrified gasp, ducked out of sight, and then crept closer to make sure she hadn't been mistaken. She could see Otto's bride on the receiving end of Keefe's greedy thrusts. He was with her? Of all people, Keefe was banging Callie? Anger consumed Gilda as she crouched behind some shrubs and watched the entire encounter, listening to every grunt from *her* man! When he finished, he zipped his pants and gave Callie a somewhat disinterested look as she pulled her dress down and faced him. She avoided looking at him while her anger boiled over.

"Your old room in the servant's quarters is still vacant," he informed her without emotion. "I suggest you spend the night there and let Otto cool down. I'll come up with something by morning."

"Yeah, whatever," Callie snarled and turned her back on him while folding her arms across her chest.

"Don't be so dramatic," he scoffed with annoyance while rolling his eyes. "You've given a piece of ass to others for less in return. I'm a prince compared with the hundreds of men you've fucked."

Callie didn't respond and kept her back to him while silently seething. Keefe chuckled then left the gazebo. Gilda watched him leave while remaining hidden. She looked back at the blushing bride with her back still turned. Gilda looked around the area surrounding her. She picked up a large, decorative rock, slipped out of her shoes, and crept up the gazebo steps.

"Think you can steal my man, bitch?" Gilda snarled from behind her.

Callie was about to turn when Gilda struck her on the back of the head with the rock. The bride let out a quick, shrill cry as she collapsed to the wooden gazebo floor with a thump. Keefe spun around on the stone-paved path and saw Gilda in the gazebo with the rock in her hand. Keefe looked around, didn't see anyone, and then ran for the gazebo.

"Gilda," he gasped in a hushed tone and stared at Callie motionless on the wooden floor. He met Gilda's gaze. "What the hell--?"

"I saw you," she snarled and dropped the rock, which only contained a little blood on it. "You were fucking her." She pointed demandingly at Callie, who remained motionless. "Her of all people!"

"Keep your voice down," Keefe shushed her then looked around.

There wasn't anyone around to hear them. He crouched alongside Callie and checked for a pulse. Keefe sat back on his feet and stared in horror at the motionless bride. He then looked back up at Gilda.

"She's dead," he gasped.

"Good," Gilda scoffed while folding her arms across her chest.

"Good?" he demanded. "Do you have any idea what you've done?"

"Yeah," Gilda snapped. "I killed the whore who was sleeping with my husband." She glared at Keefe. "And fucking my lover."

"We can't let anyone find her like this," he insisted while staring up at Gilda, who seemed to be returning to her senses. "They'll put you away for life."

Gilda nervously ran her fingers through her hair. "You're right," she gasped as reality swept over her then stared into Keefe's eyes. "What are we going to do? You're not going to let them arrest me, are you?"

"No, of course not," Keefe insisted. "Give me a minute to think."

Gilda sat on the bench, held her head, and stared at the dead woman near her feet. "I don't know what came over me," she gasped.

Keefe glanced across the garden and toward the house. They were still alone. He indicated the gazebo railing in the back.

"Over the railing," he announced and picked up Callie, who lay draped in his arms. "I'll pass her off to you."

Gilda nodded and climbed over the gazebo railing. She landed on the other side. Keefe lowered Callie over the railing and into Gilda's arms. She was a strong woman and was able to hold her up. Keefe jumped over the railing and joined her on the other side. The gazebo and dark garden would offer cover for them all the way to the crypt. Keefe held the dead bride draped in his arms.

"We'll take her to the woods behind the crypt," he announced. "Keep watch for anyone outside the house."

As Keefe carried the dead bride, Gilda watched the house and surrounding area while following him. He saw the gardener's workshop not far from them.

"There's some rope alongside the gardener's workshop," he informed Gilda. "Grab it and that small stool next to it."

She nodded, ran for the items, and returned only a few minutes later. They headed toward the crypt.

"What are we going to do?" she asked with concern.

"Distraught over ruining her marriage to Otto, Callie decided to take her own life," Keefe informed her. "I'll take care of setting the scene in the woods. I have the wedding program in my jacket pocket and a pen."

"What do you want me to do?" she asked with surprise.

"I want you to jot down a quick suicide note," he informed her. "Guilt over what happened with Nole and how sorry she is for what she did to Otto. She can't live with herself. The usual suicide note stuff. Write in print not cursive. She always wrote in print."

Chapter *66*

A Bitch to Remember - Part 2: The Sleepy-time Memorial Service

The memorial service for Callie was still going strong in the game room, although almost everyone remaining was just about wasted. Dane and Raina talked while heading into the kitchen, passing the partially open study door. As they turned the corridor for the kitchen, the study door opened the rest of the way to reveal Keefe. He peered into the hallway, made sure everything was clear, and then entered the hall. Nole stepped out of the library, startling Keefe. He was surprised to see Otto's business partner, considering he'd been escorted out half an hour earlier.

"I just realized what's been bothering me," Nole informed Keefe. "It's you."

"What are you talking about?" Keefe asked while acting bored.

"I know you deleted that video from my phone," Nole announced. "The one incriminating you."

"I don't know what you're talking about," Keefe insisted. "I don't know anything about a video, and your reputation around here is about as good as shit, so no one will believe a word you say."

Keefe was about to walk away when Nole stopped him. "Yeah, well, we'll just see about that," Nole remarked. "I was questioned by that Detective Payne, and something he said finally makes sense."

Keefe leaned against the wall looking bored and impatient while staring at Nole.

"When he questioned me about my indiscretion with Callie that night, I had to admit we had sex," Nole informed him. "When he mentioned semen samples and DNA, I never even thought about it until now."

"I don't know what you're getting at," Keefe remarked with little interest while glaring at Nole, "but I wish you'd get on with it."

"I had a friend read the police report to clarify what the coroner had found," Nole announced then cocked his head with a strange look on his face. "He told me the report said they'd found semen when they did the autopsy, and they also found traces on her wedding dress. I realize I had a lot to drink that night, but I know for a fact they couldn't have found my semen on her. We were interrupted by Otto." He raised a cocky brow. "That leaves me to wonder who she had sex with *after* me. After what I'd recorded with my cell phone before the wedding, I think I have a pretty good idea who'd be a match for what they'd found."

Keefe continued to stare at him with little reaction, although his body twitched slightly.

Nole grinned and nodded. "Yeah, that's right," he announced with a chuckle. "You just assumed I would accept responsibility for that since there were witnesses, but I think the police should do some DNA tests on you and see if they come up with a match."

"They'd be wasting their time," Keefe announced while straightening. "I didn't kill Callie, and I certainly didn't have sex with her after you were found with her."

"I'm going to talk to Otto whether he wants to listen or not," Nole insisted and made a motion toward the noisy game room. "Otto and I may have had our differences, but he's still my friend. I won't let you railroad him into a murder charge. No, I suspect you were blackmailing Callie and maybe even killed her."

"I could say the same for you, Nole," Keefe informed him with little interest while taking a step closer to him.

"Does your girlfriend know you were doing her sister?" Nole demanded. "I'm willing to bet she doesn't. I say we get Otto and Elana together and let them compare notes on you. I think you're attempting to frame Otto for Callie's murder, and I won't let you get away with it."

As Nole turned toward the open game room doorway, Keefe suddenly spun into a high roundhouse kick and struck him on the back of the head. Nole dropped to the floor not far from the game room, but no one heard it since it had been so noisy inside. He looked around with concern then dragged Nole into the nearby study. He found some duct tape in the desk drawer and bound the unconscious man's hands and ankles before placing some tape across his mouth, just in case he came to. He hid Nole behind the door and hurried back into the hallway while fixing his jacket and hair.

Keefe cursed softly to himself and then entered the game room while attempting to look casual. He saw Gilda looking bored at the bar and slipped alongside her but kept his eyes focused elsewhere.

"Nole has incriminating evidence against us. He was going to tell Otto everything," he muttered to her, causing her to react. He placed a hand on her shoulder in an attempt to relax her. "Just remain calm. I have him contained for the moment, but we're going to be exposed. We need to do something fast."

"Like what?" she asked while sipping her drink and avoided looking at him.

"Do you have any pills on you?" he asked. "We need to knock everyone out, so I can deal with Nole unnoticed. I can't do anything with so many witnesses."

"Yeah, I have a bottle," she replied. "What do you want me to do?"

"Give me the bottle," he instructed.

She made sure no one was watching them then removed the bottle of pills from her purse and slipped them to him.

"I'll crush them up and return the bottle to you," he instructed. "I need you to spike the pitcher of martini."

"That's going to take an hour or longer to work," she reminded him. "It's going to depend on how much they drink."

"That's good enough," he replied. "That'll give both of us enough time to establish alibis with our partners. Once Farley finishes his drugged drink, lure him up to the bedroom. Stay there with him and don't come back down. I'll handle the rest."

§

Half an hour later, Keefe and Elana were in the sunroom aggressively kissing and groping each other. The excessively drunken Elana suddenly pulled away from him and grinned with enthusiasm.

"Let's do it in the gazebo," she announced.

Keefe was less enthusiastic and was about to protest when Elana giggled and stumbled out the French doors onto the terrace. Keefe groaned his reluctance and hurried after her. For someone who was stumbling down drunk, she made it to the gazebo in record time, keeping two steps ahead of the reluctant Keefe. They reached the gazebo when she turned to face him. She threw her arms around his neck while grinning and suddenly sank against him out cold. Keefe caught her, stared a moment with surprise, and then sighed with relief. He lowered her to the gazebo floor and hurried back for the house. On his way back to the house, he saw the garage lights were on. He could make out people within one of the garage bays. Keefe groaned with annoyance.

He hurried into the kitchen and found it abandoned. He entered the grand hallway and ran for the basement steps. Keefe hurried into the basement and switched off the backup generator. He then approached the fuse box and shut off the power. Anyone left who was still conscious would be fumbling around in the dark. He returned upstairs. As he approached the study, he saw Otto passed out just inside the study doorway. Keefe groaned with disgust then came up with another idea. He grabbed Otto and pulled him toward the kitchen. He heard voices in the kitchen and approaching fast. Keefe panicked and deposited Otto in the hall closet, where no one would look with the lights out. He darted back into the study as Dane and Raina appeared from the kitchen and headed for the basement.

Once they had headed down the basement steps, Keefe grabbed Nole, placed him in a fireman's carry, and hurried along the hallway. He carried the unconscious man into the sunroom, out the French doors, and into the dark garden. By the time Keefe reached the crypt, he was nearly out of breath. He dropped Nole just behind the crypt, hurried for the gardener's workshop where he found a pair of gardening gloves, and slipped into them. He then fumbled around in the darkness until he found some more rope and an old hunting knife belonging to the gardener. Keefe hurried back to the woods, threw the rope over the same branch Callie had been hanged, and tied the excess around the trunk. He then made a noose and placed it around Nole's neck. He untied the rope from around the tree and hoisted Nole from the ground by the rope until his feet were a foot above the ground.

Nole came to and struggled while gasping against the rope tight around his neck. Since his neck wouldn't break, he was slowly suffocating to death. Keefe stood before Nole and looked into his eyes. Nole attempted to muffle a gasp. Keefe raised an arrogant brow.

"Feeling pretty foolish right about now, huh?" he announced.

Keefe gritted his teeth and plunged the knife into Nole's abdomen just beneath his ribs. Nole managed a slight, breathless gasp. Keefe put all his weight against the knife and allowed his body and gravity to pull it down, deeply slicing Nole down to his groin. He pulled the knife free and let it drop to the ground. As Keefe stepped back while grinning, Nole's midsection opened up, and his insides plopped down to the ground beneath his feet. Keefe held back his startled gasp and placed his hand to his mouth while dry heaving. He had to turn away to keep from throwing up. Keefe returned to the gardener's workshop and hid the gloves, which surprisingly didn't have much blood on them, and then headed back for the house.

§

As Keefe slipped into the kitchen from the back door, he could hear several creaks from the second floor, indicating someone was moving around upstairs. He considered his options then hurried into the staff wing and darted down the corridor. He paused outside of Dane's bedroom door, grimaced, and then tapped lightly on the door. When there was no response, he opened the door and slipped into the nearly dark room. He turned on a small pen light and approached the closet. The locked box was exactly where Callie had mentioned. He grabbed the locked box, set it on the bed, and removed the key from the small, wooden jewelry box on the dresser. Keefe unlocked the box and opened it. To his surprise, the box was filled with old girly magazines. He cursed under his breath.

Keefe returned the locked box to the closet then placed the key in the wooden box on the dresser. He heard Sloan in the corridor. He grabbed the jewelry box, darted behind the open door, and waited. Sloan shined her flashlight into the room and hesitantly entered. Keefe crept up behind her and struck her on the head with the wooden jewelry box. He stood over Sloan a moment and contemplated his next move when he heard voices from the kitchen. The staff wing door opened. Keefe again cursed and hid behind the door.

"Sloan," Titus called out. "Sloan, where are you?"

Titus could be heard in the corridor. He peered into Dane's dark room and saw Sloan lying face down on the floor with the lit flashlight not far from her outstretched hand.

"Sloan," Titus gasped and ran into the room.

As he fell to his knees alongside her, the bedroom door shut behind him. Titus spun on his knee toward the closed door in the nearly dark room and reached for the flashlight. Keefe struck him on the head and watched him fall alongside Sloan. Keefe replaced the jewelry box, opened the bedroom door, and peered into the dimly lit hallway before slipping out of the room.

§

Keefe entered the gazebo where he hastily removed Elana's clothes and discarded them along the lawn leading from the sunroom. As he approached the gazebo, he removed his own clothes, tossing them haphazardly around the lawn, and then ran up the steps to join his naked girlfriend. He made himself comfortable alongside Elana while breathing heavily for several minutes. His body finally relaxed.

Chapter *67*

Don't Get Jimmy Love's Boxers in a Bunch Part 2: The Night Elana Died

The night Elana died. Just before dinner, Keefe slipped inside the empty, dimly lit library and shut the door behind him. Gilda threw her arms around his neck, momentarily startling him, and then kissed him quickly but passionately. Keefe returned the brief kiss with less enthusiasm and pulled away. His look was serious.

"You know what you need to do?" he asked while staring into her eyes.

She grinned and nodded. "Is everything ready?"

"You'll find everything you need hidden under the bed in your room," he informed her. "Remember, it's important that you don't put the sedatives into Farley's drink until right before you head upstairs. We can't have him passing out in front of everyone."

"Are you sure you can encourage Elana to drink enough?" Gilda asked then appeared giddy. "I can't believe we're finally doing this."

"I have Elana, don't worry," he replied. "The chauffeur had energy boost in the limousine glove box. One of those in her drink, and she'll be guzzling the hard stuff." He eyed her and smiled. "Are you ready?"

She eagerly nodded. "I've been ready to be a widow for years."

"Good luck," he announced then kissed her quickly. "See you tonight."

§

"You bitch!" Elana screamed alerting the entire game room to her fight with Gilda.

Dane attempted to hold Elana back as she clawed at Farley to reach the woman behind him.

"Everyone settle down," Dane announced without releasing Elana then eyed both women. "The bar is officially closed to the two of you."

"Fine," Gilda scoffed in a drunken tone. She snatched her drink and glared at her husband. "Finish your drink. We're going to our room."

Farley frowned but obediently did as he was told. Both finished their drinks in a few swallows. As Gilda stumbled toward the game room door, Farley followed with less enthusiasm. The Nixon's left the game room and headed up the grand stairs in silence. They continued along the second floor hallway and approached their bedroom midway down the corridor. Gilda entered the bedroom as Farley lagged behind with less enthusiasm. She glared at her husband, who didn't bother looking at her. He removed his shoes and shirt in silence.

"You never side with me," she announced in an angry tone. "That little twit says and does whatever she wants, and you just let her."

"What was I supposed to do, Gilda?" Farley asked with a defeated sigh. "Create a scene. We fired her. She's not your problem anymore. You'll never have to see her again after we leave here tomorrow."

Farley tossed his shirt onto the nearby chair and stood to open his belt. He suddenly clutched his head, attempting to remain steady on his feet, and fell backward onto the bed.

"I don't feel right," he announced and attempted to sit up. He again fell back down, and his hand fell to the bed.

Gilda stared at him a moment then approached and nudged his arm. He didn't move and appeared to be unconscious. Gilda grinned then kneeled alongside the bed and removed a kitchen butcher knife and a plastic bag containing a pair of gardening gloves from Hanson's workshop. She set them on the bed then collected her husband's shirt and shoes. A few minutes passed before she heard the bedroom door next to her's close. Gilda hurried to the closed connecting bathroom door and listened. She could hear Elana fumbling around within the bathroom. She listened for the connecting door on the other end to close then entered the bathroom and listened at the connecting door to Elana's room.

The emergency light went out in Elana's bedroom, indicating she had gone to bed. She was so intoxicated; she'd undoubtedly passed out the moment she hit the bed. Gilda hurried back into her room, slipped into the gardening gloves, and grabbed the butcher knife. She returned to the bathroom and opened the connecting door that wasn't locked. Gilda slipped into Elana's bedroom and saw the young woman lying naked beneath the covers. She crept up to her bedside. As Gilda raised the knife above her head in both hands, Elana's eyes opened. She gasped when she saw the woman standing over her bed. Gilda plunged the knife into her abdomen, immediately ripped it back out, and watched her gasp and wheeze while clutching her bleeding stomach. Elana stared at Gilda with horror.

Gilda smirked. "Guess what, Elana?" she announced while raising clever brows. "Keefe was using you all this time. He used you to spy on my husband for me, and after I had Farley fire your sister, Keefe and I became lovers."

Elana stared at her with horror in her eyes while gasping and clutching her abdomen.

"That's right," Gilda informed her. "I killed your sister. That whore didn't just fuck Nole on her wedding day; she was fucking Keefe as well." Her twisted smile faded to a psychotic look. "And I wasn't about to tolerate that."

As Elana continued to wheeze, Gilda leaned closer to her ear. "Every time Keefe fucked you, he was thinking of me," she whispered.

While straightening, Gilda slashed Elana across her forearm. Elana could barely cry out. The psychotic woman grinned and slashed the dying woman's forearms several more times while Elana could do little more than whimper and clutch her bleeding midsection. Gilda pulled her hand away from the wound and stabbed her right hand, piercing her palm. Elana cried out, but it wasn't very loud. As Elana remain staring at her while slowly dying, Gilda grinned. She set the knife on the bed and removed her gloves before heading back to the connecting bathroom. She returned only a moment later with Farley draped across her back and his feet dragging along the floor behind her. She dropped him onto the vacant side of the bed next to Elana, who attempted to speak but couldn't.

Gilda removed Farley's pants and underwear, carelessly tossing them to the floor, and then returned to the connecting bathroom. She came back a moment later with his shirt and shoes and set them on the floor as well. Gilda easily rolled her unconscious husband onto Elana, who softly cried out now almost unable to breathe. Gilda put the gloves back on, removed Elana's hand from between their bodies, and ran her blood-covered hand over Farley's face before rolling him back to the other side of the bed. She then reclaimed the knife and smiled sweetly at Elana.

"It's too bad you and Farley got into a lover's spat," Gilda informed her with a psychotic look in her eyes. "You tried to fight him off as he stabbed you. Fortunately, right before you died, you got in one, fatal blow."

Gilda placed the knife in Elana's hand, clutched her hand over the knife, and rolled her onto her side. She held the knife in Elana's hand as she plunged it into Farley's neck. He jerked in his unconscious state but never roused. Gilda pulled the knife from Farley's neck, while it was still clutched in Elana's hand, and forced her to drop the knife between them. Gilda released the dying woman. Elana collapsed onto her back and gasped several times before she finally stopped breathing. Gilda grinned with satisfaction.

"Well, that was fun," Gilda announced then removed her blood-soaked gloves and headed back to the connecting bathroom, shutting the door behind her. She entered her bedroom and returned the bloodied gloves to the plastic bag on her bed. She stashed the bag under the bed and made herself comfortable until Keefe would join her.

§

Gilda impatiently looked at the bedside clock several times while lying seductively on the bed wearing a sexy satin nightgown. A little after midnight, others could be heard in the hallway, but their voices were faint and muffled. She possibly dozed off. When Gilda again looked at the clock, it was nearly one thirty in the morning. Keefe was late. She stood and started to pace. The bedroom door quietly opened. Gilda breathed a sigh of relief when Keefe slipped into the mostly dark room from the dimly lit hallway.

He looked at her and grinned. "Is it done?"

She nodded and threw her arms around his neck. He returned the smile and kissed her passionately and with aggression. He pulled away and smiled while touching her cheek, pleased with her.

"We have to be careful while stuck in this house," he informed her. "One drink to celebrate, but then I have to return to my room."

"I've survived this long, I can go another day," she informed him.

Keefe approached the small refrigerator in the elegant cabinet and removed a bottle of wine. She eyed the wine and appeared pleased.

"When did you put that in there?" she asked.

"When I brought the other things to the room," he replied while grinning. "I thought you'd like to celebrate."

"Oh, yes," she replied eagerly. "I'd like to do more than have a glass of wine though."

"Tomorrow, I promise," he replied. "When we're away from here." He nodded across the room while removing two glasses. "Did you put the gloves in the bag? I'll take them with me and dispose of them."

She nodded and removed the bag from under the bed while Keefe poured them each a glass of wine. He removed a small bottle from his jacket pocket and dumped a clear liquid into one of the glasses. He slipped the bottle back into his pocket before picking up the tainted glass of wine and extended it to her. She accepted the glass as he picked up his. Keefe headed for the bed with Gilda eagerly following. They sat on the bed together and held up their glasses.

"To revenge," he announced while grinning. "And to us."

"Forever," she added.

They clinked glasses then drank their wine. When he made a point to finish his entire glass, she did the same. Keefe sprang to his feet.

"I should go before someone finds me here and ruins everything," he announced. "Remember; wait for someone else to find the bodies."

She nodded and attempted to stand but couldn't. Gilda suddenly made a face and gasped. She looked at him with horror.

"What did you do?" she attempted to cry out but could barely speak.

Gilda gasped several times and again attempted to stand. Keefe made comforting sounds and gently guided her back onto the bed.

"Don't fight it, baby," he announced while smiling. "Trust me; it's better this way."

Gilda collapsed to the bed and couldn't move. She gasped several times before she stopped breathing. Keefe lovingly shut her eyes then sprang into action. He slipped into a pair of latex gloves, removed his handkerchief, and wiped the bottle of poison clean of his fingerprints. He placed the bottle in her hand, pressed her fingers against it, and set it on the bedside table. He then wiped the outside of her glass clean and also pressed her fingerprints on it, setting it on the table as well. He hurried to the small bar, wiped his fingerprints from the bottle, and brought it to her bedside. He placed her fingerprints on the bottle and placed it on the bedside table alongside the other items.

Keefe grabbed his glass, ran into the bathroom, and hastily washed and dried it. He returned to the bedroom and replaced the clean glass to the bar. He grabbed the plastic bag containing the bloodied gloves and hurried back into the bathroom. He opened the bag, dumped the gloves into the bathroom trashcan, and then entered Elana's room through the connecting bathroom door. He eyed the scene, grimaced a moment, and hurried for Farley's body. He easily removed Farley from the bed, careful to keep from getting blood on his own clothes, dragged him across the floor, and deposited him near the bedroom door. He returned to the bed, picked up the blood-covered knife and approached Farley on the floor. Keefe drew a deep breath.

He sucked up his courage and stabbed Farley in the back several times. Keefe made a face, placed his hand to his mouth, and nearly threw up. He collected himself then hurried for the bathroom, dropping the bloodstained knife in the sink. He returned to Gilda's room and wiped the blood from his gloved hands onto her nightgown. He then removed the latex gloves, placed them in the plastic bag, and hurried for the bedroom door. He took another moment to assess the room and make sure he hadn't forgotten anything. Keefe gently opened the door, peered into the hallway, and slipped out of the bedroom.

Chapter 68

If I Tell You; I Have to Kill You

Present day. Keefe leaned on the island counter across from Dane within the kitchen and continued with his story. Dane listened to him for the longest time without interrupting or even commenting.

"After Gilda took care of Elana, I killed Gilda and made it look like suicide. Everyone would think she was the killer," he announced then sneered. "When you concluded it wasn't suicide, I knew I had to eliminate you and frame Miller. You confessed your suspicions about Miller to Raina, who would reluctantly tell the police what she suspected happened." He grinned seeming proud of himself. "End of story."

"My God," Dane boldly announced while shaking his head in disbelief. "I thought you'd never shut up."

Keefe appeared bewildered by the comment while staring at the butler.

"For the record," Dane then announced, "the house's PA system has been turned on this entire time." He nodded to the stairs behind Keefe. "Everyone in the house just heard your detailed and, may I add, long-winded confession."

Keefe looked over his shoulder at the box on the wall. When he looked back, Dane had pulled the shotgun out from under the counter and aimed it at Keefe. The dining room door suddenly burst open, and Jimmy Love charged into the kitchen like a flashy gladiator while clutching the baseball bat.

"Jimmy Love is here to save you, honey!" he cried out while raising the bat, prepared for combat.

Jimmy Love's dramatic entrance was enough to startle Dane and give Keefe the opportunity he needed to raise his own weapon. He fired haphazardly at Dane while leaping across the kitchen table as Dane simultaneously fired the shotgun at the moving man, mostly missing him. Stray buckshot caught Keefe in the arm as he disappeared behind the table. Dane ducked behind the island counter, narrowly avoiding the stray shot that hit the cupboard behind him. Keefe aimed his weapon above the table and fired at Jimmy Love as he attempted to dive to the floor. The bullet hit him in the arm, helping him to the floor a little faster. Raina crouched in the dining room doorway and watched the unfolding scene while casting looks at Jimmy Love, who clutched his bleeding arm while writhing on the floor in agony.

Keefe aimed the gun at the island counter and waited for Dane to reappear. He shifted looks to the outer kitchen door then made his move, bolting for the patio door. He threw open the door to reveal Miller, who escaped the staff wing linen closet and exited through one of the servant's patio entrances. Miller grabbed Keefe's wrist to keep the gun away from him and punched him in the face. Keefe stumbled back a step and was again forced to bolt behind the kitchen table before Dane could take another shot at him. Keefe aimed the gun at Miller, who gasped and leaped into the nearby stairway. The gun fired and struck the wall not far from where Miller had been standing.

Jimmy Love was now on his knees while still clinging to his bleeding arm but seemed paralyzed by the sound of the gun firing. Raina leaped across the kitchen floor and tackled the injured wedding planner to the opposite end of the island counter to keep him out of the line of fire. They sat with their backs to the counter and remained hidden. Keefe stared at the open kitchen door to the patio and freedom then bolted for the open door. Dane popped up over the island counter and fired at Keefe. The buckshot exploded the relic ham radio but missed its intended target.

Miller leaped from the stairway and tackled Keefe to the floor before he could reach the open door. The gun flew from his hand upon impact. Miller landed on top of Keefe and aggressively punched him in the face. Keefe managed to throw Miller off him, and both men simultaneously leaped to their feet. Dane stepped out from behind the island counter and removed two additional shotgun shells from his jacket pocket to reload the shotgun when he saw the face-off.

"You killed my family," Miller cried out in rage that had been repressed for two years.

Dane saw Keefe take an aggressive karate stance and knew what was about to happen. "Miller, no," Dane cried out as Miller attempted to punch Keefe.

Keefe spun into a roundhouse kick, nailing Miller in the face, and sending him to the floor. Dane cast the shotgun aside and bolted for Keefe before he could do any further damage to Miller, who writhed around the floor. Raina and Jimmy Love stared at the empty, discarded shotgun not far from where they hid. The two shells had rolled beneath the kitchen table and were just out of reach. Keefe spun to face Dane, prepared to fight him. He kicked out, attempting to stop Dane's approach. Dane blocked his kick with his forearm, surprising Keefe. Dane then spun into his own roundhouse kick and struck Keefe in the face, knocking him backward into the wall. Keefe was slightly dazed and stared at Dane with surprise.

"Top in your class my ass," Dane scoffed. "You're an MMA fighter wannabe."

Keefe sneered and lunged for Dane, attempting to throw an aggressive punch. Dane blocked the punch, struck him with his own fist, and kicked him in the abdomen.

"No style, little form," Dane informed him and then kicked him in the ribs while sneering. "And you've absolutely no flexibility."

As Keefe hit the nearby doorframe, Dane gracefully slipped out of his jacket, which had been hindering his movements, and tossed it aside. Jimmy Love and Raina both eyed Dane's stylish yet aggressive jacket removal and marveled simultaneously.

"Lordy lordy; have mercy," Jimmy Love muttered while sizing up Dane.

Raina scrambled across the floor for the discarded shotgun shells beneath the kitchen table. Keefe again moved to his feet with a little less energy, faced Dane, and now panted.

"If you were smart, you'd stay down," Dane informed him then kicked him again, striking him in the chest.

Keefe was thrown backward and struck the floor. He writhed in agony a moment then saw the discarded gun and scrambled for it. Dane saw him go for the gun and lunged for him. Keefe grabbed the gun, took little time to aim it at Dane, and pulled the trigger. The bullet grazed Dane's arm, only momentarily surprising him but kept him from attacking. Keefe aimed the gun with more conviction at the butler.

"If you were smart, you wouldn't have missed with the first shot. Now you die," Keefe snarled back at Dane.

Keefe was about to pull the trigger when he heard the familiar metallic sound of the shotgun closing. Keefe spun with surprise to the sound. Jimmy Love had the shotgun aimed at Keefe and pulled the trigger. Raina and Miller ducked to the sound of the shotgun blast. As the shotgun fired, Jimmy Love squealed and flew backward from the recoil. The full brunt of the buckshot struck Keefe in the chest and threw him to the floor. Jimmy Love caught his balance, lowered the shotgun, and flamboyantly pointed at the dead man.

"That was for ruining my favorite jacket," Jimmy Love squealed.

Dane hurried across the kitchen where Raina was huddled near the kitchen table and helped her to her feet. She threw her arms around his neck and hugged him.

"Hey," Jimmy Love cried out while holding the shotgun in one hand and placing his free hand on his hip. "How about a little love for the real hero here?"

Raina laughed and hugged Jimmy Love. He immediately squealed with delight to the embrace. When she released him, he looked at Dane, smiled boldly, and opened his arms.

Dane rolled his eyes and snatched the shotgun from him. "Not happening, J.L."

Miller approached and opened his arms to Jimmy Love. He squealed with delight and hugged Miller. Miller pulled away then looked at Dane.

"You do realize those intercoms haven't worked in years," Miller remarked.

"Yeah," Dane replied. "But Keefe didn't know that, and I needed a distraction."

"Honey," Jimmy Love announced to Dane and gave him a sweeping glance, "*you* are a distraction."

Chapter 69

Ultimate Happy Ending

Within the game room, Jenna held ice to Miller's already swollen face while Otto stared at his stepson and shook his head.

"A little brave," Otto remarked to Miller and patted his shoulder, "but a lot stupid."

Sloan finished wrapping Jimmy Love's injured arm while he watched with fascination. Dane had a matching wrap on the same arm. Raina clung to Dane's good arm while sitting on the sofa with him, relieved it was finally over.

Dane glared at her with some disappointment. "What happened back there? The plan was you listened in on the confession while staying out of sight," he announced then indicated Jimmy Love. "You certainly weren't supposed to bring J.L. as your enforcer."

"He didn't give me much choice," Raina informed him. "I needed an exit, and he insisted on coming along." She gave him a condescending look. "And, correct me if I'm wrong, but when I agreed to that entire 'flush out the killer scheme' by having a heated argument on the patio with you, we never discussed you being alone in the kitchen so far from the rest of us."

"Keefe wasn't going to try anything within earshot of witnesses," Dane protested in his defense. "I had to locate myself far enough from the rest of the house for him to make his move."

Before they could finish their discussion, Titus hurried into the game room from the front door and appeared out of breath.

"Hanson made it across the bridge in his pickup truck," he informed them. "He'll be back in an hour with Detective Payne and the police." Titus hesitated and looked at the injured men. "What happened?"

"It's a long story," Dane reported.

"I'm a hero," Jimmy Love announced cheerfully while bouncing in his seat.

"God, we're never going to hear the end of that," Dane muttered and eyed Raina, who sat alongside him.

"Let him have his moment," she announced with a laugh as she affectionately patted his arm.

Levi entered the game room looking upset and shook his head with disgust. "My kitchen is officially a crime scene," he remarked.

"Yeah, sorry about that," Dane replied.

§

By the time Detective Payne finished his investigation, and the bodies were removed, it was nearly three in the morning. Tia and Olivia accepted a ride home from the detective while Jimmy Love opted to stay at the mansion and get a ride home in the morning. The paramedics examined both Dane and Jimmy Love's wounds. Since Sloan had done such a wonderful job tending to their wounds, it was determined they didn't need to go to the hospital. After their ordeal, Otto ordered the staff to take the rest of the week off to recover from their injuries. Hanson was the first to turn in with Levi bringing in a close second. Once the detective left with Tia and Olivia, Sloan linked onto Titus' arm and smiled sweetly.

"I'm heading to bed," she announced. "Care to walk me to my room?"

Titus grinned and nodded. Everyone cast a glance at the affectionate couple as they left the game room.

Otto managed a tiny laugh then approached the bar and refilled his glass. "They realize they're not fooling anyone, right?" he teased.

"They were meant to be together," Miller informed his father. "Their relationship just got derailed for a little while." He looked at his watch and groaned. "I'm sleeping until noon, and then I'm getting out of this house." He eyed Jenna and smiled. "I know the Maui beach house is vacant. Maybe a few weeks on the beach is what I really need."

Jenna affectionately linked onto his arm and returned the smile. "Hmm, that sounds romantic," she teased. "Want some company?"

"Absolutely," he announced while grinning and leaned in to kiss her.

Otto groaned with annoyance. "My God," he scoffed. "Take it upstairs already."

Miller pulled back before kissing Jenna and smiled with embarrassment. "What a wonderful idea," he teased. He then looked at Raina and Dane. "Are you guys turning in?"

Dane shifted and appeared uncomfortable. Miller cringed with embarrassment.

"Sorry," he replied timidly.

Otto rolled his eyes then sipped his whiskey. "All of you; just go to bed," he grumbled. "I already stated my feelings on who's sleeping with whom. You have a thirty-minute head start before I turn in, so I'd better not hear anything disturbing after that."

Raina eyed Dane and raised her brows. "I think that was the official green light," she informed him and extended her hand to him.

Dane offered a warm smile and accepted her hand. "It's going to take a little getting used to," he remarked then leaned closer and whispered into her ear. "I'm still not convinced he won't kill me in my sleep."

She laughed and pulled him toward the doorway after Miller and Jenna. Jimmy Love joined Otto at the bar and smiled cheerfully while extending his empty glass for him to fill. Otto glared at him then groaned and reluctantly filled his glass. Raina and Dane were just about to the doorway when Otto turned on his bar stool and looked back at them.

"Dane," he gruffly announced causing them to stop.

Dane looked back at Otto. "Yes, Sir?"

"About that question you asked yesterday morning," Otto announced and offered a tiny smile. "I'd be honored." His look then hardened and turned demanding. "Sooner rather than later would be nice."

Dane smiled and nodded with understanding. "Thank you, Sir."

Raina gave Dane a strange look. He clung to her hand, smiled warmly, and led her from the room.

Otto sighed into his glass of whiskey and glanced at Jimmy Love at the bar alongside him. "Ready to plan another wedding?"

The End

Coming Soon!

"Midnight Requisition 2"
Amateur Night

&

"Witness Protection 7"
Bravo Foxtrot

Other books by Holly Copella!
Reviews left on Amazon are appreciated!

"The Battle for Andrea Maria"

A cruise ship attack turns six survivors into overnight celebrities after they take credit for the heroic act of a stowaway who died saving them.

The cruise is just what Jess needed--a bit of harmless fun far from her daily grind. But what begins as a relaxing vacation turns into a desperate fight for her life when terrorists take over the ship and start piling up bodies. Teaming up with a mysterious stowaway, Jess attempts to send out a distress call but knows they cannot wait for help to come. If she or the few remaining passengers have any hope for survival, Jess must act now. The papers dub it "The Battle for *Andrea Maria*," but to Jess it is the moment she fought side-by-side with her enigmatic Romeo, saving the ship--and losing him. She thinks the story ends there, but really, the nightmare is just beginning...

"Insanely Deadly"

When the dead return to life, it's up to an admiral's daughter and a mildly insane, former war hero to save their small town.

Jetta Cross, a Navy Admiral's daughter, is tasked with keeping her father's comrade, a former war hero turned town crazy, grounded in the real world. Capt. John Hunter is still fighting the war in his head, where imaginary dead people are part of his world. When a viral outbreak brings about a zombie uprising, Hunter is left to his own devices. He must resume his role as a one-man commando unit in order to destroy the ravenous undead. With Hunter still fighting his own inner demons as well as the undead, the townspeople fear their zombie neighbors may not be the only threat. Stranded at the island's luxurious resort with a handful of workers, Jetta is forced to live up to her father's reputation and take charge of the deteriorating situation at the hotel. She must wage her own war against the infected before the government declares her hometown a total loss.

"Deadly Institution"

A town recluse suspected of killing his wife teams up with a young woman in order to stop a killer.

After being accused of murdering his wife, Konrad Asher turns his back on the town that once adored him. Ten years later, he still holds his grudge and the title of the most feared man in town. With the reopening of the burned mental institution, where his wife had died, former employees are now murdered one-by-one, throwing suspicion back on Asher. A young local reporter, Jacey, is forced to reveal her long-time friendship with the infamous recluse in order to clear his name not only in the recent murders but to exonerate him in the death of his wife as well. Will Jacey's relationship with Asher invite the killer closer to her? Or is the killer already in her life?

"Death Displacement"

A grief-stricken man travels back in time to seek revenge on the woman who murdered his girlfriend but inadvertently falls in love with her.

Kane is about to marry the woman he loves. His life is perfect. A few weeks before the wedding, a vindictive woman from his girlfriend's past mysteriously arrives and kills her. He learns of a traumatic accident that happened five years earlier, which triggers Riley's hatred for his girlfriend. Distraught over his girlfriend's death, Kane uses an antique time machine to travel into the past in order to find and destroy the woman responsible. When he runs into Riley's younger self, he realizes she's not the monster she later becomes, and he can't bring himself to destroy her. With a little help from his oddball friend from the past, they formulate a plan to prevent the accident that sends Riley down her destructive path. Kane's plan backfires when he falls for the younger Riley. His new tortured existence is further complicated when future Riley, his girlfriend's killer, shows up with her own devious agenda that doesn't include him. Will he be able to stop the time ripple, which ultimately ends with his girlfriend's death? Or will future Riley take him out of the timeline forever--

"Dead Village"

After strange happenings isolate a small resort town from the rest of the world, nearly one hundred residents seek refuge at the closed hotel. Only eight survive the night. And that's just the beginning...

One day after the entire population of Fox Ridge Village disappears, a car wreck forces several unsuspecting crash victims to seek help at the closed summer hotel. Within the hotel, they discover the grisly aftermath of a brutal slaughter. Crash victims Vander and Devon, a reluctant clairvoyant, team up to solve the riddle of the "haunted hotel" and the mass hysteria plaguing the remaining survivors. By the time they discover the hotel's secret, they're already drawn into the hysteria. As the body count continues to climb, it's a race to isolate the source and bring everyone back to reality before they kill one another. Will Devon be able to communicate with the traumatized spirits before their fate becomes her own?

"Town Darling"

After surviving a brutal attack that claims the lives of those she loves, a young woman seeks revenge on a corrupt town.

Going back home is never easy, but for Casey, it means returning to her corrupt hometown where she barely survived a brutal attack. Accompanied by two family friends, she seeks justice for the night that destroyed her life. Her physical scars are nothing compared to her emotional ones, forcing the local sheriff to believe that the town darling is back for revenge. As the conspiracy for her revenge appears to be leading up to the coveted town fair, the sheriff is determined to stop her from fulfilling her vengeful scheme...but guilt over his role on that fateful night continues to haunt him. Will his desperate need for Casey's forgiveness be his undoing? Or will Casey's desire for revenge destroy them both?

"Basement Dwellers"

A viral outbreak at a hospital leaves a mortician, sheriff, and coroner fighting for their lives against a horde of undead and the CDC.

After a massive car wreck leaves several survivors in critical condition at the local hospital, a surgeon uses experimental drugs on his critical patients and accidentally causes a zombie outbreak. When local mortician, Lexx, receives an infected corpse as her client, she becomes stranded in the hospital basement during CDC quarantine along with the local sheriff and the coroner. The infamous surgeon struggles to find a cure for his infectious blunder by using the other survivors as test subjects. Meanwhile, Lexx and the sheriff attempt to locate his missing sister, who's stranded somewhere in the battle zone that once was the emergency room. It's a race against time and the ravenous undead. Can they survive the undead before CDC sanitizes the hospital of all infection?

"Misfits, Inc."

A seemingly ordinary, young woman meets four misfits who claim she has given them supernatural powers.

While on a business trip to a remote island paradise, a bored secretary, Hailey, has her world turned upside down when her path collides with a psychic freak, Skyler. He attempts to convince her that they had met in his dreams, and she had chosen him as one of her four mystic warriors. After Skyler foresees a woman's death, they discover an unidentified creature has killed one of the guests. They are joined by a lounge pianist and a rich playboy, who also claim they had met her in their dreams. If Skyler's prophecies are genuine, the evil entity controlling the ravenous creatures needs to destroy Hailey to ensure its survival. Reluctantly accepting her fate, Hailey has to locate the last and most powerful of her chosen warriors, The Guardian. Their fate is in doubt when The Guardian turns out to be a self-absorbed, former cat burglar with a bad attitude. Can Hailey turn her company of misfits into an elite team of mystic warriors? Or will The Guardian's secret agenda destroy them all?

"Deadly Institution 2"

When blackmail turns into murder, a young woman finds herself caught in the killer's crosshairs.

The small town of Stony Ridge is no stranger to scandal and persecution of the innocent. When a brutal killing shakes the town's prestigious country club, Jacey McMurray seeks help from a self-proclaimed vigilante, Konrad Asher. As her professional and personal worlds collide, Jacey fears the stress of the country club killings have finally taken their toll on Asher. Can a stressed out vigilante stop the killer before he strikes again?

"Witness Protection"
Also available in audiobook!

After witnessing an execution, a resourceful young woman attempts to disappear while being pursued by a hitman and a handsome federal agent.

A helicopter pilot, Jackie Remus, reluctantly agrees to go on a date with one of her clients, but her date is unexpectedly cut short when she witnesses a man being murdered. After narrowly escaping with her life, she is placed into protective custody. When the safe house is breached, Jackie makes a daring escape from both the hired killers and the handsome FBI agent, who wants to return her to protective custody. With a little help from her sly and crafty friend, Monroe, Jackie is convinced she can disappear until the trial. While on her journey to meet with her friend, she solicits help from a few shady but lovable characters along the way. Although she manages to stay one-step ahead of the hired killers, the federal agent remains in hot pursuit. Will Jackie reach Monroe before she's captured by the FBI and returned to protective custody? Or will the hired killers silence her first?

"Unconditional"

A young woman puts her life on hold to care for an unstable, highly skilled combat soldier, who believes someone is trying to kill him.

A botched military coup leaves a team of elite fighters injured with one clinging to life in a coma. When Harlan wakes from his coma, he's left with no memory of his past life. His commander's daughter, Indy, takes it upon herself to care for the fallen war hero. She's challenged with more than just his physical care as she combats with not only his memory loss but also his newly found desire for her. His infatuation with her becomes the least of her worries when he sinks back into his role of a combat soldier. Believing his life is in danger, his fighting skills surface, turning him into an unpredictable and dangerous man. Will his memory return to him before Indy is forced to commit him? Or will he finally find his nemesis, "the coyote", and possibly claim the life of an innocent person?

"The Pen Pal"

In order to save her friend, she must enter the mind of a serial killer.

When her best friend is abducted, no one believes Jolynn saw it in a psychic vision. With nowhere to turn, Jolynn reluctantly joins Agent Harris Slade and his team on their hunt for a sadistic serial killer known only as "The Pen Pal". Finally confronted with the killer, Jolynn realizes she must enter the mind of the psychopath in order to stop the brutal killings. But when her vision reveals a particularly disturbing death, can Jolynn sacrifice her lover for her friend?

"Witness Protection 2"
The Return of Whiskey Tango Foxtrot

Believing she holds the clue to millions in missing laundered money, a young woman is placed into the protective care of a former Navy SEAL team.

Feeling sorry for her recently separated co-worker, Leeann invites Wiley to join her and her friends on their night out. Little does she know that finding her co-worker murdered is just the beginning of her nightmare. Leeann unknowingly holds the key to fifty million dollars in potentially laundered mob money. With hired killers pursuing her, the FBI places her into a different kind of protective custody. Former Navy SEAL team Whiskey Tango Foxtrot reunites to keep Leeann alive at their secret hideaway. What should be an easy assignment takes an unscheduled turn when secrets, lies, and betrayal threaten to derail their mission. Is the team prepared for a war on their own doorstep? Will Leeann's misguided trust endanger the lives of those sent to protect her?

"Witness Protection 3"
Alpha Mike Foxtrot

A helicopter pilot risks her life to help a team of retired Navy SEALs rescue two girls from a killer.

When former Navy SEAL team Whiskey Tango Foxtrot asks for a simple favor, Jackie reluctantly offers her air-taxi services. What could go wrong? What begins as a search and rescue for two girls turns into a fight for survival against a heavily armed drug cartel. Wanted by the law with the cartel in hot pursuit and their home base breached, the team is forced to call in a favor from a questionable ally. Unfortunately, their new safe house isn't what it seems. Without knowing who the real enemy is, can Jackie and the team save their young witnesses from the hands of a killer?

"Already Dead"
Supernatural Collection

From the already dead to the undead. Three supernatural tales of "things that go bump in the night".

"Bloodletting" - A vampire themed resort allows guests to *participate* in their Bloodletting Ritual to celebrate the island's legendary vampires.

"Reaper of Souls" - A young woman must outwit an evil sorcerer in order to save her brother or become one of his minions forever.

"Already Dead" - When Flight 220 crashes, ten passengers make it to an isolated island, but only one man lives to tell the lie.

"Witness Protection 4"
O-Dark-Hundred

A simple assignment turns deadly when a retired Navy SEAL team uncovers a plot to kill a notorious mob boss.

When Whiskey Tango Foxtrot embarks on a simple stalking case, they're not prepared for a trip to a private island paradise owned by an infamous mobster. With one of their own suffering from traumatic head injuries, the team is left scrambling to decide what is real or imagined. The situation escalates even further when they uncover an assassination plot where everyone is a suspect. Now targets themselves, can the team survive their trip to paradise?

"Witness Protection 5"
Outside the Wire

After suffering several casualties on their last assignment, a retired Navy SEAL team discovers their misery is just beginning.

When Whiskey Tango Foxtrot returns home after suffering a devastating loss, they're hit with even more bad news regarding the rest of their team. Their grief is cut short when they discover their names are all on the same hit list. Hunted by relentless assassins, the scattered team must decide whether to remain safely hidden or find the man who put the price on their heads. Against the wishes of her teammates, Jackie strikes out on her own in order to save a friend who wants her dead. In a kill or be killed situation, will Jackie's emotions finally betray her?

"The Murder of Emily Fisher"

After finding their favorite teacher murdered, the lives of two teenage girls are forever changed.

Everyone loved Emily Fisher. While walking home one afternoon, two teenage girls, Sidney and Trisha, stumble upon a gruesome murder scene. The brutal murder of Emily Fisher, a young, attractive schoolteacher, shocks the small town of **Marilina**. After graduation, Sidney moves far away from the memories of the small town while Trisha retreats deeper into denial. Eight years after the murder, Sidney receives a desperate call from her childhood friend, forcing her to return home. Trisha believes Emily's killer was falsely accused and she manages to turn the entire town against her while attempting to prove it. When Trisha receives a death threat, Sidney realizes there may be some credibility to her friend's wild accusations. Is Trisha's mental breakdown a result of childhood trauma? Or is the real killer actually attempting to silence her? In order to save her friend, Sidney must answer the eight-year-old question. Who murdered Emily Fisher?

"Once Upon a Disaster"

A young homicide detective finds herself at the mercy of a hitman in the aftermath of an earthquake

While investigating the murder of a hitman, Detective Jade Wesson pursues a lead connecting the dead man to a break-in at a computer programming company. She's drawn into the world of nightclub owner and front man for the mob, Cody Riley. Her investigation keeps pointing to Cody's right-hand man and possible hitman, Vahn Lott. Despite her efforts to keep her investigation on track, Vahn has plans of his own for the attractive detective. When an unprecedented earthquake rocks their east coast town, Jade must put her life in Vahn's hands if she wants to survive. Can she trust a man who might be the killer she's hunting?

"Awaken the Dead"

A grieving innkeeper struggles to keep her haunted hotel out of foreclosure.

After losing her parents in a suspicious boating accident, Harley Brandon is determined to keep the family hotel out of foreclosure. Unfortunately, the hotel ghosts have other plans. Built with tainted money, the century old Horizon Hotel thrives on a tradition of murder, scandal, and suicide. As the paranormal activity increases to alarming levels, Harley discovers the truth about the hotel and its residents. Can Harley save her friends from the hotel's frightening hidden secrets?

"Castle Bloodshed"
Murder Collection

From a deadly island paradise to haunted castles. Three novella length tales of murder, mystery, and malicious intent.

"Castle Bloodshed" – A tour of Wesley Castle turns into a fight for survival as six stranded tourists discover the haunting secrets within the castle walls. A mystery writer teams up with an uptight butler in order stop a killer who may already be dead. Novella length paranormal murder mystery.

"Fleshies" – Is Uncle Rutger crazy? Five years ago, four business partners died within their newly purchased, fixer-upper castle. Their bodies were never found. The surviving partner, Rutger, claims a demon keeps him as its slave. Rutger's nephew schemes to save his uncle by sacrificing the lives of a group of stranded motorists and a high-profile novelist. Novella length supernatural murder mystery.

"Demon Island" – A group of strangers are invited to a remote island for the reading of a will. The guests soon discover they were brought to the island to be executed one-by-one. It's up to a private detective and a tenacious young woman to solve the murders and find a way to escape paradise. Novella length murder mystery.

"Brighton Island"

When a psychic visits a haunted island mansion, he inadvertently awakens the ghosts' tortured souls.

Something's not right with Simon. When Jacklyn brings her eccentric friend to her uncle's island mansion, she didn't expect him to slip into psychic overload. As Simon attempts to solve a decade-old, double homicide, Jacklyn is confronted with the possibility that she could be next to join the mansion ghosts. When they find themselves stranded on the secluded island, her Uncle Hyland wages his own war to save them from a flesh and blood killer. Will her uncle's "shock and awe" military tactics save them or get them killed? Can Simon bring peace to the tortured souls or unexpectedly join them?

"A.L.F. Resort"

A fantasy vacation turns into a nightmare when the resort's artificial life forms are compromised.

Welcome to A.L.F. Resort where you can live out your fantasies with safe, state-of-the-art artificial life form robots! When a young journalist and a photographer are sent to A.L.F. Resort to do a story for their magazine, Shay and Becka believe they've hit the jackpot of all work-cations. The engineers pull out all the stops to make their fantasies memorable. Unfortunately, the newly designed A.L.F., the Gen X, is smarter than his programming and creates havoc within Shay's fantasy. A computer malfunction removes their safety inhibitors and the A.L.F.s play out their own hostile fantasies. Zombies, bikers, and mobsters run amuck, turning fantasies into nightmares. Shay gets more of a story than she anticipates, but will she survive long enough to write it?

"Jungle Princess"

While stranded on a prison island, a young woman discovers a creature of "unknown" origin.

After their cruise ship sinks, Alex and two of her shipmates are stranded on a deserted, tropical island. Unfortunately, the castaways soon realize they're not alone. They discover an abandoned prison with over two dozen inmates living on the island's south side. While avoiding the prison on the far side of the island, Alex discovers a strange but loveable creature of unknown origin. When one of her fellow castaways is in trouble, Alex reluctantly seeks help from the prisoners. After the brutal murder of several inmates, their questions surrounding the abandoned prison are about to be answered. What really killed over one hundred prisoners? And is it still out there?

"Murder in Wax"

A series of brutal murders plague a quiet farming community when beautiful women audition for the same acting job.

While all the young women in town are fighting over a once-in-a-lifetime acting opportunity, Devon Vincent is excited about her new job at the local wax museum. Although supportive of her friend's acting aspirations, Devon has a hard time understanding the rivalry among the women in town. When the aspiring actresses are brutally murdered one-by-one, Devon fears her friend may be the next victim. Devon finds herself in the middle of a murderous revenge plot that leads back to the wax museum's doorstep and possibly implicates her boss as the killer. Will Devon's newly found feelings for her boss bring a killer closer to her? Or is the killer already in her circle?

"Witness Protection 6"
Alpha Dogs

An easy rescue turns into a wild ride for retired Navy SEAL team Whiskey Tango Foxtrot when everyone wants to kill their client.

It was a simple task. Rescue a young woman from her mob boss father-in-law. Little did Jackie and company realize that rescuing the young woman was the easy part. Keeping her alive would be a massive undertaking, especially when everyone wants a piece of the mafia heiress. The team fights for survival against their toughest adversaries yet. How many innocent people must die in order to save one woman? Can the team survive the ultimate battle between mercenaries and assassins?

"Midnight Requisition"

A series of brutal murders leaves a traumatized young woman on a hunt to find a killer.

When they were just babies, Scorpio and her twin brother, Kane, tragically lost their parents under mysterious circumstances. Refusing to accept his father was dead, Kane set off on a mission to find a man he'd never met. A home invasion gone wrong leaves Scorpio grieving the loss of those she loves. Out of the tragedy of her loss, two fallen heroes are thrust upon her. Scorpio soon realizes someone wants her dead and the killer may already be in her circle. As her entire life unravels in a web of betrayal and lies, can Scorpio trust her new, slightly questionable friends?

ABOUT THE AUTHOR

Holly Copella has been writing since the age of twelve when her frustration at a book's poor plot drove her to author her own story. Over the last decade, she's written a number of screenplays, some of which she's now adapting into novels. Her fascination with zombies and other darker material lends an edge to her writing, which tends to lean toward horror. As a fan of Agatha Christie, she appreciates the craft of a good plot and the importance of creating significant characters.

Hailing from Pennsylvania, Copella lives in the Endless Mountains on a farm with her rescue horses and other animals. In addition to writing and reading fiction, she enjoys riding horses and traveling to Las Vegas and Disney World.